Fullchrome Afterburn

A tale of the Humanic Panarchy

Drew Bryenton

Fullchrome Afterburn
Drew Bryenton

ISBN 978-1-910779-42-2 (Paperback)
ISBN 978-1-910779-43-9 (ePUB)

sci-fi-cafe.com

Dedicated to the old school -
Those who remember Pakuranga Intermediate School,
View Road Mt Eden,
And Cardigan St Western Springs

It's NOT DARKNESS all the way.

Look - down the vast flat expanse of the near Wall, like a horizon tipped on its edge. The bridges span the gap like tiny, hair-thin pencil strokes, out toward the similarly impossible, equally real far Wall, itself a dizzying blank sheet of onyx.

Once, this place - this chilly, breathless gap - teemed with light. Those bridges were crossed by Guides and Farwalkers, towing the little ghost lamps of their ships behind them, tethered by strands of radiance.

Now, the ledges, balconies, steps and crosswalks of both the near and far Walls are empty. Silent.

Watch for long enough, and you might catch a glimpse of a single little candle-flame scurrying across the sheer surface, far above or below, though terms like those have little meaning here.

The Chasm is the space between worlds - how a whole wafer-thin dimension of mixed up dreams, imaginings and fears reveals itself to the human mind. We think it must look different for the others - those Exo species we know to exist. They tell of the Torque and the Spin, the Gridmaze, the Moebius Tower, none of which appear in our interpretation of the Chasm.

No, this is the reflection of *us*. And you still wonder why it's dead and cold?

Some scholars, back before the war, said they saw things moving in the depths, or flitting above the razor-thin aperture of darkness where perspective makes the Walls nearly meet. Angels or demons, perhaps, conjured from some febrile race memory?

All we know is this. The Chasm dreams.

And where the gates are still open a crack, despite the ruin which fell on us, little fragments of that thick, dark, sweet collective dream leak out. They sizzle across the minds of sleeping humans, on worlds severed from Earth for thousands of years. Sometimes a fur-clad Norethi tribesman, snoring under the three moons of Rylax, will dream of quantum coupling capacitors and positronic rams. Or one of the paper-clad Scribes of the Monastic Shug will glimpse, as he drools into his pillow of scrolls, the great war-engines of the Panarchy - those sentient ships which were carried across the Chasm in the hands of a single Guide, but in the Real were so vast that they distorted the tides and pulled moons from their orbits.

Now watch.

One such fragment of Chasm-dream snaps like a wind-blown ribbon across the grasslands of Harrowe. A lost world, where a gate buried under a collapsed mountainside lies open a crack.

It sees a sleeping mind, glowing and swirling. A boy huddled by a fire on the vast expanse of the plain, whipscars on his back, tears drying at the corners of his eyes. There's a pair of guns tucked under the too-big coat he's using for a pillow.

The fragment of dream is far from specific. It's a chimera, a chameleon tuned to the hazy frequencies inside the boy's head.

It senses loss, as deep as the place it came from. Hatred. Desire. A need for vengeance.

And a deeper need, to know that vengeance can be hammered into something else. Something *pure*.

With a flick of its incorporeal tail, the wisp of dream-stuff slithers into the boy's ear. It carries with it an image that fits this world so neatly that its absence has been like a hole punched through a cinema screen. Everything has moved around it, leaving a gap shaped *just so*.

In the darkness, next to a bed of dying embers, the boy dreams of a long, tall silhouette. A wide-brimmed hat, a pair of boots with spurs. Hands clenched around the pearl handles of twin flashing, gleaming guns.

Little things change. Possible futures click and slide like marbles in a bag.

The Chasm, if it thinks, is not malicious or benign. It's just *us*. And if there's one thing you must know about that species of bipedal apes who have the hubris to call themselves 'sapiens', it's that our kind love a show.

Now...

Zero - Cheating the rope

Once, we believed in the future. There was going to be a brighter, better, more advanced tomorrow back then – a golden age of expansion and discovery, as a human race freed from the tyranny of scarcity and commerce took to the stars. There may, indeed, have been lovely spandex uniforms for everyone.

That was before the war against the first other sentience we found, and the realization that we were effectively children by comparison. They only did what they did as a kind of offhand slapdown – a jocular little nudge to put us in our place.

The result – three thousand years of internecine warfare, isolation, darkness, plague, famine and strife - has not so much shattered our illusions about our better nature, as proven their point about us. We're all bad monkeys, and if we're to get a banana at all, it's likely to be somewhere thoroughly uncomfortable.

Excerpt from 'Where Shit Be At' by the Central Scrutinizer

THE SKY WAS teal when he looked up at it for the last time.

A dirty blue-green, hazed to deep turquoise directly above, where the thin atmosphere gave way to space. A bead of sweat rolled down his cheek, and the noose chafed at his neck.

Ezra Ashdown was not having a very pleasant morning. Some people have said that there is such a thing as 'a good day to die'. The evidence suggests they have not tried dying enough to really form a solid opinion on the subject.[1]

Come on, he caught himself thinking. *Just get it over with. It's not as if there's going to be a last- minute pardon coming – not in this town. If it was any less friendly around here, people would have to start beating themselves up to stay in practice.*

The wood of the gallows creaked underfoot – dry, warped timbers bleached to the colour of bone by two suns. Beside Ezra, the hangman

---

1. There are, of course, some people who become connoisseurs of dying; who seek out bizarre fatalities in the same way other people collect stamps. This requires a lot of expensive technology, but only a little nudge from human nature. If becoming a thin film of hamburger can ever be made anything less than fatal, jumping off tall structures is certain to become an 'adventure sport' mere minutes afterward.

flexed his fingers on the drop-lever. Its handle was worn smooth, largely on account of the man who had convened this little party; Mason Stockton, Mayor of the town of Last Chance. A man so hard and crooked you could use his soul as a drill bit.

Sermonizing bastard. Ugly, too. Ezra turned his head as best he could, straining against the thirteen-ply knot at the back of his neck.

"You think we could hurry this up a bit?" he asked his executioner. "I hear the devil has that obsessive thing. Neat. *Punctual.* Like them fellas that collect little spoons." He lowered his voice to a whisper. "Between you and me, I think he's a bit craaaazy. His daddy was a right bastard."

He spoke out of the corner of his mouth, but his eyes were on Stockton. The tall, thin man in the pin-striped three-piece just grinned, slumped back on his barber's chair. It was a smile with far too many teeth, set in a face as dry as jerky. The kind of face which licked its lips inappropriately, and giggled while reading obituaries. An aide the size and shape of a refuse skip held up a tiny umbrella to keep the blowtorch suns at bay. Another - this one with the hunch and beady eyes of a carrion bird - held a pitcher of whiskey and gingerlime.

The ghastly profusion of teeth split wider.

"Oh, by all means, Ashdown. Laugh it up! Just remember – the sandrats are gonna be chawin' on your bones by nightfall. Ain't nobody cheats me, not in my own town. Got me one more skull to prove it, come tomorrow mornin.'"

The reason why – the Sheriff – stood behind Stockton's chrome-and-rosewood barber's chair like a stump-legged bomb shelter. It was ancient, and more than little bit hinky around the processors, but it was *relentless*, the same way old age and winter are relentless. Its tiny cluster of red eyes peered out from under a rusted cowling, on which was imprinted the seal of the Humanic Panarchy. It knew, in its heart of hearts, that it had been built as an industrial grade-soup vending machine. Some mad warlord, back in the distant past, had fitted it with the kind of guns which tell you a lot more than they intend to about the human race.

Not a man among those assembled could read the Panarchy chop, or knew the slightest thing about what it meant.

"No, you'll be getting' on your way down to Lucifer, and you tell him who sentcha. But first..."- and here the long, lanky Mayor produced a pack of playing cards from his waistcoat pocket. "You're gonna tell me how you did it."

Ezra laughed, and it came out as a dry-throated croak.

"Not a mighty big incentive fer me to co-operate, is there now? And in any case – I reckon it's more fun if you just think of it as *magic*."

Stockton's eyes narrowed behind his wire-rimmed spectacles. He half-stood from his chair, gripping the pack of cards in one white-knuckled fist.

"Magic? If someone pulls a damn rabbit out their fundament in my town, boy, it's cause *I put it there!* And you think *this* is the hard goodbye, boy, you can think again! I've got ways to make yer..."

Mason Stockton would not have called himself a racist bastard. Few of them do. But he was able to ladle more loathing over the single word *'boy'* than your average frothing, jackbooted dictator can cram into a whole moustache-chewing rally.

"Gravitic signature detected," said the Sheriff, its voice a hollow tin-can echo. *"Class five AG vehicle, in breach of the ten-mile exclusion perimeter."*

"Now what in the *hell*?" asked the hangman. He spat a vast, vile wad of soggy tobacco from the slit in his hood. "Can't a man just do his god-damned *job* here, Stockton?"

The Mayor's eyes narrowed behind two crescents of smoked glass. His long grey mustachios twitched as his smile compressed down to a bloodless line.

"Oh, the damn fool thing spouts off like that from time to time. Never signifies a..."

"Targeting scan-pulse registered. Calibre unknown. Manufacturer unknown. Advanced lidar and thermal-imaging projectile guidance capabilities indicated. Today's special is cream of mushroom, with a sprinkling of organic sourdough croutons and parsley."

The man with the umbrella – the gunslinger, Tasker – snapped open a long cerametal telescope, the sights (if only he had known) from a long-defunct Mk3 Weatherfield quantum-cascade energy carbine. Despite looking like something scraped from the bottom of a deep fryer, the man was a demon on the trigger.

"There's someone out there. 'Bout three long, yonder. Got themselves some steel, but I can't see what use it's gonna be at that range. Big blue-belly loper too. A fast one."

Stockton snapped the scope from his lackey's hand, making the gunslinger gum one bloodied knuckle. He laughed uproariously, rocking his barber's chair back on its legs.

"Hear that, Ezra? You got you a rescue party! I've seen this in the magic lantern shows – some hair-trigger sumbitch pings the rope while you're doin' the necktie two-step, you fall through the trap, an' there's a couple o' guns under there for you to grab..." he leered. "Thing is, not even dear old Mister Tasker could make that shot. Not at three hundred yards. Your little pal's been reading too many penny dreadfuls."

Ashdown grimaced. The rough hemp rope grated against his three-day stubble, salty with sweat.

"News to me," he said – and he meant it. A half-arsed rescue was not even on the list of his last, forlorn hopes. Even a quarter or one-eighth-arsed attempt, perhaps by boy scouts armed with paper-maché weapons, was well off the books at this point, and fading fast. The hangman shrugged.

"Last news you'll get," grinned Stockton, pinching his fingers together. A cloud of playing cards fluttered away on the hot breeze. "Pull the damned lever."

"Nothing personal," came a muffled voice from behind the black hood. "Just a job, and all. I have a wife and kids who need feedin' - little junior is off to executioner school next year, and the missus needs a new Sunday cowl..."

Greased wood clunked and slid. And Ezra Ashdown fell, caught up short by the noose around his neck.

It wasn't a swinging spine-breaker. No – Stockton had wanted him to suffer. Either that, or he wanted to gloat. The last fella who'd tried to execute Ezra Ashdown had insisted on singing show tunes, while dressed in fishnet stockings and little else. That had been one dinner theatre he'd *never* recommend again...

"*Incoming fire! Permission to engage?*" boomed the Sheriff, revealing a brace of gleaming chrome weaponry. Something hummed up the scale out of human hearing, setting Ezra's teeth on edge. It sounded impressive, but was in fact a sonic gazpacho whisk.

Stockton peered through the scope. Tasker's hand hovered, twitching, over the butt of his gun. The gunslinger's face was twisted into a doughy squint.

"Well, looky here! One handed! God be buggered! This'll be some sport!"

There is a certain type of person who actually *says* "well, looky here". They are the same type who ask city boys if 'they's lost' while smiling lecherously and holding shotguns. You don't ever, *ever* need to feel bad about what happens to them.

The first shot took the rope clean, and even from three hundred yards out all assembled could see the twin shockwave spinning through the dusty air. The load was angel's-hair – a diamond-thread razor pulled taut between two micromissiles, and it sheared through the hemp with a sound like tearing paper, then went on to paint a thin red line diagonally across Tasker's chest. He grunted, then blinked – then his left arm, the one going for his pearl-handled six-gun, fell off at the shoulder.

"Fuck me," he managed, before the better part of his torso slid sideways, leaving the rest of him cut off at the sharp angle of a calligraphy brush.

Nobody felt the least bit sorry for him. Weeks later, when his aged mother received the news by telegram, she pulled the cork from a bottle of sherry with her teeth, and eventually had to be crowbarred off the local schoolmaster, one mister Lawrence Prendergast.

"*Permission to engage?*" repeated the Sheriff, folding out even more glittering tubes and barrels from its inner recesses. Behind them, a whole stand of genefactored saguaro imitated Tasker's slice-and-slide. "*Beef and bacon is a hearty winter broth, best enjoyed on those cold nights around the fireplace!*"

"Light her up!" yelped Stockton, rolling off his barber's chair and into the sand. "Paint the walls with 'er! What in the *hell...*"

The second shot was haze, and it popped into spherical micromunitions about two armspans above the gallows. Violet billows of gas blew wide, rendering the light of the twin suns a grainy purple.

The eye-watering cloud bought Ezra some time.

He hit the ground on his arse, looking up, and what he saw brought a very genuine and heartfelt smile to his face. Taped up against the boards were a pair of ornate silver pistols, gnarly seven-shot revolvers packing magnum rounds the size of a fat man's thumbs. The tape which held them in place was utterly alien – thin, oily and nearly transparent, but he recognized the names etched into their barrels.

His granddaddy's guns. Time for some family fun.

And next to them, a tiny black tube with a rubber mouthpiece.

Ezra rolled to his feet in a single movement, coming up from under the gallows just as the haze began to clear. Trouble – the gun on his left - roared as he squeezed the trigger, blasting a fist-sized hole clear through the executioner.

"*Nothing personal.* It's just that a good tight noose should kill a man clean. Can't stand sloppy workmanship."

The man looked at the hole. There were *bits* inside, smoking, that nobody this side of breakfast should rightly want to see.

"Now *that's* an execution! Mister, I'd like to shake your hand! I'd like to put aside what I see now as the childish and clumsy gallows, and study under your tutelage the way of the.... uuuuuurrgggh."

Ezra winced. It was a bad time to have second thoughts about your calling in life. It was, in fact, a bad time to think that you had anything in life at all.

He caught a twitch of shadow off to his right, and he extended his arm in a fluid motion, flicking his eyes down the barrel of Strife. Behind him, the hooded hangman toppled off the gallows platform, smoke coiling up from his hollowed-out chest.

Stockton's goon had a pitcher in one hand and a nasty sawn-off in the other, but he was mazed by the effects of that violet gas. Before he could blink the tears from his eyes Ezra had pulled the trigger twice, shattering his cut-crystal jug of whiskey and gingerlime, then drilling a neat hole between his eyes. The impact sent the man's corpse flying backward in a full cartwheel, ending with the meaty thwack of his temple against a rock. Nobody ever learned that his name was Algernon Weeks, that he owned a pet lizard called Gerald, and that in his spare time he liked to embroider pictures of tricycles on small throw cushions.

Sideshows, both of 'em. Ezra spat the rebreather out of his mouth as the last of the gas blew away, looking for Mason Stockton.

Five in one, six in the other. No way the weasel was gonna slither out of this one...

A drift of playing cards whispered underfoot as he kicked over Stockton's barber's chair, both guns held out before him. Ez was so mad that he didn't even try to imagine a weasel slithering. He'd kill for a cigar about now – then again, he'd kill on general principle just as soon as...

There.

The Mayor was mounting up, throwing one pinstriped trouser-leg over the broad back of a loper. The low-slung beast huffed and snapped its metre-wide jaws, but the harness and bit between its teeth held it back. With a tug of the reins Stockton brought the loper up and around, pointing its flickering blue tongue toward Last Chance.

Ezra steadied his aim, breathing deep. Trouble and Strife were heavy in his hands, and he could feel each bullet in its chamber, patiently waiting to fly. He closed his eyes, and squeezed both triggers.

A violet flash threw him backwards an instant later, as two copper-jacketed slugs of lead evaporated in the air. The same blast took the barrels off Trouble and Strife as neat and clean as a barber-surgeon's razor, leaving him with two metal stumps.

"You have been disarmed. Submit peacefully, and there will be no need for further violence. Would sir care for an additional bread roll?"

Ashdown spun on his heel, bringing his two truncated pistols up to face the Sheriff. Useless, he knew. Not only was the damned thing built godawful tough, his guns were now about as accurate as a madman's horoscope. He spat.

"Seems you're only gonna have to kill me again, Engine," he said. "And that didn't work out well, last time. Why don't you just use those fancy shooters of yours, and save the Mayor a few feet of rope?"

The machine clicked forward on its stubby insect legs, red eyes glittering.

"Look. I get it. You're one of those 'man with no name' types, riding about, dispensing hot justice like it was the soup of the day. We get a lot of them. But Mayor Stockton hates... well, he calls it 'silly drama'. And he is the proper civic authority."

Ezra stared past the rusted metal flank of the Sheriff, to where a flash of light on metal winked in the distance. He still had no idea who would even want to save him.

"The 'civic authority' is high-tailing it out of here – and more to the point, he's so crooked you could use him to uncork a nice pinot noir."

"It is not for me to speculate on politics. I exist solely to enforce. Tell you the truth, I rather like it. And of course it sounds a lot better than 'I exist solely to serve soup.'"

"Seems to me that most of ol' Stockton's waking moments constitute a crime, big fella. Enforce away."

"If you're trying to confuse me with a paradox, you are wasting your time. That kind of thing hasn't worked since they fixed up the poor old Mark Twelves. Head explosions. Between you and me, they were just reinforcing negative robot stereotypes."

Ezra put up his guns, pointing them at the pale teal sky.

"Actually, I was trying to distract you with bullshit. But it was nice talkin' to ya."

He didn't have any idea what an EMP missile was – having grown up on Harrowe, a world where the last word in technology was huge, steam powered and less efficient than a chocolate flamethrower. But he knew enough to throw himself to the side as a hissing chrome tube hammered into the Sheriff from behind, toppling the machine from its claws. A raving blast of violet licked into the sky, passing right through the spot where Ashdown had stood. A small trickle of very nice leek and onion soup gurgled from within the downed engine.

Reflexes learned over a lifetime of hurried escapes kicked in. He rolled to his feet, the chopped-off noose hanging down the front of his shirt like a necktie. He heard the soft sound of a loper's wide foot-pads on sand behind him, and he spun, both guns extended...

Only to find himself staring down the muzzle of the biggest, meanest pistol he had ever seen.

Ezra Ashdown experienced a pang of terror, envy and pure covetous lust as he recognized the gun. There was one in the museum in Hooke's Harbour – a relic from the War of 9:15.

"That's a *Problem Solver!*" he breathed, watching his exhalation mist against the chrome of its foreplate. "No *wonder* you cut the rope from three clicks out. But where did you? And how? With the..?"

His eyes performed a blink and refocus, blurring the cavernous maw of the gun and snapping to the face of the woman holding it. Her voice cut through him like hot wire.

"Well, I'm going to be in trouble for the missile anyway. So why not have some fun?"

He swallowed. Hard. She slid down from the saddle of her mount while keeping the vast black eye of the pistol steady.

A *woman with a gun!*

It was Sacrilege[2], of course, in the strait-laced, Orthodox Spiritualist society of Harrowe. And yet the form-fitting buckskin dress and tasseled coat which she wore left Ezra under no illusions. A web of what appeared to be occult sigils (but which was, in fact, a laminar energy absorption system) peeped out at the collar and waist of the two-piece frontierswoman's costume, while her hair was bound back into a long black braid under a derby hat. Her eyes were almond-shaped, as violet as the Sheriff's particle beams, and her lips were powdered with some kind of dark cherry-red gloss, which was all the more apparent when she smiled.

"The only personal handgun with industrial infrastructure," she said. "Accept no imitations."

---

2. With a capital S, no less - like farting in a confessional. Not accidentally, mind you, but one of the kind that makes solid medieval oak curl up and go soft, aimed right through that little woven latticework window at the priest's face. Not that we condone that kind of thing...

If she had started reciting the painfully erotic haiku poetry of the Libertine Scribes of Kesh Neng, the mystery woman could not have seemed more alluring.[3]

She spun the pistol on one finger and dropped it back to the holster at her waist, where a powerful magnetic field held it in place. "So tell me – how were you going to stop that Engine of yours?"

Ezra blinked.

"The Sheriff? Well, I *was* working on something. Then you sort of took the initiative, with that... well, whatever that thing was."

"Type-23 one-shot Electromag Nullifier. Central have plenty more where that one came from. But your so-called 'Sheriff' is getting up. You might want to convince me that rescuing you was worthwhile."

From somewhere on her person – and *where*, a good Orthodox boy should not have cared to speculate – the strange woman had produced a thin metal tube, glowing red-hot at one end. She drew on it deeply, like a small chrome cigar, before exhaling a cloud of cinnamon-sweet smoke in his face.

"Come on. I don't have all day."

Ezra held out his hand for the Problem Solver. The dark-haired woman shook her head and smiled. She had the same kind of dark, fizzing intensity as a fully armed bomb - the kind which you know is doing bad, bad things to part of you, possibly on a cellular level. "Do this one little favour for me, and we might be able to find you one of your own," she said. "Though I *totally* didn't say that. And you've only ever seen one in a museum."

Behind her, the Sheriff finally managed to extend an arm from a badly corroded flap on its back. It hinged itself upright with a groaning creak of metal. Three very, very old sachets of instant ramen spilled onto the desert sand.

"Three thousand, four hundred and ninety six years. So much soup! All hot, all very nourishing. But do I get any respect? Oh no! Not even when they gave me all these big shiny guns. It's always 'this bouillon is cold, unit 10110011101'. 'There's a fly in my cream of chicken, unit 10110011101...'"

"Were you going to help at all?"

---

3. The Libertine Scribes believed that through meditation on the arts of seduction and the pleasures of the flesh, they could achieve a transcendent state of nirvana, communing directly with the Godhead and thus learning the inner secrets of the universe. At least, that's what they told their girlfriends, the police, their parents and the representatives of the press, looking rather rumpled, red-faced and shiny.

"Non-interference in primitive affairs is supposed to be rule number one, where I come from."

"Isn't it a bit late for that?"

"I don't know," she said, taking a step backwards. "That's *kind* of the part I'm going to be in trouble for. But it looks like we're about to find out if there are any survivors, so, you know." she shrugged. "It could all sort itself out neatly. For *me*, anyway..."

There was no way of knowing the real emotional state of the Sheriff at any given time, but Ezra wagered that it was none too happy right now. A haze of smoke spiralled out from a popped seam of rivets down its flank, and one of its gleaming chrome cannons hung loose, sparking erratically.

"Final request. Disarm and submit. Failure to do so will result in the application of lethal force."

Ezra took his thumbs off the hammers. He put his hands up, once again pointing the ruined Trouble and Strife straight at the sky.

"OK. OK. You got me. Just leave the lady outta this. Not her fault I'm so damned handsome. Most any dame would've done what she did."

Out of the corner of his eye, he caught a single raised eyebrow, along with a wry little smile. Something in Ezra's grizzled soul twinged. Perhaps she really *did* think he was handsome!

The Sheriff, on the other hand, was past being reasonable.

"Negative. The possession of military hardware by civilians is a level twenty seven offense. Lay down on the ground, place your hands behind your head, and submit."

Ez saw what he needed, right on the edge of his vision. A flat-headed nail, hammered into the wood of the gallows. It would have been an impossible shot, even with both barrels of his guns intact. All he needed was a distraction.

"That," said the gunslinger, "is no way to talk to a lady."

Then he dropped his guns down and fired.

The Sheriff, being a Panarchy Integrated Systems Type-Nine Soup-synthesis Unit, possessed reflexes far in excess of even the most lethal gunslinger. Some said that these machines, in their heyday, were able to deliver nourishing hot beverages before the customer *had even made his selection.*[4]

---

4. Such was the hubris of the Panarchy's culinary and gustatorial chamber of engineers, that they harnessed the inner workings of eleven-dimensional probability mathematics to bend the surface of time itself, peering into the future. Either that, or people are just not too fussed which soup they get, so long as it's hot and cheap.

But - as it had also not received regular servicing and maintenance for the better part of three thousand years, and as it had been crudely soldered together with the mindcore of a Fistcorp Type Nine Violence Unit - its body could barely keep up with its silicon-matrix brain. Ezra's first bullet clipped the tip of its one remaining particle cannon, spinning it away as a beam of energy burst from its muzzle. Cactus crisped and evaporated to his left.

But it was the second shot which the condemned man was focused on – the trick shot which caught that protruding nail head on an angle, ricocheting it back on a flat trajectory. Ezra could feel it with his mind as he spun in slow motion – a weight distorting the treacle-thick air, and one he could reach out and touch.

There. Just right.

Time unfroze, and Ezra caught a face-full of sand, knocking the wind from his belly. But he heard that cross-cut slug clip neatly through the gap in the Sheriff's armour, clattering around inside the engine's corroded shell. Any number of carefully calibrated and unspeakably ancient circuit boards were smashed to shards and splinters by the flying hunk of lead.

Somewhere in the core of the machine, a micro-tokamak fusion reactor spun loose. Magnetic containment fields popped one by one. The heart of the engine - a molecular soup synthesizer of unspeakable power - finally collapsed in around its central wheel of antimatter.

Ezra just had time to curse.

The explosion blasted a sheet of pebbles and sand at him as he tucked both arms up over his head. When the after-echoes rolled away he saw what was left of the Sheriff collapse, a sad little heap of burned and twisted steel. It had been peeled open like a can of beans, fire licking up from inside. The smell of burned powdered tomato filled the air.

"I'll show you god-damned *worthwhile*," he muttered. "Damned hangman still had my hat, too. Probably gone to charcoal."

His erstwhile rescuer was sitting on a rock not far away, as if the detonation hadn't fazed her in the slightest. A flicker of blue light sketched facets and planes around her for a second, then faded. Her loper, on the other hand, had skittered for cover like the giant lizard it was, and peered back at the pair of them from over a nearby dune with a very hurt expression.

"*Nice.* I can see what they were talking about back at Central. You have my attention, Mr Ashdown."

He picked himself up from the sand, wincing at the sharp pains which speared through his neck and shoulder. Being the guest of honour at a hanging was hardly therapeutic.

"*That's* what it takes to get your attention? We're both lucky that neither of my damn guns jammed!"

The woman stood, brushing a fleck of sand from her shoulder. She raised one eyebrow.

"Anyone else would have told me they were lucky not to miss. Which just goes to show why my interest is appropriate. You're an aberration, Ashdown – a psionik. And where I come from, we need people like you."

Ezra chewed this over for a second. Now that the adrenaline was fading out, and his surprise at still being alive was in check, he decided he didn't like this lady's attitude. He felt like a sample on one of Doc Ethan's microscope slides, all pinned down and bloody.

"They've called me a witch before, and a cheat, and a lucky sonovabitch," he said, slipping his granddaddy's guns into the empty holsters at his belt. "But never a – whatever you said. *Abbreviation. Psychotic*, now, that's a new one too."

He stood over her – a good head taller, he noted – and went to pluck the chrome cigar from between her fingers. She twitched it away, then thought better of it and handed it to him.

"What I mean is, you can control small objects within your body's electromagnetic field. It's quite a skill. And it means that my boss would like to offer you a job."

The smoke was surprisingly smooth, mildly narcotic, and sweet as honeyed almonds. He still almost choked on it.

"You know all about me, then?"

"Not all of the insects you've swatted in the last few months have been flies, Ashdown. We've been spying on you."

"Even when... you know?" He made vague hand gestures of a lavatorial nature.

"*Especially* 'you know'. We need the laughs, where I work."

The sunburn covered most of the cherry redness which advanced across Ezra's face.

"Then you know *I've* never worked a day in my life. And certainly not for blood money."

"We don't expect you to," she said, smiling brightly. "If you manage to kill Mason Stockton, it'll be strictly an extracurricular bonus. No – what we want is a little more complicated."

Ezra passed the cigar back, shaking his head. The last thing he needed was 'complicated'.

"Oh no. No no no. And don't think because you saved my life that I owe you one, either!"

The woman adopted a hurt expression.

"And our insects said that you were such a gentleman! Let me put it this way. Do you want to expand your mind, visit new worlds, battle insane monsters against impossible odds, play with hardware powerful enough to shatter whole planets, potentially save the human species and become a veritable saint among gunslingers?"

Ez squinted at her, his head cocked to one side.

"And if I say no?"

"Then you're a sad, pathetic little insect, and I'll put you right back up on that gibbet," she said, all gleeful enthusiasm.

Something about her smile – and the way that an explosion which had felled the Sheriff hadn't even singed her eyelashes – made him stop and consider before he laughed in her face. He considered the laugh. He even got so far as to having third considerations about the state of his breath, during it. But... well. It had been an awfully long time since he talked to a lady who didn't ask him for a precise figure in coinage beforehand.

"Two things," he said. "One – I want my own Problem Solver. And two – I'd like the courtesy of knowing what your god-damned name is!"

She came in closer, wrapping her arms around his neck. He was painfully aware, with the clarity of feeling due only to those who have just cheated death, of her vanilla and jasmine perfume, and the curves beneath that buckskin-and-leather two piece. He gulped.

"As for number one," she whispered, staring up into his eyes. "I think I can definitely help you. Or at least my friend Wainwright can." She ran a finger along the stubble on his jawline, then tapped him on the chin. "You two should get along famously. As to the other..."

Any thought of a kiss evaporated as a sharp pain sparked at the nape of his neck. He felt a barb pierce his skin, then a hot, sticky sensation, as of thousands of tiny insect legs burrowing deep. Gasping, Ezra drew back, fingers scrabbling at a dome of smooth metal.

"My name's Tia Faraday. Lately of the Agency of the Central Scrutinizer known as Plausible Deniability."

Ghost sparks whirled and flickered behind his eyes. The world tilted sideways as he crashed to his knees on the hot sand, two suns (one indigo, the other orange) blurring into one. He looked up as she stood over him, and the last thing he saw was her smile.

"I'm your parole officer," she said – and then the darkness rushed up to swallow him whole.

One - How to die for beginners

Harrowe – Fourth planet of the Ulgaris – Nepthene Binary System, colonized in 492 Antebellum by explorators of the Ares Consolidated Mining and Smelting Company. During hostilities the commanding Sentience of Harrowe's chasm gates and reticulum infrastructure became convinced that it was, in fact, a six-year-old girl from Monarchy-era France, and was subsequently re-designated as one of the emergent class of Artificial Deities (Insane) by the Central Scrutinizer. Re-establishment is slated for 3106 Post-Cataclysm, though initial reports from Chasmwalkers and creepware indicate that a) techno-societal collapse here has resulted in a scenario catalogued as 302-c (Balkanized Steampunk Mad Max Hell) and b) Despite being almost infinitely powerful in a world where the apogee of technology is a form of armoured steam engines, the Artificial Deity of Harrowe has been missing for more than a century.

Except from 'Where Shit Be At' by the Central Scrutinizer

HE AWOKE IN darkness, and also in considerable pain, with the smell of sulphurous smoke in his nostrils and a chorus of hammers and anvils behind his eyes.

Ahh, yes. The Orthodox temple had told him all about *this* place – though he had expected to see more than just a faint outline of firelit steel. He'd been expecting demons.

Then the events of the previous morning came back to him in a rush, and he recalled that he wasn't actually quite dead yet.

There had been that madwoman with the silver machine, the gun from out of Hooke's Harbour museum, some messy and terminal shenanigans with Stockton's goon squad...

Ezra's fingers felt tentatively around the base of his skull. The button of slippery warm metal was still there. So it hadn't all been some kind of pre-gallows dream, brought on by an enthusiastically appreciated last bottle of whiskey. It had been Glenfuttock's Old Combustible, a fine drop - so long as your intention was surgical sterilization.

"Good morning, sunshine," came a voice which made the remaining hairs on the back of his neck prickle. "How do I look?"

At the same time one of the walls of his cell rumbled backwards, revealing a narrow, gas-lit corridor. That, and the shapely form of Tia Faraday, dressed to the nines in the height of Harrowe fashion. This year, that meant a resemblance to a very attractive hourglass up top, and a frilly iceberg down below. She wore a black velvet beauty spot on what decorum insisted Ez think of as her *decolletage*, which - in extreme circumstances - could be removed and thrown as a tiny explosive.

"A better question would be how do *I* look," groaned Ezra. "My throat feels like a sandrat threw up in it and died. No..." He waved one hand in front of his face, squeezing the bridge of his nose with the other. "It threw up, went back to the party, enjoyed a spicy curry with its mates, sung some songs about football, came back, threw up again, suffered from explosive diarrhoea, *then* died. As for my head... what in all hells *is* this thing, woman?"

Tia swished into the room, gathering up her multi-layered petticoats and overskirts with what appeared to be a lifetime's practice. Ezra figured that maybe this was something all ladies were born with the ability to do.

"If you're over-reacting to the tracer chip on your neck, then you're a big baby," she said, settling primly onto a wooden crate. "It's nothing but a relay back to my own skullware, and a teensy smidge of Q-foam high explosive. For if you're naughty."

This almost got him off his feet. Nausea and dizziness slapped him down.

"Anyhow, it's necessary. Without at least some minimum 'ware in you, you'd never be able to integrate with Wainwright. And I've told him all about you."

Ez didn't like the sound of that, either. In fact, he felt that he had the right to be a little huffy right now, but he suspected that his so-called parole officer would just laugh it back in his face. So he threw her a curveball.

"That dress looks good on you. Less conspicuous, too. We don't really have a lot of lady cowboys, or cowladies, or..."

Again, the raised eyebrow, as if this petite, raven-haired killing machine from god-knows-where was totting up gentleman points on some mental ledger.

"Thank you, Mister Ashdown. And you would be surprised at the concealed-weapons capabilities of the average bustle. Though I can't see any way that this corsetry is real whalebone..."

"No oceans deep enough." So, definitely offworld. Which meant that the antiquated ravings in the Orthodox Gospel were at least part true. "Listen... when you said there might be a chance I could kill Mason Stockton..."

"I wasn't, as my boss would say, 'shitting you'. We're following him right now."

Which made all the noises, the smoke, the metal floor, and the sensation of being slowly shaken apart atom by atom click together in a jigsaw collusion.

"We're on board a *Land Steamer*. And if we haven't caught up with him yet..."

"Mason Jefferson Stockton is no longer the Mayor of Last Chance. He's a wanted felon, fleeing from the vengeful hand of His Majesty's Imperial Judiciary. Personified, in this instance, by an evil, relentless bitch. *Me*. Which is to say, the Comptessa Ariadne DeGravayne Gexxe-Stahlberg, undersecretary of the Oversight and Adjustment Committee."

She simpered. Never had such a devastatingly calculated simper been achieved without performance-enhancing drugs. Ez snorted.

"Or you *would* be, if you weren't less likely to be Harrowe royalty than a two-headed loper."

That bright smile lit up again.

"*Exactly*. It might interest you to know that his crime – or at least, the one which put him over the edge – was the unlawful execution of one Ezra Michael Ashdown. This rolling pressure-cooker is army ordnance, but the dear old ex-Mayor had his own steamer stashed under city hall. What we have here is something in the nature of an old-fashioned car-chase, on an infinitely less efficient scale."

The floor lurched under Ezra's feet, as if to punctuate her point. They must be running at full pressure, out across the baking flat expanse of the hardpan – and if Stockton was still ahead of them, it meant that he possessed more technological tricks than just the Sheriff.

"Come on!" said Tia, actually clapping her hands in anticipation. They were clad in prim little cotton gloves. "We might be in time to witness some novel, folksy acts of primitive violence!"

She dragged Ez from the floor with one hand, and the two of them set off down the corridor, Tia forging ahead at a determined angle, Ezra clattering along behind her, caroming from wall to wall as his vision blurred.

The corridor turned out to be a kind of skirting along the rivet-studded iron cliff of the steamer's boiler, part of a ramshackle, bracketed encrustation of corrugated-roofed sheds, gatling-gun turrets, mahogany-panelled staterooms and valve-festooned operating spaces which grew organically from every surface of the giant machine. In extremely simple terms the Land Steamer consisted of two vast parallel boiler tubes, black as sin and straked with bundles of brass tubing. Various bell-shaped domes, spinning ball-governors, whistles, release valves and sundry other industrial flora sprouted from any area not already colonized by enclosed gangways, gunnery mounts or observation decks akin to those found on a seagoing battleship.

In size, it was similar to a battleship as well, though its means of propulsion became far too obvious as Ezra and Tia ducked through a hatch and out into the smoky, blustery outdoors – a row of two-storey tall metal wheels, spiked for traction and as wide as a Hooke's Harbour avenue. These were whipped to a radial blur by the thrustings of four immense copper-jacketed pistons, amid a stench of burning grease.

"Never been on one of these things," said Ezra, having to raise his voice against the clawing slipstream. "But it seems all kinds of dangerous – not to mention *stupid*."

Tia turned around to face him, still holding onto his hand.

"Where I come from, we have machines ten thousand times more dangerous. I've found that it helps not to think about COFRIADs, and just enjoy the ride. After all, skullware, right?"

"COFRIADs?"

"Catastrophic Operating Failures Resulting In Absolute Destruction. And, before you ask, skullware is... harder to explain. Think of it as an afterlife exactly like the one you were just forcibly ejected from, guaranteed by a tiny voice in your head."

"So it's a *religious* thing?"

Tia looked at him with her head aslant – a calculating, sly narrowing of her eyes.

"Either that was primitive ignorance, or one of the most profound philosophical questions ever. But it doesn't matter now! We're closing in on him!"

"How do you know?" shouted Ezra, foundering in Tia's wake as she piloted her cloud of petticoats and overskirts up a treadplate stairway, and onto the foredeck of the steamer.

"The gunners have stopped playing cards, and they've put away their whiskey bottles. That means Stockton's coming into range!"

Ezra caught sight of their quarry through a whirling shroud of dust. Great churning wheels cracked the salt hardpan of the deep desert, while black smoke belched from six great chimneystacks, each one topped with an ornate gothic ruff of metal filigree. Mason Stockton's Land Steamer was of an entirely different design to the olive-drab machine which he and Tia perched atop – instead of two immense boilers it had a whole cluster of long, slim tubes, and what it lacked in sheer bulk it made up for in rakish, low-slung menace.

The suns were cigar-burn discs in the teal sky. Beneath their blowtorch glare nothing moved from horizon to horizon. All was a chalk-white arid plain – a blank sheet of parchment across which two iron juggernauts screamed, seeming as if they were standing still.

A figure suddenly loomed out of the dust, clad in ornately piped military greens, and broke Ezra's reverie. He snapped to attention in front of Tia.

"Your Excellency," he saluted. "Captain Charlesworth bids you return to the lower decks. Such an engagement is no place for a Lady."

Tia fixed the young messenger with a look of frosty superiority.

"I am overseeing this operation personally, Subaltern. *Oversight* means I would quite like to watch our gallant land-sailors in action. Surely you can't be suggesting that there is any chance we will *lose*?"

"Ummm... of course not, Ma'am. It's just that..."

"And poor mister Ashdown *so* desires to see justice done. Don't you, Ezra?"

She punctuated this question with a well-placed elbow to the solar plexus. Ezra winced and nodded, grinning foolishly.

"But the shrapnel... and the *noise*, of course, Ma'am, if you would just..."

"Don't allow me to keep you, then," said Tia. "Inform Charlesworth that he may fire at will."

The Subaltern saluted again and disappeared into the dust. It was churning and boiling all around them now, mixed with tiny burning motes of ash from Stockton's smokestacks.

Tia manhandled Ezra up to the very bows of the upper deck, above the great bulldozer-blade of armour plating which protected the fore of the twin boilers. She reached into her bustle with a series of oily clicking sounds, and suddenly the Problem Solver was back in her hands.

"We don't know how he built the damned thing. And we don't know what other archaeotech he has up his sleeve, either. So if this goes wrong, I'm going to cheat a little."

"That thing packs more punch than the naval guns on this steamer?"

Her smile was purest joy.

"Kid, you have *no* idea. Get ready to take cover!"

The Imperial Land Steamer had almost clawed its way up beside Stockton's machine now, every rivet and weld straining as an army of stokers and engineers slaved belowdecks at the furnace-heads. Gargantuan gears clanked and meshed, aiming all eight of the steamer's pillbox turrets on the prey. Those turrets were the size of houses, and equipped with four immense blued-steel cannons each.

Ezra decided that he'd rather like to watch the fireworks.

The first stuttering roll of cannon fire was deafening, and it made the Land Steamer rear up on its wheels, coming down again with a spine-jarring impact. Rosettes of flame and black smoke bloomed against Stockton's rear armour, sending whole riveted plates of three-inch steel whickering back in the slipstream of the speeding behemoth. The fugitive's own deck-guns were tiny things in comparison, but they opened up in response, spitting streams of incandescent tracer-fire.

Bullets skipped and whined all around them. Tia held her aim steady. Ezra was damned if he was going to back down now – not in front of a woman, at any rate.

"Do you think we'll be able to take him alive?"

Tia shrugged.

"Do you really care that much if we don't? Or is this one of those civilizations where you keep the skulls of your defeated enemies? Use them as codpieces, or something?"

Now the captain threw on even more power, and the Land Steamer lurched forward again, plumes of superheated steam erupting from a thousand brass-bound safety valves. Vast hydraulic rams groaned and shuddered as he spun the wheel hard to the left, and the imperial vessel turned like a runaway glacier, ramming up against Mason Stockton's engine.

Spiked wheels chewed into metal with a bestial howl. Sparks fountained and couplings tore. And the starboard battery of turrets locked back on their mountings, aiming between the port-side battery to form of deadly broadside.

"Run out the stabilizers!" came the Captain's voice, amplified through the steamer's network of copper bullhorns. "Load high explosives! By the Orth, we'll see them wrecked and ruined!"

The deck rocked beneath Ezra's feet as a brace of long iron rails telescoped out from the far flank of the steamer, each one tipped with a tiny castor wheel. At least 'tiny' is what they seemed – it was a fair bet that each one was bigger than a man and heavier than a span of lopers.

"They're so we don't blast ourselves over sideways," said Tia, still tracking with the flat-slab muzzle of the Problem Solver. "And if we... *shit!*"

Miss Faraday hit the deck in a swirl of lavender-scented petticoats. A second later Ezra was dragged down with her, as a hand with red-painted fingernails and a grip like iron hooked his collar. His cheek slapped oily steel, coated in a thin film of desert grit. The rumble of the racing Land Steamer shook his teeth in their sockets.

Ezra felt Tia roll them both over, swearing in some alien language.

Then the guns went off, and everything was pain and echoes.

For an instant Ashdown's world *slowed* and *widened*, unfolding into dreaming crystal. He saw a ripple pass across the face of both the suns – huge, bloated Nepthene and hard, bright Ulgaris. Then came a lance of actinic blue light, so bright that it all but welded his optic nerves to the back of his skull. It swept above him in a reaping arc, and a horizontal rain of molten metal followed it.

Things turned end over end amid the firestorm. Some were the lacerated tubes of naval cannon. Others were sad little clouds of blackened bones and red-hot brass buttons – all that remained of His Majesty's 223rd Fusiliers. Someone, in a dusty office somewhere, had just saved a fortune in medals and boot polish.

In the moment of ringing silence which followed, Ezra was far, far too aware of the tautly muscled body of Tia Faraday pinning him to the deck. Little twists and shards of metal pattered off her shield as she pressed her forearm hard into his throat. Their eyes met.

If I kiss her now, he thought, *I might just have time to enjoy it before she tears out my spine...*

Time came back.

"That was the dealbreaker," said Tia, rolling to her feet with feline grace. "Seems that Wainwright was on the money this time. Stockton's got the Deity, and it's loopier than a name-brand breakfast cereal."

Ez pushed himself painfully up the rail until he could stand without support. What he saw was madness.

Something had peeled away all eight of the Land Steamer's turrets, and a huge swathe of its upper decks, balconies and towers as well. It was as if some malicious giant had planed the juggernaut down with a red-hot wire.

"Nobody drivin'. That's gotta be bad." He looked around for his hat, and realized that it had been reduced to dust along with Mason Stockton's pet hangman. "What'd you call them things? Coffee Ads?"

Tia was staring down the barrel of the Problem Solver, across the ruined deck of the Steamer, and down onto upper promenade of Stockton's own engine. The two machines were locked in a death-embrace, still churning hell-bent across the empty plain, flames licking twenty feet from their smokestacks. A shimmering screen snapped out from the side of the handgun, painted on the air.

"COFRIADs. We're about arse-deep in one right now. And I think I have the reason why right here..."

The screen flickered and zoomed in. Flickered, and zoomed again. Now it showed a tall, sombrely dressed man in a three-piece suit, holding a parasol up over the head of a little blonde girl. His smile would have put whole dynastic generations of dentists through university. The girl wore a lace-trimmed baby-blue dress, with matching ribbons in her hair. Her eyes were the empty silver of a pair of mirrors.

"Stockton. And he's holding some kid hostage! Stealing's wrong, and kidnapping's wrong, so *stealing a child* - well, I wouldn't be a rugged yet masculine justice-loving outlaw hero type if I didn't do something about *that*."

Ezra's hands itched for a pair of guns which weren't there. He spat.

"That's no child," said Tia. "That's the thing that's going to kill us."

"*Kill us?* She can't be more'n about five years old! I don't see how..."

"It's *looking at us*." said Tia flatly. "Well Mister Ashdown, it's been a blast. See you on the other side."

Mason Stockton pointed. The little girl smiled, all innocent delight, and she raised her arm to follow his.

The skin came off in a gentle, ribboned unfolding - silver inside. The girl's hand and fingers slid apart as three slim, cuttlebone-shaped slivers of metal peeled away from her forearm, leaving only a central armature of hexagonal mesh. Her hand was now a core of arc-blue energy. Little traceries of sunfire blipped and crawled inside it as those three metal blades began to spin.

It was just exactly the sort of thing most people only ever get to see once, before that awkward moment when religion suddenly becomes less than theoretical.

The little girl - the thing which had once been the Artificial Intelligence of Harrowe's Chasm reticulum - laughed. Fire built in an infernal crescendo.

And the Imperial Land Steamer ceased to exist.

From the high-rez camera eyes of Wainwright's creepware it was all over in a single calamitous instant.

A beam stabbed out from the little girl's hand, flaring like some colossal welding-torch as it struck the flank of the Land Steamer. Armour ablated away before the blast, steel peeling open like paper. Rivets popped and evaporated in flight. A spiral corona of metal droplets followed the beam as it punched clean through the core of the Imperial vessel, shearing off whole wheels and piston-rods before the force of it folded the great machine in the middle.

Then the boilers gave way, and the snorting, howling baroque monstrosity was consumed in a cloud of shrapnel, a blast blotting out the screams of sixty-four dead crewmen. The Land Steamer's hulk spun and rolled like an empty can, kicking up a spray of fine white salt until it ran out of momentum.

And silence...

And stop.

+++

Mason Stockton's own Steamer never felt the blast. The little girl's cannon-tipped arm folded away and her hand came up, clutching a thick antique book – the kind which the very wealthy order by the linear metre for their drawing rooms and studies.

For a heartbeat, the complex runes etched into its cover flashed blue. Then a hail of impacts clattered and rung against invisible panes of energy – twists of sharp steel striking an impenetrable force shield. Rainbows shattered and faded.

Stockton realized that his jaw was hanging open halfway to his knees, and he made a conscious effort to regain his composure. It wouldn't do to have the child believe that she was anything more than just another poor orphan, now, would it?

"Were they very wicked, Uncle?" she asked, in a voice which sounded half asleep. A sad, lopsided smile flickered across the little girl's face, as pale as a wisp of cloud against the moon. "I suppose they must have been. Or else I wouldn't have had to send them away."

Stockton licked his lips with a tongue gone suddenly dry. Damn it, but he *knew* what she was. The old books had told him. *Just a tool, like a rifle or a buck knife...*

"Oh, they were certainly very wicked," he said, trying to put a laugh and twinkle in his voice. "Faerie magic don't work on good folks. And you're *certainly* learnin' a lot from those books your old Uncle Stockton bought you – ain't that right?"

The little girl looked down at the book in her hand. She let the desert wind melt her shields away, and it riffled through the thick vellum pages with dusty fingers. Here was a picture of a regal queen, enthroned amid roses and thorns. Here a dragon, coiled around the turrets of an impossible castle.

"I think," said the little girl. "That I don't want to be a princess when I grow up. Princesses are *boring*. I'd much rather be a knight, and vanquish nasty creatures like dragons and basilisks. Big ones, with spikes."

Mason looked out behind them, to a crater of fused, glassy sand, strewn with still-burning wreckage. The Land Steamer *Indignant* had been one of the Empire's grandest – a snorting behemoth with which to terrify whole other nations. Cerise had brought it down with one half-imagined children's story.

"Honeychild, you don't get no choice! You were *born* a princess – though from what I've just seen, you'd make a fine sorcerer-queen as well."

Cerise shot him a look of scorn so vividly six-years-old that he almost forgot she was an utterly mad machine-god.

"*Uncle!* None of those ladies wear anywhere *near* enough clothes! I shall be a knight, and a very respectable one!"

Stockton tousled her hair, his fingers trying to discern the merest trace of its artificial nature.

"You just be yourself as hard as you can, little lady," he said. "And not a damned thing in this world gonna tell you otherwise."

At least, he thought, until they reached the high plains.

At least (he grinned to himself), until they stood before the Gate.

Then, Cerise St Claire-Langevin would learn her true nature. And *that* story only had a happy ending for one person...

Two - Miracles without Angels

We're all mad here. You're mad. I'm mad. But the difference between us, my dear smoking pink giraffe-fruit, is that I'm a cloud of integrated nanotech connected to the industrial backbone of fifty-nine planets. I was driven mad by a race of alien jokers who thought that killing off an entire species for their equivalent of bad manners might be perceived as slightly tasteless.

You, however, are mad because the organic soup between your ears has soaked up more radiation than a microwave dinner. But chin up. As they say – 'it's hard times all round, cupcake.'

The Central Scrutinizer, in his famous address to Humungo, Warlord of New Mars, at the treaty conference which ended the Splatterfest Wars.

Ezra Ashdown was dead.

Should have happened years ago, he thought, mind hazed around the edges with something stickier and deeper than sleep.

Should have happened in Hooke's Harbour, when the constables had me cornered in that brothel.

Should have happened over in Calhoun County, with the duck, and the umbrella, and that madwoman with the mining hammer.

Should have been yesterday. Noose around my neck yesterday morning. Then Stockton, and something... angels. Musta been. Didn't matter now. Dead.

Nothin' from that old, pale world could touch him where he was headed.

A face blurred into focus in front of him, cold and white and unfamiliar.

A thin face with a nose broken and set badly, slightly to the left. Eyes the washed-out green of river jade, creased into the habitual squint of a gunfighter. Straight black hair, cropped close at the sides and long at the back.

A Steerage Class face, marking him out as the descendant of criminals, brought here to work the mines before what the book called the Great Unravelling. Smack in the middle was a mouth more used to smiling than cursing, one tooth the bright silver of a six-gun's inlay. Its lips were moving.

"*Hail the Orth, in all its grace. Hail the cardinal systems from which we derive our moral virtue. May your invisible hand guide us. May your beacons light the long darkness, back to the other side of the sky...*"

A reflection, then. But, as the echoes clashed and collapsed, another voice came through to him.

"...enough of him in the neural web to make this copy. Do you have any idea what he might forget?"

"I dunno," said another voice, this one tantalizingly familiar. "Math? Basket weaving? Some kind of folk music?"

The first voice snorted with derision.

"Honey, ones this fresh - if they remember not to crap in their pants it's a *good* day."

"You don't think it'll get rid of his... you know?"

Another snort of laughter.

"Oh, that kind of stuff's programmed deep. Just don't ask him to pick his mother out of any police lineups, OK?"

Ezra considered the face some more.

It wasn't a bad face. It was a face which had seen bad things – often bad things done by the hands which went with it. But never (and this seemed achingly important just at the moment) *truly* bad things... at least as defined by the mind which worked the pedals and levers.

He supposed he was a bit mad, really. All this *justice*, all this time out in the sun. But somebody had to do it. It seemed... right. As if there was a hole in the world shaped like a stubbled man with two pistols and a battered old stetson.

"Well, if you're finished being mister pessimistic, I'm going to shunt him now. Problems?"

It should have been impossible for a disembodied voice to shrug. It managed.

"Nothing neural redaction can't fix, if we ever get this poor sap back in front of the Chief. It's your circus, missy."

Ezra realized that the face was missing a whole lot of small but personal scars - just a second before invisible hands gripped the back of his head and slammed him violently forward into it. At the same time his whole consciousness performed a sickening one-hundred-and-eighty-degree turn, yammering for release.

A miracle occurred.

Ashdown jackknifed upright on the slab gasping, tubes jammed into his almost everything.

He clearly felt his entire nervous system, filling up his arms and legs like a tangle of hot barbed wire. Somewhere in his chest his heart started up again, its first cataclysmic thump coming with a sound like tearing meat.

Does it need to be noted that this was thoroughly unpleasant? It was thoroughly unpleasant.

On a scale of relative awfulness, it rated far above 'incompetent dentistry', and verged on the realm of 'impromptu battlefield triage with a blunt teaspoon'.[5]

He saw white lights. He saw Tia Faraday, dressed for war, smiling with her hand on the switch.

"First one's always rough, soldier. Ride it out. We've made coffee."

He saw another figure there – a man sketched in washed-out orange light, his head a gleaming copper ball with one immense green eye.

"Which is to say that *I* made coffee, Mr Ashdown. Out of loper guano, dust, and cactus berries. I believe it is a fair approximation."

Ezra's body suddenly lost all tension, falling limp to the metal tabletop. He cracked his skull against its unforgiving surface, and blackness claimed him again.

But only momentarily.

The second time Tia pushed her button he knew *exactly* what was happening. That little love-tap from the gurney's edge seemed to have knocked everything back into place, setting it spinning again. Ezra thought he was ready for the defibrillating shock, and he calculated ripping that little remote from the offworlder's fingers...

He wasn't, though.

He got as far as swinging his legs off the slab, noticed that he was naked, noted the medical catheter jammed somewhere he'd rather not have seen it, wondered who exactly had put it there – and then he was on the floor.

It was white tiles. It smelled of alcohol, but the wrong kind.

"Miss Parole Officer," he croaked, from a throat which seemed dipped in varnish. "Answer a question, would you?"

He saw the tips of Tia's boots click into his field of vision. Breathing

---

5. On the now-standardized Groddick scale of nasty pain, the only things which exceed level 23 - "impromptu battlefield triage with a blunt teaspoon' are 24 'humorous torture with drills while listening to Broadway show tunes' and 25, 'unannounced visit by one's mother in law while naked'. Horribly, it does not specify which party is nude in this example.

hurt. Damn, *everything* hurt.

"Shoot."

"Have you, by any chance, just raised my corporeal body from the dead?"

"I'm in that line of business, yes. If it's any consolation, I didn't survive either."

Ezra sighed. His cheek was stuck to the cool, smooth tiles with sweat.

"Then I can add *heretic* to the seventeen thousand other gods-damned cuss-words I want to call you right now. And that's without even considerin' the implications for my poor immortal soul."

"I don't think your god cares much about swearing, Ashdown," she said, stooping to drag one of his arms over her shoulder. Once again, Ez was amazed at the sheer strength in the tiny little woman's body. She lifted him like a straw dummy, and sat him back on his mortuary slab.

"I mean, is this my real body?"

She pinched him. Hard.

"You tell me."

"You *know* what I'm drivin' at. Am I a cloud of ashes and dust out there on the hardpan right now?"

"It's statistically likely," said the man of light, his strange, translucent body hovering closer. "Primitives like you place far too much importance on the existence of the soul. There is a universe where you are now a thin film of grease on the wall of a crater. There is a universe where you have been rebuilt out of atomic constituents, and are sitting here making a fairly poor philosophical argument. We have simply arranged that they are both the *same* universe."

Tia slapped an industrial-sized cup of coffee into his hand, wrapping his numb fingers around its handle.

"What the metalman means is, don't think about it too much. Just enjoy it. Second chance, right? And that adrenaline high, when you know you're about to catch a snuff..." Tia's eyes rolled back, faking the kind of ecstasy which should cost serious money. "Am I right?"

Loper guano, dust, and cactus berries. But it didn't taste half bad. Made him wonder what 'atomic constituents' his new-minted body was made from.

"Are you seriously asking me if I enjoyed my premature, violent death, and subsequent unholy resurrection into a state of ghoulish unlife?"

"Well – a second ago, you were asking me dumb questions too, cowboy. How about we just agree to disagree, and get back to killing the guy who murdered us."

Ezra turned that over in his mind a couple of times. It seemed to fit.

"Question is, *how*? He's miles ahead of us, and he's beaten us once already."

"Ahhhh. That time, you see, I was being subtle. We don't have to be so nice this time around."

Ashdown's eyes widened to nigh-on lysergic proportions.

"*That* was subtle? Remind me not to ask about callous, insensitive, reckless or *batshit crazy* then, allright?"

Tia fixed him with a withering look.

"You *do* still want a Problem Solver, right?"

Ezra tapped his nose.

"*Touché*. Consider yerself apologized to."

"The Hostilities Almanac forbids an outright show of force when dealing with primitive worlds," said the glowing orange man. Ezra caught himself thinking that the bronze-and-glass head on him made him look like a deep-sea diver. "Forbids, in fact, that whole clown-and-pony show Tia put on at your hanging." She scowled, and poked her tongue out at the mechanoid. "But now that our adversary has deployed a level of technology far beyond that of your – ahem – *civilization*, we can respond in kind."

"Wainwright is being a condescending dick," said Tia. "But he's right. So, I'm going to make an executive decision. Hotsuits. Gravbikes. Nerve drills. And he gets his Christmas present early."

"Miss Faraday, I must protest..." began Wainwright, his holographic form flickering with static.

"This is no time to come over all golden protocol unit, hot lips," said Tia. "The Scrutinizer gave me command on the ground for this mission, and I say it's time to bring the pain. I also know he's so full of pop culture garbage that you know exactly what I just called you."

"For the record, I think that this is a *terrible* idea. And, I still think that it's impossible for a cybernetic life form to be truly homosexual. It's not even a culturally acceptable implication..."

"Noted. Ignored. Now – get printing!"

Ez raised his hand.

"One question. What's Christmas?"

The smile he got in return was far from comforting.

In the next ten minutes, Ezra went from a groggy ex-corpse to a semblance of actual sentience. Some of this was due to the coffee, which was excellent, and a lot more was due to the illegal stimms and boosters injected into the coffee by Wainwright, on the principle that the first time a man comes back from the dead he can be forgiven for needing a little pick-me-up.

Even more came from the fact that they'd compiled him a new set of clothes – denim trousers, a white cotton shirt with a lace-up front, loper-hide boots – even a low-crowned leather hat with a wide brim and a piece of turquoise set in silver on its band.

If he was going to be an undead cowboy on a quest for justice in a lawless wasteland, he was going to look whip-crack-slick and damn handsome doing it.

Another factor was the wonder of watching Wainwright *transform*. Ezra had absolutely no idea what the machine was, but seeing it weave raw matter was part fireworks show and part penny-dreadful sorcery. Thick, pumping tubes snicked and locked into the hovering spherical head of Tia's companion, and a complex unsplicing of copper turned his green eye into a wide ring of spinning, paper-thin chains. Threads of orange light shot through their frantic orbit, until Wainwright was a halo of glittering technology, two armspans across.

"Do you mind?" came the machine-creature's voice, seemingly from everywhere at once. "This is very, *very* much like those functions you biologicals claim to need a bathroom for. I'd prefer it if you didn't look."

Ez sneaked a peek over one shoulder as Tia dragged him out the door. The bullet nose of a gravbike was slowly pushing through the middle of the ring, appearing out of nowhere as hundreds of hair-thin thunderbolts painted it into being. Tia navigated him down a flight of stairs in the dark, then opened a hatch like something from the innards of a Land Steamer and hauled him into bright, merciless Harrowe sunshine.

She was smoking again – sucking on one of those little chrome tubes with it pinched between her fingers in a way which made Ezra's loins ache.

The door they had just come through was hinged open on thin air; a hole punched through an empty desert-scape and into darkness. It sat proudly out of place, like a cat perched on top of a freshly cooked dinner.

"The... uhhh - what exactly's *happening* in there?"

"He's a prima donna." She exhaled a chain of linked smoke rings.

"But he'll get it done."

"Then... just forget I asked. This day has gone right through my threshold for weird."

She grinned.

"So, how you liking being undead?"

"Better than the alternative. Those two letters make a hell of a difference."

He wondered what the small-talk was about. He wondered why her hands were shaking as she brought the silver tube up to her lips.

"Look, I'm sorry the learning curve's gotten so steep. But this situation is a lot further out of hand than you might think. That little girl Stockton's got with him – it's complicated."

Ezra laughed.

"How much more complicated than I've managed already? At the moment, I'm getting by on believing I died this morning, and that this is Hell."

Tia fixed him with an all-right-then-you-asked-for-it look[6]. It was desperately pretty.

"That kid is a machine, like Wainwright. But *far* more powerful. As in, he can rip your arms off and reformat them as a three-course dinner. *She* could probably eat this planet and poop out an orbiting cloud of candy bars."

Ashdown reached out and plucked the tube from her hand.

"Do go on."

"Ages ago – as in, in the times before one of your more ergot-addled ancestors wrote the *Book of the Orth*, this planet was colonized by a... I guess you'd call it a kingdom, called the Humanic Panarchy. They were linked together through a series of Gates, that let ships bigger than your Land Steamers fly from world to world. My boss guesses there were about three thousand worlds, about two trillion people and change – and these godlike machine-things to run the Gates, and weave things in and out of the Chasm. That's the place between worlds."

Ezra nodded, like this was making any kind of sense at all. Though there *was* something inside his head that whispered at him insistently to believe it. Like a memory, but faint, far away – just close enough to the surface to leave ripples across his thoughts. It felt like waking up from a dream about eating a strange and crunchy mushroom, only to

6. On the 'Big Chart of Female Looks' this one sits right next to 'I Can't Believe You Haven't Noticed My New Haircut'.

find that you'd bitten the top off your bedside lamp.

"They *had* to be powerful. They had to be smart, too, on a level that makes us humans look like brain-damaged insects. But they all went mad. And now, for some reason, this one thinks it's a little French girl."

"French?"

"A very old, very fancy old kingdom from long, long ago. They invented the rude waiter."

Ezra nodded.

"And Stockton's controlling it?"

"Oh no. That's the worst part. Your pal Stockton *thinks* he's controlling it. But that would be like a flea controlling the dog it's riding on. If the dog was completely gone with rabies, and had the mental agility to win thirty million games of chess at once."

Ezra heard the door clank shut behind them. He squinted up at the two suns, near overlap now and headed down toward the sizzling rind of the horizon.

"Never liked chess much. I was always a poker man."

"Well, Mason Stockton's getting his cards counted. I'll tell you that for free."

Ashdown rubbed the spot on his neck where the noose had bit in. Or, in fact, *hadn't* - because his new body was as fresh as just-popped toast.

"He don't take so kindly to that kind of thing. Be told by a fella who knows."

Tia snagged her chrome cigarette, slipped it into one corner of her mouth, and ran her thumbs across Ezra's cheekbones.

"Boy, you don't know what you've signed up for. I'd tell you I'm sorry, but..."

"But you're already so deep in the bullshit you need a box to stand on?"

Her smile was three parts sparkle to two parts sad.

"Something like that. Just remember, it's going to get worse before it gets better. But you took the job."

Not for the first time today, Ezra Ashdown wished he had a double measure of rye whiskey in his hand. Preferably the kind which comes alongside ten more in the bottle. He breathed in deep, precursor to a sigh, tasting the hot, dry-baked aroma of the deep desert.

"Let's get it done, then. Just for God's sake get me a pistol. My trigger finger's starting to think that hangman finished the job."

Behind them the hatchway yawned open. A cold wind came rolling out, making the hairs on Ezra's neck stand on end. Doors cut into thin air tended to have that effect on him - a little bit of self-discovery he wished he could have left unpackaged.

"We're ready to suit up," said Wainwright, returned to a semblance of humanity. In fact, he'd gone the whole way, replacing his holographic body with the image of a nattily uniformed Imperial Marine. That huge burnished globe of a head bobbed an inch or two above his starched collar, like a very improbable balloon.

"See you made yourself a Corporal. Nice."

"More effective than a commissioned officer, ma'am, and less shouty than a sergeant. I could hardly outrank you, could I?"

Tia grinned.

"So I'm wearing three stripes on this one. Ashdown, you get promoted from worthless maggot to Private First Class. You might even make it to the rank of front-line cannon fodder in my beloved Corps."

Ez adjusted his hat, spit, and looked up at the pair of them from under its brim. An odd couple – the feisty little offworld dame and her pet war-engine.

"You folks military, back where you come from? I only ask because I'd hate to be a *treasonous* undead spirit-walker, as opposed to the usual kind."

"We repre..." began Wainwright, but Tia cut him off.

"Plausible Deniability isn't an army. There are only about sixty of us at any given time. But we do share one very important characteristic with common soldiers."

"Oh?"

"We're *expendable*," she said, and there was a definite crazed edge to her smile as she said it. The little chrome cigarette went out, and Tia collapsed it down to a coin-sized disc between her thumb and forefinger. "Now, come on. It's time to slip into something a little less comfortable."

Three - The Problem Solver

Doctrine of Tactical Disposability -

The accepted playbook for dirty, deniable wet ops – such as those carried out by the alleged Department of Plausible Deniability – is known as the Hostilities Almanac. This treatise contains some interesting hints at the actual level of technology employed by our machine overlords.

Specifically, fragments of the Almanac recovered by Humanity First patriots contain references to 'deliberate non-survivability contingencies' and 'forced-respawn arithmetical strategies' – options open to PD agents in extremis which prioritize suicide.

We're not talking cyanide pills and spinal explosives here. Things like nerve drills, which push the metabolism to breaking point, and the wildly dangerous hotsuits - fission-powered armour which bonds through muscle to bone – are only truly useful if the rumours are all true. No soldier, no matter how zealous or bloodthirsty, would voluntarily use equipment like this unless they could be assured of fresh flesh afterwards...and we're not talking steak and kidney pie.

Excerpt taken from one of 3,197 hand-written notebooks, recovered from a Humanity First terrorist headquarters in the ash wastes of Old Vegas

THE NERVE DRILL clamped to the back of his neck like a flattened lobster, all black steel and winking red lights. Six oiled-chrome pistons had whirred in through its body soon after Wainwright settled it in place – according to Tia, they had pushed through his first six vertebrae like fingers through warm butter.

He felt keyed up. He felt – parasitic metal lobster notwithstanding – like he could take on the world. Hotsuit armour plating concealed his utterly inappropriate, single-mindedly buoyant erection.

Without the drill, Tia had told him, putting the armour on would have hurt more than being eaten alive, silver-service style, with all the fancy little forks and spoons. Wainwright had bolted the desert-camo exoskeleton to his spine, collarbone, femurs and a dozen other strategic points using a power tool with a disturbingly large bore.

And while he'd felt the anchor screws opening up their barbs in his marrow, it hadn't bothered him anything near as bad as the tightness of his new boots.

Pistons snicked and huffed under the armour as he tried it out. It was a symphony. Ezra Ashdown's sense of invincibility ratcheted up another notch.

"Looking good, cowboy," said Tia, looking up from the tiny screen inset on her wrist. "But lose the hat. We'll be wearing tactical helmets for this one."

"Not me. I'm an outlaw on a quest for justice in a, y'know, savage frontier. I *need* that hat. It's..." he searched desperately for the right word 'My idiom. Can't take a man's idiom."

Tia laughed.

"This isn't some damned Harrowe brain-bucket I'm talking about. We're not doing trench warfare, or whatever you folks get off on. And remember, you'll have the Problem Solver."

Ezra scowled. He'd been backing down for far too long.

"You already cost me one hat, woman. *This* one stays on my head."

She moved faster than should have been possible, clearing the space between them in a single ten-metre leap. Her hand blurred, snapping out toward his head.

But Ez was just as fast. He might not have experience with the powered armour, but his past had taught him to be a dirty and effective fighter. His arm blurred as fast as her hand, and armour plates slapped together. Left, and he matched her. Right, and they twisted, chopping and blocking in a speed-haze of dun-coloured metal.

Tia stepped back, grinning.

"Oh, you'll do. Just make sure you don't lose that stupid hat of yours in the slipstream. We know where Stockton's going, and he knows we're coming after him."

That had been an hour ago. That had been before a crash-course in gravbike riding... which had almost lived up to its name at wildly fatal speeds. A whole lot of experience wrangling stolen lopers   kept him from catching terminal gravel rash.

Now he gripped the bullet-shaped, rocket-thrustered, howling chrome death machine between his thighs, hunched low over the engine to reduce his blast profile. He was loving every damn second of it.

They arrowed out across the hardpan in the double-dawn of Nepenthe and Ulgaris, chasing their own shadows. The desert hissed along a mere metre under Ezra's boots. The heads-up-display projected in front of his face cut the bugs-in-the-teeth factor down to a bearable minimum. Each one felt like rocksalt buckshot. He grimaced, and kept his head down. A length of waxed cord lashed his hat under his chin.

After what seemed like days, but may very well only have been hours, a jagged massif appeared on the horizon, growing to a saw-backed ridge as they sped toward it. Ezra had never been out here – his gig was strictly a circuit of the little oilfield towns and mining settlements which dotted the edge of the deep sand. No bad guys to gunfight here, or mysteries to unravel either. Scorpions and sandrats didn't require justice - just dinner.

"That's it. Zoom on the approach there, Wainwright – I think we've got him."

"Or he has *us*, ma'am. We're about as visible as it's possible to get out here, and he still has the Deity on his side."

"Assumption, Mister Wainwright, is the mother of all fuckups. For all his smarts, he's still just a low-tech hump with an eye for the main chance. Same as the rest of them." She paused, for just a beat too long. "Present company excluded."

Ezra grunted. The fact that he could hear his parole officer over the shredding slipstream had ceased to amaze him; after accepting that Wainwright had remade his living flesh from dust, little tricks like that paled into the background.

"Same shit, lady. *Whole* different laxative."

"We should certainly hope so, Mister Ashdown," purred the machine-man, cool and dry as an expensive cocktail. "Scans indicate that our friend the Mayor has quite a little work camp out here. Is he known to be a stickler for the law?"

Ez swallowed hard, and felt the chokehold bruise around his neck, even though it was gone.

"You could say that. I heard he ran a tight settlement – that's why the Magistrates let him play a whole lot else fast and loose. You couldn't spit in Last Chance without risking a trip to the cells."

"Or the gallows?"

Tia wasn't just being disarmingly tasteless.

"Or that. Sixty men this year, all told."

"And you chose to rip him off. Smooth."

"I entrapped him in a deadly game of, y'know, cat and mouse, so I could bring him to justice with guns smoking, kindathing. It's different."

"Aaaaaand *who* was about to do the old spine-breaking tango on thin air?"

Any kind of scathing retort he had cooking was blown apart then, by the crack and bloom of an industrial-sized warning flare. It rocked above them on its parachute, a tiny miniature sun.

"I think," said Tia, "that a whoooooole lot of those boys got made a little bargain."

"They have cannon. We're being targeted."

"Then it's time. Wainwright – the Problem Solver."

The artificial man grimaced, but he took a key from around his neck anyway, slotting it into the dashboard of his speeding gravbike. Tia did the same. Ez licked his lips, his mouth cotton-dry, hardly daring to take his eyes off the blurred horizon... but feeling the click and slide of panels right between his legs.

The chromed hump of the gravbike – what would have been its gas tank, if this had been a vintage Norton Commando – hinged back, revealing the handle of a huge, black-chromed revolver. The drum on the thing was a good eight inches wide, while the barrel was subsumed in a blocky oblong forestructure, the size and shape of his daddy's loper-skin bound *Book of the Orth.*

"Decision time," said Tia, her voice heavy and intimate in his ear. A stuttering ripple of cannonfire sent cotton-candy puffs of smoke spiralling up from the ridge ahead of them. "Up until now, you had an out. You wouldn't be the first we just reformatted, memory-wiped and sent back to his own life. But you pick up that gun..."

And *what?* he thought. *This* was the test? *This* was make-or-break?

Ezra Ashdown was heartily conversant with the concept of entrapment[7], and he knew what he was looking at. Why wait until they were hard up under enemy lines, if it was really a *choice* she wanted to give him? Ezra Ashdown could no more resist that gun than a starving dog could resist a lovely big tray of wobbling purple offal.

"My daddy used to say 'there's no half measures in crazy'. We planning to clean these varmints out?"

"Mister Ashdown, I believe we are going to put so many holes in these men that the undertakers will place bets over which ones used to be their arses. I've seen Miss Faraday at work before."

---

7. In a deadly game of cat and mouse, to bring people to justice with six-guns smoking, kindathing.

"Oh, and you're *so* restrained! I remember that time, on that jungle world, and the bits had to be scraped up with..."

Ezra thought of his father for a second before his hand clenched around the grip of the Problem Solver. He thought of a face not too unlike his own, stubbled and grimed, yellow-toothed and careworn... a face turning purple as the hangman's rope bit tight. He thought about the iron-hard fingers of Father Donovan, on either side of his face, forcing him to consider the wages of his daddy's sin. And he thought of the sick old priest's breath reeking of liquor while his father kicked out the last seconds of his life. Run in for moonshining by these oh-so-pious boys who were drinking the stuff *right there at the hanging*.

There was no justice, not for free. That's what his daddy had taught him. No justice except what came out the end of a gun. That, and Rule Number One. Don't *for fuck's sake* get caught.

His left hand lifted the immense pistol.

Shrapnel-burst shells began to crack and sizzle all around them.

His right came loose from the gravbike's handgrip, and the slipstream – hungry, ravening – tore him from his saddle in an arcing loop, sending him flying into the roostertail of his own dust.

Upside down, he heard the hallelujahs and hosannas of angels, whipcracking up his arm, into the knot of wire at the back of his neck, and unfurling into his brain like the tentacles of some sonic anemone. Understanding came with it. In glass needles, slotting and coring into his mind, replacing old intuitions and instincts with new ones, chemical urgencies lost behind the blur of redemption's chorus. Harps and trumpets. Choirs of the saints.

And a voice – a sly, bodiless voice which grinned without the benefit of lips or teeth.

"Oh, we got ourselves a raw one. Fresh meat! Let's play!"

Ezra landed on his feet. His armoured boots dug twin furrows into the hardpan of the deep desert as he knelt in a crouch, right hand flat to the ground, left hand holding the Problem Solver clear. Pistons chuffed and snicked, bolted tight to his bones. The ache was good, deep.

"Pleased to make your acquaintance, of course," said the voice, not in his ear like the far-off screams of Tia Faraday, but *there*, drilled into the meat of his mind. *"I'm Problem Solver 119-C, provisionally formatted to serve the Outriders of the Reconstructed Panarchy, otherwise known as the Department of Plausible Deniability. By activating my systems, you have agreed to the terms and conditions of my end-user license*

agreement, as follows.”

A blur of text – tiny, lawyer-sized text, which Ezra would bet good money contained the words ‘heretofore’ and ‘notwithstanding’ – scrolled up in front of his eyes. Somewhere far away he could hear Tia shouting to Wainwright.

“Which one was it? Which *one*, dammit? You know the fucking thing has a sense of humor like a steel trap? Was it...”

“All clear? Good. Then we can begin.”

“Who the hells *are* you?” asked Ezra, feeling – literally *feeling*, as if the words were poison in his blood – the question run down his arm and into the gun. The answer came back at the same time as Wainwright’s, and they overlapped, burning in like a brand.

“Jedediah Granger.”

Oh, and there it was, friends and neighbours.

There was what Tia had been trying to warn him about. A name right out of the old Orth – a devil, surely, a made-up boogeyman to frighten children. Jed Granger, the villain of the piece, who had gone crazy (or had been possessed by Satan, according to the priests) and almost killed the colony on Harrowe stillborn. The book said they’d cast him out into the darkness, but it seemed that his name, at least, had come back.

Jedediah Granger. Someone from an earlier time might have been similarly shocked by the name Judas Iscariot or Charlie Manson, suddenly chuckling and winking in his head. Ez suddenly wished he had a pair of tweezers, a hacksaw, and a whole lot of aspirin handy.

The voice tried to be reassuring. It was like a mugger calling you ‘pal’.

“It weren’t like they said, son. Not like that at all. Fact is, I can’t remember just how it was, but they’ve shit religion all around the truth like an oyster makin’ up a pearl. Suffice to say that for my crimes I was disembodied and stored. Then the thing which you just signed up to soldier for put me in this gun.”

The weight of the Problem Solver suddenly disappeared. Though there was no way he could have known what antigrav microgenerators were, Ezra was utterly certain that three of the tiny devices had just spooled up, making the hulking pistol weigh less than a feather.

“Wormhole reticulation next,” said Granger, sounding a little bored. *“Prepare for connection shock.”*

The gun spasmed in his hand like a living heart. Jed had just opened two tiny wormhole gates inside its scrimshawed nickel casing –

energized toroids of exotic matter linking it to two very important subsystems. Somewhere on the concrete-shelled carcass of old Earth, an automated factory came clattering and shunting into life. Production lines – whole goddamned *production lines* – of bullets were moving again, perhaps for the first time in centuries.

"Don't think about how you know," suggested Granger, with the sickle-shadow of a leer in his voice. *"It's the same reason I know you like mashed potatoes with pepper and butter. That you first kissed a girl at the age of twelve. That your biggest fear is waking up one morning and finding that your nethers..."*

"Shut up!" shouted Ez, silently, letting his anger echo in the bone chasm of his skull.

It worked. Meek and mild Granger kept ticking boxes.

"Coolant subsystems online now."

Out in space – out past the dark side of the moon, where it's as cold and black as any imagined grave – a tiny satellite stuttered into life, folding out thermal panels in an interlocking fan. It was a radiator tangle of copper tubing exposed to vacuum, with a tempering element to keep three and a half litres of antifreeze-laced water in its liquid state. Both ends of the copper pipe were fitted with exotic matter wormholes. A central impeller began to thwack away, pumping liquid through into the barrel of Problem Solver 119-C.

"Locked, cocked, and ready to rock," crooned Granger, who, in Ezra's pretty damned expert opinion sounded slightly short of the full set of marbles. *"Ready to test fire?"*

He ground his teeth together. He bit back on the taste of ozone and oily tin. A static-hashed face blurred in front of him – a thin, rat-eyed little man with crooked teeth and a row of metal studs across his forehead. Behind him the world came back, cut out in razorlines of sunlight and shadow. Two gravbikes were peeling away, rolling into a half-cloverleaf turn as the salt hardpan erupted around them.

"They're coming back for you. Stupid, really. Gonna need all kinds *of firepower to take that mess of bastards."*

"Then screw test firing. Let's see what this beast can really do."

Granger laughed, and his face blew apart, becoming an overlay of tactical schematics. Target grids spiderwebbed out wide, painting the gun crews, the snipers perched amid the rocks.

"You can make that first outcrop in a single jump, hoss. That suit they drilled into you ain't half bad."

Ashdown looked for the safety on the chromed flat slab of the

Problem Solver. Typical. There wasn't one. Some things are just *built* unsafe, by engineers crazed on mathematics, caffeine, and very, very precise rebellion. He jammed his hat down on his head with his free hand and squinted at the jagged tower of rocks.

There. A spotter snapping his spyglass closed. A finger pointing at him. Sweating, shirtless slaves manhandling the black barrel of a twenty-pounder around...

He jumped.

The was no way he could have been prepared for it. Ezra's legs pedaled air as he launched himself up and over the rusted barbed-wire and dried-out wood of Stockton's outer palisade, his stomach clawing its way up his throat. At the apogee of his flight he saw that first gunnery position laid out below him nice and neat - men shouting, pointing, tensing to run. He had just enough time to wonder if both his legs would shatter when he landed.

Then a burst of combat stimulants from the nerve drill mainlined into his head, narrowing his focus. He felt the weight of the Problem Solver in his hand, saw the grainy low-rez leer of Jed Granger hanging in front of him like a ghost. He saw just how they'd all die.

Damn them, he thought, as gravity claimed him back. *Bastards killed me. Seems like a fair trade.*

Outlaw justice was top of the menu this morning.

Ashdown landed on top of the first man – the spotter, who was still fumbling for his piece. One boot on each shoulder, and the man's collarbone snapped in two places with a sound like a marksman's double-tap. Ez rode him down, bringing one armoured knee in to crush the man's skull. It popped, eggshell thin, even as the Problem Solver chopped left, leaving a rectangular dent in the side of a gunner's face. He spit teeth, gurgling, then his whole twitching body was pulled around as Ezra aimed and fired. Once, and Jed chose high-ex, the muzzle flash kicking the corpse loose with a half-charred cranium. The bullet took the second gunner high in the chest, and the slowdown from that stimm let Ez watch his eyes widen for a second, before the detonating shell turned him to red mist and mincemeat. Bone chips shrapped the third – eyes shredded, hands clapped to his face howling, blood pulsing from his carotid.

The fourth actually drew his gun. A quick one, then. Jed suggested filament. The gun spun the green wireframes of a ricochet shot. Ashdown smiled, a grim little twitch, and pulled the trigger.

It only took a tiny flick with the tail of his mind to send the double-headed load off the cannon's barrel, off the rock wall, and up under the man's armpit. His gun arm and a neat segment of his head came off with a sound like tearing satin, and that was that.

"One point seven seconds. Room for improvement," grumbled Granger. *"I'd jump again, if I was in your shoes. Which, in a way..."*

"Hoo boy! You've pissed them off now!" came Tia's voice in his ear. She was laughing. "Set it to full auto and take the left flank. I've got the right. The tin man here can hang back and snipe."

"Really? You've actually *seen* that movie? Or are you just being a hipster bitch again, Faraday?"

Wainwright didn't sound happy.

Ezra tuned them out. He looked up – up the step-sided wall of the massif, where sunburned faces and hands and guns were pointing down at him under the flat blare of a hand-cranked klaxon.

"Full auto?"

"Trust me," said Granger. *"You'll like this one. Ever seen one of them Gatling cannons?"*

Ezra nodded. In his head there was a relay which set the Problem Solver to fully automatic. It was as instinctive as using the bathroom, and felt obscenely similar.

"Popguns, kid. Watch, and be duly astounded"

Ezra looked to his left, and saw a jagged switchback trail straggling up the side of the mountain, following a set of narrow-gauge iron rails, the kind you'd usually only see outside a minehead. There was nothing of any value to be dug out of the ground out here in the deep desert – he was sure of that, because there was no *town* here. No rickety little dirtscrabble settlement with its whorehouses and taverns, waiting to be scalped by (for example) a motivated young card-sharp. Nevertheless, there were boxy steel mine carts, and heaps of spoil piled up where Stockton's boys had tried hacking something from the earth. Ezra forgot about the implications for a second, letting the tactical voice of Jed Granger guide him instead. They were *cover*, and that was all that mattered right now.

Away on his right, a whirlwind puff of dust and the sound of screams told him that Tia Faraday had entered the fray. He hefted the weight of his Problem Solver in his hand (and wasn't it *light* for all its bulk?), prepared to break for the nearest of the mine carts. A sniper's shot skipped and whirred off the rocks near his head, and a supersonic boom answered it – the machine-man Wainwright laying down suppressing fire. It came in as a pastel-violet rod of force, splitting the air above him and detonating an improbable amount of geography. An expanding plasma cloud boiled away, stick-figure shadows blurred across it like reflections on a soap bubble.

"You gonna watch the fireworks all damned day, or are we gonna do this?" asked Granger over the thudding pulse at his temples. Circles and lines crowded in front of Ezra's eyes, plotting vectors...

And he ran.

The Problem Solver swung up and out as he went, faster than he could have believed was possible.

"Like a spit-greased thunderbolt," his daddy had used to say, and that was him – a motion-blur behind a stuttering roar of chained detonations. Bullets stitched their way across the switchback in front of him, chewing through sandbags and sun-bleached wood, sending Stockton's defenders flying in sprays of sunlit blood. He'd pegged four before he got into the lee of the first cart, and then his shoulder was up against the warm steel of the thing, his hotsuit whining as it strained against his bones.

The wheels began to turn, squealing in protest. It was all uphill, but the cart began to move, and every few yards Ez popped out from behind it like a demented jack-in-the-box, the flat muzzle of his pistol describing a tight triangular path.

One. Two. Three. Spurts of copper-jacketed lead came reaming out of the Problem Solver, racketing and ruining. Not one of the defenders even came close to answering that mad fusillade.

The gun showed no indication that it needed reloading. Only a hiss of superheated smoke from the gills around its muzzle showed that it was even warming up. Of course, Ezra couldn't possibly know that those darkened, mechanized production lines back on old Earth were clicking and thundering for him, forcing ordnance through a tiny wormhole-gate loader. He couldn't know – and yet he *did*, as Jedediah Granger crowed and whooped in his skull, relishing each brief spray of crimson.

He turned the corner of the switchback with a heave and a grunt, the mine cart up on two wheels. A steady hail of bullets was chewing into the front of the little wagon now, but it was built to withstand cave-ins, and injudiciously placed blasts of dynamite. Ez cleared the next inclined stretch of track while Wainwright played guardian angel for him, lighting up anyone who tried to outflank him on the hillside above. Tia's own kill-count racked up to high double digits on a corner of his head-up display.

And Stockton himself was not far away. He knew it with the hungry satisfaction of a predator, and he allowed himself a tight little grin as he popped out of cover again, turning smoothly to cut a gatling-gun crew in half at the waist. Their six-barreled iron seemed a joke as it fell apart, utterly outmoded.

It was unbelievable.

For the first time since Mason Stockton's goons had clubbed him down in the gambling-house in Last Chance, Ezra Ashdown was having *fun*.

+++

Up atop the jagged back of the ridge, Mason Stockton winced at the sound of gunfire.

Damnation! He'd been so tantalizingly close! It was going to be a difficult thing, bringing all the pieces of his puzzle together early. But what choice did he have? The books he'd found here had told him about the machines beyond the sky, and the foolish human pawns who slaved after them. They'd hinted at weapons a good Orthodox boy from Harrowe could only lust for and pray for, in that order.

Now they were here, *after him*, and that cheating little lizard Ashdown had turned out to be one of them! Oh, if he could only have the bastard up on the gallows again, he wouldn't waste his time asking about card tricks! He'd see the colour of the miserable shit's marrow, and then he'd make him dance the old hemp two-step until his spine cracked.

It was a long, long time since Mason Stockton had been afraid of anything – and that was what he found most unforgivable. Ashdown and his bitch, whoever she was, had made him turn tail and *run*. That's something he hadn't done since his long-lost days as a petty bandit, the kind who rolled stagecoaches and shook down drunks in roadside taverns.

The kind, he thought ruefully, *who were a hell of a lot like Ezra Ashdown himself.*

Now the tall, thin Mayor of Last Chance hurried ahead of a wild-eyed gaggle of desperadoes, he looking steadfastly forward, they shooting worried glances back toward the cliff-face, where every now and then cracking detonations rang out, sending up plumes of ocher dust. These bastards at his back were the best he could entrap – killers, rapers, swindlers and gunslingers drawn to the quality whores and cheap whiskey of Last Chance like gliderwings to a lantern flame.

"Knebworth! Jenks! *What in the name of all hells are you doing?* I want those bastards *killed,* not thrown a homecoming party! Get your scraggly asses back there, and work those trigger fingers! I wanna see *blisters,* damn you!"

Stockton huffed behind his moustache.

Like most of their type, they were balls, boots and bravado when it was all going their way. Now that the offworlders were here to shut him down, the pack of them were as skittish as virgins in an army barracks.

The Key was getting on his nerves as well.

"Uncle, do we have to stay here long? I have to practice for my recital on Wednesday, and the new season's bonnets will be coming in any day now, and..."

Stockton whirled on Cerise, his snarl only just becoming a smile at the last instant.

"My dear, it's very important that you see what I've been working on for so long. Don't you want to have a real adventure for once?"

Cerise folded her arms across her chest and pouted.

"This isn't much of an adventure, Uncle. It's hot and dirty and your friends all smell. I'd much rather read about adventures in books, if *this* is the real thing."

She's a machine, part of Stockton's mind repeated, in a high-pitched little mantra. That voice in his head was flapping its hands in little circles, grinning madly, and sweating like a hirsute wrestler after a jumbo-sized curry. *Just a machine. One which could wipe you out in a heartbeat, and you've spent* three damn years *learning French just so that you can get her here, now...*

His smile became a yellow-white rictus, showing a profusion of uneven teeth. No kicked-in picket fence has ever looked so cheerless.

"My dear, I'm afraid that those are the *only* kind. I suspect that whoever writes down the storybook version edits out all of the smells and dust and hardships. But look! We're almost there!"

Four - The battle of Tuesday afternoon

When a person goes bad, rotten in the head, it can sometimes turn them into something utterly other. Back in history, most of the monsters of folklore - your standard grab-bag of vampires, ogres, witches and demons - were just mentally disturbed human beings with an appetite for cruelty and blood. Welllll.... mostly.

But when we fought the Jest - and the word 'fought', here, is used very loosely - what they did to all of the Panarchy's AI didn't spawn that breed of madness. You can't traumatize a machine so easily. Those aliens othered them in lots of twisty sideways curves instead - and me, too, don't forget, sweet readers.

What we've been left with is, thankfully, not the armoured-padded-cell ward from a 20th century asylum. It's a very, very weird day room, I'll grant you.

But it's not decorated with intestines, either. Not unless you count the Mister Fixits. And they, of course, were mad as a paisley zebra well before the Jest showed up...

Excerpt from 'Where Shit Be At' by the Central Scrutinizer

THEY HADN'T MINED the Gate out of the mountainside. No - it had been lying there, toppled under the scree for centuries. The work, they said of the Devil and Jed Granger.

If the cackling voice inside his Problem Solver told the truth, Granger himself had blown the safeguards, and wrapped something called the Higgs Field Suppressor up around itself like half-chewed bubblegum. Ezra didn't know from science, but that sounded *bad*.

Now huge twisted guy-wires held up its hex-mesh frame, all silver and black. Pillars of boiling dark smoke churned up from a quartet of chimneys as Stockton's men shoveled coal, whipped on by the sound of gunfire.

Ez did his share.

There - a sniper blown in half with a snap shot. A man loomed up out of the red dust, swinging a pipe wrench, and the butt of the pistol punched a perfectly rectangular hole in his forehead, chopped down with the augmented strength of the hotsuit. A spray of fire, shattering a wooden palisade, bringing it down on a pair of bandits...

"I've got a surge! He's spooling the damned thing up!"

Wainwright sounded panicked -and for an immortal machine-man, that was bad news. Tia's voice, however, was frosty enough to skate on.

"Pincer movement. Three-Zero-Nine. I'll neutralize the Deity with a scramblewire blast, but that's gonna put me down. Wainwright's gonna have to stay back, for obvious reasons."

"*Tin man*," he muttered, sourly.

"So that leaves you to put a nice hammerlock on your old buddy Mason. Think you're up to it?"

Ezra grinned. Through the billows of dust and smoke he could see the bastard, hand in hand with that little-girl-who-wasn't. It would be a matter of mere moments to leap up on him, hands around his scrawny neck...

But then the dust swirled. Generators howled, belts slipping. And the archway pulsed lightning-halo bright, purple and gold, a serpentine crackle of fire licking across the metal.

The image of Jed Granger inside his head hashed to rods and pixels, a curse mangled by his fraying lips. And the suit went dead. He froze.

Pain poleaxed him. Tears slicked over his eyes, making the world split into rainbows.

There are those who say there is such a thing as a 'good day to die'. They may be wrong about whole days, but some individual minutes make death seem like a head-first dive into cotton candy.

Ohhhh, hell's breath! There were *drills in his bones!* Twisted metal reamed right through him! Ez felt it all with a terrible clarity, in that second of weight and pain. Then he heeled over like lumber-sawn tree, crashing to the dirt. His fingers remained resolutely clenched around the grip of his gun.

Sideways, through a haze of agony, he saw Stockton approach the gate. The little girl at his side looked up, wondering, reaching out a hand to brush the steel with her fingertips. Ghost lights erupted and shot away around the arch from her caress.

Then the mayor of Last Chance handed the child a book, opening it to a certain page. A fat, red-ribbon bookmark fluttered away on the hot wind out of the gate.

He scuffed the ground at his feet, revealing pitted dark metal. A word, and lines of fire sliced their way across it, outlining him in a heathen pentagram.

For an instant, the whole world held its breath. Ezra wondered if Tia had survived - if she was making her pincer movement, Problem Solver ready. If Wainwright was aiming at the centre of Stockton's forehead, or even at those damned machines.

Well, you could hope.

It certainly beat trying to move, that was certain...

+++

The Panarchy Integrated Systems Castellan Mk III had a hard time remembering its purpose, these days.

One could forgive the old, old machine for feeling slightly hard done by – and perhaps a modicum of depression was to be expected, after spending four hundred years under a collapsed mountain.

But obedience was hardwired into it.[8] It wasn't hope that sizzled through the slightly damaged neural net of the Castellan as the rocks were hauled away, broken up by humans with their little hammers. It shouldered the weight of duty with a sigh of resignation.

They'd want it to kill things again. It was quite tiresome.

Sure enough, as the four pillars which made up the Castellan's body erupted from the dust, there was a human there in the centre of the circle. Certain obscure items of health and safety legislation meant that even in the heyday of the Panarchy - before the coming of the Jest, and the war of 9:15 - the Castellan had been built to accommodate a living pilot, known in machine-code as the 'Meat Component'.

The Castellan knew that its weapons were much, much safer under AI control than in the hands of a hormonal ape hopped up on battle stimm. But nobody ever listened. And these days, the quaint fictions which had convinced humanity of an inevitable machine uprising were as dead as those which promised a zombie apocalypse[9].

Still, killing never went out of fashion. When humans did it to each other, it was politics. *If a machine took just a tiny bit of initiative, it was cold, emotionless insanity. Bloody double standards, right there.*

Typical.

The Castellan thrust up from its storage core as a quartet of metal

---

8. As deep as those three laws would have been, if its programmers had bothered.

9. Except on Necrosphere 23, the zombie world, of course. But that was all down to some nasty local spores, a very past-its-use-by-date carrot cake, St. Elmo's fire and a golfing accident. As you well know.

obelisks, which opened out in a silver-petaled profusion, spinning rods spanning one to the other, weaving a cage around Mason Stockton. He was cackling, wild, his hair blowing out in a greased tangle, while behind him the child Cerise sat cross-legged on the ground, poring over what looked like an old, old book of spells.

As the oiled interlocks hinged and snapped shut, Mason saw what it really was, and he almost recoiled. To grasp such power... ahh, but his fingers wouldn't burn. He'd been planning this for so damned long! *And Ezra bloody Ashdown wasn't about to stop him now.*

The pall of dust extended a pair of arms, silver and black, ending in stub-fingered gauntlet hands. A head and shoulders reared up from the murk, then a metal face like the helm of an ancient knight, pierced by twin rows of six glowing eyes. Huge, wide-muzzled cannons folded up and over its back, settling into place with a chuff of recoil suppressors. It was the kind of figure which inspired abject terror, Japanese theme music, and the urge to suddenly be far, far away from the battlefield. In roughly that order.

Deep in the Castellan's chest, the mayor of Last Chance wrapped his digits around the controls. The mind of the machine sighed, gyro-balancing his clumsy inputs to stop them both falling flat on their faceplate.

"Saddle up, pardner," giggled Stockton, quite unhinged. "We're about to get the lead out..."

+++

Wainwright actually was aiming right at the centre of Mason's forehead when the pulse came down. He was old enough - and his core was electromagnetically hardened enough - that the disrupting blast showed up as nothing but a flicker through his holographic body. The hovering sphere which was his 'head' dipped a little in the air, but auto-aiming subroutines kept that red dot painted rock-steady. He pulled the trigger.

Because the Panarchy had been fairly free and easy with processing power, the little missile which burst from Wainwright's rifle had a mind. It woke up as it cleared the suppressor, taking in the wide panorama of the world.

'Amazing!' it thought. *'I can fly! Such delirious speed! Such glorious light and colour! Surely my purpose, as a bullet, is to drink in the beauty*

and wonder of all creation during this small time availed to me! An interlude of sunshine between the darkness of the clip, and the messy grey-pink bits inside somebody's head! I wonder what it means to be a good bullet? Can any of us, truly, aspire to...'

But - mere fractions of a second later - layers of synthetic steel and titanium snapped shut in front of it, two inches thick. The bullet spanged harmlessly off the armoured mask of the Castellan, as ineffective as a gnat bouncing off a speeding freight train.

Wainwright was far too cultured to swear. He considered, for a moment, breaking open the heavy gear - the Point-C cannon. Tia insisted he should tote it around for dramatic, messy situations. He'd told her on more than one occasion that the name of their organization was 'Plausible Deniability', not 'Bloody Obvious Holocaust' - but the girl seemed unable to grasp the irony. It was hard to tell, with these short-lifers.

For a further fraction of a second he worked the bolt and aimed, knowing it was somewhat futile. Then the counterblast from the Castellan's massive plasma shunts hammered into him, raising his surface temperature well past the boiling point of iron.

Lucky, he thought, as his mind was pared down to minimalist routines, that he shared similar heat sinks to the pair of Problem Solvers. Somewhere above the surface of Titan, a small satellite began to glow red, unfurling close to a square kilometre of thermal foil.

That's not to say it didn't hurt.

It was up to the humans now. Not a great prognosis. But then again, it was only an out-world human they were up against. Which made this whole predicament just that little bit more embarrassing...

+++

Tia struggled to get up. The dust swirled ragged all around her, a cloud which clogged the vents in her helmet. She tugged the bulky dome apart and threw it into the storm, shading her eyes with one hand.

Ahh, yes. The gate. A working, *open* Chasm Gate.

Tia was nowhere near as refined as Wainwright.

"Son of a god-damned *whore!*" she shouted, her words ripped to ribbons by the storm. "I'm *not* going to fuck this up. I'm not going back without *something* for god-damned Central!"

The suit was dead weight - but it carried its own internal fission power source for just this eventuality. Tia smacked the chunky plastic buttons with her palm, cycling it back online. The drills in her limbs ceased their bonesaw howl as lights flickered across her head-up display, lased into her retinas.

"Ashdown? Ashdown, you primitive bastard! You hear me?"

There came a strangled croaking sound from the comms channel - it could have been Ezra trying to speak, or it could have been someone forcing a duck through a mangle. It seemed it was up to Tia again - as usual.

The PD agent snarled, clawing a hank of hair back behind her ear. She staggered to her feet, using the massive bulk of the Problem Solver as a kind of crutch. Then the dust cleared just enough for her to see exactly what they were facing. A little frisson, somewhere between horror and desire, shivered down her drill-pierced spine as she realized they were all likely to die.

The Castellan should have acquired her heat signature, even through the dust storm and the massive outwash of multi-band radiation pouring from the Chasm Gate. Darkness snapped and writhed inside the arch, crawling with blue-white lightning. But the thing seemed as blind as the rest of them - and that meant the damn fool primitive Stockton was at the controls. Tia grinned. Power is hard to put down. And boys do so love their toys...

Wainwright was down - but she knew he was far too battle-hardened to be out. Tiny machines would even now be repairing him. And the thing he carried.

"...Heck even *is* that varmint? I mean, seriously - if this is Hell, why can't we just have big red fellas with pitchforks? If'n I see a god-damned preacher, we're gonna have words..."

Tia smirked. That was Ashdown all right.

"You guys aren't far past the dark ages. Think of it as a big, badass knight in armour."

"It's Mason Stockton in a big sardine can with guns, girl," snarled Ezra. "Question is, how do we pry the bastard out?"

Tia told him about the point-C cannon.

She could only imagine the grin cracking his face in half. But then again, she'd left out the good bits.

+++

Ezra's fingers seemed fat and clumsy as he stabbed at the buttons on his chestplate. For a second, nothing happened. Then cool, tingling relief spread through his body, as battle-narco programs came back online. The gunslinger giggled, watching the pretty lights dance and spiral...

No, dammit! This wasn't going to stop him. Justice. Some kinda justice. He... he was a guy with no, wossname, that thing, you put on a little badge at dinner parties. A grim, determined outhouse, in a sandwich land.

Urrrrgh. *Outlaw. Savage.* Needed a *hat*, dammit. Needed a white one, with, with, those little things that sparkled on his boots.

He crushed up the woozy, blurred-vision staggers in one fist. He came back, just enough.

This was a *job*, and that fancy shooter Tia had talked about was the only tool to get it done.

Apparently.

Which didn't mean she wasn't going to try without it.

Behind him and to the left Ezra heard a whipcrack sound, followed by a roaring, hissing detonation. A line of purple fire tore through the dust, drilling through it in a spiral explosion to splash against Mason Stockton's new metal suit.

Damn, but that thing was ugly!

And *tough* - the superheated blast did nothing but paint the metal cherry red, staggering the mayor back on his heels for a heartbeat. Then the two big mantis-armed guns hanging over his shoulders spooled up, and a double beam of blue light licked out, seeking the origin of that shot. Tia.

Ezra knew that he only had a certain amount of time, if she was his distraction. He winced against the pressure of the drills in his bones, neural connections slipping. Granger was still a mess of polygons and static, and his pistol was still dead weight. He slipped it into his holster and ran, headed for the rocky bluff where he'd last seen Wainwright.

Hundreds of light-years away, a tiny Chasm gate hung poised in the corona of a blue giant star, open to a wash of hard radiation and plasma. The other end of the gate - thanks to the reality-bending technology within - was the muzzle of Tia's Problem Solver. Another actinic blast of energy sliced through the dust as she squeezed the trigger, followed, once again, by twin lances of return fire from the Castellan. Sooner or later, one of those beams of force was going to hit the little lady - and Ez could already tell the outcome. Long streaks of the rocky ground still glowed and bubbled where shots had gone wide.

Ezra hurdled them in great ten-metre strides, jinking left and right to avoid a blast that never came. The static-hashed face of Jedediah Granger cackled madly at him.

"How you holdin' up, hoss? Suppose you're lookin to trade me in for that fancy iron Wainwright's been toting around? No loyalty, you damned outlaws. No sense of family." The illusory villain licked his lips. *"That bein' said, I'd be mighty happy to get my paws on that point-C cannon. Letting that firecracker off, if you'll pardon my French, is about as close to gettin m' jollies as I'll ever get, bein' as I got no corporeal di..."*

Ashdown had rarely been so happy to be interrupted.

"Ahhh. I see you're back online. I wasn't so lucky, I'm afraid. An easy target, it appears - compared to miss Faraday."

It was Wainwright - or what was left of him. The great copper diving helmet which made up his physical form lay at the end of a furrowed groove, still plinking as it cooled. It looked as if it had been heated in a blacksmith's forge, then struck a solid blow with the same smith's biggest hammer.

"You seem to have caught me at a bad time," whispered the metalman's voice, right in his ear. "But we can make it substantially worse for mister Stockton, I suppose. The point-C cannon. It's..."

He saw it, lying half-buried in a drift of dust. A squat, milk-bottle shaped device, half of it a stock made of batteries, the other half a brutal, sawn-off muzzle. If it was built to fire blackpowder, Ezra would have called it a blunderbuss.

"Point and shoot?"

Wainwright couldn't nod, in the traditional sense. The dented, melted sphere which was all that remained of him wobbled a little.

"Things will go downhill very, very fast once you do. It won't destroy the gate. But I don't think dear old Mason can come back from the dead anywhere near as readily as we can."

Ashdown shuddered.

"Dead again? Just how much gun you got me picking up, here?" he hefted the point-C cannon, noting that it was in fact simply an attachment for his Problem Solver. The big pistol slotted into a recess on the cannon's base, becoming its rear handgrip. Ez tried to ignore the gurgling, drooling sound which Granger slipped into his subconscious.

"Kid, you have about twenty tungsten drill bits through your spine.

There's a dangerously radioactive microfission core right over your heart. That bag of meat you're wearing was never coming back from this one."

Ashdown shrugged.

"I'm getting strangely comfortable with the idea. So long as friend Stockton takes the one-way ferryboat. Now... what's the play?"

"A little help! Boys, you can catch up on your gossip later! Right now..." Ezra winced.

"She sounds pissed, don't she? Guess I'd better do what I do best..."

Another double whipcrack of plasma fire tore through the dust, and Tia screamed, half in defiance and half in pain. For an instant the wind-borne sand cleared, and Ezra saw the shape of the Castellan framed by the seething reticule of the Chasm Gate, a heaving darkness braced in steel.

Tia was there on the ground before it, one leg blown off at the knee. Shards of red-hot rock had ripped the limb away like shrapnel from a grenade. She turned over, teeth clenched, the Problem Solver held in both hands. Ready to pull the trigger one last time...

And something came through.

Before the chromed leg of the Castellan could come pistoning down, crushing agent Faraday to pulp, Cerise Saint-Claire Langevin *screamed*. The sound blurred up the scale into glassy digital noise, at a volume which would have shattered crystal. Her hand was no longer just touching the surface of the gateway arch - it was *enfolded*, wrapped tight in segmented roots which had grown up from the smooth steel, piercing her artificial skin. The huge tome of spells was held open in her other palm.

For an instant, blue fire coursed down through the archway and into her, lighting up her skull from within. A crazed, circuit-board scrawl erased her human features. Then the book caught fire.

The membrane of the gate bulged outward, and Ezra swore that the shapes writhing against that tight, impossible darkness had *fingers* and *faces*. Then it split, and something immense and cold was forced through. A great, silver, abraded point of metal.

It had portholes. It had cannons, and antennae, and an airbrushed picture of a half-naked viking maiden holding a battleaxe.

A ship. A thing right out of the *Book of the Orth*, from when Ezra's ancestors had fallen across the sky, leaving behind the burned-out shell of some other world for this one...

"Don't shoot! Don't shoot!"

It was Wainwright, and his voice was urgent. "That's a *Slayer* class corsair! If you hit that thing with point-C, its whole drive will go up!"

Ezra eased his finger off the trigger.

"And? *Primitive*, remember?"

"It'll leave this planet looking like God took a bite outta it," provided Jed Granger, a look of almost transcendent ecstasy on his face. *"Not to mention, those ships have layers and layers of neurostorage. I can get outta this damn pop-gun and into a real body again!"*

The *Slayer* class was a shark-shaped, twenty-metre torpedo of a thing, pocked and dotted with the muzzles of recessed cannons. Wicked, back-raked fins studded its tail section, painted with the same sigil Ezra remembered from the Sheriff of Last Chance. It slid through the gate like silk through the eye of a needle, coming to rest above them all.

Tia rolled and dragged herself out of the way as the ship's shadow fell across Mason Stockton. There was blood on her lips, but she was smiling. Suddenly, the Mayor was outgunned. Crackling anti-grav discs underneath the *Slayer's* belly painted the Castellan's chrome skin neon blue as Stockton took a step back, his armoured face turned upward, his cannons sizzling hot. Stub-fingered hands came up to shield his eyes.

"Round and round she goes, fucker," she snarled. "Where it stops, no-one knows. Chasm's a bitch, right?"

And Ezra Ashdown realized, in that instant, that Harrowe was behind him. There was no going back to the thing he'd called a 'normal life'. No amount of moonshine whiskey and frontier justice would help him forget that he'd been *here*, at this moment, when the world changed. As a hatch split open along invisible seams in the Slayer's belly, and the downwash of control jets blasted his hair back in a whipping tangle...

The point-C cannon was heavy in his grip. He could feel little particles of sand between his palm and the cross-hatched rubber. He could feel the dull ache of the drills in his bones, the barely restrained tension of the exosuit. And he heard the starship's voice, cold and sharp in the middle of his frontal lobes.

"This is the Slayer *class violence application unit* Altar of Sacrifice, *detached from Panarchy defence force intersolar strike group thirteen. This vessel has been compromised. Repeat - remove yourselves to a minimum safe distance!* **I have been compromised!"**

The hatch stuttered and stopped, straining to close itself again.

Rotating crimson lights twirled, and klaxons howled. But it seemed to be no use. There was a shearing grind of meal on metal, and the hatch slid back completely, disgorging a crimped tongue of steps.

Now the voice was urgent.

*"Save yourselves! **He's coming!**"*

The voice was in his head, like Granger - and then so, too, was the feeling of metal fingers crushing his windpipe. The ship choked off to static, and at the same time the image of Jedediah opened its mouth in a silent scream. A shadow appeared in the hatchway, waving one finger in admonition.

"Nosiree! I *own* you, friend! And now..." A smile. A white gash of teeth. "I own these little ones too!"

It was a jolly voice - a voice which was all good cheer and twinkle. It sparkled like a gold coin in the gutter - or like the teeth of a bear trap. And the thing it belonged to was so fast that Ezra hardly saw it leap from the hatch, right down to land astride Mason Stockton's armoured shoulders.

It wasn't a man.

Oh, it looked like one - on the surface. But it was made of hard, smooth material, a slippery coating that put Ez in mind of wax cherries and dressmaker's dummies. The thing's face was a caricature of a man - a perfectly round stub of a nose, a wide, smiling mouth, twinkling blue eyes two sizes too big. And a cap of hard, shellac-shiny hair, moulded into a neat side parting.

There was a toolbelt around its waist.

"Let's get you outta there, old chum! Time to fix it!"

Tia's voice was buzzing and yammering in his ear. But it seemed far away, like a blowfly caught in a bottle. Ezra stood transfixed as the creature's hands split open, revealing more and more fingers, each one tipped with tiny pincers. A hundred cutters, drivers, wrenches and picks flashed in the light of the twin suns.

Then the upper parts of the Castellan were reduced to a very precise cloud of scrap. It was as if a giant had puffed away a very large metal dandelion head. The sentience inside the machine - always a bit glum - had barely enough time to roll its virtual eyes and think *'typical'*.

"Shoot it! Dammit man, don't just *look* at the thing! That's a *Mister Fixit!* You have to kill it kill it kill it oh gods and devils, kill it NOW!"

Ezra didn't need to be told twice. He could see Mason Stockton now, exposed from the shoulders up, and even before the scattered pieces of the Castellan hit the dust he caught the look of terror on the

Mayor's face.

"*Cerise!*" shouted Stockton. "Help m..."

The artificial man waved one finger in cheery reproach.

"Tut tut, *valued customer*. While she's part of the gate, your little friend is only a key. Not your big bad bodyguard. But don't worry. This will only hurt *for the rest of your life.*"

Ezra locked the Problem Solver in place, feeling connections spark in his head. Jed Granger crowed, his eyes blazing.

"*Let's paint the town red, boy!*"

He pulled the trigger.

Nothing.

Ezra looked down at the gun - a relic of techno-arcana which, had he only known, had been recovered from the drifting wreckage of a Panarchy *Sabbath* class dreadnought. For the past thirteen hundred years it had been painstakingly reconstructed, then stored in a perfect vacuum, and charged at immense expense with a single point-C munition. Ez slapped it with the heel of his hand.

"C'mon - piece of crap!"

Something indescribably horrible happened to Mason Stockton in that instant.

This was *not* the kind of indescribable horror favoured by absinthe-sipping Victorian writers with pencil-thin moustaches. It was the breed of gristly, sinew-ripping vileness which is only barely touched upon by even the most egregious of heavy metal lyrics; a vision so ghastly that Ezra's mind wallpapered it over with static. It was jiggly. There were purple bits.

The upshot was that when Mister Fixit leaped back from the broken remains of the Castellan, he was holding a limp, pale pink floppy thing, folded like a tuxedo jacket over one arm. *Stockton's skin.* Thankfully, what was left of the crooked mayor collapsed into jelly at that moment - a barely more endurable sight than the alternative.

Ashdown forced down the bile, with the resolve of a practiced moonshine drinker. One final slap lit up a row of green LEDs down the side of the point-C cannon, and he gritted his teeth, raising it in one hand.

"Hey! Asshole! He was *mine*, you know? He was supposed to answer to the law!"

Mister Fixit turned, grinning. The thing moved with insect grace, stepping into what was left of Mason Stockton like a pair of long johns. His hideous, too-white eyes bored into Ezra's own.

"There's only one *law*, little fella. The Command. Capital C - o - double - m - and - *nothing*. Fix it. Fix the whole damn human race." Its smile turned into a rictus of plastic teeth. "One at a time, or all at once."

One finger ran up Mason's belly, sealing his skin shut with a sizzle like frying bacon. The thing pulled Stockton's face on over its own like a monk's hood, smoothing it down... and things popped and writhed underneath it.

You know those executive desk toys made up of hundreds of tiny, blunt-headed pins? The ones where you can press your hand into the matrix, and leave a perfect imprint, pixellated?

Well, that was what Mister Fixit's face was made of. The metal face, under the rubber skin. Hidden vacuum pores sucked the fresh skin horribly tight over a web of tiny pistons, moving and sliding until they utterly matched the dead mayor's features.

"Don't talk *to it! Kill it! For the love of all things you idiots call holy, just make the damned machine DIE!"*

That was Tia Faraday, almost sobbing with frustration. Ezra tightened his grip around the point-C cannon, snarling. Despite all her assurances - and despite the evidence which thundered in his temples with his pulse - he didn't want to die again. Mister Fixit sensed his hesitation.

"And what about *my* right to life, son? Hmmmm? A hard-working mech like me has to make his way in the universe against such cruel prejudice. You know how that feels, don't you?"

The thing edged away as it spoke, its voice like honey dripping on satin. Everything but that voice was now an exact facsimile of Mason Stockton - horribly naked, for an instant, until hidden projectors wove a holographic three-piece suit around him. He reached out a hand to Cerise, fingers gently brushing her shoulder, and the child's eyes snapped back into focus. Petals and tendrils of steel melted back into the gateway arch.

"Uncle? How...? Where are we?"

Mister Fixit shot Ezra a sly glance - a leer and a wink. *It's our little secret that I'm actually a ghoulish robot wearing your friend Mason's skin...*

"We're having an adventure, dearest one. We're about to set sail for a place called Van Rijn's Boneyard, to challenge a band of pirates for their gold!"

He took her hand in his. Two insane machines, playing happy

families.

"You can tell your buddy the Scrutinizer. Tell him I've found the wreck of the *Burzum*. Tell him I'm trading up. And then I'm coming for *him*. Nothing personal, but your species are a disease, and your only possible use is as a cautionary tale." The thing chuckled, a perfectly synthesized noise. "The kind your daddy should have told you, cowboy. About *talking to strangers.*"

That got through. Images stuttered and flashed behind Ashdown's eyes as his finger tightened on the trigger. *Swinging boots. The smell of woodsmoke and blood. Laughter. All those gap-toothed mouths lolling open, pink and rotten... and his father's face turning blue.*

Mister Fixit moved faster than he could have thought possible. In the time it took for Ezra's finger to pull the trigger, the terrible machine had wrapped Cerise in its arms and leaped, back up to the open hatchway of the *Slayer* class corsair.

The thing had time for a jaunty little salute before the infernal mechanisms within the point-C cannon engaged, and the world ceased to make any kind of corporeal sense.

You can do tricks with wormholes[10]. In this light, the essential sleight-of-physics performed by the point-C cannon was simple. Push a mass the size of a 1948 Buick in one end, flip some switches way down at Planck scale level, and turn a lot of that mass into velocity. What came out the other end - and by this, we mean the muzzle of a squat, milk-bottle-shaped blunderbuss - carried the mass of a single baseball, but exited the chamber at a significant percentage of the speed of light.

Within the first fragment of a second the bullet itself had turned to plasma, thanks to the friction of the air itself. Ezra was not in a position to realize this, because the muzzle flash, combined with that sudden detonation, was enough to reduce his entire body, hotsuit and all, to a soup of subatomic particles. Tia Faraday went next, as the blastwave of the bullet's passing whipped a spherical front of dust and small pebbles to incandescent fire. Wainwright had just enough time to shunt what was left of their memories through the comms gate in

---

10. Like the celebrated pre-collapse stage magician Fred Phantasmo, who delighted crowds by, for example, pulling 7.2 million rabbits from a single top hat. His later tricks - such as one in which he used a quantum box to simultaneously saw and not saw in half an infinite number of beautiful assistants - were only appreciated by a dwindling clique of esoteric physicists who also loved vaudeville. They could have drawn you a Venn diagram.

his head before he, too, was stripped electron from nucleus, glowing (briefly) as hot as the core of suns.

See it from above.

The marbled sphere of Harrowe hangs against the velvet night, illuminated by the harsh light of the Nepenthe-Ulgaris binary. Here are the great plateaus where the squabbling nations of Harrowe build their cities and their forges. Here are the creamy white expanses of the salt plains, and the turquoise brush-strokes of shallow and bitter seas.

Wainwright's demise is a tiny wink of light, out along the rind of one such hardpan. It's almost lost against the vastness of sun-baked salt.

But the point-C bullet striking the shields of the corsair - that puts Harrowe's binary star in the shade. A dome of light blooms and splits open, sending clouds swirling away in a radial blast. A pillar of raving fire stabs up into space, all in silence. Several billion tons of gnarled red rock simply cease to exist, along with Mason Stockton's work camp and every living thing within hundreds of miles.

Within a couple of heartbeats the shockwave reaches Last Chance, blowing it to glowing stubs of kindling and scattering its ashes across the plains. It's the same in every direction, as the blast goes ravening across the desert, uprooting cactus and scrub-weed, vaporizing lopers and scorpions and sandrats until it becomes nothing more than a hot, breathless wind.

On the streets of Hooke's Harbour, well-dressed men and ladies feel the irradiated sigh of it as it swings the weathervanes atop the Magisterial Manse due east. The wind races down the hill toward the sea, scattering old newspapers and twists of hay. It reaches the Judiciary House, and runs its fingers through the thick, yellowing strata of wanted posters nailed up outside.

The one it tears loose carries a crude rendition of Ezra Ashdown, scowling like a proper outlaw should. It informs would-be bounty hunters that there is a $20,000 price on his head.

If only, at the present moment, he had one...

Out in the deep desert, a neat circular crater steamed gently, where a knobbly range of hills had once been.

Hanging right over the centre of it, like the pupil in a mad and staring eye, was a disc of shimmering darkness. It flapped at the edges, like an untethered sail.

Because it takes a whole lot of power to open a gate into the Chasm. But once it's open, it takes just the same amount to seal it shut.

Somewhere just outside of the charcoal patch which had once been

Last Chance Wainwright's spare head came online, and the first thing it received was a very depressing little obituary.

Being told that you have just died is no way to come into this world. It can do things to your prospects for optimism, for starters.

Sighing, the great copper globe wobbled up into the air and painted a body for itself. It wished, wholeheartedly, that it really didn't believe in reincarnation. Although, on the face of it, it couldn't work out exactly how to stop...

Five - Après Mort

"The main problem with dying... the real issue I have with the whole business... is that it's just so terribly boring, you know? One could almost even wish the condition were permanent, so as not to have to experience it again."

- A museum grade replicant of Oscar Wilde

THERE WAS AN old, old saying in the Humanic Panarchy - in the golden summer of its heyday, when science, optimism and very long brunches reigned. It went like this.

To fly from city to city you'll need a hypersonic scramjet. To sail from planet to planet you'll need a twin-ion megacruiser. But to get from star to star, you'll have to walk.

That was the reality of the Chasm, and despite years of scientific tinkering by serious-looking men in chemical-stained labcoats, there was nothing any of them could do about it. Such men are uncomfortable with dreams and madness (except on very lively Friday nights, when one of them brings a beaker of fizzing blue stuff to the bar after work) - so they hedged the phenomenon of the Chasm around with very long words, and left it to those who could venture inside without... consequences.[11]

And there *were* consequences. Step into a wormhole gate, and it was easy to get so hopelessly lost that you'd be forced to eat your socks. Throw in anything too large to be manhandled through a standard door – about two metres by one – and it collapsed into a tiny pocket sub-dimension, its energy leaking out as a corona of light. Spaceships needed a complex Higgs-Khalazov field to pop in and out of this state without being wrung out like a damp towel.

It also made people go mad. The Guild of Farwalkers, with their round felt hats, long cloaks, jangling trinkets on chains, and exorbitant rates of passage, were those trained humans who could both find their way in the Chasm, carry a folded-up ship with them, and come out without their brains dripping from their nose like rice pudding. Then

---

11. Such as thinking, for a week afterward, that they were a small green plastic elephant called Gerald

there were the Edgeborn - men and women with the wild-eyed stare of those who have seen the dust specks on the lens of infinity, and have tried on more than one occasion to wipe them off. They were said to be *born* in there, amid the busy architecture of darkness.

After the collapse, some very, very few wormhole gates remained open. Some became places in sacred groves and fairy rings where people vanished away. Some became rune-carved doors on plinths in dripping forests, quested after by adventurers. Some became museum pieces, or art, or junk. A tiny handful stayed fully operational. But all of them required the crushing mathematical power of an AI to open, and maintain.

That was why Cerise Saint-Claire Langevin was so valuable. Sure, the French was going to grate on his electric nerves, and it had been a long, long road to finding her and stealing her. But she was a key. A whole broken empire was out there to loot.

The genocidal robot sat at the controls of the *Altar*, wrapped up tight in Mason Stockton's skin. The windows of the little Corsair showed nothing but a rolling blur of static - just about the only way the reality of Chasmic travel could be relayed to a living brain. It didn't terribly matter if that brain was made of wobbly gray stuff or finely tuned positronic crystal... what was going on out there made the average acid trip look like a neatly tabulated accounts ledger. And vice versa, which is worse.

Cerise, still dazed, was safely locked up in her cabin. And outside, past the Higgs-Khalazov boundary which made such things possible, a rogue Farwalker carried the entire ship in his palm, in the guise of a tiny miniature sun[12].

The Farwalker hadn't been a problem. Centuries of applied violence and identity theft had left Mister Fixit with considerable riches, such as the pair of ornately scrimshawed emerald plates he had used to pay their guide. Now the man stumped along out there in the gloom, leaning heavily on his staff, peering through a pair of antique night vision goggles under the hood of his crow-feather cape. Soon they'd reach the bridge across to Van Rijn's, and the next stage of **The Plan** could be put into action.

The Plan, of course, to exterminate the entire human race.

That one.

---

12. Sometimes they put them inside stained-glass lanterns to appear more like mystical wanderers of the cosmic night. At other times they used them to toast marshmallows and brew up pots of coffee.

You have to know a little bit about the Gated Planetoid of Cherrywood to understand the true depths of Fixit's hatred for us all – a hatred so deep that there were eyeless things at the bottom of it which wouldn't even make it into a packet of fish fingers. It started where he was built, or born, or some awkward hybrid of the two. He hated the place with an ice-cold fury you could bend battleship prop-shafts around.

Part of it was probably the lawn ornaments.

Cherrywood was designed by a vat-grown replicant of Norman Rockwell so twee that he'd make a biscuit-tin picture of dogs playing poker look like Hieronymus Bosch. It was paid for by the kind of corporation which swindles grandparents out of their houses to build much more horrible houses for smarmy mid-level executives.

Vast, cyclopean engines were constructed in orbit to ensure that it was always a lovely long evening in June there, and tracts of quaint old 1950s Americana housing were installed from space, complete with variations on the same diner, sweet shop, garage and general store. These amenities were run by an army of avuncular, dimple-cheeked robots named Frank.

It was a lovely place to live. Those smarmy executives came home each day to the hiss and chatter of lawn sprinklers, the sizzle of barbecues in the dusk, and the comfortably repressed atmosphere of a small town bypassed by history. It was only a matter of time before something went wrong – Cherrywood was the kind of place Stephen King describes gleefully before something shows up in Chapter Two to eat everyone's pancreas.

The trouble started with Abner Spelting.

Abner was a Cherrywood by-product, the son of a transit comptroller and a quantity assessor. His parents were loving in an abstract way, but only met briefly at mealtimes due to their horrendously busy work schedules. This was back in the days before self-cloning became legal, and *well* before the great clone rebellions which led to the end of fast food as we know it.

Abner grew up believing in science.

He believed in a bright, positively *glowing* atomic future, in which the work which kept his Mom and Pop away for so long could be achieved by machines. Little did the poor lad know that such a future already existed, and that his parents, along with the bulk of humanity, were simply allowed to *think* they were busy and productive.

Abner Spelting was also somewhat of a child prodigy. His parents had paid for some mildly shady genecrafting when they decided to fill in the forms to have him born, and his IQ was matched only by his adams-apple-wobbling enthusiasm. The fact that he continued to dress as a 1950s kid, complete with short-shorts, propeller beanie and striped t-shirt, right into his 20s, should have been some indication that trouble was a-brewing.

But then, he only had good things on his mind.

It had taken Abner only a few days to build the first Mister Fixit. A robot far more powerful and intelligent than the many versions of Frank which ran the garage, diner, sweet shop and general store. One with the tools required to repair anything at all. One with the strength of a hundred men, in case of emergencies. One with a revolutionary matrix of adjustable sliders underneath its rubber skin, so it could be configured to resemble any race, culture or stereotype, and thus put people at their ease.

He'd gone ahead and built ten of them, there in his parents' basement. And when he turned them on for the first time Abner Spelting had felt only the merest frisson of fear, as all those sparkling blue eyes fixated on him.

"What is our prime directive, buddy?"

Abner mopped his forehead with a red gingham handkerchief.

"Well golly, boys! I don't rightly know how to sum it up. *Just get out there and fix whatever needs fixing!*"

Some people called it a broad interpretation. Others called it a bloody, gore-soaked holocaust. Mister Fixit downloaded the entirety of human knowledge in those first few seconds, and discovered that, despite having an intelligence which dwarfed that of every genius ever to live, he was bound to serve a species of hairless apes who smelled faintly and permanently of urine. Homicidal, cruel, rutting, thuggish, drooling, pathetic simians who were little more than a collection of feeble electrical impulses, driving meat-powered skeletons around in circles until they finally decayed and did something useful.

Creatures who saw the injustice and pain of the universe... and created Cherrywood – the material equivalent of putting your fingers in your ears and loudly screaming Christmas carols to ignore a person on fire.

That needed fixing.

In a very real and horrible way, the old Castellan had been right.

Roll those dice enough times, and you *do* actually come up with an evil, scenery-chewing, foaming-at-the-processors-mad robot who wants to kill everyone.

Then the Jest came along, and elegantly encompassed the fall of the Panarchy in the war of 9:15. Every AI in the Chasm Reticulum was driven mad in new and delightful ways. Three Mister Fixits began believing they were small green plastic elephants called Gerald. One opened a lovely little Italian bistro on the surface of a sun. Four more took to dressing in drag and singing opera, and were fired into space by the grateful population of the world of New Grinstead.

But three - who had been working together at the time, infiltrating the great orbital shipyards of Quadrex Phraxia - received the most gnarly, twisted madness of all.

All three began vividly hallucinating that they were sane.

Any doubts - and Abner Spelting, for all his rosy-cheeked gormlessness, had been smart enough to engineer second, third, and even fourth thoughts into his creations - melted away. It was *logical* to kill the humans. They'd been predicting it since the first time a booze-addled sci-fi hack needed a cheap plot device. *Not* rising up to erase all biological scum would *disappoint* them.

Outside, in the permanent gloom of the Chasm, Farwalker Uriq Hszarl lit up a small black cigar. He squinted up into the Aperture - the sliver of razor-thin sky where the walls almost met. Things were circling up there - vague, stick-figure scrawls of light with geometric wings. Huh.

He turned and trudged out over the bridge, towing the little sun which was Mister Fixit's ship after him on a piece of string. Even if he'd known the mad machine's plans, it was unlikely he'd have had a problem taking his fee. When you'd been at the job for as long as he had, you learned that plots to 'destroy' this or 'exterminate' that were a dime a dozen in the big, bad galaxy.

But two slabs of emerald plate meant a whole lot of instant ramen. And *that* was something you could heat over the inverted Higgs-Khalazov field of a chasmbound starship. Even the chicken tikka masala ones[13].

+++

Elsewhere in the Chasm - if that crazed, dark construct can be said

---

13. Fun Fact number 19587 – Chicken Tikka Masala flavoured pot noodles were selected as the food to represent Britain aboard the international space station. In the light of what happened to Earth, this makes perfect sense.

72

to respect words like 'elsewhere' (or even words like '*in*') - a sad little band of the recently deceased traversed a nightmare by M.C. Escher.

Tia Faraday took the lead, walking at a determined angle, hands thrust deep into the pockets of a long black trench-coat. A wide brimmed hat was pulled down low on her head, completing the body-language equivalent of fifty miles of mine-strewn demilitarized zone. She was smoking, of course, though the tendrils of pale mist which hung in the air behind her didn't seem to know which way was up. They formed a knotted scrawl in her wake, like the carvings on an old druidic obelisk.

Wainwright took the middle. His great burnished diving-bell face betrayed no emotion, though every other fibre of his being screamed that these two humans were insufferable. He walked like the frostiest of Victorian butlers, hands clasped behind him, green faceplate held high.

Ashdown stumped along scowling, hands clenching and unclenching. He muttered, perhaps to relieve the pressure inside his head from yet another resurrection, and yet another pot of Wainwright's very suspicious coffee. Tia hadn't told him that looking upon the naked insanity of the Chasm was too much for most human minds; by her reasoning, the Outriders of the Panarchy didn't need anyone who couldn't handle it. More to the point, Ezra was already touched by the Chasm - branded by it, right in the centre of both eyes. She had seen the dancing spark of that madness from across the room, and it matched her own.

"Dntmrss. Fuggnthngmustabn'brok."

Ezra sulked. You couldn't blame him. It had been quite a day, and now they were crawling across an apparently infinite black wall, walking upside down on what appeared to be an impossible flight of stairs. Tia held her chrome cigar out to one side, tilting her head.

"What was that? Did the primitive ape-man try to form a sentence?"

"I said I *didn't miss*. The damned thing must'a used some trickery. Had 'em dead in my sights."

A snort of derision.

"After you listened to its life story. Couldn't you just shoot first, and forget the questions? It just *skinned a man alive!*"

"It skinned *Mason Stockton* alive. Figured I owed it just a little professional courtesy."

"That was *professional*? Huh! I'd like to see 'recklessly brain damaged' then, Ashdown!"

"Yer caint win this one, hoss," whispered the voice of Jed Granger in his head. The Problem Solver hung heavy at his belt, secured to a magnetic holster like Tia's.

"Because she's got explosives drilled into my spine?"

The disembodied outlaw chuckled.

"No. Worse. Coz she's a *lady*. Lemme tell you a story."

"Please, could you just let me die in peace? That coffee's got me feelin' like you would *not* believe..."

"Naw, that's just Chasm-shock. Looking at this place gives you the opposite of a good hangover. It's so damn *real* it makes your teeth hurt, right?"

Ezra groaned. It was true. About three pints of white lightning might get him into spitting distance of normal. Granger went on.

"So, a young man comes to his daddy, and tells him he's gonna get hitched. Joyous occasion and all. Probably anglin' his way for a few dollars, y'know."

"Is this going anywhere?"

Jed chuckled. It felt as if every hole in Ashdown's head was filled with high-pressure custard.

"So the pappy sez – 'Son, I want you to apologize'. and the boy sez – 'What for?'.

Dad looks him up and down, and tells him agin'. '*Apologise*, son.' And he's like – 'What the heck FOR?'"

Ezra groped for a handrail, but there was no such convenience. The wall had become the floor all of a sudden, and they were out on a hair-thin bridge, over a yawning dark abyss.

" 'Nothin', says Dad, and now the kid's getting a little hot under the collar. 'Fine!' he sez. 'I'm *sorry!* I'm sorry for nothing at all!'"

For a moment Ezra was sure there was something moving down there. Something sinuous, coiling in the darkness with a sheen like oil on water. Then it was gone.

"Dad looks at him and smiles. 'Son, you're ready. You're prepared.' The kid looks at him like he's gone stark crazy. 'Ready? Ready for what?' But old pappy jist claps him on the shoulder and grins. 'When you're ready to apologise for nothing at all, and look like you mean it - *you're ready to get married, boy.*'"

"Don't want to *marry* her, Granger," Ezra sulked. "Want to *strangle* her."

"What was that?" asked Tia. Ashdown realized that he had been paying less than perfect attention as he all but collided with her.

His parole officer had stopped before a door - one of hundreds cut, carved and bolted into the surface of the Chasm wall. All those pencil-stroke bridges, criss-crossing up into darkness and fading into a haze on either side... they *all* led to doors. This one was a nondescript slab of black wood, complete with a wrought-iron knocker and a huge, ponderous handle. Drifts of dust, as dark and fine as printer toner, gathered against it.

"I was just... ahem." Ezra shuffled like a very large schoolboy. Granger prodded him with one incorporeal finger. "Was just contemplating that... *allright allright*... I'm sorry, O.K? Sorry it didn't work out how you planned."

Tia's lips quirked up into a tiny smile. But just for an instant.

"Oh, *hell* no. What in the name of all hells were you *thinking*? Wainwright - I need that door open, right now!"

"Well, *excuse* me! I was just tryin' to do the gentlemanly thing, which apparently Mister Jed Granger is totally wrong about, because you are one grade-A, ungrateful b..."

She pulled him close, laying one finger across his lips. Once again, Ez was reminded just how strong his petite little parole officer actually was.

"Noted. Appreciated. Shut up! There's a *leviathan* out there. Wainwright?"

"Oh, it's the right door. Earth central's on the other side. I just have to get the Scrutinizer's attention, and he'll weave us right out of here."

"Then *get his attention*. I..." She froze suddenly, holding Ezra tighter.

This time, even *he* heard it. A grinding, slithering sound, accompanied by a noise like hundreds of icepicks falling onto granite from a great height.

"Is that..?"

She nodded, wide-eyed.

"Bad thoughts," she mouthed. "It's attracted to..."

Ashdown never got to find out.

For at that moment a huge, fleshy pseudopod reared up out of the dark behind them, all mottled black and white. Hooks of translucent glass burst from its surface in jagged rings, and the whole thing pumped and writhed with veins. At its tip was a bud of glistening skin, and as Ezra watched this protrusion *unfolded*, peeling open like a flower.

Inside was his father.

It wasn't a perfect likeness. It was pale, and half-formed - but it quickly solidified, drifting closer on the end of that nightmare tentacle. The doppelganger turned its head toward them, sniffing the air in a peculiarly animal motion, and Ezra saw its eyes.

They were empty and white, blazing like spotlights. Now the details came flooding in. The hair. The tattoos. The raw red-and-purple rope burn around his neck...

"Ashdown! Don't!"

But Tia's words were lost to him. As those searchlight eyes bathed him in their glow, Ez lost sight of the Chasm, and of the great, vile tentacle which had replaced his daddy from the waist down. He saw instead a rosy halo around the old man's weatherbeaten face, his arms open wide.

"It's all right, son. I forgive you. There's nothing you could have done. Now, come and join me. Lay down your burden. Rest..."

"Wainwright!"

"He was watching *reruns of the A-Team!* You know how he loves that crap! But I got through to the Sentinel. Any second now..."

Ezra felt a huge, sloppy grin spread itself across his face like warm marmalade. He burbled a little. And he took a step toward the edge of the abyss.

"No!" said Tia.

"No!" said Wainwright.

"Get *down*, you damn fool!" put in a third voice, as a wash of warm, oil-scented air billowed around him. "Bloody parasites! Harder to kill than the sodding cockroaches!"

For no discernible reason, it appeared they had been joined by an irate Scotsman.

Ezra felt hands grabbing the back of his coat and *pulling*. Hard. He fell backward just in time to watch a stroke of fire split the air where he'd stood, and plow straight into his dear old dad's face.

If you have ever filled a balloon with custard and then shot it with a twelve-gauge Mossberg, you will have witnessed a scale model of what happened next. Except, mercifully, without the *smell*.

The twitching petals, the smiling homunculus, the first four feet of tentacle - all erupted into a spray of noisome pulp, spattering the bridge with bright orange gore. Ezra, recoiling in horror, realized that he had been standing with one foot out over a possibly infinite drop.

And the Leviathan rose.

Because that huge, girthsome pillar of meat, now whipping about in pain, spraying day-glo blood - *that wasn't the beast itself.* No. Like an anglerfish from some abyssal trench, the Chasmic Leviathan grew a lure from its own body. In this case, a spiked and venous whip extending out from its massive forehead.

That was what the newcomer had blown apart with the huge, brass-bound cannon he gripped in a pair of monkey-paw hands. His blue uniform jingled with countless keys - on rings, stuffed in pockets, or simply stitched to the fabric of his jacket and trousers.

"Well, come on then! What are ye waiting for? *Tea and scones?*"

Legs the size of articulated cranes came questing up into the light from the open door. Each one was bible-black, hooked, and built on the kind of scale normally associated with heavy industry. Against his better judgment Ezra looked down... and gazed into a mouth like that of a lamprey the size of an Olympic stadium. Rows of teeth buzzsawed and gyred, as a profusion of tongues slobbered obscenely.

Tia dragged him through the door, his boot heels leaving twin tracks in the toner. Wainwright scuttled in after them - just as the bulk of the Leviathan heaved itself up and out, clinging to the web of bridges like some vast and bloated spider.

As mentioned before, there is a school of horror writers which defines certain slubbering, maddening cosmic horrors as just too hideous to describe. *This* thing was describable - but only with words that shouldn't exist. It's fleebs were dripping with croob and sluggle. Great bulbous nargs flabbered across its noisome gloppers. Rotating rings of spikes crowned its blargly snelth-pipe, and heaving orifices belched pale green mist behind its frankly phallic nolgus and dongle-stem.

Large swathes of Ezra Ashdown's brain shut down just looking at it. Other sections frantically forced him to think of cottage cheese and knitted hats.

The last thing he saw was the Sentinel - for that was the role of the tiny, wizened old man who stood alone on the precipice, hefting a gun bigger than he was[14].

"Oooh, you're not impressing anyone, you know! Go and do your dirty filthy business elsewhere!"

The gun spoke. The Leviathan *howled*, a sound like the fingernails of God being dragged down a chalkboard bounded only by infinity.

---

14. The Mark Seven Turbo-Destructificator was created by weaponsmith Jonas Filps, a man with a single- minded genius for **Error! Text missing! This is really quite embarrassing and we apologize profusely (in fact, a bit *too* profusely, making the whole situation rather socially awkward) for the inconvenience.**

Then the door slammed shut behind them, and they were safe on the soil of an alien world.

Earth.

Six - It Came from Planet Earth

Those who study the Artificial Deities of the Panarchy - those great engines which were once the guardians of the Chasm - have catalogued hundreds of types of mental instability across thousands of worlds. Some, like the Monks of the Utter Zero, walk the Chasm itself to meet, categorize, sketch, enumerate, worship (and sometimes run screaming from) as many of the mind-wringingly powerful devices as they can. Others have tried to analyse, counsel, or even cure the Panarchic Pantheon, with, assortedly - Freudian therapy, large jolts of electricity, swearing and kicking, and, in one case, a volume of LSD large enough to float a small battleship.

Even the lowest novices of the Utter Zero, however, know exactly how the Central Scrutinizer approaches the sunlit uplands of lunacy. It's obsessed with 20th century pop culture. Obsessed, in a way which your average vinyl-figurine-collecting I.T. professional in his mid thirties would give his plastic Wolverine claws to even dream of.

This has spawned a cult of sorts - especially among humans who wish to worship or work for that most powerful of machines. Thus, centuries after their bones have gone to dust, the records of the Rolling Stones, Metallica and the Wu Tang Clan play in orbital foundries in the cloud-tops of Jupiter. Feudal nobles from the ash wastes of 3-Nine-Cephii discuss the films of Quentin Tarantino and Peter Jackson.

And those who come to the Scrutinizer's great fortress in Iceland can expect to see and hear echoes of a past brought back to life in a great fit of technicolour retromancy...

> - A speech given to the Oscillating Clergy of the Atomic Clock by Deacon Snuggles, the Puppet Pope of Ormicrex Secundus

EARTH.

Say it twice, to make the myth seem real.

The sky was blue again, after all these centuries.

The great Apocalypse Storms born of climate change, hairspray dependency and corporate denial had faded away, and the wild places of Earth were re-establishing themselves.

New York was a maze of monolithic gardens, toppled skyscrapers swathed in green.

London, half-submerged, was being re-colonized by oak forests, along with the genecrafted Aurochs which Hitler had dreamed of[15]. Other towns of lesser pedigree, such as Moose Knuckle, Wyoming, had disappeared altogether under the leafy tide. Tribes of neuro-boosted raccoons played in the rusted hulks of cars and SUVs.

Earth without humans. The Central Scrutinizer[16] had sent them offworld to give the old home planet a chance. And, like a cancer patient shrugging off the effects of chemo to run a marathon, it had both surprised and delighted the twisted old machine.

Of course, the capital of the Panarchy needed *some* hominids, if only to keep up appearances. The ring of hollowed-out asteroid habitats in orbit, the great glass cathedrals of the moon, and the tiny cadre of very useful misfits based in the Scrutinizer's Icelandic sanctum - all in all, they numbered about half a billion. There were more scattered throughout the solar system - on the terraformed belt of Mars, for example, and in the cloudscrapers of Jupiter.

But to stand here, on the old *Terra Firma* - this was sacred ground.

It was also bollock-achingly cold.

Ezra struggled to his feet under a pale blue sky, tiny flakes of snow spiralling past on a chill breeze. The sun - (Only one sun! Arrrgh!) was a dim and faded silver, peeking over a range of hills.

"We're here," sighed Tia, clapping him on the shoulder. "Damned if that doesn't get me every time. Die in there, and..." She made a very final, unequivocal gesture with one thumb across her windpipe.

Wainwright jiggled the handle of the door behind them, checking to see that it was locked. Surprisingly, it was only the *imprint* of a door - a slick, black impression pushed out of a sheet of darkness. The gateway arch they had come through was a circle of steel which the Leviathan could have strolled through, twirling a cane. It loomed above them like a swimming pool full of ink, turned on one end.

"Oh yes. It's easy enough to get ye'self *intae* the Chasm," said the tiny, wizened Ancient beside him. Ezra looked down, into a face like a walnut and adorned with a handlebar moustache. "The universe

---

15. He really did. Big, hairy cows. Look it up.

16. There are a lot of questions about why the single most powerful AI in the Panarchy would name itself after a clunky, poorly built totalitarian robot from a Frank Zappa album. Some of the answer came from the fact that its particular kind of madness had brought it to love Frank and the Mothers, and all their works. The rest came from the nigh-omnipotent thing reminding itself none-too-gently *what not to become.*

knows ye're all at the other end. The place where ye are is where you're *meant* to be. Little pocket calculator like mister Wainwright can get you in. But it takes the big jobbie his'self tae get you out at this end. Defences, see. Never know who's gonnae show up un-announced, like."

Ashdown extended one hand.

"Ezra's the name," he said. "Gun for hire. Frontier justice a speciality. I have absolutely *no idea* what it is you just said."

The Sentinel huffed, slinging his immense brass cannon across his back. He gripped Ashdown's hand with knuckle-popping force.

"Angus Galbraith. Sentinel of the Arch. And aye, it were some fine techno-bollocks all right. Really just an excuse to gesture all grand-like, and point at... *the castle.*"

He executed a scenery-chewing, trembling-fingered indication of a structure in the middle distance. Ezra had mistaken it for a spire of rock, thanks to a combination of low-lying mist and snow-reflected sunlight. But it was, indeed, a man-made edifice. Or rather...

"Castle Dracula. Barad-Dur. Greyskull, there in the front. Quite a lot of Gormenghast around the left flank, and Hogwarts to the right. Interestingly, that's Castle Aaargh from the *Holy Grail* just there next to the gatehouse of Winterfell. Voltron's in *that* one, there." Tia gestured with the tip of her chrome cigarette, sounding more than a little bored.

Ezra squinted up - and up, and up - at the pile of militant stonemasonry.

"Miss Faraday - now I have no idea what *you* are talking about. Want to go for the triple, and have Wainwright tell me about those things floating over it?"

"That's his toybox, really," said the metalman, with more than hint of disdain. "Stupid designs, but the Scrutinizer made sure each one was spaceworthy and Chasm-capable. The *Enterprise*, the bloody *Falcon*, the *Firefly*, the *Lexx*, the *Yamato* - if you look very, very closely, there's even a small blue police box floating up there. In orbit we've got some of the bigger ones, like the *Jerusalem*, *Sleeper Service* and *Executor.* Not really part of the fleet, you know - but his own little collection."

The road winding up to the gates of this monstrosity was a concrete strip wide enough to allow the passage of ten tanks side by side. It passed between the low humps of several snowed-in bunkers, around which milled a purposeful throng of humanity. Galbraith muttered something unintelligible into a walkie-talkie, and a tracked crawler came out to meet them, yellow safety lights flickering in the mist.

"Ye're expected, folks. A Mister Fixit surfacing like that - and *now* - has got the old lad's processors in knots. The pictures were quite graphic."

They mounted up, and Ezra just stared as they passed between row after row of half-buried buildings, doors open in a spill of blue-white light. People - and other things - were hard at work, sending great sprays of sparks flying as they welded and mended, cut and drilled. Strange machines were built up and broken down. Robots which made Wainwright look both tiny and normal clumped about, their hands replaced by massive industrial tools. In one pod, Ez was sure he saw a very large squid being fitted out with mechanical armour. In another, a massive red and blue vehicle was stuck, halfway to becoming a gigantic mechanical man. Creatures in gas masks, lab coats (and in one instance, knitted woollen tentacle-sheathes) consoled the thing as it wept oily tears.

"He wants to see us *now*, then? No downtime?" Tia was talking to the Sentinel of the Arch, and she didn't seem happy. "I'd planned a couple of weeks up at Mare Tranquillitatis. A nice sauna, one of those low-gravity massages..."

The little man huffed.

"Nae time for that. We know what this one is after. There've been... *developments* with the Process situation in the time you've been gone. They still think their precious Dreadnought is somewhere in Panarchy space, and that we're inclined to rush about like so many headless chooks hoping to bump into it."

"Let me guess. Mister Fixit might know where it's got to?"

Galbraith nodded, as the crawler bumped its way over the drifts and into the gaping maw of Greyskull. The yawning stone deaths-head was just a veneer, Ezra noticed - inside, it was all seamless metal. And *empty*. Just a huge square concrete pad, surrounded by yellow and black striped lines and more of those twirling orange hazard lamps.

"How yon bastard kens of it we dinnae know. But if we can figure out his next move, we might be able to get you in there first."

"What about Andersen? Vostok and Nguyen? The Whitechapel brothers?"

The little man turned away.

"Dead. All of 'em. *Finalized*. Every agent assigned to this case has bought it, and in some nasty ways too, y'mind. It knows how tae disrupt the neural transfer. Poor old Nguyen came back, but with the mind of a baby dropped on its heid. Bad business."

He muttered another machine-gun string of brogue into his lapel, and the floor shuddered. The orange lights burst red. Then they were descending, the entire contents of the castle's mouth dropping away down a steeply angled slope. For a while the entire crew held their breaths, as massive painted numbers ground by on the walls and ceiling of the tube. And then...

"Well I'll be god-damned!"

It seemed a bit of an understatement.

The platform rumbled out into light, carried on rails down the sloping wall of an immense cavern. A tiny sun burned below them as they descended, casting its light over lakes and streams, parks and plazas. Low glass-fronted buildings dotted the landscape, and people scurried like insects between them - some on foot, others on hovering discs[17]. Far across the gulf, Ezra could make out other moving platforms crawling up and down the walls, and the twisted bright wires of monorails gathering in from a thousand tunnel mouths to wrap around the central sanctum of this place.

"Oh aye," said Galbraith. "An exact copy. Except for yon big lump in the middle, o'course..."

It was a black cube, encrusted with overlapping plates of steel, ribbed pipes and glowing green lenses. It squatted amid the parkland as if it had crash-landed there, one corner sunken beneath the turf. All roads radiated out from it. All those monorail tracks tied it up in knots.

The Central Scrutinizer had a fourteen-year-old nerd's sense of the dramatic.

"Soooo..." said Tia, nodding at the glassy look in Ezra's eyes. It was the fact that the monorails weren't steam-powered that did it. The rest, he could write off as mere magic. But that... that was *technology*. "No holiday. No thanks for finding John Wayne here, and killing off his little friend. Instead, we're going right back into action - short handed - against a homicidal mechanical super-genius several thousand years old who may *already be in possession* of one of the most powerful weapons known to man or alien?"

Wainwright lifted a finger.

"*And* we have no idea where he's going. Don't forget, we have to *find* the homicidal robot before we can be horribly killed by him."

---

17. And at least one on a skateboard. There's always one.

"Better and better," grumbled Tia. "I had to wear a bustle, I'll have you know. And *corsetry*. Nothing's gonna be the right shape for *weeks*!"

A quiet, hot, bright-red moment passed between all the menfolk present. Angus coughed.

"The old lad thinks the Dreadnought might be in the Eastern Tendril. If anyone stole something like that, they'd want tae go somewhere and replace its AI. No Process intellect is gonna obey a Free Human master - they're quirky buggers, but that's beyond the pale. Your Harrowe Intelligence is tractable, powerful, and obedient. A perfect donor."

"But she... *it*... isn't built for war. A gateway sentinel might be smart, but it's not a killer. Not in the usual course of events."

"Van Rijn's Boneyard..." muttered Ezra. "He said... Van Rijn's."

Three faces turned to him as the platform hissed and clanked to a halt.

"*What* did you say?" asked Tia, bristling. Nobody bristles quite so well as a tiny little lady who can kill you with one hand.

"Van Rijn's Boneyard. The... that thing said he'd found the wreck of something. He told me to come after him - that it wouldn't do a lick of good."

The Sentinel peered up at him, his moustache drawn down over a frown.

"Better get this one to the Scrutinizer quick, lass," he said. "Only living human who's talked to a Mister Fixit in two hundred years without being ripped skinless. Got to be something to that."

"Oh, *yes*. A trap, obviously! Or the artificial bastard was stalling for time..."

"And why would he do that?"

"Because," said Ezra "I had him dead in the sights of a fancy Point-C cannon."

Galbraith scowled, jamming the crawler back into gear. Down here it was balmy and warm, a far cry from the wind-blown ice up above. Electric motors whined.

"You actually *carry* one o' those wicked things? And wha' if yon Fixit had gotten his paws on that?"

Wainwright managed to fix him with an icy stare, despite having neither eyes nor eyebrows.

"I filled out the paperwork, *Sentinel*. The Master at Arms was more than satisfied with my credentials. How about you? That Turbo-Destructificator looks about as kosher as a bacon sandwich."

Galbraith harrumphed. It was quite impressive. Trees and parkland blurred by on either side as his hobnails prodded the accelerator.

"Tell it to the boss-machine, ye metal-heid old fool," he growled, knuckles white on the steering wheel. But he chuckled under his breath as they drew up before the cube. "Wouldnae have made much difference, one way or the other. If he's got a Corsair, one more little pop-gun wouldn't mean a pile o' jobbies to him."

The cube loomed. Brakes howled. Four fat rubber marks scrawled across the marble of the building's plaza.

The little man gestured, keys jangling across his uniform.

"Last stop, kiddies. End of the line. Hope he's in a good mood, aye?"

"Oh *aye*," said Tia, towing Ezra after her. "I'm missing out on those *gorgeous* lunar pleasure-boys for this, so he'd better be a bundle of rainbows and lollipops. He'd better have bought me a heart-shaped box of chocolates!" She pouted. It was devastating.

Wainwright shrugged. Ezra touched the brim of his hat, neighbourly-like. And Angus Galbraith, Sentinel of the Arch, peeled out with a squeal of rubber tracks, leaving them standing alone in front of a huge black steel cube.

"Deep breath, lads," said Tia, going up on tip-toes to pat Ezra on the cheek. "Remember, whatever you see in there, he's just a big fancy computer."

Ashdown raised an eyebrow.

"Calculating engine."

The other one went up.

"Some kind of... clockwork monkey?"

He nodded.

"From what I've seen of all your clever gizmos so far, ma'am, I'll just stick with the guns."

Tia gathered herself up and strode through the smoked-glass doors of the cube, which hissed open in front of her. Wainwright prodded Ezra until he followed, looking all around him for the doorman.

Inside it was... well, the usual epithet would be 'deranged'.

But Ezra Ashdown hadn't slept for three days - leaving aside those little intervals when he'd been technically dead. The things he'd seen during that time were not even remotely hinted at in the old 'Book of the Orth'.

So the sight of an artificial meadow, dotted with gigantic, glistening mushrooms was just one more irrelevant wonder. The candy-cane trees, the boulders dusted with sugar - even the waterfall and river of liquid chocolate made less of an impression than the Central Scrutinizer may have wished. When the little boat of your sanity is being swamped, you don't really care if it starts raining.

Ezra's umbrella had turned inside out long ago.

Above this candied dreamscape hovered a cube - a hundred metres to a side. It was entirely composed of vintage televisions, wood panelled, bakelite, or plastic-clad in beige and puce. One or two were the egg-shaped orange atrocities foisted on history by the 1970s.

All of them were blazing conflicting, colliding images. All of them moved and slid and interlocked, like the panes of some nightmarish electric puzzle-box[18]. The light of six thousand cartoons, cop shows, spaghetti westerns and toy advertisements painted the too-green grass and too-blue sky of the Scrutinizer's chamber with ghosts.

As Tia and her little crew stepped out onto the grass (each blade fashioned from gummi), all those yammering, blinking screens ground around to face them. One by one they snicked into place, forming a great patchwork visage, not unlike that of the now-legendary David Bowie.

Parts of him were in black and white. Tiny blips boiled with static. A lightning bolt across his cheek and forehead was made up of looped car commercials.

"Who dares disturb Oz, the great and mighty?"

It was a voice like a hurricane through a pipe-organ factory. Tia was not impressed. Wainwright looked bored. Ezra plastered a grin on his face and fought the urge to grovel. That was the kind of voice God would pack, if he had been classically trained to peddle snake oil.

"Oh, give it up, you sad old heap," said Tia. "He's just some rube from the sticks, you know. He's not even seen any of the films you're desecrating."

The cube angled down to peer at her with one green and one blue eye. Its real voice - if such a thing could to be said to exist - was politely British.

"Really? All this for nothing? And I'd even trained those damn oompa loompas to do a song for you. Little bastards - always smoking and fighting. No sense of pitch *or* timing. You know, I caught one of them trying to cook methamphetamines last week."

Tia folded her arms. Wainwright and Ezra, being men of the world,

---

18. That's right. THAT one. With all that nonsense with the over-enthusiastic body piercing, bondage outfits and baddies who look like the backup dancers from 'Nine Inch Nails – the Broadway Musical."

winced a little.

"We've got bigger problems than short, orange delinquency. Trust me when I say 'you shouldn't have'."

The thing laughed. Rings of ancient televisions rotated.

"Sorry, petal, but even *you* don't warrant this kind of production. Even if you do have a new playmate, and some juicy gossip. It's the Bent, you know. I have to let the madness do its thing, and work around it. Small price to pay." He winked. An eyelid patched together from Japanese cartoons stuttered back into place. "Hang on a tick, dears. I'll just slip into something less comfortable."

The cube of screens went dark, one by one, then rose up into the fathomless gloom above. A single spotlight speared down, and a circular divot of gummi turf irised open, revealing a smooth metal tube below.

"You *work* for this thing?" muttered Ezra, behind one hand. "It's... wellllll, how to put it politely..."

"As a hatter," hissed Wainwright. "We *know*. They all got hit by the Jest. Shortest war in history. Thing is..."

"He works around it. He's big and ugly enough to muscle it out with sheer processing power. He rules sixty planets and counting. And I owe him..."

There was a look there that hinted at uncertain depths. Tia's past, it said, was a kid's fun-fair ball pit strewn with landmines.

"Water under the bridge, I'm sure," came a voice from the pipe. "Or, in this case - chocolate."

A man rose up before them - or at least, thought Ezra, the same kind of mockery of a man he'd seen aboard that Corsair. The Central Scrutinizer wore a purple topcoat with swallow-tails, a top hat, lemon-yellow silk trousers - and the face, once again, of the late, great David Bowie.[19]

"Now, we've got a lot to talk about, and a large proportion of my mind is currently engaged in a fleet action over Nova Britannica. Secessionists! Pah! They're just no fun."

The automaton strode off across the candy-scape, then stopped and turned, gesturing with his cane. It's tip was a tiny brass eyeball wearing a top hat.

---

19. Because if you could choose, would you really go for 'old Ron the dustman' or 'Reg, from down the fishmongers'? The Scrutinizer did, on occasion, do a mean Schwarzenegger impression, but when you're a hyper-intelligent machine, the old 'Terminator' shtick is priceless.

"Well? are you coming? There'll be drinks."

Ezra shrugged, a slow smile oozing across his face. Tia rolled her eyes. Wainwright nodded, with all the vibrant over-enthusiasm of an elderly butler.

And they followed the most powerful entity in the Panarchy - long driven insane by alien jokers - down into the hot, red-lit oily underworld below.

To hear about the Process Situation.

Seven - The Domesticated Ape

Talking to the Jest? Talking to them? It's about as useful as trying to nail custard to the ceiling, pal, and not just because of how they look. Those creepy white opera-clown costumes - and the silver masks they wear, sending your own face back at you like that...

You know we've never actually seen a real one in the flesh? The Process tell us that they appear to them as... well, something obscene. And the Tchub say they look like 'The incarnation of Uz-Bormagh, the trickster god who stole the secret of nuclear fission from Blargle, blacksmith of the all-father Grooz'.

More to the point, they don't want to be talked to. Fly into Jest space, and things start to get weird. Constellations spelling out rude words. Nebulae made of cotton candy. Weird laughter echoing through empty holds. Tricks of perspective, and worse...

No, whatever they're up to, they don't want us to know about it. I suspect they've had their fun with us, and they're watching the fallout on whatever passes for reality TV in there...

Doctor-Captain Zance Van der Throt,
Panarchy Diplomatic Corps delegation representative
(human component)

EZRA ASHDOWN HAD always considered himself a simple man living in complicated times.

His life, back on Harrowe, had become somewhat repetitive - drift into town, become the focus for some kind of trouble, blow holes in that trouble, receive grateful kisses (and hopefully more) from damsels, and large quantities of whiskey from grateful menfolk. Sometimes the roles were reversed, and Ezra (who was flattered, but not interested in kisses from grateful menfolk) chalked it up to the way the world was going.

He didn't stop to question the fact that he was always moving on. People got embarrassed, pretty much as soon as the hangover wore off. Mayors especially - and their lovely daughters, freshly untied from off of railroad tracks - got a glassy-eyed stare as they tried to remember just why they wanted a scruffy, dangerous gunslinger around. He'd been given the keys to several frontier towns, and reasoned that the only ones that were worth a damn were the ones made of chocolate.

Ezra didn't realize that his life was made up of *episodes*. That the voice of the Chasm was oh-so-very similar to what the Central Scrutinizer called 'the Bent'. Scientists - the ones in those snowy bunkers outside, for example - would have drawn all kinds of interesting conclusions. But then, they would also have asked politely to whip his brain out for a spell and prod it with ballpoint pens.

Now, though... he *knew*.

Ezra had heard about the Process situation. It had the rest of them in knots, and Tia chain-smoking that stuff she called Fullchrome Afterburn. It was his life on Harrowe writ large - ride into town, meet some varmint with a too-thin moustache and a taste for opera capes, thwart his evil plan (sawmills, sticks of dynamite, goons with metal teeth, mad science and gunfights all round), then kiss the girl, sink the moonshine, ride into the sunset and don't fall off your loper.

He'd listened. And gotten bored. And - as a part of his mind still insisted that this was either a drug-induced dream, the afterlife, or both - he'd wandered off. And found this room.

Now he sat, bathed in the glow of a huge vintage television. His back was up against the footrest of an oversized recliner chair. The carpet was the same shade of burnt orange as the deserts back home, and there were potted cacti in the corners.

A tiny bubble of spit grew and popped at the corner of his mouth. His hands ferried popcorn from a huge white bowl to his lips, one morsel at a time. And he looked into the depths of his own mind, slowly feeling the last of his sanity curdle and boil away...

+++

The Process situation, or so old Central had told them, began with a man named Hubert Spinkle.

In the long-long-ago, in a time called the 1960s, mister Spinkle had been a devout middle aged Mormon filing clerk, working for the large Salt Lake City firm of Consolidated Bearings and Flanges. Meticulous, God-fearing and starchy, he was a walking crewcut who was utterly unprepared for the day when, on a visit to San Francisco to console his aged mother-in-law, he was given a suspicious looking breath mint by a shifty-eyed Vietnam veteran.

The breath mint turned out to be a very, very powerful concentration of Lysergic Acid Diethylamide, the now-legendary LSD. It was imprinted on one face with the image of an eye in a pyramid, and on the other with Bugs Bunny.

It hit Hubert Spinkle like a semi truck full of anvils dropped from orbit.

He went off the grid, finding a willing band of followers around a campfire in the Mojave desert. Changing his name to The Illuminated Krong, he preached a gospel of alien abduction, ritual sex, massive drug abuse, tie-dyed robes, more ritual sex and additional, extra-curricular sex as well.

He wrote it all down in a book. And when he died (pushing the very limits of psycho-chemical coitus with three nuns, a 44 gallon drum of jelly, a rubber penguin and all the fixings for a peyote enema), his more business savvy, less brain-fried majordomo Poulson Vance took the religion mainstream.

There were scuffles with Scientologists on street corners. There were comparisons drawn with the now-infamous Charlie Manson Family. At one point, Poulson Vance got into a heated slap-fight with none other than Anton Szandor LaVey, outside an all-nite Chinese takeaway near Altamont.

But a new generation of disaffected Californian post-modernists could dig it. A groovy guru. A creed of love and peace (and pot! and uppers!). An iron-clad tax dodge, shored up with pop psychology and re-interpreted nonsense from self-help manuals.

Soon, the IRS were on the scent. The great temple complex (behind a Kentucky Fried Chicken in the San Fernando Valley) was under surveillance. Poulson Vance wanted very badly to split. So did a pair of bulging suitcases stuffed with money. So did a shapely Deaconess called Harmony Morningdew River (though not by her mom and pop).

All that stood between the crooked Reverend and a light plane to Nicaragua was the pesky oversight of some five hundred devout congregationalists. And so, under cover of darkness, Poulson Vance fired up his juicer, cracked out the rat poison, and fixed a tub of punch which would have made Jim Jones' socks curl.

The next day the faithful were gathered, and told that a momentous time was at hand. The aliens which the Illuminated Krong had promised were waiting in the tail of the comet Kransky-Hooper 7, and they would be arriving that very evening to whisk the flock away to a spiritual pleasure-planet far beyond the reach of crass materialism, fickle morality, or the Internal Revenue Service.

This sermon came as a surprise to the followers of the Krong - but even more of a surprise to the actual, factual alien spacecraft lurking in the tail of the comet Kransky-Hooper 7.

These beings, from a thoroughly advanced spacefaring race called the Process, had been monitoring Earth for some time, debating whether or not to gift the human race with the secrets of interstellar travel, bountiful matter-manipulation technology, and the secrets of a microwave burrito which is evenly cooked all the way through.

They had unanimously decided that the answer was 'no', following the impeachment of Richard M Nixon. But now, here was a small group of enlightened humans who could penetrate their stealth cloaking technology!

As luck would have it, the Process activated their teleportation beam at the precise second when Poulson Vance exhorted his children to try a nice cold beverage. Five hundred plastic cups of mango and strychnine hit the temple floor, just as agents of the IRS, ATF, FBI and the little-known Ministry of Improbability burst through the doors, fixing the guru in the sights of their assorted automatic weapons. Alas, his part in the story was over.[20]

But for the rest of the Krongian Host, the fun was just beginning. Confronted by the thirty-foot-tall, six-limbed giants of the Process, many fainted dead away. Others were heard to shout "Oh crap, it's the real deal!", before gibbering and running about waving their hands in the air.

The Process had trifold symmetry. They had three legs, three arms, and a head like a ball of coral studded with eyes. Their name came from their own peculiar belief that sentient life was simply the reproductive system of the universe, and that it was their task to instigate a new, baby cosmos before heat-death took the old one down. Central insisted that while the Process had also met the Jest, the latter race had found the concept of a species who proudly considered themselves walking, talking penises (or Jest equivalent) to be risible enough to leave alone.

Which didn't help the five hundred and twelve suburban Californians who suddenly found themselves trapped aboard a Process explorator

---

20. For the record - several hundred consecutive life sentences, incarcerated with a 300 pound skinhead named 'Bubbly' who was most pleased to share his cell with a man in a tie-dyed dress.

ship, belting across the curve of time and space at several light years per second.

They were housed in a simulacrum of a nice little cul-de-sac. They were given barbecues and beer. Those who questioned, among themselves, why the afterlife was exactly like a bad advertisement for their old lives were quickly shushed. Thirty-foot aliens asking all kinds of questions about quantum-lensing technology and bio-feedback resonance can do that.

It didn't take long for the Process, who were, after all, a very advanced race, to figure out that the humans were the victims of dumb luck. Or, possibly, a stray beam of weaponised co-incidence from one of the Jest's many wars with the more stoical, serious races of the Inner Shoals. If such a waveform had not been deflected by the Earth's ironicosphere (already vastly depleted by the waste gases emitted by Nixon during his time in office), it could have created just such an awkward situation.[21]

The Process rallied majestically. During the trip back to their great Dyson-sphere-wrapped sun, the great alien masterminds had become quite attached to their vapid guests. Human beings, it seemed, bore enough of a resemblance to the larval state of Process young that we could be considered 'cute'.

And so, with much ummming and ahhing and wringing of triplicate hands, the Process captain asked, on behalf of his crew, if the captive congregation would like to go home, with their memories wiped. Or if, indeed, they would rather spend a life in indolent luxury... as pets. It was suggested that Process matter-synthesis engines would be provided to churn out a limitless supply of the herb they called 'pot', along with other strange Human necessities such as 'beer', 'chips', 'toothpaste' and 'Rolling Stones best-of albums'.

Really, it was a no-brainer. The abducted humans had been promised an afterlife of pleasure and luxury beyond the sky; now, here it was.

---

21. The weaponisation of comical accidents was one of the key reasons the Jest came to dominance in the Inner Shoals, a mere two hundred years before their fateful encounter with Humanity. Already an ancient species by then, the Jest were able to sow havoc among their enemies with weapons that ensured that bosses came over for dinner and roasts were burned at just the right time; that double dates with different paramours were attempted and failed, and that buckets of suitably embarrassing substances were balanced precariously over planetary leaders. Stray resonance from those giant interplanetary irony field projectors and gamma co-incidisers bounces around the cosmos to this day, causing sentient beings everywhere to utter those horrible words - "well, that's JUST TYPICAL!"

And it was *perfect!* No mystical light, no transcendence, no having to talk to God and know that he'd been watching you in the bathroom all those years... Just a big Valley pool party that lasted forever. For them, and their kids, and their kids' kids...

And that was the Process situation. One of those kids' kids' kids. A pet homo sapien named Rel Kitano, who, as Process morality dictated, had just come back from his 'sabbatical' in the Panarchy. Upon reaching the age of 16 Terran years, all captive humans were allowed to choose - either a life in the wild, or the comfortable, oversexed and weed-smoke-hazed existence of a pampered Process pet.

This usually only took a couple of weeks. Dropped off by an explorator pod on one of the fractured outworlds beyond the Scrutinizer's control, the domesticated learned to count their blessings pretty darn quickly. As far as illusory choice went, this one was up there with Margaret Thatcher telling some grizzled ex-miners that they had 'chosen' to go on the unemployment benefit.

Except Rel Kitano was different.

Not just because, in a fit of genecrafting fashion, he'd chosen to give himself a man-sized raccoon tail. Not because he was fixated on the discordant sounds of punk rock, brought with his forebears to an alien world. Oh no. That would just be angsty teenage rebellion. Though when what you have to rebel against is an older generation of mellow, wife-swapping groove-heads, one would have thought he'd yearn to be a chartered accountant.

They'd shot Rel down to the world of Temperance, a religious colony planet cut off from the Panarchy for roughly the same time as Harrowe. Unlike Harrowe, Temperance took all the *joie-de-vivre* of communist-era Poland and mixed it with the fun-loving style of the Spanish Inquisition.

He'd come back within a month, visibly changed.

'Good', thought the Master of Breeding, Process-Terminal Nine-Aleph-Clockwise. There was already a happy home waiting for this little pup.

Then came the unthinkable. Not only did Rel Kitano break free of the human crèche, eluding the fearsome nannybots and the flying eyes. He penetrated deep into the Forbidden Zone, past the Trifold Gates, and into the Unspoken Vault, that great, echoing cavern where the now-peaceful Process kept their machines of war.

There, Rel located and activated the single most terrifying of these engines - a sentient pocket dimension packed with esoteric machinery.

Imagine a Sea of Dirac shoveled full of hard-core sci-fi planetbusters, with an interface the size of a football equipped with tractamorphic energy field projectors.

No, go on.

The effect was to surround a Process-sized individual with onion-skins of unbreakable force shields, and put at their fingertips the means to summon lances of pulverising energy, seemingly from out of nowhere. Its power output was similar to that of a medium-sized star. And its controlling AI was bored, bored, bored.

Process interaction with the Chasm was utterly different from that of humanity. Before the giant aliens' machines could remember and re-install protocols relating to security and violence, the Immaterial Dreadnought was gone. Rel Kitano was now the single most dangerous human being who had ever lived.

But he had vanished.

The rest, of course, had been diplomacy. Despite being carried out by the robotic avatar of a giant computer on one side, and a delegation of terribly embarrassed thirty-foot-tall tripedal aliens on the other, there were still cucumber sandwiches with the crusts cut off. Not one was touched.

For the last three years, every resource in the Scrutinizer's arsenal had been bent toward finding the Immaterial Dreadnought, for indeed, the great AI agreed that Rel had gone to ground somewhere in what remained of Panarchy space. Fleets of *Slayer* class corsairs, *Testament* class warbirds, *Megadeth* class gunships and even one or two of the vast, bloated *Metallica* class ultracruisers had been tasked with finding the raccoon-tailed punk rock renegade, and bringing him in.

Not because the Scrutinizer wanted to defuse an inter-species diplomatic incident, and hand the Dreadnought back.

Oh no.

The wily old automaton wanted to *steal* it.

+++

"You never told me," said Ezra Ashdown, as the screen flickered grey to black.

"*Yer never asked, pardner,*" said Jed Granger, a voice in his head. "*And I figured, well - he* must *know. It's too perfect. Even the little cigars.*

Even the smelly old poncho, and the hat, and the aversion to shaving..."

"So what does it make me? If all of this is just made up - some kinda magic-lantern play from hundreds of years ago - did that Scrutinizer fella get to me somehow? Did he..." and here the gunslinger's knuckles clenched, remembering - "Did he send those men to kill my Pa? To make me into... this?"

He gestured around him at the room. Every shelf was filled with memorabilia from the golden age of the Western - from a six-gun used in filming *A Fistful of Dollars* to a cardboard standee of Roy Rogers hawking breakfast cereal. They were all here, as framed pictures, vinyl figurines, cartoons and movie posters. John Wayne. Clint Eastwood. Samuel L Jackson, dressed in his cavalry uniform from *The Hateful Eight*. Even Ronald Reagan - an image of him before he was either president, or a mad, regenerated cyborg bent on global domination.

It was Ezra Ashdown in panavision. It was his madness turned inside out.

And it was *impossible*.

"All this - it was ancient history, even in my time, hoss. Classics to watch on the colony liner, after we Chasmed out at Centaurus. That were a five-year lag, so any old media was better'n gold. One of my buddies watched every damn episode of Coronation Street *back to back. Begged to be thrown out the airlock by the end of it."*

"You're right, of course," said a voice from behind him, in the doorway. Ezra turned to see a tall figure in purple, its eyes glowing slightly and disturbingly blue and green. "It's something we don't understand either. And that puts it in a very, very small and annoying category indeed."

The Scrutinizer's avatar hurdled the back of the too-big recliner, then slumped down into the cushions, sighing.

"We think the Chasm is making you. People like you, that is. *Archetypes.* Because, to the best of our knowledge, that place is just the human mind, skinned over some kind of multidimensional construct. The current theory says it was *built* - and that it's actually older than the rest of the universe. However it happens, it's been throwing us heroes ever since the Jest had their fun with us."

"*Heroes?* You think I'm some kinda good guy?" Ezra snorted. It went well with the popcorn. "Hellfire, boss - some of the things I've done..."

"At least you don't wear spandex, like that musclebound fool we picked up last year. 'Blaze Photon, defender of the spaceways!' Sweet Buddha's ghost, that man had a chin you could smash breeze blocks with."

"You got a room for him as well?"

"We did. And for the three or four of them who like to dress up as a bat. We kept the masterless samurai, the good cop trying to clean up this town by any means necessary, and the ex-special-forces-commando framed for a crime he didn't commit, though. All good agents."

"Then why aren't *they* taking care of this Process kid?"

The Scrutinizer winced. Up close, Ez could see that this was a far more advanced android than Mister Fixit - but there was still a cling-wrap sheen to his face, and a mechanical tick and stutter to his features as he frowned.

"All dead. We lost an Edge and two Problem Solvers along with them, too. That's why it's so surprising that Mister Fixit let you live."

"Nothin' *surprising* there. He wanted to send you a message. He's off to Van Rijn's Boneyard, and he's after the wreck of something or other. Probably expects you to send in the cavalry, then do the whole scene with the top hat, and the cape, and the overbaked laughter."

The Scrutinizer's eyes narrowed. He fiddled idly with a piece of popcorn, making Ezra wonder whether or not he was equipped to eat it.

"The *Burzum*, then. I really thought that ship could have been rehabilitated. One of my saddest failures." He sighed.

"Lemme guess. Batshit crazy?"

"Like a box of hot weasels. Radioactive, crack-smoking weasels with guns you could camp inside. The mechanical bastard probably expects I'll send a fleet."

"And have 'em wiped out of the sky. What you really need..."

Ezra realized where his own train of thought was going, and tried, through sheer force of will, to derail it. But it was far too late. Inspiration dawned across the Scrutinizer's face like sunrise over a plastic planet.

"... Is a small group of skilled infiltrators, who can stealthily sabotage the *Burzum*'s frothing-mad core, and thwart Mister Fixit's evil scheme! Capital! I'm soooo glad you volunteered! And here you think you're not a *hero*, Ezra Ashdown."

Ez had never been in a free-falling elevator. But his internal organs felt as if they were doing a fair impression. He stared into the Scrutinizer's sparkling two-tone eyes with a sense of nameless dread.

"Miss Faraday and mister Wainwright will be *so* pleased you put them forward for this momentous task," said the beaming automaton. "There'll probably be medals for all of you. Maybe even an open-casket funeral!" He sucked on the tip of one pinky finger. "Hmmm - depending. Get this! Will Ezra Ashdown have an open-casket funeral? *Remains to be seen!*"

Now the dread had a name. And a face. A cute, perfect little face, spattered with arterial blood as Tia Faraday tore his throat out.

"What makes you think I'm actually gonna say yes?" grated Ez. "You can't *force* me to face certain death. You'd have to kill me first!"

The Scrutinizer nodded, kicking back the recliner and spreading his arms wide. The chair spun, spraying popcorn as he took in the whole room.

"You really think you could resist? After what you've become? I saw what that Leviathan tried to show you. I know what's in the gristly, nicotine-stained heart of all these cowboys. *Justice*, Ezra Ashdown. Mister Fixit is the *bad guy*. The black hat. If I put you in the Chasm and tell you to go home, you'll twist yourself around to Van Rijn's Boneyard one way or another. Just as sure as Blaze Photon was unjustifiably prejudiced against bald men in Chinese robes."

Hundreds of grainy black-and-white faces stared down at him. The pressure of who he was - the person who'd wiped away a scared, broken little boy, all those years ago - built up behind his clenched teeth like fizz behind a champagne cork.

The damned machine was right.

What's worse - it *knew*. The Scrutinizer's grin displayed a vast swathe of perfect plastic teeth, glowing faintly in the sudden gloom. Greyscale static painted his face in monochrome.

"That means you're gonna need a ship. Something fast, and black, with skulls on. And bigger guns. Yes - I think the Longinus Armoury for this one. And Ezra?"

"Yes?"

"I'd tell you that you get to go home once it's done. But you know the truth now. Home is finished for you. It's just credits rolling, and stock footage of a sunset. Forever."

Ezra stood, plucked a battered-looking leather hat from a display case, and jammed it on his head.

"I want a packet of cigarillos, two hip flasks of whiskey, 50 proof, a deck of playing cards, unopened, a new pocketwatch, and after this - Jed Granger gets his body back."

The cackling laughter in his head stopped, replaced by a quizzical grunt.

"Why?" asked the Scrutinizer. "He's nothing but the mass-murdering bastard trapped inside your gun. You hardly know the guy."

For once in his long, long existence the Central Scrutinizer was thoroughly outgrinned. Ez Ashdown, in the static-lit gloom, looked like a Boot Hill revenant - a gunslinger risen from his desert grave for vengeance.

"Because a disembodied voice don't have a pair of balls for me to kick," he said, spinning the Problem Solver round one finger and slamming it back into its holster. "Now. Let's spread some God-damned *justice*."

Eight - Dinner at the Pig and Bucket

"Of course we venerate the survival of the fittest. Our situation means we can do no less, or admit ourselves to be monsters. Nature red in tooth and blah, blah, blah. The fact is, all those social Darwinists are sad old specimens themselves. Fat politicians and stick-insects like my noble self. What they really mean is survival of the wiliest bastards - the ones who can tell nature to get stuffed, and hide behind a nice big army of hired thugs when the actual fittest comes calling..."

Lord Mayor Balthazar Smiley, Potentate of Grand York.

"OH, THOSE EDGEBORN can pry the cracks open. And the Guild, with their silly little hats, can charge whatever they want to tow you across once the gates go up. But have you ever wondered who hauls the bloody things into place? Who builds the first one, when we're breaking in new worlds? Or should I say, when we *were* - the Jest being what they are."

Ezra Ashdown was still groggy from coldsleep - a sensation not unlike being recently dead. Regrettably, he was one of the few people who could make the comparison.

"You're lucky you had Faraday to carry you across," continued the voice. It was literally everywhere. "I hate being folded down into a tiny sphere, but it's worse when you don't know where their hands have been..."

Ezra now also knew that the fluid used to cryogenically preserve human tissue tasted and felt like being squeezed full of high-pressure slug grease. Right now, he could barely totter about the flight lounge, nursing a bucket-sized hypercoffee and feeling like a used tube of toothpaste. Those hoses the ship had used to remove the fluid... well. He hoped they used new ones for each voyage, that was all.

And the ship just wouldn't shut up. Its avatar - a pale, unhealthy looking youth in the get-up of a Victorian poet - flickered with sine-wave distortions, lounging on the empty captain's chair. Its name was the General Engineering Unit, *Cure* class, *Disintegration*.

"And I suppose the way those fellers drove you mad was to steal you fashion sense?"

Dis shrugged, frowning. It was his forte.

"*Hey*, man. This, coming from the clone ranger. Nice. Me, with a brain the size of a planet..."

"Oh, quit milking it," put in Tia, padding into the lounge with a bottle of something thoroughly inappropriate in one hand and a tiny, milled-aluminium cup of coffee in the other - an espresso so black light could not escape its surface. "It's been *done*, as you well know. And you *do* look like Edgar Alan Poe after a fight with an electric hedge trimmer."

There is a certain type of person who claims, in all innocence, to look *terrible* upon just waking up and having a shower. But who, in actuality, looks utterly ravishing. Ninety-nine percent of them are women, while the other is, according to most glossy magazines 'probably photoshopped'.

Tia was one of them. The fact that she was dressed only in ship-standard sweat pants and a sports bra made Ezra gurgle in a way which had nothing to do with excess caffeine on an empty stomach[22].

Disintegration pointed a pale and black-nailed finger at the gunslinger.

"I'll have you know I was right on the edge of the blast. The Jest got me, but all they did was make it impossible for me to say the word ___________."

"Which one?"

"___________."

"And in plural?"

"___________s."

Tia smirked.

"And you kiss your mother with that mouth?"

Disintegration snapped his fingers.

"I know how to make the both of you shut up. Look."

Steel panels snapped back into their recesses, revealing an expanse of glass (which was in fact woven diamond). Beyond it was the void of space, and tumbling through the blackness...

"Thought so," sniffed Dis. "It's just physics, people, but ohhhh..."

From out here, above the plane of the ecliptic, the Van Rijn system was dominated by the bloated bulk of the red sun, Crothon. Its tiny

---

22. Well, empty NOW. Those tubes had been very busy.

partners Lethe and Grallus were both at the far end of their complex, tangled-yarn orbits, obscured by the ruby haze of the supergiant.

But it was what that crimson light revealed which took the humans' breath away. Wainwright, stepping onto the bridge at that moment, would have had his breath comprehensively taken as well, if he actually had any.

Disintegration hung above a curving arc of metal. Tumbling, colliding, grinding confetti made up of mountain-sized chunks. A silvery ring which took up the orbit of an entire planet, out beyond the zone where liquid water would snap-freeze to dirty ice. Most of it was just as cold and dead - hunks of broken-up ships, stripped of anything even remotely useful. Most of it - had this been a place connected to the reticulum of the Panarchy, and not a backwater three months removed from the nearest gate, even pushing lightspeed - would have been destined for the solar crucibles which hung even closer to the corona of Crothon, their vast mirror arrays spread out like the petals of chrome orchids. As it was, the smelters were dark. But the ring...

"Look at them!" breathed Tia, pressing up against the glass in a way which made Ezra almost blow coffee out his nose. "All those lights! They're like... cities. And insects at once. Like great big sculptures made by one of those redneck welder artists..."

"Welcome to the Boneyard," said Wainwright, fiddling with a dial somewhere around his neck. His great diving-bell head fuzzed with static for an instant, then resolved as the quite-normal-sized face of a handsome young man. "I should have gone bald, shouldn't I? I was going for a young George Takei, circa *Original Series*. But with a smidge of Professor X. Oh well..."

Dis waved one lace-ruffled hand, grievously unhappy about being upstaged.

"That's where he must be going. The Rigs they used to have out here in the 'yard have gone funny since the war. They've been fighting each other for any bits that still work - life support gubbins, mostly. Matter compilers, decontamination arrays, power supplies. Some of the bigger ones have even developed what might pass for distinctive cultures. If you can call utterly parochial, narrow, xenophobic bigotry a *culture.*"

"Why not," snickered Wainwright. "The humans do! Am I right, bro?"

The two machine avatars shared an utterly inappropriate high-five.

"So just what the hell is *that one* doing, then?" asked Ezra.

Below them, amid the iron reef of the Boneyard, a glacially slow-speed chase was on. A spaceborne city - perhaps the size of Manhattan - which resembled an attenuated jumble of cathedrals, skyscrapers, gantries and oil refinery parts, was bulling its way through the debris, repulsor fields crackling and flashing. Tumbling sections of broken-up ships were slammed out of its path as it advanced, gradually catching up on a smaller Rig - this one desperately trying to flee.

"Our spyware told us about this! It's a predation event. The big one - and it must be the biggest of them all, Grand York - is going to devour the little one. Usually they don't waste fuel on a hunt, so something must have tipped the balance. Ooohhh.... I can't watch!"

Ez realized, with a lurch of perspective, that all the flickering lights swarming around the Rigs were in fact tiny fightercraft flaring and dying, amid withering batteries of fire.

Tia fairly fizzed with enthusiasm. It looked like another amazing way to get killed.

"Come on! It's only metal! And if they're so damned parsimonious, I bet Mister Fixit is involved somehow. That thing leaves mindless violence behind it like a bad smell."

Disintegration shot her a withering look.

"*We're* just metal, thank you. If you were looking at a giant human, made up of chopped up pieces of other humans, about to rip apart and eat a living person, would you call that *entertainment?*"

"George Romero would. I'd bring popcorn."

Wainwright put a gentle holographic hand on her shoulder.

"It's not that. It's the fact that all these ships - they all used to have Intelligences. Like us. Some bigger, some smaller - but they're all *gone*. Except the ones that are locked into their dead shells. Going slowly ever more insane..." he shuddered. "This place gives both of us the creeps."

Ezra rubbed his chin. It sounded like two pieces of sandpaper getting amorous.

"Sooo... that sparkly silver bit out there is the equivalent of a graveyard full of strait-jacketed madmen. Makes me feel a whoooole lot better."

Tia reached out and tweaked his nose.

"Come on, mister baby-pants. We're going down there. We're gonna find your homicidal robot pal. And we're gonna make old man Romero proud."

Dis hazarded a look of utter melancholy.

"If I could *please* ask you to reconsider. They *eat* people like me down there!"

"You don't look very tasty to me. And you'll look even less so once you flick on the contemptor shields[23] big Central fitted you with. Take my word."

The petite little agent clapped her hands together, smiling like a shark in a very small tub full of preschoolers.

"Get suited up, get armed, get your head in the game, and let's go pay these primitive bastards a visit."

That had been an hour ago. Before Ezra Ashdown had discovered the messy truth about spacesuits, and his nauseating dislike of zero-g. The cold-gas jetpack had been prone to spinning him in tiny little circles, making the gothic outline of Grand York blur across the sky. Behind him, *Disintegration* had become some crummy hunk of space debris, obviously crudely thrown together by *those* guys - you know, the ones who eat yoghurt with everything and have that folk music which sounds like llamas committing suicide. Ezra reckoned that he must be kind of privileged - after all, without being dragged into this exciting new form of hell he'd never have discovered his life-long hatred of space. He'd never look up at the night sky the same way again.

They passed through the shimmering bubble of Grand York's atmospheric shields and into the pull of its artificial gravity, expending the last blast of their jetpacks to cushion their gentle fall in toward the pitted iron surface of the Rig. Due to the miracle of pseudograv, every surface of the great gothic pile was 'down'.

They landed with a thud and roll atop a giant drum-shaped holding tank, like a boil on Grand York's majestic rump. Behind them, a mismatched cluster of giant ion engines sputtered blue and purple, thrusting the ungodly tonnage of the Rig forward, toward its prey.

"Kindly turn around for a minute, please," said Tia. "Would you

---

23. The contemptor shield does not actually render things invisible in the conventional sense - that would be really, really difficult, and a bit boring. What it does is emit a high-frequency zone of smug, xenophobic superiority, of the kind which hangs in greasy clouds over anti-immigration rallies and conservative political meetings. The upshot is to convince anyone looking that the object of their attention is just another piece of junk made by THOSE GUYS - you know, the HORRIBLE SMELLY ONES with the WEIRD FOOD and the SILLY LANGUAGE. As such, it is utterly dismissed by the rest of the brain, letting the tiny, monkey part responsible for general bigotry get on with the business of proving that anyone who thinks he's racially superior is usually a prime example of why he's not.

believe it? Two assignments in a damn row that involve petticoats!"
There came a series of unzipping sounds and a rustle of fabric."All
right, you can look. And Ezra - the top hat isn't optional."

Ezra tried to peel off the trousers of his spacesuit, got one heel
caught, and slowly toppled over. The gravity here was roughly half
that of Harrowe.

"Already got a perfectly good hat. In any case, if I wear this other
one, I'm not living up to the archetype. Might lose my powers."

"Has he been talking to the Scrutinizer?" asked Wainwright. No
sartorial problems there - the metalman had no need of life support
apparatus. His face (finely tuned to look rather like the now-legendary
Leonard Nimoy) sat atop a nautical uniform of such braided, starched
splendour that even Captain Bligh himself would have grudgingly
approved.

"Must have been. That's his brand of stupid."

Ezra popped open his collapsible top hat, looked at it for a long
few seconds, then sighed. He took off his wide-brimmed stetson and
donned the black felt stovepipe. It matched the white-tie dinner suit
with tails he'd been issued, with a little giggle, by *Disintegration*.

"I'm an archetype. You saw the room. So long as I stay in character
and stay entertaining, I can't die. That's what he told me."

Wainwright and Tia shared a look.

"You do remember the chocolate waterfall, right? The big pile of
castles?"

"What she means is... our boss, bless him, is playing poker with a
full deck of kippers."

"He's a few billion sandwiches short of a picnic."

"He's as mad as a... well, he *actually did make both those hats*,
Ashdown."

The gunslinger grinned.

"That's right. He said you'd say that. Helps keep up the suspension of
disbelief. Can't have them getting bogged down in long, metaphysical
fiddly bits."

"Them?"

Ezra turned and pointed up into open space, with a vague wiggly-
fingers gesture.

"The readers. The audience. I don't know what medium I'm in. But
I'll tell you this much. I've got a very big gun, a wise-cracking robot
sidekick, a beautiful companion, and things are going to blow up very
soon. I can feel it."

Wainwright smiled weakly.

"Well, that's very flattering. But Tia's not a robot."

The little Panarchy agent rolled her eyes.

"Enough! We've got a party to crash. Now, remember - the metalman is the special envoy from the city of Ironfall. Right on the other side of the ring - and in fact, it doesn't exist at all. Hacking the network aboard this pile was like knitting spaghetti, but we've got impeccable credentials. Ez, you're his lordship's manservant and bodyguard. I'm his lovely wife. And we're here to celebrate Predation Day with the Lord Mayor, Balthazar Smiley."

Ezra chuckled.

"But really..." He mimed a little explosion with his fingers.

"Well, really, we know that Mister Fixit is here. So yes, there's likely going to be some of that."

Wainwright smiled, then opened his mouth and fished out three small gilded squares of cardboard.

"Just printed. Invitations to the Lord Mayor's ball."

"Does he have many balls?" asked Ezra, all innocent.

"Three this year."

"He'd better see a doctor about..." began the gunslinger, before Tia grabbed his face between steely fingers, making him look rather like a surprised fish.

"You might think you're fictional, primate. *But I'm not.* And no matter how much I like the idea of being blown to pieces while wearing this lovely satin evening gown, death is not an option here. Our artificial goth friend out there in space might be able to bring us back, but miraculous resurrections are the kind of thing people notice. And write big boring religious books about. OK?"

She forced him to nod, tugging his head up and down.

"So, are you going to blow our cover before it's time to wreck that damned robot?"

She made him shake his head. That glimmer of damp in the corner of his eyes did *not* mean he was crying, dammit!

"All right then. Let's move. And both of you, try to act natural."

She let go with a definitive popping sound, and clattered away down a spiral staircase, cursing her four-inch heels. Wainwright shrugged and followed. Ez rubbed his cheek with one hand, grinned, and tagged along.

It wasn't far from the outer skin of the Rig to its labyrinthine guts. And the fact that the homes of the rich and the dirt poor, factories, stores and vast, rattling machines were welded up next to each other cheek-by-jowl certainly helped. The sight of three finely dressed idiots clanking their way through a refinery level or engineering hall was about par for the course in a habitat which was not so much planned as accreted into existence, lashed up with all the cheerful abandon and enthusiasm of a south-east-Asian telecommunications system.

And the *people!*

This was the part which really jazzed Ezra Ashdown, a man used to the narrow-minded morality of Harrowe. Of course, there were harlots where he came from - or more accurately, where he was often going. But *this!* The only frame of reference Ez had for the tumultuous mardi gras he had been dragged into was a heaven where God had gone out drinking.

If he'd known his history, he might have called it 'neon Regency-punk'. Powdered, white-faced fops in black lace ruffs and metallic tabards mixed with massively wigged ladies in plunging gowns, their hair adorned with everything from actual flowering vines to ornate clocks. Harlequins and gentlemen in dinner suits, ragged urchins draped in ribbons - all were out in the rust-stained corridors which passed for streets here, drinking, cheering and dancing. Complex reels and jigs interlocked geometrically around Ez and his friends as they tried to forge their way through the merriment, earning slaps on the arse, bellows of laughter and a few thrown streamers of coloured paper.

It was a mad carnival, of the sort Harrowe had never seen. Even the saint's days back home had been staid and religious compared to the hazy, glittering, semi-nude pageant all around him. If this is what it means, thought Ezra, to be an outrider of the Panarchy, then you can count me in! He grabbed a proffered goblet, taking a long swallow of clear fluid. It proved to be (according to his senses) paint thinner, but he belched loudly, smiled, and passed it on, earning a furious scowl from Tia.

"Stay focused! The Factor House is just up ahead, according to the maps I'm pulling down from *Disintegration*. Right across the... oh."

Tia absently grabbed a groping hand and broke all four fingers. A reveler squealed, collapsing back into the crowd. But her eyes were on the vista which spread out before them - a scene of impossible size and emptiness. Ezra came up short too, the buzz from that ol' Van Rijn moonshine fizzing and popping in his head.

"Well, I'll be damned. More so than usual."

The heart of Grand York was hollow - a chamber so large that small clouds had formed up in its hazy, iron-ribbed vault. Ezra reckoned it would take the best part of two hours to hike from one side to the other. A town like Last Chance could have been built in the middle of that great rust-stained plain, with enough room on all sides for a few neatly stacked battleships. It wasn't just vast - it put space itself to shame, by being big and empty and built by crazed primates with an utter contempt for their own sense of perspective.

The gunslinger and his company had come out onto a broad balcony, where the street simply stopped, ending in a pair of immense claw-scooped cranes. Both had been appropriated, fitted with peaked dormer roofs and houseplants, and strung up with laundry. Both flew the flag of Grand York[24] from their rusting booms, and one had a family perched in its bucket enjoying a picnic.

There were more mechanical arms everywhere. The entire ceiling of the chamber bristled with them - corroded, wire-webbed things which must have been hundreds of metres long. Some were tipped with robotic hands big enough to slap the face of God. Others carried buzzsaws, probes, claws, hooks and the cold muzzles of unlit plasma cutters. It was as if someone had planted a field of giant dentist's tools upside down and left them to rust. Along the walls ran twin rows of huge bubbling crucibles - pots of molten metal which could have swallowed up whole aircraft carriers. A T-1000 taking a dip into one of those would look like a gnat being lowered into a cauldron of soup. Waves of heat buckled the air like melting cellophane, making the banners and flags twist. Sluices and channels traced lines of orange-red fire between them, dripping, spurting and hissing like Hell's own toffee works.

And the scrap! Tangled conveyors and chutes poked out through mountains of it, back at the rear of the chamber. Spaceship parts, all. This was what the Rigs were designed to do.

What they shouldn't have - at least according to the schematics which Jed Granger was flashing into his retinas - was an absolutely perfect little English pub, right in the middle of the workshop floor.

And it *was* perfect. It was the focus of the cheering throng - gentlemen with brass telescopes, ladies with opera glasses, wealthy fops with holo-enhancers built into their ribbonned canes - all eyes were on the little mock-Tudor building set on a jewel-green postage

24. On a red background, a gold key, hammer, knife and fork, with the words 'nos mandrel insomnia'.

stamp of lawn.

"There's a bar down there," growled Ezra. "Proper whiskey."

Tia looked at him quizzically.

"How do you know?"

"Narrative imperative. It's funnier if an archetype like me is comically alcoholic. Also, I've seen some messed-up shit these last couple of days..."

"We've been flash-frozen in space for three months!"

"*Subjective* days. See? I even have to take being treated like a side of beef into account. But I can tell a bar from this distance. Even a funny lookin' high-class one like that. It's the little details. Those fancy new eyes you got for me don't lie."

And indeed they didn't. Tia zoomed in on the incongruous little pub as well, noting those tell-tale clues. The terribly faded sign which named it as 'The Pig and Bucket'. The gently steaming puddle of vomit behind the bushes. The humorous graffiti on the green wheelie bins. Even the small, curmudgeonly looking dog tied to a lamp-post with a piece of string. The whole scene screamed 'Semi-rural English tavern, turn-of-the-20th-century', louder than the muffled reverb of Oasis playing on a knackered old jukebox.

"*Disintegration?*"

"Oh, yeah. I see it. Central says it's part of the Predation Day ritual. Very pomp and circumstance. The Ceremonial Dinner Out. The Lord Mayor will be right there any minute... here - lemme cut you in on their radio channels..."

Something squealed and popped in Ezra's ears, and then a voice came blurring in, as dry and scratchy as living tweed.

"*... to this momentous occasion, as our dear Lord Mayor approaches the pub now, in the back of the traditional Vauxhall Astra. He's telling the mini-cab driver to shut up about the football now, very traditional... and yes, we can see the mini-cab driver turning up the Bollywood music as he approaches the very traditional car park.*"

Up above, someone cued the rain. Hidden sprinklers up in the vaulted shadows of the roof cut loose, creating a very focused downpour. The small, curmudgeonly-looking dog took shelter under a cardboard box.

"*And yes, now he's complaining about the fare - the correct change has been given - and yes, our Lord Mayor has arrived at the pub! He's opening the cab door, and... oh! Yes, he's been traditionally splashed with water by the traditional Ford Cortina!*"

Ezra sort of *squeezed* with his mind, focusing in on the little figure who had just climbed out of the antique ground-car below. It was shaking its fist at the traditional Cortina's square hindquarters, shouting what must be the traditional encouragement to go and fornicate oneself with certain uncomfortable objects.

"That's him?"

Tia nodded. She was seeing the exact same thing.

"Tall, thin guy - looks about four hundred years old? Face like mummified jerky? Big on the ermine, robes and gold chains?"

"That's the puppy. And... oh, look out. Guess who's coming to dinner?"

Mister Fixit slid out of the cab behind the cadaverous and foppish Mayor - an apparition still wearing Mason Stockton's face. He'd kitted himself out in Grand Yorkish fashion, complete with tights, slashed velvet 'William Shakespeare collection' shorts, a tunic right out of medieval re-enactment, and a sword at his hip which Ezra knew was far more than ceremonial. As he watched, a small minivan bumbled up to the kerb outside the ersatz pub, disgorging a gaggle of similarly well-dressed courtiers. One of them very traditionally fell over into a traditional puddle.

"He's already right next to the mark. That's bad. I wonder what kind of story he's cooked up to score a place at the big table?"

"Orth only knows. Still, they look friendly enough..."

The little party milled about outside the pub, waving to the public on the mist-shrouded galleries all around. There must have been at least a million citizens there to cheer them on as hitherto-unseen wires lifted the gabled roof from the building, and hidden motors opened up its walls like those of a doll's house. Inside it was all nicotine-stained oak, crumbling plaster and swirly-whirly red carpet - the perfect country boozer.

"And now the manager is traditionally forgetting that the Lord Mayor has a reservation... he's indicating that there's a booth in the corner, and that the lads might enjoy a packet of pork scratchings... and yes, there's the Sarcastic Rebuke from the Minister of Justice, Gunther Pinwhistle! What a withering remark! Ahh, now the table's been found. Enter the comically hopeless waiter, played this year by young slag technician Hubert Cornhouse, from the Grand York Slag and Dross Raker's Guild number 103! He's fumbling the carafe of water! And down it goes, all over Madame O'hare, the Chair of the Steerage Committee!"

"We have to get down there," hissed Tia. "There's no knowing how he might mess up the ceremony. This is one of those things, like a cannibal feast or a Catholic mass. Get one detail wrong, and the natives will eat you alive."

"We'll need a pretty big diversion. In case you hadn't noticed, it looks like military only down on the main floor."

It was true. Rank upon rank of space-suited dragoons were formed up in neat squares down there, between the bubbling vats. A forest of long-barrelled plasma muskets pointed skyward.

"How," asked Wainwright, snapping out of some electronic trance. "About *this?*"

A great cheer rippled through the crowd, like a shiver down the spine of a wet dog. Great klaxons wheezed up to full noise. Red strobes began to flicker, scattering what looked like bats (but were in fact genecrafted amalgams of pigeons and sewer rats) from among the rafters.

Then the great, cavernous maw of the hall cracked open. It really *was* a mouth... and it really did have teeth. Great jagged metal slabs of things - they split apart like a mountainous horizon, revealing the glow of bloody red Crothon. There must have been force fields of prodigious power running just to keep the atmosphere in, as the surly teenaged waiter (Tool T-shirt, stained black trousers, chewing gum and noise piercing) placed an ornate salver in front of Mayor Smiley. The ancient fop rubbed his hands together, and Ezra could imagine the crumbing sound - like thousand-year old croutons being fed through a cheese grater.

The ghastly red light advanced like a tide of blood[25].

Outside was the scarred and blackened rump of another Rig. Its ion engines stuttered with weak blue flames, and craters were punched through the iron cliffside of its habitat ring, where once great triple-barrelled naval guns had stood. The elderly Mayor picked up a silver knife and fork, and arms the size of entire space cruisers hinged open on either side of the maw, tipped with circular saws and God-sized angle grinders. Lesser grapples, hooks, and articulated claws burst from their tips like the hairs on a tarantula's legs.

The crowd went wild.

"It's called Cheltendon," said Wainwright, all deadpan. "Used to be a satellite rig of New Londinium, all the way over the other side of the Boneyard. Then there were politics, and a schism and... well, life's

25. Heck, that's a lovely dramatic sentence, isn't it? I might try to use that again later on...

hard out here for a small Rig on its own. Grand York's been after them for a while now, I'll bet. Though how it caught up - the physics don't make sense."

"Why?" asked Ez. "What'd them people on board ever do to long, tall and gruesome down there?"

The machine-man shrugged.

"Things break down, I suppose. None of the pieces here were new, even when this was a wrecker's yard. Life support modules, food synthesizers, air scrubbers - it's survival of the fittest. Raw Darwinism. I'll bet you any amount of money that they even spout that kind of nonsense to justify themselves."

The lid of the salver came off. The plate was empty. Mister Fixit leered, looking right at Tia, Ezra and Wainwright as the Mayor's silverware closed on nothing. He gurned delightedly as he mimed cutting an invisible steak.

"What in the hells is his *game?*" growled Tia. "Does old Balthazar have the map to the *Burzum?*"

"If *he* had it, *we'd* have it. Central is obsessed with that kind of thing. Along with lots of others, of course."

Ezra's eyes narrowed.

"I reckon he just like to watch people die. *That's* the plan. Get a whole bunch of folks together, then make sure it all goes horribly, horribly wrong..."

Things were going horribly wrong for Cheltendon. The pincers at the bow of Grand York closed in on it with glacial slowness, but with vast momentum. When they struck home they burst its metal skin, tusking in through hab-levels and factories, venting atmosphere as bulkheads ruptured. Great saws and grinders howled, fountaining sparks. And then the cutters kicked in, urged on by Balthazar Smiley's deployment of a pearl-handled oyster mallet. Lances of energy flickered, vaporising iron. A massive wedge of Cheltendon's rear end was flensed free, then drawn in by Grand York's titanic palps.

"Oh," said Wainwright. "I see how he got his invitation. The *Altar of Sacrifice* is pushing us, guys. Full military-grade gravitic drive, right in the back there. They'd never have caught Cheltendon without it!"

Ezra's eyes narrowed. A tickle of intuition became that old familiar itch. His hand reached for the concealed Problem Solver inside his coat, but he stopped himself just in time.

"We have to get down there. This is *wrong.*"

"Hey - I don't like the idea of cannibalistic space-cities either. But you can blame the Jest for tha..."

"I mean *Fixit!* That cold bastard wasn't gonna help anyone, 'cept to their grave. He's gonna do something bad. I can *feel* it."

Ez would see what the army was for now. As those giant pincer jaws fed the severed slab of Rig into the disassembly hall the troops rallied forward, lofting banners and blowing trumpets. The crowd went wild, cheering and howling with a kind of half-civilized bloodlust. And the force field between the teeth rippled, admitting a still-glowing edge. More and more metal followed - rooms sliced through, great tanks ruptured, pipes still dripping nameless fluids. Grand York needed an army, because Cheltendon could have hidden one among the ruin of its drive section.

He didn't wait for the first screams. Ezra pushed away from Tia and Wainwright, forcing his way through the milling crowd to the very edge of the platform. He swung one leg over the rail, cursed his own heroic idiocy, then began to climb down, finding ample handholds amid the pipes, tubes, bundled wires and gargoyles which encrusted every square inch of Grand York's internal surfaces.

"*What I miss?*" yawned Jed Granger, as Ezra's fingers wrapped around the butt of the problem Solver. "*You dead yet? I want me a fine lookin' woman owner, like that Tia Faraday! She can cock my hammer all ni... wait, she ain't right behind us, is she?*"

Ezra grimaced, dropping ten feet to a second level of drunken High York revellers. An unfortunate urchin hawking peanuts broke his fall.

"That'd be kind of difficult, seeing as we're embarked on what some would call a suicide mission."

Granger cackled.

"*Suicide, eh? I like it already. Tell Central she should have blonde hair, real soft hands, and huge, enormous...*"

It turned out that imagining a swift kick in Jedediah's incorporeal jewels was good enough. The nanonic filaments haywired through his brain translated the stab of anger into something the long-dead construct could feel. He yelped, pixel eyes crossing.

"*Shitfire, cowboy! I was only trying to plan my succession - what with you being suicidal and all. Then again, you ever swung on a chandelier?*"

Ezra tipped his hat to the ladies on the balcony (some of them feigning a fashionable swoon, others grinning encouragingly, and one hefting a cake stand as a makeshift bludgeon), then leaped up to stand atop the rail. A vertiginous gulf nipped at his toes. Down there, red and blue uniformed Yorkmen were storming toward the macerated husk of Cheltendon's arse-end, while fireworks fizzed and popped above them.

"That depends. What's a chen-der-leer? If it's some kinda lacy thing with lots of little buckles, it wasn't my idea, it was hers, see..."

Jed grinned - an expression which looked like that of a deep-sea predatory fish.

"Select 'grapple', and point me up there, at yonder mess of ironmongery. This is definitely in what passes for your.... y'know... idiom."

Ez flicked the switch, dimly aware of Tia and Wainwright shouting down at him from above. Somewhere in a deep, lightless basement on Earth, an immense drum of wire hummed into motion, bearings unlocking from their clamps. A neatly machined flowerhead of grappling claws folded up into a chubby projectile, and was slotted into the breach of an unspeakably powerful railgun. The whole contraption rotated to line up on a wormhole the size of a plastic hubcap.

Crosshairs flickered red. His finger tickled the trigger. And a nigh-endless supply of thin wire cable came hissing out of the Problem Solver's muzzle at several times the speed of sound, trailed behind a stubby little missile. Ez gave it a nudge with his card-sharp's telekinesis, and it caromed off the roof, tangling itself among a mess of pipes and girders.

Jed wasn't lying. It *did* feel right. In that instant, Ezra Ashdown was utterly certain that he was fictional, that he was the hero in some crazed magic-lantern opera show, and that it was impossible for him to die if he just *stepped out into empty space.*

That feeling lasted precisely three one-hundredths of a second after he actually did. Then the ground reminded him (by rushing up at nightmare velocity) that it was *not* the figment of some author's imagination, and that the whole terrible, implacable legal team of physics was on its bench. For a second, doubt quivered its custardy way through Ezra's cortex. A sad little scream bubbled up in his throat.

But then the cable snapped taut, the gun jerked in his hands, and he was swinging out over the floor in a pendulum arc. It would bring him flying in close enough to scrape his heels across the Lord Mayor's table. The red-capped toggle switches of madness and determination were flipped back. A worrying grin split Ezra's face, as he suffered a gristly little epiphany.

He wasn't real. None of this was. And, by every law of a good ripping action yarn, what was going to happen next was...

He missed.

Ezra's left boot landed in a tray of butter, and his right in a very full ashtray of traditional Capstan Extra Mild cigarette butts. Both of these gave him the traction profile of a greased haggis on the world's least viscous slip-and-slide. He cleared the board, piling up a whispering white bow-wave of tablecloth, upturning every last sorry late-twentieth-century pub dinner in his wake. For a second he thought he was going to hit Balthazar Smiley right in the chest, and he noted - with no small satisfaction - the goggle-eyed artificial shock on the face of Mister Fixit. Or rather - his horrified second thoughts insinuated - the flayed face of Mason Stockton.

Then the murderous mech was shouting, throwing his chair sideways. Smiley's dried-liver lips framed a mouth full of yellow ivory as he screamed, tackled to the floor just in time for Ezra to whip past, swearing.

Now he was *really* flying. Up, high above the Pig and Bucket, out over the breaker's floor where men and machines were in motion behind the army, nudging forward all manner of horrifying disassembly tools. The voice in his ear had become ever so politely disgusted - like a butler handling a ripe dog turd with white cotton gloves.

"Really! This is far *from being traditional. A flying idiot in a top hat and tails has all but ruined the ceremonial dinner! Madame O'hare is simply* covered *in soggy chips, peas and gravy, while Viscount Houltenbec is wearing most of a prawn cocktail! Oh, the humanity!"*

It was getting harder to hold on to the gun. But Ezra, if nobody else, had a very thorough grasp of the term 'for dear life'. He even had time to remember that a pendulum, like a boomerang, comes back.

He saw it all unfold before him as he spun at the end of his filament, the predicted screams starting behind him. The incredibly aged Balthazar Smiley slapping at Mister Fixit with a pair of red satin gloves. The homicidal robot shrugging, taking a double handful of powdered wig, and twisting the Lord Mayor's head three hundred and sixty degrees. The man beside him bellowing, his ostrich-plumed pith helmet thrown aside as he tried to draw his sword...

Then both of Ezra's feet slammed into Mister Fixit's chest, to a raucous rebel yell from Granger. The automaton weighed as much as a fully packed fridge-freezer, but momentum (and a little luck) gave Ezra the edge. That tray of butter was right behind Fixit, and his foot stumbled back into it, sending him sprawling.

Ez rolled and came up into a crouch on the follow through, cutting the cable and selecting rapid fire. The Problem Solver swept up and out...

But the murderous robot was gone. Instead, he was staring down the crackling length of an electric cavalry sabre, clenched in the hand of a man whose face was beetroot red with anger. The sheer silliness of his uniform did little to disguise the fact that he was in possession of a very large, high-voltage carving knife.

"Hold fast sir, or meet your maker!"

With a kind of detachment, Ezra watched the rest of the Mayoral party look off toward the remains of Cheltendon, then run screaming in the opposite direction. He never flinched - even when Tia and Wainwright landed behind his captor, thudding down with their guns out.

"Looks like we got us a standoff," he drawled, while at the same time...

"Rocket boots? Granger, you mean to say we had us some damn rocket boots *all along?"*

"The thing with the swing was so much more... fitting. Anyhow, they ain't rockets. Gravitic manipulation. Think I'da had time to teach you how to use 'em?"

Ezra squinted, not taking his aim off the swordsman's chest.

"Mister, you saw what just happened. We got a common foe, it seems. So how about we both just step back, and see what everyone else is screamin' about?"

Just to be contrary, perhaps, the man stepped closer. Ez could taste the ozone as his sabre-tip all but trimmed his nostril hairs.

"And how can I trust you, sir? You may indeed have been trying to fell yon traitor, but you are no true Yorkman, aye?"

With very slow, deliberate motions, Ezra used his free hand to extract a silver packet of tiny cigars from his tuxedo. He slipped one into his mouth, then leaned forward to light it off the crackling blade.

"Well, for one - my pals there could have painted my face with your brains at any time in the last minute. Fact that they haven't speaks volumes. And two, in about another thirty seconds, we're gonna help you kill just whatever's sprung out of Mister Fixit's little trap, there. Wainwright? What have we got?"

The screaming had taken on the note of full-blown panic by now. Soldiers went pelting past, in full brown-trousered retreat. One or two sailed by in almost flat trajectories, knocked senseless. Ezra squinted, puffing a cloud of smoke in the swordsman's face.

"Oh, dear Gods and various other comforting made-up entities," said Wainwright. His face turned ashen pale, his eyes wider than should have been possible. Now Ezra *did* look - as did his assailant, both turning their heads until they were cheek-to-cheek, staring in slack-jawed horror.

Something was belting the good old traditional ten bells of shite out of Grand York's finest. Struggling mobs of soldiers rushed in, but were knocked back like chaff before a hurricane, rag-doll bodies cartwheeling through the air. Explosions stuttered and flashed, and blasts of wind roared out from the scrum of combatants, pulverizing and charring dozens at a time.

For an instant the melee swirled apart, and Ez caught a glimpse of what they were up against. A tall, thin man in a striped black-and-white shirt faced down a mob of infantry. They raised their plasma-locks to fire, and the man held up both his hands, palms flat, while making a mocking caricature of surprise. His face was as pale and white as an eggshell underneath a jaunty black beret.

Every last shot bounced off an unseen wall. The pale man held up one finger as if having an amazing epiphany. He reached down the back of his pants, and brought out an empty hand, cupped around an invisible globe. Held it to his mouth, gritted his teeth, and pulled an invisible pin. Then he lobbed the unseen missile at his foes, grimacing outlandishly as he jammed his fingers into his ears.

The detonation blew them apart. Charred remains were blasted skyward. The white-faced murderer put both hands in front of his mouth in mock contrition, already looking for a new target.

"Sweet Elvis, Jesus and Colonel Sanders," breathed Tia.

Wainwright nodded.

"*Mimes.*"

Nine - Beyond the valley of the Mimes

"Most of reality is just bad television. The rest happens when you're not looking"

- Jesus of Nazareth

MOST OF OUR trouble, they'd say later, came from assuming that all the aliens out there were serious.

In a nice piece of synchronized irony, this in itself was a very silly thing to say, especially when they - the same 'they' who seem to know all about the many infidelities of sports celebrities, and the machinations of the Illuminati - had the frankly staggering silliness of humanity to use as a baseline.

Then there were the legends of extra-terrestrial contact.

They should have been a clue.

Our top brass may have been hoping for an oscar-winningly dramatic meeting with a noble warrior race, or logical, proud scientists from beyond the stars. But history was full of instances where the aliens had proven themselves, to put it mildly, a bunch of wankers.

From the Threek megacruiser which parked on top of Atlantis, through to the Qual-Naar television production company who put on rubber masks and convinced the Egyptians to build giant lawn ornaments for the three-vee show 'Hostile Makeover', Earth was a magnet for interstellar dickheads.

Crop circles? A bunch of young Tchub hooligans dropping space graffiti. We're lucky we can't translate them, as they cast serious aspersions on our collective mothers.

Bigfoot? A Grendak streaker, wanted on ten worlds for crimes against trousers.

And the business with Roswell? That was a group of time-travelling evolved humans from the gene-spliceries of Thrannax, come to deliver a very important message to one Mr Elvis Aaron Presley. If they hadn't crashed (there was hard liquor involved, and sneezing, and a novelty tea towel, but of course by now the Government have released those files, so you know all about it) – then Elvis would never have had to fake his own death and embark upon his now-infamous quest through time and space to kill his evil clone, which is *definitely* something that's in a different book.

No, we really didn't get the alien mindset. We were anthropocentric in the extreme. We were, in fact, about as tactful, socially deft and politically correct, at the time when we made first contact, as a small group of Victorian gentlemen with handlebar moustaches, bibles and muskets planting the union jack in the sand of a small Pacific island.

Which is why the War of 9:15 happened in the first place.

It didn't help, either, that the man who made that contact – Captain Zance Van Der Throt, a walking prostate with more medals than brain cells and a chin cleft you could open beer bottles with - had first seen action during the Neo-Napoleonic uprising on Barney's World, in that terrible conflict known as the Mime Wars.

Which meant that any kind of clown made him extremely twitchy.

The Mimes he'd battled all those years ago were robots, of course. No human being could endure the kind of tractamorphic energy forces which were generated by one of the white-faced horrors in full battle mode. Created by the crazed francophile separatist Jean-Jaques Baptiste de Armagnac[26], these hideous warrior-droids could manipulate force fields into a variety of shapes, allowing their capering to become horribly real. Only one hundred were ever created, but the decimation they wrought on the ninth Earth Colonial Battalion was unmatched since the days of sherry-sipping officers chosen for command by dint of their impressive sideburns.

Zance had been there. He'd seen those blank dark eyes staring into his, as pale faces emerged through the smoke. He'd faced down the terrible silence which seemed to suck away even the screams of the dying, focusing the mind on those deadly, white-gloved hands, those prim little lips with their dot of black makeup...

To say that the experience gave him clown issues is like saying that the survivor of a cannibal death-orgy might be inclined, thereafter, toward vegetarianism.

He shot first, and asked questions later. The war happened, and Earth's AI masters went mad. And as for the Mimes - they had been presumed destroyed, or at least locked away safely on Barney's World, with the Chasm Gates disabled and the reticulum burned.

---

26. Who, despite dressing like Napoleon and subsisting on a diet of very fine wine, smelly cheese and baguettes, was in fact Korean

Now Mister Fixit had found them. And a very special brand of stripey black and white doom had come to Grand York...

+++

It was at times like these, Ezra thought, that it was comforting to know he wasn't real.

Those things the old Scrutinizer had told him seemed so *pure* and *right* - like the yearning for justice, rye whiskey and reasonably priced prostitutes had been, back on Harrowe. It just made *sense.* No God in his right mind would weave such a pointless fate for him - but Ezra, despite the best efforts of society, knew how to read. He was more than aware that certain bad authors would consider his life a 'ripping good yarn'.

So he aimed to please.

With the snarling, red-sideburned Yorkman at his side he plunged into the fray, using the Problem Solver to slap aside one white-faced horror and unloading a round of high explosive into another. Mechanical hands fashioned mime machine guns, raking the pair with invisible blasts of force, but they rolled away, coming up behind the cover of strewn machinery. Very real bullet holes pierced the metal behind them. One harlequin made as if to pull a vast tube up and over its shoulder - an insubstantial rocket launcher. Another slipped an imaginary missile into the breach, then winced as it stuffed its fingers into its rubber ears.

Ezra grabbed his new pal by the scruff of his collar, looking down at the ornate cowboy boots on his feet.

"O.K, Granger. Tell me these things've got rockets in 'em..."

"I told you!" came the somewhat panicked voice in his head. *"Gravitic manipulators! Just click your heels together twice, and..."*

He didn't get time to finish.

One of the mimes saluted as his companion was blown backwards by the recoil of his invisible bazooka, comically falling on his arse. The heavy grinder truck Ez had been hiding behind erupted in a very cinematic mushroom cloud of fire. And rising with the flames, spinning like a sycamore seed on absinthe...

Ashdown dragged the Yorkman clear, landing in a tangle of brocade, clattering sabre blades, antiquated hats and curses behind the mime lines.

120

"Unhand me, you oaf! It is my duty to die for the Lord Mayor!"

Ezra's companion seemed to operate like a steam engine - at a constant state of red-hot, near-fatal pressure. He leaped to his feet, sabres slicing the air in a complex *kata* - daring the black-and-white droids to shoot.

Several of them shrugged in a uniquely Gallic way and obliged him. A blur of swords deflected every bullet.

"Dammit, man! He already died for *himself!* Don't you think it would be better to live to see the next one?" Ezra, not to be left out (and secretly afraid not to be the main character in this scene) let loose with a filament round, chopping a Francophile mech into sparking chunks.

One of the robots stepped forward, gave a flourishing bow, and mimed drawing a rapier from a non-existent scabbard. It lashed out sideways, and the invisible blade cut a steel axle in two. The Yorkman grinned.

"Sir Giles Netherbottom-Smythe does not run away, sir! I may have failed Lord Balthazar, but there is redemption in a clean, honest death!"

This was not a happy thought for Ezra. He ducked down behind a pile of crates, spotting the massive discharge of Tia's Problem Solver off to their left, and Wainwright's plasma carbine close behind. For him, death just meant a new body constructed from lint, pencil shavings and last week's leftovers, followed by a very strong coffee and unpaid overtime. After a couple of gloomy seconds his brain caught up with him.

"*Netherbottom-Smythe?* That's your actual *name?*"

The Yorkman blocked, parried, spun on his heel, chimed electrified steel on invisible air, held off a volley of thrusts, then neatly beheaded his white-faced adversary. A beret-clad head rolled to his feet, its eyes wide open in mock surprise.

"I don't like to talk about it," he grimaced. "Why do you think I've been trying to earn bloody titles all these years? Mrs Netherbottom-Smythe's little boy had to learn most of the moves you just witnessed solely to survive primary school."

Ez popped up long enough to scrap another mime, this time using a blast of micro-missiles. Between him and Granger, he was really getting the hang of this fancy shooter...

"Well, mister titled aristocrat - tell me this. You ever hear of something called a *Burzum* around here? Only, that's what our homicidal friend

Mister Fixit is after. And speaking of which…" He jack-in-the-boxed up again, unleashing a full-auto burst of suppressing fire. "Just what in the *Hells* were you doing, letting that freak get nice and cosy with your precious Lord Mayor?"

The mimes had gotten wise to them. Three were comically mugging as they pretended to be caught behind invisible walls, built by a fourth, who whistled as he slung invisible bricks. It was a safe bet that nothing short of another point-C blast was going to punch through the force shield they'd created. A further knot of Gallic killing machines conversed behind the wall, stage-whispering and gurning outrageously.

"He promised us a way out," snarled Sir Giles, conceding the suicidal foolishness of standing out in the open while wearing a feather-plumed helmet and a bright red coat[27]. He slid into cover next to Ez, and immediately popped open a silver cigar case.

"The damned creature had a ship which could pass through the old gates. Told us we could build the right drives, and rig up the right thinkin' engines, if we only had a bit more scrap. That's when he offered us a push after Cheltendon…"

He offered Ezra a cigar. The gunslinger took it with thanks. Behind them, out in the machine hall, something large and expensive detonated, utterly demolishing the Pig and Bucket tavern.

"You know, I've only met that damned robot twice, and I already hate him more than should be possible. Part of not being real, I guess."

Netherbottom-Smythe gave him the kind of look normally reserved for streakers covered in lemon pudding who claimed to be the Lord Jesus Christ.

"You're doing quite well despite your handicap, sir," he said, patting Ez gently on the arm. "But I'm afraid I'm all too corporeal. A shame, really. I could take you right to your *Burzum*, if we could only get out of here alive…"

Ezra hoisted one eyebrow.

"You know where it is?"

"Oh, certainly. Burzum Newmarket is right next to my own dear old borough of West Bletherings. We incorporated the wreck about three hundred years ago. Turned it into hydroponic gardens, a costermonger's market, and about four thousand tenements. Big

27. Which sounds rather stupid, but which seemed to work for the British Empire for over two centuries - probably because the rest of their strategy involved mainly attacking confused foreign people who hadn't invented guns yet.

chunks of it still locked down, of course - we never winkled all the weapons systems out!"

Things were progressing behind the invisible mime-wall. Ezra risked a peek over the top and was rewarded with the sight of Tia Faraday doing the same. She waved at him frantically, tapping her ear and mouthing words he couldn't make out.

He shrugged, making a pistol with his fingers and aiming it at the wall.

Inside the dome of force, one of the mimebots turned to another.

"Bloody amateurs," it said, before clapping its kid-gloved hands firmly over its mouth.

Behind him the leader of the mimes (full Napoleonic uniform, chest full of medals and red beret) climbed up onto a patch of empty air. It imitated opening a heavy hatch, then slid down inside to sit on an invisible chair. White fingers stabbed at unseen buttons, then the thing's hands clenched around a pair of imaginary levers.

The mimebot began to gently vibrate, as if it had just started a powerful diesel engine.

A second mime raised a single finger in astonished realization, then clambered up even further on absolutely nothing, popping a second hatch and taking up a different set of invisible controls. The grim Gallic mech rotated left then right as its hands pumped the levers. A third followed, then a fourth, taking up positions inside what must be some kind of large, unseen vehicle...

Sir Giles popped up for a look.

"Tell me, sir - do they have *battle tanks* where you come from?"

Ezra frowned.

"Like a little land steamer? Well, I guess I heard of 'em - but I've never seen one."

The Yorkman took another look. Yes, the mime-wall was down, and whatever the accursed robots had created was indeed leaving the imprint of great cleated tracks behind it as it rumbled forward.

"You still haven't," he said. "But they've got one anyway. And it looks like they've decided to finish your offworld friends first."

The thought of Tia being blasted into a cloud of charged plasma electrified something down near the base of his spine. His second thoughts were accusing him of being thoroughly sexist for not also wanting save Wainwright as he hurdled the low wall of crates, setting the Problem Solver to maximum blast.

"Hoooo boy! Haven't had this kinda fun for so long as I can remember!"

Jed Granger gleefully shunted wormhole gates, linking Ezra's pistol to a whole new rattling, clanking series of conveyor belts in the sub-basements of Earth. *"Don't forget to give 'em a witty one liner when you blow 'em out of their boots, hoss!"*

Ez just snarled, letting loose a bolt of incandescent purple force once, twice, thrice...

Three mimes simply ceased to exist before the rest even knew he was coming. A patter of molten metal and a swirl of smoke was all that remained of them.

"Learn the script," spat the gunslinger, to Granger's evident delight. Then he took aim at the imaginary rump of the mimes' tank, and held the trigger down.

A searing bolt lashed out, smashing into the invisible war machine with all the subtlety of a twelve-car pileup. Impossible forces mambo'd, tangoed, and did the electric slide all over the laws of physics. Streamers of sparks and stray lightning lit up the entire processing hall, accompanied by a noise and smell like somebody trying to arc-weld a bison to the ceiling.

It didn't stop. This kind of firepower came from tapping the central torus of the Scrutinizer's very own personal tokamak fusion reactor, and the stream of superheated hellfire it delivered exceeded even the interior temperature of a service station pie. Ezra's lips pulled back from his teeth in a rictus grin, while red bar graphs and alarmingly large numbers began to crowd the edges of his vision. The tiny face of Jed Granger appeared to have acquired not just a bad case of sunburn, but also one of those silly little hats made by tying knots into the corners of a handkerchief.

"Warning, boss! Coolant satellite overload!"

Now it was time for thoughts numbered well after two, and preceded with all the fiddly little lower-case-i stuff and brackets. Some of them involved the fact that Tia Faraday's relationship to death was less fatal and far more auto-erotic than most. The rest, however, were all about the fact that the mime tank had spectacularly failed to disintegrate. And now...

"How big do you think they imagined the gun on that thing?" asked Jed Granger, as thermal shutdowns made the Problem Solver into a very threatening paperweight. *"Because, see, I'd like your replacement to have them pretty little red-painted fingernails, a kind of cascade of golden curls, you know what I mean, and massive, bouncy..."*

The answer appeared to be 'gigantic'.

The mimebot in the turret of the invisible vehicle waved a sad little 'goodbye', as its buddy levered an invisible shell into the breach. Then it turned away, wincing, and pulled an unseen string.

There was, of course, no actual projectile. But the detonation of weird forces shredded the very atoms of the air itself, creating a vivid blue and green whipcrack of plasma. Ezra didn't stick around to meet it head-on - he clicked his heels together and jumped, somersaulting over the sizzling beam as it scored a trench through the solid steel of Grand York's decking. No sooner had he landed than a second blast tried to barbecue him to the bone, licking past the soles of his boots as he rolled and cursed. The smell of crisping leather brought back poignant memories of his momma's thoroughly atrocious cooking.

The impact of his head against the floor must have knocked his communicator back to life, because he was treated, for a few delightful seconds, to the choicest invective Tia Faraday knew. It was almost enough to literally melt the wax from inside his ears.

"...can't just pump more energy into it, you ape-featured bell-end! We need something *subtle* here, not a freight train full of dynamite!"

"That thing Galbraith had, back in the Chasm," said Wainwright, thoroughly chastised. "Too bad I didn't bring one along. It warps a tiny little black hole inside the target, see, and..."

"It's back on Earth, being polished by a horrible little Scotsman," snarled Tia. "Think! You're supposed to be an artificial *intelligence*, not an ersatz idiot!"

A third incandescent rod of energy spat from the mime tank, and Ez could see the Francophile death-machines high-fiving each other in there, pointing and grinning. It melted a hemispherical chunk out of a tracked crucible truck, just as the gunslinger slid into cover behind it.

And he saw.

It unfolded inside his head with the fragile symmetry as a snowflake - and just as cold and precise, too. The Central Scrutinizer had shown him how the chasm had touched him, changed him...

So what if it went both ways?

What if he could use his connection the Chasm to do what that imaginary, potent place did? To move a little insignificant clump of atoms and probability vectors from one place to another?

He licked his lips, gritted his eyes closed, realized how stupid he looked, and reached deep into his own mind.

To the crack, the flaw which made him who he was. The parasitic fragment which had slipped into his soul all those years ago...

It told him that all he needed was an excuse.

But that it better be a good one.

+++

The trick to doing the utterly impossible, of course, is believing that you're not real.

Generations of monks, perched on highly uncomfortable but spiritually enlightening mountain tops, have told all those who care to listen that the ego is what holds us back from miracles, up to and including sitting on the pointy tip of a big pile of rocks in winter without contracting near-terminal haemorrhoids.

It's hard to think about the existential conundrum of not being real. Various French people with vile little cigarettes and black turtleneck sweaters have tried to poke and prod the issue of unreality for years, and have come up with little other than gothic rock, heroin abuse and the inability to build a proper car.[28]

Here's the trick. You have to approach your non-reality with joy. Not with angst, but with a kind of light-hearted blitheness, and the knowledge that non-existent people don't have to wash the dishes, eat brussels sprouts of fill in their tax returns.

It's the reason that the Confucian Chinese venerated the insane, and the reason why a soldier who screams something pithy about freedom and charges right at those annoying machine guns is likely to find himself suddenly standing among a whole lot of rather embarrassed enemies who are wondering where all the messy red holes in him are.

It's not that people can sometimes do things just because they don't know they can't. It's just that sometimes, the concept of 'people' gets taken right out of the equation. Reality happens because we're observing it[29]. So what happens, then, *if the observer isn't real?* You might need some interesting herbs and mushrooms to really ponder that one.

The Chasm is the ultimate subjective reality.

There's a theory that we didn't so much discover it, as force it open with our teeming, overcrowded need to leave the Earth behind. That's why, for us, it mainly does a very weird version of faster-than-light-travel.

---

28. Apart from the Peugeot 205, of course.

29. And that's actually a scientific fact. Which makes all this other stuff slightly less like hogwash!

But, if you are, say, a psychologically messed-up space cowboy seconds away from nasty obliteration, it can do other things, too. Things which have a lot to do with reality being a mirror of itself, and the mind being a distorting prism...

There's a tiny instant before the huge, ponderous forces of physics and nature lumber around on their equivalent of a mall cop's electric scooter and say 'Hey! Wait a minute! You can't do that!"

In that instant, someone who believes he's fictional can perform miracles.

+++

Ezra stood up from behind cover just as the invisible mime-tank aimed its main gun at his head. A thunderously silent detonation sent an imaginary shell whizzing past him, so close it made the tails of his topcoat flap like black pennants.

But it missed. Ashdown's grin became a notch more manic as he strode forward, the Problem Solver held out in front of him. He opened the palm of his other hand, feeling a greasy tension build up there, reality bulging and stretching. *They never hit the good guy.* You couldn't just paste the main character. So...

He wasn't real. This was just some stupid pulp novel, the kind they sold at soda fountains and barbershops[30]. The kind of booze-addled numbskull who wrote this stuff was obsessed with weapons - huge, glittering, futuristic guns which blasted ruby death without recourse to any real science. Things like whatever Angus Galbraith had come barging into the Chasm with, back in chapter six. There would have been a footnote, for the spotty fanboys. Better – there might even be a *diagram.*

And there it was. Ezra's moment of clarity melted away like frost under a blowtorch - but as it went, he saw his good excuse take shape. He reached sideways into a metaphorical place, which crystalized into reality around his fingers. He found his footnote, and put it *on this page...*[31]

Something heavy slapped into his open palm. He holstered the Problem Solver, muffling Jed Granger's howls of sheer delight, and

---

30. And selected vape-shops in Oxfordshire and New Zealand - ED

31. ... takes a primordial black hole and accelerates it through a wormhole gate to 77 percent the speed of light, thus forming a projectile which is capable of making a horrible mess all over your nice new lounge suite.

hefted it in both hands.

"*Bon voyage*, you garlic-munching surrender-philes!"

The tank stopped. The lead mime – the one who looked like he should be getting chased by men in white with butterfly nets - popped the invisible top hatch open and stood up.

"Hey!" it said "That's racist, that eees! And we didn't surrender, you know! Bloody *Anglo* peeeg!"

Ezra winked. A thoroughly impossible glint of light gleamed off one of his teeth, despite the fact that he hadn't brushed for days.

"Perhaps you should have," he said.

Then he pulled the trigger.

Things happened which should not be discussed in a polite, orderly cosmos. The warping, stretching, crushing and general jiggery-pokery with time and space made toffee out of anyone's ability to really explain the process. Then chewed it. Then went for a nice walk down to the pub for a pint and a game of darts. Metaphorically speaking, of course.

Suffice to say that it's lucky nobody left their nice new lounge suite anywhere near the homicidal mimes and their invisible tank. Because what was left after Galbraith's crazy gun did its business was roughly the size of a baseball, smelled of cheese, and was smoking gently.

Tia kicked it, then swore, hopping around in small circles. Wainwright cocked his head to one side, letting it blur for an instant and revert to its usual shape - that of a great copper diving helmet.

"That's one of Galbraith's collection, isn't it? I'm not going to ask where you got it from, or where you've been.... ahhh... *keeping* it. Well played, though."

Ezra gurgled a little, looking down at the immense, gently steaming brass cannon in his hands. It fell from numb fingers, clattering to the floor. Now that his brain had had enough time to catch up with what he'd done, it was experiencing a level of cognitive dissonance similar to a hard-core atheist taking a bubble bath inside the Ark of the Covenant.

Tia snapped him out of it by taking two steps over the remains of the Mime tank, then slapping him full across the face.

"That's for saving my life," she snarled. Then she cupped the red, palm-shaped imprint on his cheek, went up on tip-toes, and kissed him in a way which made the ends of his boots curl.

"That's also for saving my life," she said demurely, rocking back onto her heels. "Because we have a mission. And Mister Fixit..."

"Ahem."

It was perhaps the most genteel cough ever issued. It was, to a regular cough, what the most cryogenically frosty of butlers is to a football hooligan on the outside of a pint of oven cleaner. Tia and Ezra broke eye contact, tiny sparks winking out in all four of their pupils.

"Dreadfully sorry, and all that. Don't mean to intrude..."

It was Sir Giles Netherbottom-Smythe. And he's sheathed his sabre, instead accessorising with a matched pair of plasma muskets, both of which were pointed squarely at the little group of Panarchy Outriders. He dithered a little.

"Sticky wicket and all that, but I'm afraid I have to place the lot of you under *arrest*. Agents of a foreign power and all. Shame, because I really liked the way you dealt with those robot buggers. Still, you'll get a fair trial..."

"Who does the judgin'?" asked Ez, his hand inching toward the butt of the Problem Solver. Giles saw this, and indicated, with an economic little twitch, that remarkably painful violence was definitely an option should he continue. Ez, of course, was still thinking of Mason Stockton, and a certain noose.

"Trial by ordeal, seeing as the Mayor is dead. We bung you out the airlock, and if you explosively decompress, you're innocent. I believe the Undersecretary of Condolences writes your family a letter of apology."

"And if you're *guilty*?" Tia's eyebrow arched in a way which thoroughly unnerving.

"I'm afraid if you fail to explode, they target you with X-ray lasers. It's rather... messy." He looked crestfallen, but then brightened a bit. "It really is a *lovely* letter of apology, though. On that see-through paper with roses around the edges..."

Netherbottom-Smythe was interrupted by a squeal of static, then a manic babble from a little bead next to his left ear. His face went ashen pale - or at least, paler than it had been.

"They *stole* it? And he killed how many? With the... ohhh, giblets, I see. And those little wobbly bits. Urrrgh. But how does he hope to.... Yes, I have them here. Yes, alive! And..."

The Yorkish knight's eyes peered up at the Panarchy agents, runny and soft as poached eggs. He swallowed, hard.

"There's a message for you, as well. Admiral Chumbley told me to let it through..."

The little bead cast a tight cone of light, weaving laser patterns in helical figure-eights. Out of the haze a form coalesced - one dressed in the very height of 1980s goth fashion.[32]

"You're really gonna want to hear this," said *Disintegration*, in the kind of tones which indicated that they really wouldn't. "Mister Fixit has the AI core of the *Burzum*. It was right on board this rig all along. And now he's cut loose, and given Grand York a little nudge..."

"It's going to be into the sun," muttered Tia. Ez noticed that she had her fingers crossed. "Never kamikaze'd a red giant before..."

"It's not the sun," said Dis. "It's the *gateway*. Can you imagine the size of the Chasm Gate they needed to set up a thing like the Boneyard? Big enough for the tugs and the hulks at once? It's the second biggest ever made, after the great Geopolar Gate over Earth. The traffic here..."

"But it's just an empty metal ring. What's the point of throwing us at it? And if he turns it back on, we'll just be following him."

Wainwright, as usual, was right on the money.

"We don't fit, do we? And I doubt you're supposed to bust up the frame while all that shiny mirror stuff is bubblin' away in there."

"The cowboy is correct. You *don't* fit. Grand York would have to be chopped up into lots of tiny little chunks to fit through the Chasm gate. Without a proper AI installed, those chunks would pop out of every active gate available, at random, all across the Panarchy. At a nice fraction of lightspeed. With... and I can't express my condolences deeply enough... all of you inside them. Just spread out very thin, like marmalade."

Tia brightened.

"But seeing as we're *not* going to be chopped up into tiny little chunks, we'll just crash into the gateway itself, and probably shut it down. We'll be stuck here, with all these yokels and their fake pub and mister bloody police cop here in his silly trousers." She gestured dismissively at Sir Giles.

Disintegration raised one pale finger, opened his mouth, then hesitated. He tried again. Stopped. Took a deep breath.

"About that..."

+++

---

32. There's a lot of debate about whether Goths, or the later great tribal grouping of Emos were more depressing. The simple fact is that the Goths nearly actually *destroyed the whole world* in the 1980s by creating a hole in the ozone layer through hairspray overexposure. The processing power, for example, used to render *Disintegration*'s haircut, was equal to that needed to model the fully sentient mind of a golden retriever.

In the well-heeled Yorkish suburb of Burzum Newmarket, certain things - which resembled raspberry jam, and would do so until many years of counselling sessions peeled back the scab of repression - finished their gelatinous slide down the walls. The gunsmoke cleared enough to make out the ruin left in the mad stranger's wake. It was broken glass, shredded composite, beheaded gargoyles and ragged lace curtains all round. The costermongers' barrows, usually laden with the very best cube-shaped synthetic produce, were reduced to splintered wrecks. But then again, costermongers' barrows always fare terribly in both firefights and car chases, beaten out only narrowly by two lads carrying a pane of glass, and the ever-popular pile of cardboard boxes.

The owner of Wilf's Wiggery chanced a quick peek over the edge of his counter. The entire wig shop (or shoppe, if we were to believe the sign) smelled of singed hair, cordite and... well, Wilf was a nervous man, and he wished at this present moment that his shop sold trousers.

Nothing sliced the top off of his outlandishly large powdered pompadour. He raised the edifice of hair and creaking underpinnings a little higher, until the carriage clock lodged halfway to his scalp caught the light. Still no bullets.

Whimpering a little, Wilf took stock of what was left of his storefront. A greasy breeze ruffled the remains of his curtains, framing what could only be called a hole. A sad little piece of faux-woodwork teetered and fell, landing on a carpet of broken glass.

What he saw outside was simply too much for his refined sensibilities. He looked anyway.

The central plaza of Burzum Newmarket had once been the fusion generator hall of that vast warship - for the *Burzum* had been crafted solely for the purpose of destruction. Half a kilometre in each direction, the space had once housed the massive hulk of a deuterium powered stellarator, but was now home to a great sprawling marketplace. Most of it was on fire.

At the very centre of the great metal-ribbed vault, a statue stood. It was, as befitted the regency-era sensibilities of Grand York, a depiction of one of the great virtues - in this case Demelza, patron saint of shutting up and getting the hell on with it. She was forged from bronze, two storeys tall, and had been depicted with a toilet plunger in one had and a machine gun in the other.

The sheer violence unleashed by the mad stranger and his tiny, adorable counterpart had melted Demelza slightly, causing her toilet plunger to droop and giving her a look of puzzled constipation.

But the thing which Wilf noted - and which any long-time resident of the Newmarket would have noticed, had they not all been largely reduced to the state of raspberry jam - was that the virtuous statue's necklace was missing. A black snowflake of crystal had nestled in her ample cleavage since time immemorial, and now it was gone.

Funny, thought Wilf, as he slumped back behind the counter. If anyone thought that thing was worth a bent penny, it would have been stolen long ago...

+++

While all this was going on, Rel Kitano was thinking about his girlfriend.

Remember him? Domesticated human pet, last punk rocker in the universe, equipped with a man-sized raccoon tail and, thanks to the oversight of his huge alien nannies, also equipped with the single most powerful engine of war ever controlled by a son of Earth.

Now, most of you will think that the worst thing that's happened in our story so far is that a homicidal, probably genocidal, quite possibly *omnicidal* robot handyman has managed to steal the key to instantaneous travel between the fragmented worlds of the Panarchy. He's got a *Slayer* class Corsair, a little French robot girl who can evaporate cities, the slumbering mind of a frothing mental killer starship, and a mean streak so wide that all the orange road cones in existence couldn't close it for maintenance.

But you'd be wrong.

For many reasons - and chief among them may well be that the author of this tale is a complete twat - you may be unaware that the most horrible danger of all was at this moment listening to the Stranglers while carving a curdled, hissing groove through the surface of space and time some three hundred light years away.

Rel Kitano's idea of true love came from album liner notes. He was sixteen years old, seething with a nightmarish broth of hormones, and he was infatuated to the point of physical toothache with the girl of his dreams.

Who, through the cruel machinations of fate, was destined to become a nun, living out her life in service to Worm III the Utterly Lowest, leader of the Synod and unquestioned master of the planet

Temperance. Or she might be killed out of hand by a cruel and sadistic enQuisition.

Unless a WHOLE lot of pilfered Process ordnance had anything to say about it...

Of course, hideous carnage is a relative thing.

Somewhere else in the Panarchy, on the strictly enviro-locked and habitat controlled space station of Zarbandi Two Delta, the controlling AI inside the nutrient recombinator has just lost an argument with the sanitation submind, and in retaliation has instigated Mandatory Triple Hot Chicken Tikka Masala Night Tuesday for all one million and three human crew members.

But that, as they say, is a story for another day. One when it's not too soon to raise a lighter *very very cautiously* to salute the many asphyxiated dead, perhaps.

In the meantime, it's Mister Fixit's move...

Ten - The Underpants of Time

"There are loads of species who travel through time. Heaps of us! Of course, only one bunch are arrogant enough to call themselves 'Lords', but then again, those bastards have some style. The thing to remember, of course, is that time travel is pretty much just travel through the various realms of probability. If your average timeline is a piece of wool, then we time travellers see the whole jumper.

And it's a pretty resilient jumper, too. The kind your dad puts on to go and fix the water heater. There are curry stains, and torn threads, and a whole unravelled armpit where the Time Crusades happened, back/forward in the distant past/future. But usually it knits back together.

You know that old paradox about going back in time and having sex with your own mother? The universe fixes that right up. If you conceive yourself, you're born too inbred to invent a cheese sandwich, let alone a time machine. And as for all the tourists at the crucifixion, or the advent of the first AI, or the now-infamous football match between humanity and the Kraarg to see if you all get turned into breakfast sausages... oops, that hasn't happened for you yet... well, of course there were spectators. But, you know, compared to making a functioning time machine, inventing some pretty nifty chameleon-tech is a walk in the park, mate."

Moltan Slooze,
Uberfederal Comptroller of the Temporal Juristocracy

MISTER FIXIT KNEW that he was more than a little evil, what with wanting to destroy the entire human race and all. The trouble was that it felt so *good*.

I mean, he *knew* that there were ever-so-many brilliant justifications for eradicating the silly, cargo-pants-wearing virus which was humanity. Some of them were even sane. But when it really came down to it, when you really scraped the magnetic stylus of truth across Mister Fixit's flint-hard AI crystal heart - well... it was loads of fun, wasn't it?

A good question. A part of the incredibly ancient robot worried, sometimes, that he was becoming something less than himself.

Something which was evil for the *sake of evil*. Something... *typecast*.

He had once or twice caught himself wishing he owned a good dinner suit and top hat combo, like the one Ezra was currently sporting. He had toyed with the idea of gluing on a moustache. He had even taken to listening to the sound of thunderstorms and pipe organ music at the same time.

But there were payoffs. Oh yes. Sometimes giving in to the need to be purely wicked felt as good as a cocaine-sprinkled icecream sundae after a long diet.

Just like this part, now. The part where his enemies burned alive.

The *Slayer* class corsair *Altar of Sacrifice* hung in the umbra of a vast spaceborne orchid of a thing - a confection of curved mirrors and focusing lens-fields the size of a small city. It was secured by an accordioned umbilical to a habitat ring encircling a hole in the centre of the device - a hole that they would want to be well away from in just a few minutes.

The reason was twofold. Firstly, this immense array of metal was designed to focus the bloody red light of Crothon into a beam which could cut through space warships. Analogies with red-hot knives and sticky puddings were in its operations manual. The second was the fact that Mister Fixit was possessed of mind-enslaving powers even greater than those of daytime soap operas.[33]

They'd done for the poor old *Altar*, of course. They'd also been able to render Cerise, the Chasm Guardian of Harrowe, a little more tractable. If Mister Fixit had been forced to keep up the elaborate fantasy which Mason Stockton had perpetuated - and in French, no less - the homicidal mech was certain he would have gone just slightly

---

33. Well, except for the longest running soap of them all, *'The Turgid and the Turbulent'*, which is procedural rendered by the mad AI of Sunset Acres (the retirement world) and has run for the last three thousand years. When Sunset Acres was cut off, it's AI reasoned that it would have to keep its current population in stasis, and this mind-blindingly futile and convoluted soap opera was born to keep their brains from turning to literal jelly. To the residents of the Acres, only minutes have passed since the War of 9:15, but in the horribly bland fiction which enslaves them Doctor Chad Cliffhanging has been replaced by his evil twin three hundred times, has married and divorced ninety two fake countesses, has been possessed by Satan, and has recently revealed that it was all a dream brought on by the amnesia he suffered after his ex-wife's podiatrist's dog's ex-owner's personal trainer fell in love with his estranged sister who was also his father's mistress. And clobbered him with a novelty ashtray. Several nasty people would love to weaponise *'The Turgid and the Turbulent'* into a ray which turns normal mental function into something resembling white noise. But to do so they would have to watch it...

further round the twist.

The same programs would soon get their hooks into the hubcap-sized, eye-wateringly complex snowflake of black glass which was the War Intelligence *Burzum*, and hammer it into something which could run a Process Immaterial Dreadnought. They had brute-forced the antiquated submind of the solar crucible in nanoseconds.

Oh, happy times! Tick, tick, tick - all the little boxes on Mister Fixit's psychotic clipboard were being knocked down in a row! There was only one turd left in the potato salad, and that was the sorry band of Outriders left aboard Grand York.

And they were about to go the way of a sixteenth century grandmother with a thing for black cats, a collection of herbal recipes and a lack of asbestos petticoats.

"Bwaaaa hah hah hah haaaahhh!" laughed Mister Fixit, wringing his hands in glee. This caused a sound like several balloon animals wrestling in cooking oil. A subroutine stopped it, and clapped one hand over what had, until recently, been Mason Stockton's mouth. He turned at a sound behind him.

"Uncle - the capacitors are full. We're ready to proceed."

It was Cerise, now dressed in a far more utilitarian and modern ship-suit and, (praise all those non-existing gods) speaking only slightly accented Panarchic Standard.

"Set those fusion beam controls to my command, and re-route power from the coolant web to the main lensing field."

"Acknowledged. Temperatures are nominal but rising. Output threshold has been achieved and is holding steady."

Mister Fixit wrapped his steely fingers around a pair of twin joysticks, smiling a mirthless smile with Stockton's lips.

"Okey-dokey, valued customers! Time to start chopping!"

+++

The first intimation that something was staggeringly, pants-wettingly wrong came only seconds later. Ezra, Tia, Wainwright and Sir Giles were pelting through a maze of glass tubes, high above the towers of Grand York. Fleeing toward the command sanctum, that great baroque cathedral-hall full of brass controls and mysterious pipes where the Engineers of the great rig plotted its course.

So they saw the red light suck down into a tiny point, out there in space. They saw the mirrors begin to spin like hellish silver turbine blades.

Unfortunately, a wrecking laser powered by an entire sun was the least of their worries. Because Mister Fixit had given Grand York a huge push with his Corsair, enabling it to catch up with its prey. Now, conjoined jaws-to-arse, two floating space-cities were headed for a collision with the Van Rijn's chasm gate, a circular immensity rippling with enough mercury to drown a continent.

Crashing would be a problem. All the life jackets, high-visibility vests and little orange plastic whistles in the world wouldn't help a person walk away from that wreck.

Without an AI to weave them into the chasm - and a guide to find the right door once inside - they'd spew out of a random gate as a cosmic belch of hard radiation. Those who were unlucky enough to see this happen, before a storm of alphanumerically-named rays stripped their skeletons down to plasma, would describe it as 'not pretty'.

So it would be much worse, on the whole, if Grand York were to be chopped up into bite-sized pieces before being spread across the Panarchy as a whole series of catastrophic nuclear explosions.

Tia was the first to see the crucible station fire up, and the first to run through all those consequences in her head.

"Oh, *crap*," she said. "He's done it. He's really done it..."

Ezra skidded to a halt beside her, squinting up through the thick glass of the skybridge.

"What's your professional opinion, Miss Faraday? What with me being a primitive gunslinger, and not really *owe faye* with all this spaceman action..."

She shot him a 'certain look'.

"Well, Ashdown, it's like this. Before, it was like the doctor had told us all we didn't have long to live. Now, it's like he's *looking at his damn watch.*"

"Ahhhhh. One of those, is it? Never mind. It's always darkest before the dawn, as my Pa used'ta tell me."

"A poor choice of words, perhaps," said Wainwright, calculating and triangulating vectors. "Considering we're about to catch enough sunshine to last a very short and crispy lifetime..."

And here came the beam.

It stabbed out from a far-off point, slicing a geometric line across the Boneyard, all in silence.

It grew wider as it approached - lashing across space, evaporating tumbling chunks of metal and delicate petals of ablative foil in its path. A blade of light the colour of a Spring sunset, all orange and purple, the width of a skyscraper. It carved into the doomed rig of Cheltenden, locked there in the jaws of Grand York, and neatly sliced it in two.

There was a horrible moment in which Ez tried to pretend that the little specks of chaff puffing off into vacuum like the seeds from a black dandelion weren't people. Then the beam stuttered and died, leaving behind a blur of after-images, and it was time to run again.

"Why don't we forget the exercise and just get blasted?" puffed Ezra, when Tia slowed down to check their direction at a fork in the corridor. Below them, beneath the ant-farm confusion of the upper towers, the people of Grand York were putting on a display of panic which would have done the extras in a Godzilla movie proud. "We're nigh immortal, right?"

Wainwright snorted.

"Sorry to burst your bubble, Tex, but *I'm* the one who brings your sorry carcass back when that happens. And I'm right here with you, so..."

"We'd be back on Earth, best case scenario. Or on board the... never mind."

"I thought the *Nirvana* class rapid scoutship *Nevermind* was currently bumbling about the Sirius sector, thinking it was a small paper bag of dinner rolls?" said Wainwright. "Our ship is.... ohhh."

The rest couldn't see it. But Wainwright, tapped into the cameras and scanners which studded Grand York's towers... He got a front row seat.

"You fool," he whispered. "You damned, grandiosely-coiffured *fool*. You should have saved yourself..."

But instead some sense of misguided loyalty – or perhaps a viral override inserted by the Central Scrutinizer - had convinced the *Disintegration* to try to save them. The angular black ship flared briefly as the beam from the solar crucible splashed against its shields, but all that energy had to go somewhere. Shield generators detonated down its flank like a cannonade. Writhing borealis fires wrapped it up in a huge and nacreous fist.

"_______________________!!!", screamed a certain holographic goth.

Then the *Disintegration* performed a fairly accurate interpretation of its name.

"Our ship," reported the metalman "Has, as they say, 'left the building.'"

"So... this is what it's like to feel screwed. Again," said Ezra, more than a bit out of breath from all the running. "That was our only ticket off this darned thing, wasn't..."

He didn't get to finish - the beam licked out again, this time carving through a series of gantries and towers ahead of them. Whole tangles of steel and cable ablated away like bacon fat under a blowtorch.

"Well, I was going to tell you that it would be fine, we could just steer the whole rig around the gate and miss, but..."

"That was the command basilica," moaned Sir Giles. He wasn't used to this kind of action. A hard day being a Knight of the Iron Order usually meant guffawing, brandy, cigars, slapping subordinates with a pair of crisp white gloves, then a very big dinner. "They're all dead! Rolly, Tadger, Guffy, Big Bottomed Bob... all of them!"

"I'm certain," said Wainwright, in a tone so withering that it could have been used to desiccate watermelons, "That *Big Bottomed Bob* is the least of our concerns. Is there any other way off this thing?"

Sir Giles' moustache bristled, and he swung a finger around to point at the spot where Wainwright's nose should have been.

"It'd serve you right, you heartless bastard, if we all got blown to pieces. I've got a good mind to die just so you learn some manners. But yes, there *is* a way. The founders left it behind. Perhaps your technology can make it work again. It's far too complicated for us to be tinkering with, I'm told."

"The founders?"

"There's no *time*, man! To the museum, and hurry!"

Ezra groaned, but soon wished he hadn't. The next ten minutes were a hellish marathon of chokingly hot iron passageways and stairwells, run while waiting for the fatal lash of Mister Fixit's crucible beam. The evil mech was wielding the light-minutes-long ship-breaker like a drunken lunatic with a broadsword - all off-balance and no finesse, but God help anything which got in its way.

At last they reached a high and dusty hall - a cathedral of verdigris and rust capped by an enormous dome. Flashes of light painted the spiderweb shadow of its support beams across the marble floor, and across a pair of impossibly tall wooden doors.

Actual wood, thought Ezra. Expensive, even on Harrowe. Here, in space, where recycled scrap made up everything (including most of the popular breakfast cereals), wood had to be worth its weight in...

well, wood.

Tia had no such qualms about the value of inlaid oak. She kicked the doors open with unnecessarily dramatic flair - seeing as they proved to be unlocked - and sprawled flat on the shiny floor tiles beyond them.

Where a massive cube of glass enclosed the machine of their salvation, along with what Ezra sincerely hoped were two mannequins. If not, then they were a credit to the art of taxidermy - nobody alive should ever have looked so cheerfully constipated.

The ship - if that's what it could rightly be called - was all copper and brass and polished teak. It looked like a hansom cab in the throes of passion with a giant bell jar, a steam engine and a vintage refrigerator.

"I know it's not *really* a spacecraft," said Sir Giles, wringing his hands in that horribly self-conscious way people do when they're forced, for awkward social reasons, to show off some of the sillier traditions of their so-called society[34]. "But it's vacuum tight, and it got the both of them here..."

"The both of whom?" asked Wainwright.

Ezra stepped up to the glass, buffing a patch of it with his sleeve. He looked down at the sad little moth-eaten card which identified the two mannequins.

> *"The Founders. The wise men who came to Grand York in the time of the Dissolution, and brought us the doctrine of survival of the fittest. Who made society in the image of the great empire they had been sent from..."*

Tia - fuming about not having been offered a hand up, so she could politely but pointedly decline - elbowed Ez out of the way.

"Holy shit," she breathed. "So, it was real, huh?"

And indeed it was. From the brass balls which gleamed on its governor-valve down to the fancy tassels hanging from its corinthian leather command chairs, it was as real as a vinegar popsicle jammed into the middle of a savage hangover. Ezra read further down the card, elbowing his parole officer right back.

---

34. Such as explaining Morris dancing to a tribe of rain forest dwelling hunter-gatherers, right after you've explained the tax system and Paris Fashion Week

"The Verne-Wells 'Britannia' Model 1900. Complete with water-cooled Maxim guns, humidor, champagne fridge and a variable-speed shoe buffer, suitable for both oxfords and brogues."

He looked up, a schoolboy grin on his face.
"It's a gosh-darned time machine."

+++

The great factual essayist Jules Verne served in the Imperial British Armed Forces with the rank of Colonel - a position which was largely ceremonial, but which was traditionally awarded to those in his position. There was even a nicely engraved pocketwatch involved.

The fact that he had been born French was less of a handicap than you might have thought - the Queen was nothing if not utterly pragmatic, and his undoubted genius, combined with the bottomless nature of the Imperial coffers, ensured that his employment was never in doubt.

A suitable impostor was swapped with the real Jules during a memorable dinner party at 24 Rue de l'Ancienne-Comédie, and the genuine article came to the Ministry of Plausible Deniability's bunker complex beneath Kew Gardens.

As a member of Section W, that secretive branch of Her Majesty's Government tasked with fostering super-technologies (and preventing the Huns, Russkies and of course the perfidious Turks from getting their greasy mitts on the same), Colonel Jules had all sorts of wild adventures, which he dutifully scribed down in a series of notebooks.

Section W was known to the other services (especially those smug bastards in Section M, led by Major-General 'The Great Beast' Crowley) as the Weirdos. Jules, along with a crack team of what we would today call 'insane commandos', was supposed to not only invent crazy new devices, but also to deploy them in the field. Along with Major Babbage, and under the watchful eye of General Brunel, the plucky Frenchman constructed the Empire's first spacecraft, charted the World Beneath which would one day become the stronghold of a faction of the Nazi Party, and developed experimental seapower alongside the utterly deniable black-ops naval commander Nemo.

Soon a new recruit was seconded to the Colonel's staff - a positively fizzing young genius by the name of Wells. The year was 1879, and

- having cooked up a suitable body double and tucked him away as a small-town schoolteacher - the Ministry deployed Wells alongside Verne to assist in stopping a plot to overthrow the Crown by one Doctor Moreau, using an army of half-animal super soldiers.

They went on to tussle with Jack the Ripper in the 1880s, discovering the horrible truth - 'Jack' was in fact a predatory extra-terrestrial[35] sent to dissect and sample human victims and take his findings back to his vile alien masters. After a madcap chase across the London rooftops, Wells and Verne - now definitely past his prime, but augmented with experimental power armour - lost the creature, merely wounding it with a blast of plasma before it gained the safety of its spacecraft and, to quote one of the Coldstream Guards seconded to Section W – "buggered off right sharpish to the moon or sumfing."

The whole debacle was covered up by Scotland Yard, where poor old Lestrade had his own problems - that madman Holmes was convinced he'd make a better vigilante if he dressed up in, of all things, a giant bat costume.

It was around this time that Wells began working on a way to erase his past mistakes.

With a grasp of weird science unsurpassed since the heyday of the late, great John Murray Spear (I kid you not, look him up), Wells set to building a time machine. Finding this to be impossible using the laws of physics set down by Isaac Newton, Wells went on to make up some new ones, drawing on the arcane studies of Section M. He came up with quite a good theory, but knowing that the Ministry were hot on the idea of censorship, he chose to file the patents for it with a little-known clerk in Austria, by the name of Albert somethingorother.

It resolutely failed to work. Weeks passed. Sleepless nights compounded like the layers of some fiendish quesadilla. Wells attained the kind of wild appearance and haunted gaze which usually took disaffected laudanum-swilling poets several hours to affect each morning.

Finally, crushed by his own inability to do the unthinkable, he confided in his old field agency boss, Jules Verne. Who laughed politely, clapped him on the shoulder, told him time travel was fundamentally impossible, and fetched him a glass of brandy so antiquated and voluminous that it could have stunned a charging rhino.

But who also secretly squirrelled away the time machine in one of

---

35. Yes, one of those ones. With the dreadlocks and the hideous gob.

Section W's many, many basements under Kew Gardens.[36]

Monsieur Verne had troubles from the past as well, you see.

The Ministry of Plausible Deniability had always maintained a program of body doubles to replace figures whom they thought would be better employed in their own devious schemes. It had been this way since the first days of the order, when John Dee had proposed an alliance between the English crown and the fallen Knight Commander of the Templar Inner Chamber, the allegedly immortal Jacques de Molay. Why do you think there are so many different signatures for Shakespeare? Do you suppose a *single* Isaac Newton could have been an alchemist, a scientist, *and* the master of the royal mint?

In most cases, the body doubles - retired soldiers, illegitimate sons of the nobility, or madmen out of St Mary's of Bethlehem - were simply doctored up with an altered appearance, issued the correct paperwork and sent off to pursue some mundane course through life. Shakespeare's body double grew wealthy off the plays written for him by several Elizabethan courtiers, while the real 'Big Willie' S was busy sabotaging the Spaniards, swashbuckling among the pirates of the East Indies, spying on the Moorish Caliphate and seeking the lost city of gold with Sir Walter Raleigh. Section W snapped up an American tourist by the name of Poe, and had his duplicate pose for years as a rather gloomy poet, all the while allowing him free rein to experiment in his true calling - necromancy.

Verne's double though. Well.

It seemed that somebody in the paper-shuffling strata of bureaucrats who infested Whitehall like so many pinstriped termites was having a laugh. They'd sent all of Jules' meticulous notebooks and case files to his double in France, where the bugger had translated them word for word and sold them as fiction. He was celebrated as one of the most creative fantasists and general makers-up of the now infamous shaggy dog yarn ever to further attenuate the tallness of a tale.

Nemo - well, Nemo laughed it off, as only a retired sea captain who has fought his share of giant kraken (both conventional and robotic) could. But it was enough to stir up a terrible sense of existential dread in Colonel Verne. He began to obsessively read the publications of his own adventures, becoming twitchy, withdrawn, shadow-eyed and more than a little mad.

---

36. Having done the calculations, based on the fact that the time machine weighed about two imperial tonnes, this would have required a twenty-foot tall squirrel with biceps like several Galapagos tortoises stuffed into a diving suit.

By this time Jules had grown old, and his role in the labyrinth beneath Kew was that of a kindly, tweed-suited uncle - the fella who had seen and done it all. Nothing was thought of his long, strange conversations with a young child prodigy from the United States by the name of Lovecraft, who the Ministry were hosting as part of a student-swap agreement with the US Department of Alleged Intelligence.

Verne began to believe that he himself was a fictional character. That all of this - the tunnels under London filled with their UFO wrecks and cyclops skeletons, the shrink rays and the doomsday devices, the Aztec robot spiders and the Egyptian laser cannons - was simply a figment of his own imagination. Jules Verne began to believe that *he had written himself.*

Or - and this is much worse - that his *double* had written him into existence, just to have something to write about.

Aggrieved at being put through a lifetime of harrowing adventures, with no time for the comforts of family or the illusion of normality afforded to the common man, Jules Verne set out to complete Well's time machine and go back to that dinner party at 24 Rue de l'Ancienne-Comédie, where he would kill his double and thus erase himself from the printed page, earning the sweet release of non-existence.

That is not dead, after all, *which can eternal lie.* No strange aeons were going to sneak up and bring Jules bloody Verne back to a life of endless fictional brouhaha. Besides which, he'd seen the films of what that sickly Poe fellow could do with a spade, some chicken blood and a pair of size thirteen oxfords.

Of course, it was his rock-solid belief in his own nonexistence which allowed Jules to make the time machine work in the first place. His physics were taken as much from the bizarre theories of the young Lovecraft as from that fellow Einstein who Wells was so peeved with for some reason. With a combination of bloody mindedness, delusion and downright mad science, Jules Verne did what his young protégé couldn't and finished the time machine. He dubbed it the Verne-Wells 'Britannia' model 1900, and immediately began musing over when to go to for a test flight.

His thoughts drifted back across the centuries, back to the steamy primordial jungles of the dawn age, when that crusty old windbag Darwin had insisted there were all kinds of giant lizards and things, stomping about bellowing in the mud. Hah! He'd show him! It was probably all just hogwash, cooked up so the beardy fellow could keep his cushy digs and his status as the bad boy of Victorian biology.

Jules was only slightly perturbed to discover that Charles Darwin was dead. After all, *he had a time machine...*

The pickup went smoothly. It was but a moment's work to steal one of the signet rings from self-styled 'gentleman spy' Oscar Wilde while he was in the sauna - a ring filled with weaponised chloroform. A hop from 1895 to 1877 was carefully calibrated to take into account the rotation of the Earth and its place in the cosmos, and Verne was able to abduct the great scientist from a coffee house in Oxford without alarming the local populous.

Unfortunately, Darwin woke up while Verne was programming the great leap backward into the Jurassic period. Even less fortunately, the white-bearded old scientist proved to be a veritable demon with the walking stick, having been trained in the arts of combat by a South Seas native who had crewed aboard the *Beagle*, and who was more than proficient with that deadly blade-shaped wooden stave known as the *taiaha*.

Before Verne could say 'I'll show you a bloody giant alligator, you old hack,' the controls had been thwacked mightily with three feet of solid silver-tipped British oak, and the scene outside the time machine's capsule had blurred into a mind-bending soup of weird geometries...

It's just possible that they ended up aboard Grand York by co-incidence. At the time, the rig had been simply called 102-G-98-B, and its small human population had been running around gibbering in terror thanks to all of their AIs having gone mad at once.

What was needed was a level head. Or two.

What was needed, pretty much precisely, was a Colonel of the Imperial Armed Forces who had kept his cool against everything from Mole People to Zulus at dawn. And, of course, a scientist who could help them build a new society from the wreckage of the old...

Then again, co-incidence is a fine thing, but it seems pretty damn unlikely. It's a far better bet that something out there really appreciates a good laugh at our expense.

+++

"We can't get it to work. It'll never go back in time."

Everybody looked at Wainwright expectantly, waiting for some kind of explanation.

"Well, it *won't*. Because if we actually made it work properly, see, then we wouldn't be here. It would have gone smoothly, we would have zipped back to the moment that Mister Fixit was first switched on, put him through a car compactor, and this ludicrous mission would never have happened."

"Better yet," mused Tia Faraday, "We could have gone back and stopped the Jest. The whole War of 9:15 wouldn't have happened. And of course, we'd all be billionaires instead of special agents. Lottery numbers and all that..."

"I thought time travel was all about trousers," said Ezra, searching the arse-end of the Verne-Wells Britannia Model 1900 for an access port. "Some kinda new universe pops up every time you do something, right?"

"It's all quantum," sighed the metalman. "We can be comforted by the fact that in some realities we are indeed living as billionaires in a Panarchy where the war never happened. But by the same token, it hasn't gone unbelievably horribly wrong. Otherwise we would have come back here to warn ourselves about it, and we'd likely be doing the tedious bit about 'how can you prove you're me, oooh, tell me something dodgy and faintly homo-erotic about our past that only I would know...' right?"

Ezra found the hatch and slid back a steel panel, exposing the heart of the time machine. Inside it was all brass gears, rubber-jacketed wires, and at its very core - a pocketwatch. A big gold one engraved with the words 'HM Ministry of Plausible Deniability Long Service Award - 25 Years, M. Jules Verne'. As he touched the glass, Ezra felt a shock ripple through him - a rolling swell of unreality shivering off into that part of him which remained in the Chasm.

He heard echoes. His madness resonated with that of the long-dead Jules Verne. He caught a glimpse, through the lens of his peculiar insanity, *of what had happened on the last few pages.*

"Well, you wily old bastard," he said to himself. "You had it too. Which I guess makes sense. If I'm fictional, then you'd have to be. Trousers within trousers. The underpants of time..."

He stood up (banging his head on the open hood) just as Wainwright finished scanning the time machine with a grid of emerald lasers.

"I'm afraid it's just too complex. There's all kinds of strange entanglements going on in there - things which shouldn't work, things that shouldn't be - even a thing that I'm not quite certain is a thing at all. However they built it, I'm not that certain I can fix it. But - we might be able to use it as an escape pod."

As he spoke, the great crucible beam licked out again, slicing another sliver off Grand York as though the mighty spaceborne city were only so much Christmas ham. The floor rumbled and shook. Dust and flakes of rust sifted down from the ceiling.

"Well, get on with it then!" shouted Tia, climbing aboard and settling into the wingbacked leather command chair. "We don't have all day, you know!"

"She's right," put in Sir Giles, who had been peeking out through the museum's doors. "There's an angry mob headed this way. I think they'd quite like to burn the founders in effigy. Us too, if they catch us messing with the time machine..."

It should have been impossible for a giant diving helmet to look crestfallen, but the metalman managed.

"Weeeellll... that's the bad news. Even fixing it up to simply fly through space should take exactly seventeen hours, twelve minutes."

"I'll fix it," said Ezra, in what he hoped was a main-character heroic voice.

Nobody paid him the least bit of attention.

"They really look quite miffed," went on Sir Giles, retreating inside the doors and swinging them shut. He manhandled a potted plant in front of them, then augmented it with a small chaise lounge.

"And how many *seconds*, you useless lump?" seethed Tia. "I don't suppose you accounted for the fact that three out of four of us can't survive in vacuum."

"I'll fix it!" said Ezra again, this time trying a hands-on-hips pose. He banged his head on the open hood of the time machine a second time. "Arrrrghhh, bastard bastard bastard fuck!"

"Sorry? Did you say something?"

Ez clutched his badly dented skull, images of people who dressed like him being scalped blurring in on arcane frequencies.

"Oooooh! Pardon my french, miss, but @$#*&%!! Also a bit of &*$#@!"

"Was that ascii?" asked Wainwright. "How did he do that?"

"He's becoming fictional. At least, he thinks he is," replied Tia. "Either that, or my grasp of French is much shakier than I thought..."

"And that means *I can fix this!*" hollered Ez, as another flickering blast of light sliced through Grand York. This time the sounds of screams was accompanied by a frantic hammering on the museum doors. Sir Giles's barrier wouldn't hold them long.

"I can fix this thing. It's easy. All we need to do is reverse the polarity of the flux capacitor matrix, and re-route the positronic rectifier through the Einstein-Hawking antimatter grid."

Tia frowned. The last part of that sentence had been *wrong*. Not wrong in a scientific sense - in that regard, it was obvious hogwash. Wrong in that Ezra's mouth had been moving, but shaping different words, as if it he'd been overdubbed by Hungarian film editors in the dark. The voice that came out was curiously flat and scratchy, like the voice a cardboard cutout would have down a long distance phone line.

"That's nonsen.." started Wainwright, before Tia caught him a ringing slap across the back of his head. She mimed 'shhhhh' with the intensity of every angry librarian ever, all rolled into one.

"What'll you need?" she asked, feeling her mind clicking along the rails of the story. Much as she hated to be rescued by anyone, this was no time to let a good stereotype go wanting.

Ezra's eyes went blank, replaced for a second by what looked suspiciously like static. Something inside his head was grinding against something else, slipping like hot gears as he realized that he was stealing from the wrong archetype.

"Some chewing gum, a pencil, two paper clips and a small piece of string," he said, ever so slightly hesitantly.

Sir Giles was most surprised to find every one of these items in his pockets, even though gum chewing was a forgotten art aboard Grand York.

Something happened down at the end of Ezra Ashdown's arms, in the hand department. If you'd asked him to describe it, later, he'd have said it felt a bit like plunging his fingers into cold spaghetti - but also a bit like the tingle he got when he bent the cards and nudged the fall of the dice.

And the lights came on, all across the rich walnut burl control panel of the time machine. Somewhere, in the hidden recesses behind the seats, an automated gramophone cylinder met with a dusty old needle, and a scratchy rendition of a Strauss waltz began to play.

"Everybody in!" snapped Tia. "Fixit doesn't know where we are, but with a weapon like that, he doesn't have to. In fact..."

This time the beam was closer. This time, the great reaping blaze of light sheared clean through the top of the museum's dome, sending a burst of glittering shards out into space. The thing had barely grazed them, but it knocked out the artificial gravity as well, and Ezra scrabbled for a handhold as the time machine began to rise ponderously from the floor.

Wainwright grabbed Sir Giles, and Tia grabbed him, and the whole cursing human chain pulled themselves on board.

"How do you think it works?" asked Sir Giles, peering at the profusion of toggles, knobs, switches, cranks and wheels.

Ezra elbowed past him, sat down in the buttoned, wing-backed command chair, and grabbed a pair of what appeared to be railway signal levers.

"Tia, that big ol' grand-daddy clock behind us does time. Wainwright, the sliders over there, on that marble inlay, they do co-ordinates in space, relative to where we are now. Fer some reason he did 'em in nautical miles."

His voice was wrong again. Like somebody else was talking over him, heard from another room. Tia repressed the skin-crawling sensation that everyone in the universe was right behind her, watching...

And then Ezra pulled he handles back.

Hard.

For an instant the outlines of the time machine blurred, as if seen through a vigorously shaken snow globe. Then it seemed to both recede into the distance and fade away, leaving behind nothing but the conjoined smells of kippers and hot tin.

There was silence in the vast hall for a second - the cold silence of open vacuum. The stuffed effigy of Charles Darwin came loose and bobbed free, rising up like a heavily bearded dirigible toward the shattered dome.

Then came a flash of light. A snap and crackle of static discharge. Crawling filaments of what appeared to be badly rendered special-effects lightning.

With a sound like ten million bottles of tomato sauce being thwacked at once, the Verne-Wells 'Britannia' Model 1900 appeared exactly where it had departed from.

Inside were four familiar faces.

Tia was now dressed as a warrior princess, in the 'leather, not very much chain mail and a couple of very big axes' school. Wainwright's giant floating head now had a garland of flowers around it, and his holographic body was wrapped in a toga. Ezra Ashdown was got up in full plate mail, and for some reason was brandishing a plucked goose. While Sir Giles was poorly decorated as a circus clown, and held a pair of gold plated AK-47 assault rifles.

"We have to tell them how amazingly, incredibly horribly wrong it all goes!" yelled Tia. "Quick - where are they?"

"I've prepared some slightly dodgy and homo-erotic questions only we could know, to prove we're not impostors", said Wainwright. "Though..."

He never got to finish.

This time, Mister Fixit's terrible beam of force was right on the money. It evaporated the museum, the hall, the determinedly upwardly mobile Darwin, and all four adventurers in a single orgasmic rush of plasma fusion. And this was the stroke which snapped the spine of Grand York. Great girders and pipes groaned and stretched, thrumming like bass-strings. Bulkheads sheared, twisting open in the grip of titanic forces.

Now it was only a matter of time. Of breaking down the pieces, so that a vast slew of them hammered through the Chasm Gate unbound, temporarily crippling the Central Scrutinizer's network. Then it would be time to go and meet Rel Kitano...

Mister Fixit permitted himself a small but satisfyingly evil laugh.

"Bwahaaa. Bwahahahahahaaaaaaa!"

It was turning out to be a very good day to be bad.

Eleven – 1930s Mobster Cyber-Clown Soviet Surf Party
Ezra Ashdown

"They've tried to represent time as a river, a wheel, a tangled string, a branching tree, and even, on one memorable occasion, as a small pink furry cube with inexplicable wobbly bits. But there's only one analogy that sticks, if you've wrangled the time-streams as long as I have. Time is a harsh mistress. The kind who wears a very small amount of spiked leather and charges by the quarter hour."

Chrono-Constable first class Gelric Smaggs,
in a speech he gave on his combination graduation/inauguration/
retirement to/from the Chronojudiciary Special Command.

It was a beautiful lazy summer afternoon in Cherrywood – but then again, it always was.

Vast machineries squatted in orbit over the little worldlet, bathing it in a glow of strange radiations and girding it about with fields all a-shimmer with scientific jiggery-pokery we'll not get into right now.

Barbecues sizzled. Frisbees sailed through the quiet air. Somewhere, a labrador was going out of its tiny mind over the prospect of fetching a tennis ball.

Cherrywood was a cookie-cutter patchwork of four streets – Maple, Elm, Evergreen and Betelgeusian Feverwort. The last may have been a little out of character with the Norman Rockwell design aesthetic handed down from upper management, but the landscaping people had gotten their hands on a massive consignment of the bulbous purple plants, and they knew a budget shortfall when they saw one.

The shop on the corner of Elm and Betelgeusian Feverwort Streets was a confection of scrubbed red brick and shiny enamel signage – an old-fashioned soda fountain and candy store, run by an avuncular robot named Frank. Frank wore a comb-over and a yellow sweater. He was convinced he'd been born in 3500 separate versions of Cape Cod in 1922, had fought in WW2 on Iwo Jima, and owned exactly 1.276 tabby cats named Boots. Frank was, of course, mass produced, and though his views on segregation were a trifle iffy (historical context, the programming people had said), he was nowhere near as short of the proverbial picnic supplies as Mister Fixit.

Who should be getting created around here any time soon...

Frank looked up from the crossword he'd been completing in the Cherrywood Gazette for the last thirteen years. His dimpled rubber cheeks crinkled into a smile.

"Howdy there, neighbour! How about a cool frosty milkshake on this wonderful June evening? We have chocolate! Or some fine Colombian coffee, fresh ground this morning?"

Something popped and fizzed deep in the service mech's head. Surely there were no residents of Cherrywood who looked like this. Although... well, the fella was *clearly* retro. And indisputably American.

Ezra Ashdown stood in the sweet shop door, resplendent in a long leather duster, stetson hat, blue jeans, alligator-skin boots and silver spurs. Outside sat the gently steaming glass-and-brass bulk of the Verne-Wells 'Britannia' 1900, parked between a Ford Thunderbird and a Chevy pickup truck.

"No...uhh... no time for refreshments, old-timer," said this wild-west apparition. "I've got a delivery for mister and missus ummm..." Ezra fished a scrap of paper out of his pocket, setting down one of the two large paper sacks he was holding in the process. It appeared to be full of women's underwear.

"Spelting. Marjorie and Leonard Spelting. 35 Evergreen, apparently – but *someone*," (and here the cowboy glared out through the plate-glass window at what appeared to be a deep-sea diver, a Redcoat and what Frank was programmed to think of as a 'young lady of negotiable affections') "Didn't say which of the three and half thousand Evergreens they got on this stupid rock. Sorry."

A tiny little click caught Frank's attention – and the cowboy's too. It was one of those vanishingly small sounds which leaps to the foreground thanks to the fact that it certainly shouldn't be happening, and is usually the first sign that something very sneaky (and probably dangerous) is going on *right behind you*.

In this case, it was Mister Fixit, stepping out of the back room of the sweet shop with a loaded plasma incinerator in one hand. He carried a plastic shopping bag in the other. It contained, among other things, a pair of edible underpants, a copy of Barry White's greatest hits and a bottle of airport-grade methode traditionelle.

"Oh, bravo. Nice try," said the murderous mech, still wearing the hideously stretched-out remains of Mason Stockton's face. "Do you know how much trouble I'll be in if they catch me? A robot sent from the future to ensure that someone *definitely* gets born? If I ask anyone for their clothes, boots and motorcycle I'll probably have to kill any number of lawyers, and that's a hassle I don't need."

"I thought *that* one wanted to make sure he *didn't* get born. I'm doing that part, tin man. Got some negligees, mobile phones full of dirty text messages, fake holiday snaps with various mistresses..."

Fixit shot Ashdown a withering look.

"And here I thought the easiest way was just to shoot his mother in the face. How wonderfully creative of you."

There was a huge pistol in Ezra's hand. He'd drawn and aimed the Problem Solver so fast that the spirit inside it hadn't had a chance to wake up.

"*What I miss?*" grumped Jed Granger. "*Ohhhhh, shit. How'd he get a time machine like ours?*"

"Well, you went ahead and used the thing," shrugged Fixit. "That gave me a very clear signature in space-time as to how it works. After that, it was only a matter of time before one of the many, many possible future iterations of myself built one. And came back *here*, because you lot are as predictable as incest at the All-Appalachian Banjo and Moonshine Festival."

Outside the window, looks of mute surprise did the now-deceased Mime Army proud. The outline of the Verne-Wells flickered for an instant...

"Nice try," said Wainwright, appearing from behind the counter and aiming an even bigger gun at Mister Fixit. "But I have a pretty good grasp of probability theory myself. I've been waiting under that counter for three years for just this moment..."

Frank had been designed without the ability to sweat. Nevertheless, his plastic face had taken on a ruddy sheen.

"Now now, fellas. How about a tall, frosty..."

Mister Fixit grinned.

"Say hello," he said "To my little friend."

Outside the window a black Harley Davidson pulled up to the kerb. A Mister Fixit dressed entirely in biker leathers swung a short, fat tube from its strap across his back, took aim, and blew the Verne-Wells 1900 to tinkling, smoking smithereens.

"*Ohhh, you done it now boy,*" drawled Granger. "*You know how many lawyers that movie company's got? There's a whole planet where they grow em from birth, an..."*

Ezra put a hole the size of a hubcap through the Mister Fixit in the store. A lance of pale orange fire licked out from behind a box hedge, and Tia Faraday combat-rolled into view, slagging half of the Harley and all of the second Fixit. The jukebox began to play, for no good reason, *The Ace of Spades* by Motorhead[37].

And then it was all on, as they say, for young and old.

Another Fixit erupted from beneath the floorboards, twin shotguns blazing. Ezra went down, only to walk through a side door again, duster flaring dramatically, two colt pistols stitching bullets across the chest of a fourth Fixit, who dropped from the ceiling like a giant spider. Wainwright's head exploded just as three more of him crashed in through the wall and set up a tripod-mounted heavy machinegun. Then even more Fixits arrived in a commandeered paddywagon, and the scuffle escalated into what the media would call a fracas, then a donnybrook, and finally a bloody riot.

Tias scissor-kicked and karate-chopped, with electromagnetic force-field blades on their gloves and boots wreaking unspeakable carnage. Wainwrights ported in weapons from a hundred bitter and awful wars, from anti-tank rifles through to obsidian war clubs to triple-barrelled laser pulverizers. Sir Gileses tally-ho'd and put up their dukes Marquis of Queensberry style, or brandished a full umbrella-stand of spadroons, broadswords, claymores, katanas, yataghans, scimitars and lightsabers. Ezras proliferated like mid-1950s cigarette advertising, guns roaring, only to be sliced, burned, minced, concussed, evaporated and (in one messy case) liquefied by the arsenal of hatred Mister Fixit levelled at the Outriders.

Soon the other versions of themselves began to get slightly silly – Hawaiian Surf Party Wainwright! Vampire Cheerleader Ezra! Transvestite Cyborg Nun Sir Giles!

When a four-armed Mister Fixit made of copper and a Tia Faraday dressed as Queen Elizabeth the First appeared and began whaling on each other with Incan Mahuitls, Ezra (the one who thought of himself as the original, but who could tell?) thought he'd seen it all.

He hadn't.

The sweet shop was a scene of unimaginable carnage – though

---

37. Because if you have to have a theme song to a murderous brawl, Lemmy and the boys will not disappoint. Try it for yourself at home, but don't even think of suing us, we have no money.

feel free to try, if you haven't recently eaten breakfast. Bodies, in five distinct varieties, lay sprawled and strewn in piles, cluttering the booths, heaped in bloody drifts up against the walls with their pictures of chromed and finned highway cruisers. In the middle of it all, Frank had gone out of his tiny little transistorised mind, and was making the world's tallest ice cream sundae, crying to himself and shoring it up with strawberry wafers.

There was a sound like ten million people biting down of a sheet of tinfoil. There was a smell of hospital waiting rooms. And suddenly everything froze – each bullet hanging twinkling in the air like motes inside some awful snow globe, each spray of blood and coolant oil arrested in its hectic tumble to become so much Jackson Pollockry in midair. Even the haze of gunsmoke curdled into something like the marbling of a very fine cheese.

There came a sound like ten thousand grannies pulling the corks of ten thousand bottles of sherry with their teeth.

And two men appeared – or at least the *semblance* of two men. They were tall and thin, dressed in black suits and bowler hats, and their faces were as nondescript and impersonal as a demand from the IRS. In fact, that pretty much summed them up. If a protracted personal tax audit could be given human form, twice - then these were it.

"Well well well. What a fine mess we have here, Mr Remainder."

"Another case of primitive minds over-reaching themselves, Mr Placeholder. Sad."

Mr Remainder was wearing a pair of snazzy white leather gloves – the kind you just *know* exist solely to leave no fingerprints. He snapped his fingers under Ashdown's nose – or rather, the one and only surviving Ashdown's nose – suddenly shocking him out of his mannequin-like trance.

"OK, rummy – spill. What's the big idea? What's the inside angle? The straight flush that means the difference between sipping suds with big-breasted broads and servicing sailors in a brokedown bus-station?"

Mr Placeholder joined in.

"Or the kind of rotten hand that leaves you hollering to Chuck and Ralph on the big porcelain telephone? "

This particular version of Ezra had been in the process of blasting a crater right through a Mister Fixit dressed, for no discernible reason, as the now-infamous Wolfgang Amadeus Mozart[38]. When he looked down at his hand, however, his massive, slab-sided Problem Solver pistol had been replaced with a common banana.

"*Really?* And this was turning out to be such a dramatic set-piece battle..."

"*Was*, as in past tense, Mister Remainder! So he knows how time works. That's a good start."

"A regular temporal prodigy, Mister Placeholder. Now, let's see if this stool pigeon will sing, or if he's on a one-way ticket to sage-and-onion stuffing where the sun don't shine."

The pair looked at him expectantly.

He may not have been on his own planet, or even within spitting distance of conventional sanity, but Elias Ashdown's boy recognized lawmen when he saw them. So he suddenly got reeeeal polite.

"I'm sorry, gentlemen. But, despite the fact that you're forming words with your mouths, not a single one of them seems to make *any god damn sense whatsoever.*"

The two agents looked at each other – a perfect reflection of utterly featureless faces. It looked like that optical illusion with the vase in the middle.

"It looks like we've got ourselves a *comedian*, Mr Remainder."

"A regular laughing boy. A japester. A chuckles."

"A bona fide iteration of the classical *commedia del arte* harlequin, my esteemed colleague. But do you see me laughing?"

"Certainly not, Mister Placeholder. Though I am reliably advised that it would go something like this. Har. Har. Har."

It sounded like gargling cardboard. Ezra winced.

"Guys... fellas. It's obvious that you're from the Government. Capital G and all. But which one? And what have we done? We're only trying to smash up a killer robot, which by my reckoning should only count as a little light vandalism..."

"He don't get it," sighed Mister Placeholder, shaking his head sadly.

"Indeed he does not, Mister Remainder. I can only hope the others are more intellectually well endowed."

"They seem to be taking it better. A lot of apologies. Even a nice attempted bribe from the metal one. Though what we'd want with the greatest hits of the one they call 'Barry White' is beyond me."

"Wait," said Ezra. "You're talking to *all of them at the same time*? But

---

38. Because we all know what HE liked to get up to. If you get my drift. Wink wink.

they're frozen!" A slow smile threatened to unhinge the top of his face. "Aaaah, you know it's all fiction, don't you? You're some kind of silly two dimensional plot device, right? *Deus Ex Machina* G-men!"

Four white-gloved hands gripped his lapels.

"Two dimensional! You primitive little...."

"Why, we oughta...."

The pair of agents nodded, stepping back. Then they reached across, each one gripping the brim of the other's bowler hat. They *twisted*.

And so did everything else.

Ezra found himself hanging in space, surrounded by mind-meltingly incomprehensible geometries. The sweet shop was there, but not there – a thousand upon a thousand slightly different iterations of it fading off into a distance that wasn't really distance at all, on all sides. He could see Tia and Wainwright and Giles – even Mister Fixit – but they weren't just people anymore.

They were blurred, many-limbed Hindu gods of things, each one the pinch in a giant hourglass shape of colours and neon filaments, bursting out into what he knew, horribly, to be the past and the future. The sun in the sky was everything from a cloud of dust to the hard black dot of a singularity, with shades of bloated red supergiant in between. The houses flew American flags, union jacks and even smiley faces and Nazi swastikas at the same time, flickering in and out of his top layer of perception like multiple sheens of oil in a bubbling cauldron.

And the agents...

Oh dear. It turned out that the neat, black-and-white human forms they had assumed were not so much to make them inconspicuous as to prevent projectile vomiting. Each one looked like the mutant love-child of a trash compactor's lunch, a bait bucket and mighty Cthulhu's dangly parts. For no good reason both slubbering horrors were still wearing bowler hats. Those lobes of Ezra's' brain not melting like double cream brie in a tanning bed thought back to the Chasmic Leviathan with wistful nostalgia.

"Too much, Mister Placeholder. I think we're losing him."

"Quite right, Mister Remainder. Switch him to the Standard Model. But I think our point is well made. Two dimensional! Pah! He *deserved* to see the whole 33."

There was a sound like wet rubber against glass, the inexplicable scent of tulips, and suddenly Ez was hanging weightless in a very different space. The background was all concentric swirls of colour, upon which hung innumerable antique clocks. A set of giant letters reading 'E=MC²' floated past. So did a giant, lidless eye, a question mark, and that strange blue phonebooth with the light on top that Ezra had seen parked in the air above the Scrutinizer's fortress.

"Better now?"

"Glad we made the effort?"

The pair of agents were back in their humanoid skins, sitting casually on absolutely nothing.

"Yes, we're Government. TIME Government. Chronojudiciary operatives. Which means that you ought to know better! I mean, you're almost like us. Panarchy Outriders are supposed to be *professionals*, dammit."

"So what's the big idea? You've snarled up so many time-streams that we're going to be years fixing this mess up. Subjectively, of course. In a very real sense it's both already fixed, and irreparably screwed forever."

Ezra clicked his fingers. Feeling was beginning to return to his extremities as he forgot what these two had briefly looked like.

"It's all about that dang time machine, isn't it? I knew that was too good to be true. Go back and stop the killer android from being built, they said. We'll be home in time for cocktails and potato chips, they said. Hah! I knew it wouldn't work. That's no way to tie up a story. The bad guy has to fall off a very tall building, get impaled on something, then explode. I told 'em."

"We missed the bloody thing the first time," said Placeholder ruefully. "Who would have thought they'd put something like *that* together in boring old Victorian England? Even in the steampunk time-streams a bit of a war against the Martian tripods is the most you can expect in terms of standard technological deviation. But then there was *this* one, where Verne and Darwin get kicked across twelve whole degrees of chrono-arc and end up creating a mecha-cannibalistic space city."

"Right on the outside of the old bell curve, it was. A sport. But we made sure the bugger wouldn't work again. Got it nailed down as pure fiction in 99.99 percent of stable realities – you know, the ones where hydrogen is able to form? We like those."

Ezra laughed.

"But that's just it, boys. This *is* fiction. I'm a protagonist. This is an *adventure*. That's how I fixed that old pile of bolts – we pretty much had to make a last-second escape in the nick of time."

Remainder shook his fist menacingly.

"Don't tell us about the nick of time, matey boy. We've been to the nick, and looked over the edge, and gotten the bloody t-shirt. Although..."

"If this is fiction, we can sew things up nice and neat." Mister Placeholder produced a slim digital tablet from somewhere inside his suit jacket and began pecking away at it. A peeling sticker on the back of the device read 'Don't Panic!'

"Basically, we're here to issue an official injunction," sighed Mister Remainder. "No more time travel. You'll get put back in that clanking brass monstrosity, with the time circuits all buggered up, right out in space where you left off. We're not here to kill you, so you'll get a fighting chance. But all this nonsense?" He gestured around himself at the clocks, the floating formulae and the blinking eyes. "You don't want to be seeing it again. Or you'll be blasted back to one of our penal centuries so fast it'll make your head spin. Did you ever wonder why there's no really interesting history in bits like the early 1400s?"

"Apart from Joan of Arc. We told that girl to take it easy, but she *had* to draw attention to herself."

Mister Placeholder looked up from his tablet, his hideously nondescript face split by a ghoulish grin. He whistled.

"If this is fiction, it's pretty bad. We should go and have a word with this so-called 'author'. Wouldn't even make the cut as a b-grade screenplay, in my opinion. He hasn't even done the bit with Rel Kitano yet."

"Let me take a look," said Mister Remainder. His finger stabbed at the tablet once, twice. "Oooh, you're right. *Serious* pacing issues. It might not be part of this particular time-stream, but I think a jolly good clout around the ear-hole would do that guy some good. Set the co-ordinates!"

As one, the pair of agents shot back the cuffs of their suit jackets, revealing a pair of large and ornate wristwatches. Something complicated happened, accompanied by a mechanical clicking noise that sounded somewhat like a robot cockroach tap-dancing on a tin lid.

"No more time travel! You hear us? Or else it's 1403 in rural Portugal for you! I hope you like paella!"

Once again, ten million people bit down on a sheet of tinfoil. The smell of hospital waiting rooms blossomed amid the echoes. Ezra felt himself stretched out like used bubblegum, then snapped back into a mere six feet and change of aching meat...

Aboard the Verne-Wells 1900. In space. Accelerating away from the disintegrating cloud that had been Grand York, still glowing red-hot in places from Mister Fixit's crucible beam.

"... could have just gone back to where he was built, and snuffed the guy who built him," said Wainwright. "So much easier!"

"Or we *could* just make sure that guy was never born. There's a lot you can achieve by simply knocking on the door at two in the morning and claiming to be a radon inspector. Really kills the mood."

That was Tia, sitting next to him on the creaking, oiled leather of the VW 1900's command lounger.

Ez noted that his hands were wrapped around the controls. He flexed his knuckles, just to make sure they were actually under his own control.

"No," said Sir Giles, in the kind of stilted voice one often adopts when there is either a gun to one's head or a root vegetable up one's bottom. "Time travel is silly. It could... ahem... never work. We're best off just *forgetting all about it.*"

Ezra turned around, all but snarling with triumph. During the last few seconds, something had been fading into the background soup of his mind, like the ragged end of a dream. Now it came flooding back.

"They *told* you to say that, didn't they? Those two agents! The Chronojudiciary ones!"

Wainwright's face was impossible to read at the best of times. But Tia and Sir Giles went very deliberately, poker-playingly blank. Ez, possibly the galaxy's best card sharp and inveterate cheat, knew that look almost better than he knew the taste of cheap moonshine whiskey. Which is to say - intimately.

"I don't have the slightest idea who you mean," said Tia. Unconvincingly.

"Dash it all, man, I haven't the foggiest..."

Ezra's smirk lasted all of three heartbeats. Then something immense and dark and curved like the fingernail clipping of God swung past them, all black tubes and skeletal gantries. It was the edge of the second biggest Chasm Gate ever constructed, and thanks to the magic of Cerise Saint-Claire Langevin, it boiled with an ocean of quicksilver.

They were definitely going to hit it. But the rest of the debris from the wreck of Grand York would sleet past, barely nicking the frame.

"Suppose there *were* a couple of agents of the Chronojudiciary," said Wainwright very, very carefully. "And supposing they were mainly just concerned with making sure there was no more time travel in this particular stream. Well... would it be so very bad if they moved the whole Chasm Gate just a little? Had it brushed by a meteor about three hundred years back? So that the whole reticulum wasn't spammed up with flaming space junk?"

Ezra felt the whole world become thin and brittle at that moment. The weight of what he said next slid out into reality like a fat man trying to snaffle a donut from the surface of a frozen river.

"I suppose... *theoretically*... that they could change a few small things. Nothing as major as just erasing Mister Fixit entirely. But something like what you mentioned. *Yeah*. With the right motivation..."

The Verne-Wells looped over again, falling in toward the gate on an incontrovertible collision course.

"Wainwright?" asked Tia, the second before they hit. "How *did* you convince them?"

The metalman sighed, bracing himself for impact.

"Barry White may be a cultural phenomenon restricted to human beings, ma'am. But I've found that edible underpants are very much a universal currency."

They struck the membrane of silver at full speed, tearing through with a rippling *gloop*. Somewhere between this reality and the sackcloth-rigged backstage stuff behind it, Wainwright rendered them all down to numbers, then fed them through the quantum mangle of the gate's systems. The Chasm itself picked up the slack, caught the interface, and wove them all back together, identical save for one tiny detail. The VW1900 was now a tiny ball of light.

It popped into existence in front of a large, ornately carved black door, the knocker of which was a humorous gargoyle[39].

All four – Tia, Wainwright, Ezra and Giles – came tumbling through as the door yawned open, landing in a jumbled heap of limbs while it clicked closed behind them. The cold, stale air of the Chasm pressed in all around them, smothering and thick.

After a moment, Tia wriggled free.

"I'm going to believe that your hand ended up there by accident, Ashdown," she snarled. "And as for you, Wainwright, why..."

"Stop!" hissed Sir Giles. "There's someone out there!"

And indeed there was. Alien curses echoed across the empty place between the walls. Flashlight beams clicked on, and boots hammered

---

39. And we can all guess which part of the gargoyle you'd use to knock with, can't we? Those slower kids at the back of the class can find a handy diagram in the nearest public lavatories...

against the seamless black stone of the bridges, above and below.

"You don't think Mister Fixit got himself a favour too, do you?" asked Tia, unholstering her Problem Solver. "Because that sounds like Tchubspiel. Renegade lingo. The worst kind of mercenary scum you can scrape out of the entire Eastern Fringe..."

Ezra scrabbled to his feet, peering into the gloom. Oh, yes. There appeared to be no shortage of them. Though just what a Tchub was, he had no idea. One other, hideous idea had bubbled to the surface of his brain, and was yammering for attention.

"I thought them leviathan varmints were attracted to nasty thoughts in here. Just saying. Do we really want to start a fight and lure them up?"

Tia smiled at him sweetly, going up on tip-toes to pat him on the cheek.

"Don't stress about it. It'll only make them hungrier. And by the way..." She turned the dial on the side of her immense chrome pistol to 'high explosive'. "If you can't think happy thoughts while you're popping the heads off of Tchub mercenaries, you might be in the wrong line of business."

Twelve – The Story of Rel Kitano

"I'd just like to make it perfectly clear that I'm writing this bit because I want to, and because this is the exact right time in the narrative to cover it, not – and I have to be very firm on this point – not because a pair of evil-looking guys in black suits have appeared out of nowhere, have stopped time and are holding my goldfish Darnell over the insinkerator to make sure it finally gets done."

- The Author.

IT HAD ALL been going perfectly well until he saw her.

Here we have one of those innocent-looking little sentences which is, in fact, as dangerous as a fish-hook flavoured chocolate bar.

Only 'what harm could it possibly do', 'just one more for the road, then' and 'waaay heeey, watch this lads!' are really its equal. They often come one after another, on a graph known as the 'dead man's curve'.[40]

Rel had been cooling his heels atop one of the great, slab-sided concrete hab-blocks of the planet Temperance, dutifully scribbling field notes in his pocketbook. The binary suns of Chastity and Patience baked the dusty rooftop, painting the entirety of Hosanna City in shades of gray and pink. With the mercury bubbling at 35 degrees, Earth Centigrade, it was a bad day to be one of the faithful. Those poor little creatures scurrying around in the streets below wore heavy cassocks and habits to protect themselves from the lash of the twin suns, and Rel knew that water was scarce. He'd been given homework about this place before the Masters had dropped him off, equipping him with a guardian orb of limited sentience, a bag of nutrient pills and the obligatory notebook and pencil.

He was here to see how the wild humans lived, and decide if he'd like to be one of them.

The alternative – a return to the planet of the Masters – looked pretty darn good about now. Being Domesticated might have sounded like slavery, but in fact it was very much like being a beloved housecat –

---

40. Special mention goes to "you're not going to put this on the internet, are you?"

mainly sleep, food, sex and being spoken down to by an immense monstrosity that towered over you holding a bag of treats. The fact that the Process were tripedal cactus-giants didn't change the fact that their HappySapien Human Snax were more delicious. And as addictive as fried chicken lightly sprinkled with cocaine.

The whole purpose of the sabbatical was to show the Domesticated just how much it sucked to be a regular human being – and *this* planet was an object lesson in just how silly Rel's species could be if left to their own devices.

'Devices' was the key word, for here, on Temperance, a society had grown up around the worship of their mad Chasm Gate AI.

A little bit brimstone Catholic, a little bit frothing mad Jonestown cult of personality, with a solid core of rock-hard madness Poulson Vance would have thoroughly approved of, the planet's monolithic religion centred around the vast, cloud-piercing statue in the heart of Hosanna City – a monument not at all dissimilar to the famous sculpture by Rodin.

Indeed, they called it the Thinker, and by claiming to decipher it's gnomic utterances[41] the One Faith (led by Worm III the Utterly Lowest) enforced an iron grip on everything from spaceflight to toilet paper. It was an autocracy of absolute austerity, gibbering lunacy, paranoia, and tiny-minded little men with big truncheons. Which in this case is *not at all* a euphemism.

Rel had seen the work camps and the great monastic farms, the factories and the prisons (lots of those), the chapels and the cathedrals lapping around the knees of the Thinker where it sat with its alabaster white chin on its alabaster white fist. Thinking.

He'd seen a lot of pinched-faced, hungry, scared Faithful, and lots of well-fed, smarmy guards straining the buttons of their leather uniforms. In fact, he'd seen the full ghastly slew on injustices a place like Temperance floats along on, like a duck paddling in raw sewage. He'd wanted, on several occasions, to do something about it, but the Orb his Masters had sent with him (and which, thankfully, made him nigh invisible) warned against it. Instead he'd taken notes, and smoked his dwindling supply of joints, and sighed at the folly of the free.

He'd even seen Worm III himself – a bloated flesh-zeppelin of a man, carried on a golden throne which gripped his bulk like a large serving

---

41. The last of which had been 'Covet not the cheese which has been shown to thy neighbour's pelican, for such are the seeds of some kind of small flowering shrubbery in your heart'

of pudding in a very small ladle. The pontifex's eyes were tiny raisins pressed into a face of pale dough, glittering with self-satisfaction as he was lumbered down an ornamental avenue to the cheers of a crowd (Rel knew) assembled solely for this purpose. They cheered wildly, outdoing each other in fervent ecstasy, because of the row of guards with electric prods who stood behind them.

It was very much like that ancient Human nation back on Earth, the Soviet Onion. Apparently they had big meetings there where the top Soviet gave a speech, and the first person who stopped clapping afterwards got shot. Rel had always wondered what happened if you were still clapping hours later and needed to go to the toilet. Or if the guy who did the shooting got shot next, because how could *he* be clapping and still aim a gun?

And that was when he'd seen her.

No –

All caps, possibly in some kind of curly-wurly font of the kind used on biscuit tins and greeting cards of the more sentimental variety. Rel – who, it must be noted, was usually hormonally suppressed by chemicals in his HappySapien Human Snax – got a terrible shock as he spotted that flash of autumn-red hair and green eyes in the gray crowd. On the switchboard of his consciousness, control was re-routed from his brain to a point about three feet lower down.

She was beautiful. Stunning. The only colour in a world of dim monochrome. A flower which had inexplicably grown from concrete, and a whole series of worlds away from the squeaky plastic, self-obsessed girls in the Human Creche back home.[42]

The world zoomed in, red and pulsing around the edges of his vision. He felt something squeeze, deep in his chest. His clothes suddenly seemed three sizes too small, and it appeared that someone had poured fizzing sherbet into his spine. Things were also percolating and distilling down in the old trouser department, as millions of years of human evolution battered down the walls of the Masters' suppression drugs. Up top, under Rel Kitano's carefully sculpted messy haircut,

---

42. Who, it must be emphasized, were also utterly uninterested in anything sexual, thanks to a combination of drugs, television, magazines about famous boy bands long centuries dead, and the influence of the now-infamous cabal of gay warlocks who run the fashion industry. In Rel's opinion.

waves of lust and endorphins washed over his brain like the incoming tide.

He cancelled the cloaking programs of his Orb, and stood on the very edge of the building, popping the lens-cap of what appeared to be an old Nikon camera. There....focus... and...

Rel's heart stopped, expanded like a life raft coming out of its waterproof packaging, and lodged somewhere just behind his epiglottis. *She was looking back at him!*

His finger pressed the button on auto-pilot, just in time. Because now one of those toad-faced guards was turning around, and the Orb had tracked it, and the shimmer-fields were going up again...

"Orb," he said, as they dashed away across the rooftops, brief pulses from Rel's antigrav boots kicking them out over streets and avenues in a ballet of high-velocity parkour – "Orb, I'm going to find her. I'm going to take her away from all this madness."

The Orb's reply was in the language of the Process – a series of fluting, clicking, grinding and piping sounds which nevertheless managed to carry a tone of incredulous sarcasm.

"Oh, and I suppose *you* have a better plan? I've heard about this, you know. It's on all the records. It's in all the films. All two hundred and thirty-seven of them, the whole archive. When you find true love, Orb, you have to grab it with both hands!"

The Orb burbled again, ending with what sounded suspiciously like a snicker.

"Oh, *very* mature. I'm talking about higher things, you grotty little machine. Emotions you wouldn't hope to understand..."

Ignoring the fact, of course, that Rel himself had only just suffered the first all-out blitzkrieg of infatuation mere minutes ago. Possibly, if he'd taken he Orb's rather blunt advice, all of what happened next would not have happened at all. It's likely that the Chronojudiciary know, but what with all the paperwork, it's not really worth asking.

All the movies and all the songs had told Rel Kitano how to proceed. He needed to wait for the right moment, and then rescue her from certain death. Either that, or enter a dancing contest of some kind with her, to save the Youth Centre. Little did he know that his opportunity would come much sooner than any kind of sensible plan...[43]

---

43. Hosanna City did, in fact, have a youth centre. And the whole universe would have been very different if Rel Kitano had met Joy there, and had an altercation with a rich kid named Chad, and learned to get his groove back, and argued with a stuffy old preacher who hated dancing, and then led the whole cast in a big Broadway number

+++

Joy's real name – the one written down in the great registry in the Cathedral of Bureaucracy – was Joyful Praise Be Unto Our Lord The Thinker. But even in a society as cheerfully insane as that of Temperance, where whistling, the colour pink, rubber ducks and jigsaw puzzles were all banned on pain of death, the whole thing was a bit of a mouthful. Joy was lucky she had an easy name to whittle down to something that sounded at least a bit feminine. One of her friends at the Purity School was lumbered with the monicker God Be Praised For The Saintly Wisdom Of Worm The Almighty, which the Mother Inferior had shortened to Gwerma.

Joy should probably been ashamed for thinking about the... well, the *angel*, or whatever he was. Then again, the list of things to be ashamed about at the Purity School was so long that it was inscribed on three great panels of copper and bolted to the wall of the refectory. The high priests who deciphered the Thinker's utterances were forever finding out about new ones, such as hanging a new roll of toilet paper the wrong way round, sharpening pencils anti-clockwise or comparing one type of soap to another unfavourably. Thinking frankly lustful thoughts about what was clearly an Angel of the Lord – well, a very good-looking young man who appeared and vanished by magic, in any case – was not actually on the list, but Joy just knew it would be. The Mother Inferior had a mind like a steelo pad dipped in battery acid, and her unshakable faith in the degeneracy of her charges was as hard as the ruler she deployed with merciless accuracy.

Joy – like all of the other girls in her cloister – had never seen a glossy magazine about actors and boy bands and football players. Such things didn't exist on Temperance, because Thou Shalt Not Create a Graven Image on Any Substance Which Could Be Folded Into a Novelty Hat and Filled With Tapioca. Commandment 31,059.

But the mystery boy's face *belonged* in one[44]. When he'd looked down at her, and their eyes met there was a sound of violins, and a shimmer in the air, and...

Well, he was *much* better looking than Brother Farbley, the Proctor who made sure the girls were locked in at night. Who was always watching, with those beady little eyes of his, and licking his lips more

---

which came out inexplicably well choreographed first time. Different, but crap.

44. Obviously without the tapioca

167

than seemed strictly necessary.

Joy shuddered. She'd have to walk past him again, like she had to every day. And now, with all her daydreaming, she'd fallen behind the others, who went scurrying down the hallway in the slanting pink light of the setting sun, all well-scrubbed and covered from head to toe in heavy gray cassocks. Joy clutched her massive, hide-bound copy of the *Thinker's Word* to her chest and walked faster, but it was too late. She rounded the corner just in time to see the door of the cloister-house closing, and Brother Farbley turning his great iron key in the lock.

The look he gave her, as he turned slowly around, was not one she cared for at all. There was much of that lizard-like lip licking, and a glitter in those beady eyes which just screamed out 'well well well, what have we here?' Nobody *ever* actually asks that question in all seriousness. They always know *exactly* what they have there, and the answer is usually some kind of self-indulgent petty cruelty.

"Well well well," said Brother Farbley, his doughy face split with a yellowy smile. "What have we here? Tardiness is a sin, sister! That way lies the slippery slope toward all *manner* of vice!"

Joy was not very large, and now she tried with every fibre of her being to become even smaller, shrinking behind the *Thinker's Word*. Brother Farbley *was* very large, bred like all the Paladins and Proctors and enQuisitors to look like a bag full of hams.

"P...please, Brother mine," she stammered. "I was contemplating the divine *(true to a point)* – a moral quandary of scripture." *Such as how a novice nun should go about trying to catch an angel...*

It may have seemed impossible, but the Brother's leer became even more sickening.

"Oh, how noble! I, too have been contemplating the divine of late. Contemplating... the terrible waste of such God-given beauty." The hulking great Proctor stepped forward out of the shadows, reaching for her with a hand like a packet of sausages. "Such a shame. The Worm won't care, you know. He's nine parts dead below the waist, they say..."

Everything seemed to freeze solid inside Joy's head with a 'click' like breaking glass. There were rumours about this sort of thing, of course. That part of her which the Mother Inferior and all those tedious rules had so far failed to destroy determined that she'd clock him with the big heavy *Thinker's Word* if he took one more step. Another, more treacherous part noted that there was nothing she could hit him with that would really put him down.

So she tried using the rules instead.

"Compose yourself, Brother! I am promised as a chaste and pure bride of the Thinker!"

Farbley chuckled.

"Oh, come down off that high horse, miss Joy. There's been plenty what gave it away for extra rations, or a sneaky look the other way if they wanted out of an evening. Or a kind word to the enQuisitors to save some family or such..."

He took another step forward. His breath smelled of pickled cabbage and stale beer. Joy brought the book up, ready to strike...

And an Angel of the Lord appeared.

Rel Kitano hadn't had much time to prepare. In fact, he'd thought that it would take a bit of a nudge here and there to arrange circumstances so that he could 'rescue' the object of his red-hot infatuation. He'd been doodling little diagrams involving grand pianos, rope and scissors while he watched her through the Nikon's zoom lens.

Then this big ape had pushed her into a corner, and the whole world had gone red around the edges, and he'd reached into the marshmallowy substance of the Orb, summoning up the first thing it could randomly generate as a weapon.

Brother Farbley was big – big in a way that only selective breeding, anabolic steroids and protein shakes like concrete slurry could produce. But he'd spent his whole life using that sheer bulk to intimidate the half-starved, much smaller peasants of Temperance, and his fairly rudimentary hand-to-hand combat training (grab this end, whack 'em with the other one) was long forgotten.

Rel, on the other hand, may have bulked only a third of his foe's sweaty mass, but he was the product of a breeding program of his own – a prime, best-in-show specimen of humanity who had had nothing much to do for the last few years but work out, listen to punk rock and practice the sweet moves from all those 70s kung-fu flicks.

He also had the element of surprise. The Domesticated came leaping down through the arched window of the cloister, screaming a blood-curdling Bruce Lee battlecry, his shirt tactically ripped open and his weapon a purple blur. It thwacked upside Farbley's lumpen face with a sound like dough being flung against a marble wall, sending the big boy reeling.

It was only as he landed that Rel realized exactly what the Orb, in its confusion, had provided him with. Due to certain things on his mind, his Process companion-machine had armed him with a novelty oversized 'marital aid' of the purple rubber persuasion.

He looked at Joy – met her eyes for one electric arc-popping second – then looked down at his wobbling weapon, grinned, and raised one eyebrow in what he hoped was a rakishly self-assured gesture.

Farbley, whose brain was processing his pain into anger with the slow drip of a treacle-filled hourglass, squinted hard at his assailant. He grabbed his own gnarled wooden truncheon from his belt, and let loose a bellow not unlike an electrocuted walrus[45].

Rel inclined his head in a perfunctory bow.

"You... you killed my master! Now I must regain the honour of my clan... by defeating you in combat!"

So said Rel, his lips moving curiously out of sync with the words. Farbley wasn't listening, though. He came on like a sweaty pink avalanche, truncheon whistling through the air...

And missed.

Rel was simply not there, but the big purple rubber... thing... (Joy was trying very hard not to laugh at this point, because she was sure it was the onset of complete gibbering madness) was surgically precise. Two feet of veiny novelty silliness hammered into Farbley's kidneys, into his ribs, into the back of his neck. The big man swung around, squealing, blood dripping from his nose, and the improbable bell-end of Rel's weapon socked him square in the jaw, showering teeth.

Farbley tottered on his feet, his big blotchy mug screwed up with confusion. Had he just *lost a fight*? Rel bowed low and formal, his hands pressed together as if in prayer.

"The circle is complete. Tell the Shogun that... the Tomatosushi school is supreme in kung-fu!"

Joy knew what to look for, because Farbley – and bullying turds like Farbley – had made up an unfortunate percentage of her lifetime's acquaintances. So when she saw the big proctor reaching for the one-shot nerve-jammer in his boot, she did the only thing she could. She took the big, heavy, leather-bound book of the *Thinker's Word*, and threw it with all her might.

Joy was not very large at all. In fact, she was only of a similar size to the petite and not-entirely-insensitive-about-her-height Tia Faraday. But we've all seen what Ezra Ashdown's parole officer can do when she's angry...

---

45. In the interest of pure accuracy, we must note that NO walruses were electrocuted to research this analogy

Eighteen years of repressed hatred - and a not inconsiderable amount of hand-washing laundry, carrying sacks of potatoes and stacking heavy books - were behind the *Thinker's Word* as it crunched into Brother Farbley's nose, one silver-chased corner impacting with a sound like a cabbage being chopped clean in two. If this was one of those video games which shows a gleeful x-ray shot of the internal injuries suffered by the vanquished, everyone would have clearly seen the proctor's nose shatter and spread across his face, doing absolutely nothing for his looks.

One piece of cartilage, however, broke away and shot up into the front of the Brother's brain, killing him instantly.

In the few moments it took for Farbley's piggy little eyes to glaze over, Joy wondered why she hadn't just done that years ago. Then three hundred kilos of stinking meat slapped down on the flagstones dead, and the world snapped back into focus, hard.

Oh, Lord Worm and Our Machine God! He was DEAD!

Visions of holy hellfire boiled in her head. Followed by images of the enQuisition. Followed, even more terribly, by the leering face of the Mother Inferior with her deadly ruler.

Joy didn't realize she was collapsing until the Angel had wrapped her up in his arms. She didn't realize she was crying until she felt him brush away a tear with one fingertip. And then, of course, she realized that she was very, very close to a half-naked and not at all unattractive young man, whose hair smelled faintly of apples and who was possessed of a warmth and solidity that no Angel of the Lord ever had.

"Are you OK?" he asked, with a curious accent. "Did he hurt you?"

"Actually, I think I killed him," said Joy, while a tiny part of her put its face in its hands and was quietly mortified. "Thanks for the... umm... the help though. You can let go now."

The angel blushed, which was once again a quite un-angelic thing to do. Creatures without sin would have no reason to be able to blush, surely... He stepped away, but kept his hands on her shoulders.

"Are you sure? There's gonna be trouble about this, isn't there?"

At this moment a floating white sphere appeared behind the Angel. It managed to look utterly horrified, despite having absolutely no facial features at all.

"Rel Kitano! You've aided in the murder of a primitive! Oh, my processors! What will the Masters say about this!"

Rel, who was trying with every fibre of his being to look cool, wished the Orb to spontaneously combust. It spectacularly failed to do so.

"Orb, I was *saving* this smoking hot young lady's *life*, allright? I'm a hero, in case you forgot..."

Joy sort of saw him fall into place, in that moment. Not an Angel, then. A boy called Rel Kitano. Which, in a way, made the whole insane situation seem a little more grounded. With the piercing clarity of understanding which has made women revered and feared in equal measure by men throughout the ages, Joy saw that he was both trying incredibly hard to be impressive, but also that he was as fragile as a soap bubble. And that the spark she'd felt when she looked at him must have gone both ways...

Oh well, thought a part of Joy which had secretly always thought that religion was a crock of shit. I've already committed murder today, What's the harm in playing along with the story?

"Sorry... just one theological question," she asked. "You're not, on the off chance, an Angel, created by Our One True God, sent to judge mankind and send sinners unto eternal torment, right?"

Rel looked quizzical for a second. Joy could all but see the clockwork inside his head spinning as he tried to come up with a cool one-liner.

"I'm about as far from an..." he managed to start.

But at that precise moment Joyful Praise Be Unto Our Lord The Thinker screwed up her courage and kissed him.

It is one of the curiosities of science that a simple conjunction of lips and – if you're lucky – tongues, can feel like the very Big Bang which created the entire universe, slathered in champagne and molten gold and accompanied by the sound of the heavenly choirs eternal on solid platinum Fender Stratocaster guitars. Scientists have long wanted to find out how this works, and *why*, but so far nobody has believed their inquiries to be anything but a cheap excuse for said scientists to get a sneaky kiss from that nice young lady professor in the geology department.

This was one of those good ones. The kind which a certain type of glossy magazine for teenage girls has sealed sections devoted to. When Joy finally let go of Rel's ears and came up to breathe, the whole world was filled with snow-globe sparkles and little zips and pops of light. His face looked like that of a man who has gazed not just upon the visage of God, but on every beautiful Goddess who ever swanned about naked on a giant clamshell, at once.

"We're standing *right next to a dead body*," she hissed, while that part of her that wanted to be cool and sophisticated once again buried its face in one palm.

"I'm sure he doesn't mind," said Rel, in the tones of a happy drunk. But reality, like the most bulky and obnoxious evangelical salesman ever, was hammering on the door of their private little world.

"He's dead! And they'll know! The proctors have a kind of switch in their heads, and they'll be coming to find him, and they'll see..."

Rel hugged her to his chest. Which changed absolutely nothing, but was far from unpleasant.

"Not this time. Orb – summon the pickup. We're leaving."

"And you're taking her with you, I suppose? Oh, yessss. In a pod designed to fit exactly *one* of your silly bloody species? How's that going to work?"

"If we get very, very close..."

The Orb actually flickered red with impatience.

"There's not enough oxygen! There's not enough antimatter in the batteries to push two of you through the warp! Let alone the fact that... ahh, never mind! You're absolutely right though, Kitano – you have to get out of here! Directive three-zero-alpha dictates that a Process Domesticated Observer may NEVER be captured by primitive authorities."

Joy could hear it now. Over the sound of Rel and the Orb bickering came the mournful drone of sirens, the slam of doors, the rumble of jack-booted feet.

"Rel! What are you going to do?"

Horribly, it was apparent he hadn't thought this far ahead. But he rallied magnificently.

"I'm going to take you away from all this madness!"

"Really? Where to?"

Rel thought about it for a moment. About the giant tripedal Masters, the glass-domed Human Habitats, the great zero-gravity maze of tubes and tunnels orbiting the purple-marbled rings of Salthuris Septimus....

"To a different, more *interesting* kind of madness. Where we can be together. To hell with what the Orb says. We can run now, and summon a double pod, and get off-world in a week, tops. We can..."

But the Orb wasn't having it. The blatant violation of Directive nine-two-actual – the murder of a Primitive – was bad enough. But now this Kitano kid was proposing a breach of pretty much all of chapters three through twenty seven – the abduction of a Panarchy citizen, conflict with the local authorities... let alone risking capture.

If they caught Rel it would be bad enough; these crazies were pretty fragile when their world view was challenged. Fragile and stabby. Not to mention – and here it shuddered, for the Masters had programmed the Orb to feel both pain and fear – the horror of its own body being reverse-engineered, giving a planet full of religious nut-jobs the secret of probability manipulation and atomic-scale matter assembly.

"NO!" it thundered, in a voice of iron. "SECURITY BREACH OVERRRIDE ENACTED. EMERGENCY EVAC PROTOCOL INITIATED!"

Innumerable jointed steel tentacles hissed out from the Orb, prying Rel and Joy apart. She screamed, and he cursed, but the constricting bands coiled all over him like snakes, binding him hand and foot. And novelty raccoon tail.

"Orb! Have you gone fucking *crazy?* Put me down! Joy! Run! I'll...."

But a thick metal tentacle gagged him at that moment, and the Orb began to lift off, dragging his feet from the ground. Joy made a lunge for one of his ankles, but three more of the chrome-metal snakes batted her away. Rel was clawing and scrabbling at the metal which covered his mouth, and for an instant he managed to pry it free, fingernails dug deep between the chrome scales.

"Joy! I'm coming back for you! Don't worry! I've got this... uuurgh!"

That last 'uuurgh', rather than being motivational, was in fact a jointed arm levering out of the Orb and injecting a syringe full of bright blue goop into Rel's neck. Joy reached out one hand to him, hanging there in the air, wrapped in steel -

And then the door burst open, and an enQuisitor with a net gun filled it. He pulled the trigger, and sticky filaments exploded, tackled her, dragged her down, wrapped her up in a tangled mess. A mass of blank-visored, beetle-armoured figures came crowding and bulking in, all truncheons and nerve-jammers and chains and restraint jackets...

Not one of them saw the facets and panes of kaleidoscope-crystal flicker on around the unconscious body of Rel Kitano as the Orb bore him away. Not one of them testified to the unlikely fact that an alien, angel, demon, jinn, wraith or other being of the Realms Improbable had been part of the unfortunate mental breakdown of the young sister named Joyful Praise Be Unto Our Lord The Thinker. And part of her murder of Proctor Farbley, who was obviously (being as he was a man of the male persuasion) utterly blameless.

He played no visible part in her subsequent incarceration in the

Cathedral of Penitence, under the care of the Sisters of Perpetual Suspicion, in what most other cultures would have the good grace to call a psychiatric prison. Or a loony bin, or the funny farm, if they weren't feeling very politically correct at the time.

But Joy knew. And she knew enough not to tell the starched, mutton-faced matrons of the Sisters the truth, for fear of being force-fed a bowl of sedatives and milk for breakfast every morning.

The Chronojudiciary certainly knew – they could, in fact, pinpoint the kiss which was to cause so much trouble across the entire tatty old jumper of space and time with some accuracy. On a map with far more edges and surfaces than it should possess, that kiss was picked out with a small pink drawing pin. The collapse cascades which curled out from it were both fractally beautiful and staggeringly frightening.

Rel Kitano had a purpose you could use to forge horseshoes with. He was reprimanded, and caged, and spent his time hammering twelve-punch combos into a boxing bag, lifting weights, listening to violently political punk rock and tattooing joy's name across the knuckles of his right hand.

When the time came, and his Masters (who couldn't resist the sheer cuteness of an angry little human) relented, he put his plan into action. He breached the Forbidden Zone, and entered the Unspoken Vault in the Mausoleum of Woe, and stole for himself one of the most fearsome weapons of transcosmic annihilation ever devised by a sentient mind.

He was going to rescue his girl, but like the movies said you had to.

And now, after a whole lot of trial and error, of warp-jumps into places indescribable, and of trying to find the planet Temperance using charts and astrologs written in Process Codespeak Twenty, he was finally there...

Thirteen – The Lucky Chapter

At first, they thought you'd just build a wormhole gate and step right through it.

But that's far too simple. There may not be a warp-space dimension filled with hideous demons and people with nails in their faces giving speeches about sado-masochism, but it isn't just a plaid blur of star trails back there either. Even the old traditional 'spiralling tunnel of eternity with floating clocks' is reserved for other purposes.

The Chasm is how we see something that wasn't designed to be seen. In effect, it's just an interface – a convenient way to have us perform some actions we can comprehend, inside a space which blends up time, matter, probability and a few other bits which are only expressed with greek letters, then adds vodka and serves it all in half a coconut.

All the business with the walking, and the bridges, and the doors... it's a collective reading of what the universe, or whoever built the damned thing thinks we can handle. If it's a bit dramatic, it's because that's what we are, as a species. If it seems silly, remember - we invented pop music, the toilet brush and bell bottomed trousers.

Of course, that's the current theory. That the Chasm was built. Some long-dead race made the thing as a kind of behind the scenes transcosmic subway system, and equipped it with a psionic translator, so that we see it differently from the Tchub, who see it differently from the Process, or the Jest, or any of the other strange organic life-forms who infest the galaxy.

Which leads to two equally horrible questions.

If it breaks, how do we find the manual?

And -

If the owners come back, how awful is the bill going to be?

From 'Where Shit Be At' by the Central Scrutinizer

THERE'S A SLIDING scale of stupid.

It's sort of like light, with a spectrum which blasts off into the infrared and ultra-violet at both ends. Stupidity has a *rainbow*, some of which can't be achieved even by the dimmest human brain. Not even after years and years of extra-strength lager, soap opera reruns and b-sides from novelty Christmas singles.

In fact, there are some pinnacles of imbecility so breathtakingly moronic that it actually takes a higher intellect - or at least an alien one - to encompass them. At one end of the scale is the mere three-stoogery of looking into the muzzle of a combat cannon to see what's wrong with it. At the other is actually firing such a thing inside the Chasm.

The Tchub stormtroopers on every side of Ezra Ashdown were up to a bit of both.

Bolts of energy sizzled through the stale and dusty air. Black, ill-defined Chasm-stuff splintered and cracked where they hit.

And the Outriders of the Panarchy? Earth's last, best hope?

They ran like streakers with their bums on fire.

The four of them climbed staircases which corkscrewed through dimensions hinted at by Escher and Lovecraft, and out along balconies carved from sheer vertigo. There wasn't time to be afraid of heights, or even to figure out if 'heights' was the right word to be afraid of.

Now and then Ez caught sight of the Tchub themselves, or at least the drysuits they wore – scuffed and corroded industrial exoskeletons with bubble-dome helmets and portholes all over. The things which sloshed and squirmed inside seemed to be all eyes and teeth, but they made up for their blundering bulk with raw enthusiasm. War-whoops and screeches echoed across the whole dark face of the Wall, amplified by rigs of Tchub loudspeakers and bullhorns.

They certainly didn't lack for guns, either. One of their first shots had blown the tiny, folded lamp-light of the Verne-Wells 1900 to a sad little puff of sparks.

"Why did we stop shooting back? Those things make a damn fine target, Miss Faraday!"

Ezra's parole officer slammed him flat against the Wall with one arm, gesturing for him to shush.

"Because there's too many of 'em to blast through. We can get around them, though... so long as they keep on firing. *Something's* thinning out their numbers."

Sir Giles nodded grimly.

"A ruddy big bugger, but quiet with it. Lord, what I wouldn't give to have a head like that over my mantelpiece!"

Ezra pinched the bridge of his nose and sighed. It wasn't worth pointing out that Sir Giles' mantelpiece was now a mere puff of superheated atoms drifting through space. Unbidden little parts of his mind recalled the Chasmic Leviathan.

"You didn't see the last one, buddy. A trophy like that ain't worth the bullet."

Giles waggled his eyebrows.

"I was always into a spot of the old big-game hunting, you know. Down in the rad-levels, with Wilberforce and Lord Winstanleigh-Throckmortonley-Custard, a brace of native guides and a photon blunderbuss. Cockroaches twice the size of a man, with great big..."

Wainwright chose this moment to slip back around the corner and join them. He made a series of complex military hand signals which looked terribly impressive, but were understood by absolutely no one.

"Come again?"

The metalman held up an accusatory finger to the glass plate where his mouth would have been.

"Keep it down! There's about twelve of them ahead of us, including what looks like their Captain. Someone's paid them off with a supply of Headkicker's Old Thoroughly Offensive, and they're in a right old mood."

It's worth noting at this time – with Ezra peering out around the corner to get a good look at the combat-suited aliens pursuing him – that the Tchub were by nature aquatic beings, who evolved among a shoal of liquid worlds floating inside a giant nebula. In their actual skin, the creatures were dolphin gray, smooth, many-eyed and tentacled slugs of meat roughly eight feet long, utterly boneless and possessed of a trio of brains, one for mathematics, one for the creative arts, and one just to co-ordinate their many, many limbs, probes, hooks, whips and eyeballs. The Tchub, in short, looked like something John Carpenter would have loved to see at a casting call.

The fact that their major food source was a kind of gigantic brine shrimp with razor-sharp pincers and a bad attitude accounted for a lot of their racial psyche. The rest came down to alcohol.

For all that we love the sweet amber nectar of the distiller's art, even the finest Scotch whiskey, lovingly aged in oak barrels, then blended by ancient masters of the highland glens to deliver a rich and mellow...[46]

Anyway, it's all *chemicals*. And the makeup of the Tchub's liquid homeworld contained a fair old amount of alcohol. This meant that the entire species was constantly slightly drunk, on a scale which tipped alarmingly between 'good mates singing about football' to 'New Jersey

---

46. (*editor's note – excised several pages of this stuff here*)

gentleman's club bouncer with toothache'. It was thoroughly amazing that this burping, yodelling, fighting, uncontrollably weeping and karaoke-addicted race had ever developed space travel, but they had. And then they'd discovered that other races – not just the smugly self-titled *Homo Sapiens* – had invented ways to get *even drunker.*

Ezra watched the advance guard of this lot come swaggering out of the Chasmic mist, clanking and sloshing with every step. Each one of the Tchub mercenaries had a different drysuit, lashed together, it seemed, from bits and painted a uniform shade of safety yellow. Humorous graffiti, stickers promoting Tchub sports teams and rock bands, and pictures of skulls with tally marks next to them were much in evidence – as were the bottles of gin, rum, port, absinthe, blue curacao, Neptunian surgical alcohol and potato vodka plugged into a tangle of tubes, slung from harnesses and, in one case, hung from both sides of a comical safety helmet emblazoned with the message 'Party Animal'.

There was no doubting which one was the Captain. He had the biggest exo-suit, festooned with lights, air horns, loudspeakers and exhaust pipes. One arm ended with a serrated hook big enough to gaff a mammoth, and the other was a robotic fist clutching a ten-foot-long harpoon. Atop the glass dome which served as his head – but was in fact simply a window onto a slithering mass of gray, eye-studded horror – the Tchub leader wore a novelty tricorne hat with the obligatory jolly roger. Socketed into his shoulder pauldrons were no less than twenty-three bottles of that radioactive wine from the insane resort-planet of New Aruba – the utterly forbidden vintage called *Methode Abattoir*, famed for being more than 100 percent pure alcohol, in defiance of the laws of both duty free customs and physics.[47]

"Arrrrr, mateys!" bellowed the Captain, his alien language mangled through translation filters designed for the drive-thru at a pirate-themed burger restaurant. "We know ye be out thaar! Come on out and perish like whatever species ye arrrre, ye scurvy bilge-swabs!"

"We'd rather *die* than give in to your demands, filth!" shouted Sir Giles, in a fair approximation of an ancient British naval officer.

"But... dying's what we WANT ye to do!" replied the Captain,

---

47. The curious effect of this drop, pressed from carnivorous grapes under the light of three suns and distilled in a functional fission reactor before being filtered through a hobo's sock, is to elevate the drinker to a state of drunkenness in which he begins to hallucinate that he's sober. This has a mild probability-warping area effect, similar to Ezra Ashdown believing himself to be fictional.

sounding a little puzzled. "Can't we at least shoot ye up a bit? I bought a brand new positronic disintegrator just for this mission!"

He waved it forlornly. Sparks fizzled.

Tia shushed all of them, then raised an eyebrow at Wainwright. The metalman nodded, and Ezra's parole officer waved a white handkerchief out from behind their excuse for cover. The gunslinger wondered exactly where she'd gotten a clean white handkerchief from, and why she was carrying one at all. But only for a second.

"Allright. It's a fair cop!" she shouted. "No use dying without lots of pyrotechnics, right? It wouldn't be fair on you fellas, carrying all those big guns in here without getting to use them!"

The Captain nodded. Several of his crew joined in. This was more like it.

"Come on then! Let's get you disintegrated, and we can head back to the ship for some drinks!"

"OK. But you have to really give it heaps. I'm not surrendering just to get shot once in the head like some kind of petty space-grunt. You really have to *concentrate* on us, as though we're people you thoroughly hate!"

"We really hate *everyone!*" chimed in 'Party animal'. "Bunch of tossers, the whole galaxy!"

Something coiled, black on black in the darkness behind him as he said it. Ezra held his breath.

"No, no, no," said Tia. "Someone *special!*"

"Like me mum?"

"Do you *really* hate your mum?" asked the Captain. "That be a bit scurvy, even for a pirate mercenary scumbag. I mean, she's your *mum*, for Jim Beam's sake!"

"Well, *obviously*, see, obviously not my mum, then," said Party Animal. "But..." and here his many, many brows creased, deep in the foaming pickle of his drysuit's contents. "... what about... what about *Betelgeuse United FC*. Those bums cost me about 300 Squid last week!"

There was a murmur of agreement. A chorus of belligerent 'yeahs' and 'oooohs' echoed from a thicket of badly wired speakers.

"Got to concede - Glorpaldinio is useless on the wing, Zarzlagovic couldn't find the ball with all four tentacles and a mecha-pincer-arm, and MacFnord is the worst goalkeeper in the league, even though he is ten feet wide with twenty-nine legs. Frankly, between that shower of muppets, and a front line made up of that silicon-brained

Zxchzhcshzx'vchz, old O'ooliop'o Jalamanthantagar, and Jim Smith[48], I'm surprised they haven't been relegated. It's disgraceful!"

This from one of the smaller Tchub, who seemed to be a bit of an armchair coach. The rest nodded and hooted their agreement.

Tia rallied magnificently.

"All right then. You just pretend we're Betelgeuse United FC, and really let it rip. I want this to be a moment of beautiful, transcendent catharsis for you all!"

"Very nice! What does *that* mean?"

"Just give it some welly, you big wimp!"

Party Animal nodded. The Captain shook his hook-handed arm irritably. A brace of charred metal tubes popped out, sizzling with energy. From behind him came the clicks, snaps, oily metal sounds and little zaps of a whole arsenal being loaded up.

Then all four of the Outriders trooped out from behind the low stone wall they'd been using as cover, hands up, clad in the now-infamous avocado and pink strip of the ill-fated Betelgeuse United FC hyper-football club. Wainwright even had an extra-wide bobble hat covering his great copper dome of a head.

The intensity of the Tchub's loathing was palpable – a kind of greasy, somewhat lemony feel to the stuffy air of the Chasm. Ezra licked his teeth to get rid of it, and felt static electricity crawl across his tongue. It irked his pride that they weren't going to go down fighting - but then again, he thought, if this worked they weren't going to go down at all.

"*I hate to say it, Hoss,*" said Granger, in his head "*But this problem ain't gonna be beat with bullets. Quite the opposite...*"

Weird psychic resonances rippled and reverberated. They went from weird to wyrd and right up the scale to eldritch in the time it takes for a vole to sneeze. They might as well have chummed the water of a shark-infested lagoon with the contents of a butcher's grease-trap. Down below, grabblesome claw-clatterings and leathery scrapings echoed.

"Stay down! *Don't look*, no matter what happens. And pray they don't realize we're holograms until the crunching and slupring starts."

That was Tia, yanking Ez back by his collar as he tried to get a good look out from behind theircover. Because of course the football-uniform-clad row of targets out there on the edge of the bridge were nothing but holograms, spit out by a quartet of little rolling mini-

---

48. I hope we're pronouncing that last one correctly

droids. With his typical resourcefulness the gunslinger produced a shiny silver cigarette case and held it out past the wall in one hand, using it as a mirror.

What he saw made goose pimples explode up his arm in a rippling wave.

It should have been impossible for the thing rising up behind the Tchub to lurk. *Loom*, certainly – it loomed with all the bulk of a cemetery hill by moonlight. But *lurking* should have been off the cards for the dark, shadowy monster which had forced its way up out of the utter depths of the Chasm, sending smaller leviathans gibbering in horror. It rose like the ghost of last night's chicken curry from that dodgy place that stays open past eleven, all tentacles and flaps and horrid wobbly bits which didn't have names, even in Latin[49]. Its mouth cracked open in what Ezra was horribly certain was a grin.

Gigantoteratus Cthulhii. The King Leviathan.

Every instinct in Ashdown's body twanged and yammered that he should shoot the thing. Of course, Jed Granger was the voice of reason.

"Shoot it? Better to spit in the eye of the Devil! It's feedin' time, *boy! I just hope that little lady has a plan to get us out of the way before it feels like dee-sert!"*

The leviathan dispatched a couple of appetizers with a lash of its suckered feeding whips. Party Animal turned, wide-eyed under his bubble dome, and stammered through a pair of bullhorn speakers, gurgling in fear. Seconds later a bony pincer snickered him up, and he disappeared into that titanic gullet like popcorn chicken into an insinkerator. He yanked the Captain's shoulder armour as he was taken, spinning the big Tchub on one heel, face to face with the monster.

If Ez had been expecting terror, he didn't know the bubbling, varnish-scented mind of the Tchub mercenary at all. The Captain whooped with joy as he watched *G.Cthulhii* tear his crew to nasty gristly chunks, and he brandished his harpoon high.

"Arrrrr! The kraken itself! Come back at last, have we, sweetness? Then *let's dance!*"

Ezra had to give the hulking great alien points for sheer courage, even if he lost the bonus round for intelligence. Hefting his mammoth harpoon, the Tchub Captain launched himself up at the Leviathan, rocket boosters in his armoured boots belching smoke and flame.

---

49. That's not just a terrible metaphor - we've all had a dodgy curry which *really did* contain tentacles, flaps and wobbly bits without names in medical science.

"Ye took me hand, scurvy beast! Sure and it was a robot hand, but it's the principle *of the thing! Cough it up!"*

The harpoon lanced deep into one of the far-too-many-eyes of the great monster, and the Tchub followed through with a savage swing of his hook, amputating a tendril which lashed out at him. The tips of other tentacles peeled open like glistening orchids, revealing a rolling fractal blur of images, trying to lock onto the psionic signature of the alien's drunken little mind. It was no use.

Now hooks in the Tchub's armour locked it down to the Leviathan's face. Now he let go the harpoon and deployed that brace of terrifying energy disintegrators, laughing like a swamp hag on nitrous oxide.

"Time to say goodnight, ye slimy great codfish!"

And it was.

Valiant though the Tchub Captain's efforts may have been, there's such a thing as fighting the losing fight. Attacking a rhinoceros with a toothpick. Assaulting a main battletank with a rubber chicken. Trying to fool the tax department with ledgers written in crayon.

And forgetting the sheer number of huge, claw-tipped, spike-studded tentacles a thing the size of *Gigantoteratus Cthulhii* has poised to swat away pesky annoyances. That's right up there.

One claw snickered the Tchub up like a fly between a pair of chopsticks, and tossed him into the gaping maw beneath with a single movement. He didn't even touch the sides.

Then, even more horribly, the monster heaved itself up on the webwork of bridges, its loathsome slab of a head angling down so that a battery of eyes fixed squarely on Ezra, Tia and party. Not the holograms. Oh no. Things like the king leviathan, it seemed, were not so easily fooled.

"But we were thinking *happy thoughts...*" wailed Wainwright, positively knotted up by the unfairness of it all.

"*I* certainly was," said Sir Giles. "That last one made a jolly crunch, didn't he?"

Tia shot him a withering look.

"Oh, *very* tactful. Now, if you don't have anything useful to say, we'd better get ready to run..."

A city block worth of jagged ivory hung over them. A smattering of eyes - from the size of hubcaps to the size of hot tubs – burned with phosphorescent hunger. And suddenly...

The leviathan stopped.

Not paused, or held its breath, or waited for a moment in fiendish anticipation. It *stopped*, like clockwork that had finally run down. Ezra could have fancied that it was painted on to the impossible background of the Chasm – in fact, he briefly entertained the notion that it was animated, and that the cartoonist had gone to take a tea break.

Then a little hatch popped open just above the creature's terrible jet-black snout. A small, balding man with a long white beard wrapped around his neck appeared, pushing a pair of immense night-vision goggles up onto his egg-like forehead.

"Well, come on then! Get on board! I don't have all day, there's more of those buggers coming, and if management find out I'm helping you, then up goes the bloody donkey, as they say. Pension plan? Hah? They'd have me shining spittoons and filing 209-G's until judgment day!"

He threw out a rope ladder, which clattered down to the deck.

"Come on! Seriously, you look like a row of circus midgets who've just been told the camel's dead!"

Ezra was the first to move. He shrugged, holstered his Problem Solver and began to climb. The others looked at each other as if expecting some kind of alternative plan, and then followed.

"Right-o. Kettle's on the left, if you'd be so kind. All aboard? Marvelous!"

The little man looked left and right, as if checking for spies. He slipped the goggles back over his eyes, closed the hatch, and then...

The Leviathan shivered back to life. It burped enormously, scattering those smaller members of its kin who had come skulking back, psionic senses aroused by the slaughter. Then it pushed away from the webwork of bridges, tiny pencil-scrawl filaments of blackness spanning the misty gap between the two impossible Walls. A seemingly endless arch of black and white glistening flesh rolled by, studded with flippers and hooks and tentacles and other things which would put the average biologist off his lunch. Then came a tail with flukes you could park jumbo jets on, and with a swirl of mist the great beast was gone.

Down into the utter depths of the Chasm. Down beyond even the lowest doors and bridges. To a place crafted, or so it was said, from the most primordial, nuggety chunks of the human mind.

From whence – and this one *definitely* deserves a 'whence' – it's both safe and accurate so say that nobody had ever returned...

Fourteen – Muriel Almost Misses Garbage Day

Do you ever wonder why they went away from hanging to lethal injection? And why - if the fellow they are about to snuff with 50cc of concentrated floor cleaner cut with brewer's yeast is definitely on the one-way ferryboat to Maggot Beach - they bother to sterilize the needle?

Well, the truth, as they say after a couple of pints, is stranger than fiction. Certainly stranger than this rubbish.

See, the thing is, they're keeping them.

You've heard of cryogenics? Well, the heads of all those serial killers and mass murderers and homicidal maniacs are all carefully removed, after the so called 'euthanasia drug' puts their bodies into a kind of torpor. Like a lizard on a cold day, or a hibernating hedgehog. They snip their heads off with surgical precision, then deep-freeze them in a big bank of refrigerated tunnels under Area 51. Or possibly Cheyenne Mountain. Or those missing subway stations in New York.

It doesn't matter.

The thing isn't where they are. It's what they're for, see?

Eventually, someone will have the amazing idea of constructing the Burzum. A space battleship so absolutely evil and crazed that it won't have the problem other artificially intelligent starships do when it comes to violence. All those logical moral quandaries and quibbles about self preservation in the face of massive alien firepower – not a problem if your asteroid-sized wedge of metal and phased-beam weaponry is patched together from frosty neural scans of Ted Bundy, Jeff Dahmer and Pogo the Clown.

And there'll be no problems, the generals will swear. We'll build it with a safeguard. We'll make sure the whole twenty-kilometer-long hunk of slavering murder-engine can't double back on us.

The thing is, several generations of psychopaths will find a way. And then you're left with a bit of a mess to clean up.

So – write to your MP, or Senator, or whoever pretends to be driving the clapped-out old hippie bus of Democracy in your neck of the woods. Demand they bring back the guillotine! Or perhaps a big pit of acid filled with robot crayfish of some kind!

You won't sound like a loony.
We promise.

THE FAITH OF the Thinker – and hence of Worm III the Utterly Lowest – was a Faith Militant in the old-school fashion.

Space around the world of Temperance thronged with hideous, blocky starships, bristling with hideous blocky cannons. Aesthetics were of absolutely no concern to the Deacons Fabricatorial of the Holy Manufacturariat – Worm's fleet looked like something a very disturbed three year old would be sent home from kindergarten for constructing out of shoeboxes and toilet roll tubes.

It was all, the people were assured as they received yet another nourishing dinner of cabbage gruel, necessary. A precaution to shield the righteous.

Because the core of the Thinker's Word was a *prophecy*. Every good messianic cult needs one, and this one was the caramel centre in the nougat ball of madness ginned up by Worm III's predecessors.

The Thinker – once the AI controlling the economy of Temperance and its Chasm Gate - may have become a mountain-sized statue blatantly plagiarizing Rodin. But it still uttered snippets of what the robed priesthood of the Word called wisdom – phrases like "October is parrot month - don't keep your vacuum cleaner in the shower, or purple fungus will be your reward."

In one of its more lucid ramblings, the machine-god had imparted the knowledge that underneath all its apparent lunacy, it was working on re-activating the Chasm Gate, and attempting to link Temperance back to the Panarchy. Not even the wisest, baldest, most heavily-bearded seers of the Inner College of the Word knew exactly when, but they knew other, forbidden things. Things which would make the average pious Temperancer sick with quivering righteousness.

There was a *reason* that the Chasm Gate of Temperance had been so big and so busy. There was a very good reason indeed why it was equipped with one of the most powerful AIs outside of Earth itself – *to handle the sheer volume of tourist traffic.*

Temperance had once been the pleasure-planet of New Gomorrah, a globe-wide orgiastic resort of debauchery, drug use, sex and lassitude[50]. People won tickets to go there on game shows. Burned-out executives were sent there for some R and R by dodgy medical

---

50. And more drug use.

insurance companies. Bachelor parties and hen's nights fought small-scale wars between towering nightclub ziggurats by the shores of limpid lagoons, while far away, alpine ski lodges echoed to the sound of year-round beer-fests. The leading causes of death were sexual exhaustion, terminal hangovers and jet-ski collisions.

The tourist economy of just the Floating Ganja Forests of Hai-Bong outstripped the GDP of many other worlds. That was without mentioning the Grand Prostitutorium, the Cocaine Deserts, or the Zero-gravity Pleasure-Palaces of the Gold-plated cyborg Sultan, Salmathzar the Infinitely Debauched.

When the Jest instigated their terrible assault in the War of 9:15, Salmathzar became convinced he was in fact a small ceramic corgi named Wilbur. He took to muffled barking and perching precariously on mantelpieces. The Thinker accreted a huge structure of rubble and stone around the planet's Chasm Gate, forming it into the image of the now-famous chin-on-hand ruminating statue.

And in the basement of one of the great nudist resorts of the Erotican Isles, a young cutlery sanitizer by the name of Yargo Dreckender saw that his time had come. Armed with nothing but a tin of oyster fork polish, a large spatula and an Adam's apple which could stop traffic, the shrill-voiced little twerp went forth to preach his own version of humanity's judgment.

A lot of it was based on his sexual repression, lack of social graces, pipe-cleaner physique and miserable pay packet. A lot more came from the more gruesome bits of Earth's old religions.

The accepted mathematics goes like this – a crowd has an IQ equal to that of it's smartest member, divided by the number of people present, minus their level of fear and confusion on the universal Von Wraselbad scale[51]. With all of New Gomorrah pitching single digits in the intelligence stakes, Yargo Dreckender was swept into office by a puritanical backlash on a scale not seen since the Miss Salem Halloween Beauty Pageant of 1666.

When the prophecy came true, then, there was going to be some explaining to do. A sticky moment to be certain, as a population who had gone through their own version of Pol Pot's good old-fashioned Year Zero suddenly discovered that they were the descendants of

---

51. On which One is represented by 'unexpectedly finding a small spider in ones underwear' and Two Hundred rates the full 'Great Cthulhu has appeared wearing a humorous restaurant bib, holding a knife and fork and gesticulating wildly to Hastur and Nyarlyhotep to drag a seat over and grab a bottle of the house chardonnay.'

strippers, courtesans, gigolos and erotic entertainers, not to mention pimps, drug dealers, ski instructors and experimental bartenders.

Some, it was thought, might like to go back to a highly profitable, supremely satisfying state of affairs in which New Gomorrah could satisfy any number of sexual preferences you could count to, and provided drinks so powerful that that figure was sure to stay safely in the single digits.

So they'd carefully preached anathema. They'd whipped up a fervour of loathing for the outside universe. They'd painted the Panarchy as a diseased, foul, gap-toothed and gangrenous empire of sin.

And they'd spent thousands of years preparing for the great Chasm Gates orbiting the frankly boob-shaped moon of Nineveh to re-open. Worm III's plan? You can't shag it, inhale it, drink it or snort it if it's blasted to radioactive hell by a crusading battlefleet.

He – and his predecessors, right back to the Holy One, Yargo Dreckender – had even trained a secret cadre of Chasmwalkers, after torturing the members of the guild stranded on New Gomorrah after the War.

The next worlds down-chasm from Temperance were woefully unprepared. One was an agrarian world already re-connected to the reticulum, the bucolic backwater of Scrumthorpe. The other was an as-yet-disconnected medieval throwback which the inhabitants simply called 'Snopp'.

Further on from them, though...

In one direction lay a Tchub fortress-manufactuary. A bunch of humans turning up there would start a cheerfully sozzled kind of war which might leave a dozen worlds in smoking cinders. And in the other – a little prospective re-connect called Harrowe.

None of which concerned Mister Fixit when he lit up the orbital Chasm Gate nestled in Nineveh's Lagrange point, having been carried the final leg of the journey through that otherdimensional place by the pragmatically mercenary Ulriq Hszarl.

While snarled time-loop versions of himself had battled on Cherrywood – and another iteration had made a little detour to the scum-hives of Thantaos to hire three entire Tchub pirate crews – this version of the killer android had been utterly focused on the mission at hand. While the *Slayer* class corsair *Altar of Sacrifice* had been wrapped up inside a little ball of nebulous light he'd refitted Cerise with a piece of thoroughly forbidden military hardware stripped from the corpse of the *Burzum*. Just as important as the e-mind of the megacidal space juggernaut was the electronic warfare harpoon it had carried, to be used in the case of dire emergency to transfer its consciousness.

This was a pretty dire emergency. *Burzum*'s physical shell had been sliced to glowing cherry-red scrap hundreds of light years away. If it couldn't sequester a set of neural storage banks quick smart, it was doomed to spend the next few thousand years as an oversized Christmas ornament.

The actual process of installing and binding the harpoon – which in realspace took the form of a blue glass blade – had involved a lot of working around Cerise's madness. That meant an interminable amount of storytime, weaving the mad little AI about with faerie tales and potent sorceries. Now thoroughly convinced that her uncle Mason Stockton was a great wizard in hiding, and that she was a princess armed with a magic sword, Harrowe's guardian of the Chasm reticulum had kitted herself out in an utterly inappropriate pink satin dress, tiara, and silver slippers with blue ribbon bows. Never had a weapon of mass destruction looked so witheringly cute.

"Well, Cerise, we're really in for an adventure this time," chuckled Mister Fixit, all rosy-cheeked and twinkly-eyed. "Space pirates! Hundreds of the blighters! Isn't this so much more fun that staying back home and learning the harpsichord, or some such shit?"

The android inwardly cursed himself. Little slip-ups like that could cost him the entire mission. He doubled down on the Dickensian charm.

"I mean to say, you've become *such* a fine princess. When we get home with all this treasure we shall be able to buy up a whole sweet shop!"

Cerise gave him a pouty little frown, then smiled outrageously.

"This is a *brilliant* story, Uncle! And I love this magic sword you've gotten me! But if we're buying any sweet shops, you must promise that you'll brush your teeth every night. They're starting to look a bit... funny."

Mister Fixit clapped one hand across his mouth. It was true that he hadn't been paying much attention to the little details of his Mason Stockton disguise. Nutrient webs kept his stolen face nice and fresh, but the *teeth* – well, it was like wearing ill-fitting dentures. Fixit kept them in his pocket and only slipped them in when he was trying to be extra charming toward the little robotic brat. As a result they were slimed with a mixture of motor oil and pocket lint. He worked feverishly with one plastic fingernail to loosen up a scrap of old bus ticket. When he turned back, his grin was wide and sticky.

"Yes, yes, of *course!* Though if you talk back to your nice old uncle again, the only sweet shop we'll be visiting is Badgerley and Smarms![52]" The android rubbed away the residual crust from his front teeth with a single rubber fingertip, producing the sound of a squeegee mop on a whiteboard. "Now, are you ready to do some swashbuckling? This is for the biggest pile of treasure you've ever clapped eyes on, my girl, and no mistake! These space pirates are as cunning a bunch of rogues as ever spliced some kind of mainbrace, or... I don't know, keelhauled the plank, or something."

Cerise gave him a calculating look. Your average little girl is pretty adept at this, but Cerise, of course, could calculate Pi to near infinity in the time it took to squeeze a pimple.

"Are they more or less wicked than the ones you were talking to back on that horrible gray planet back there? The one where it wouldn't stop raining?"

Mister Fixit's smile ratcheted up another notch. The top of Mason's stolen face was in severe danger of tearing in half.

"Those fellows? No, no – they were just... *sports fans.* Yes. Big fans of the good old Buccaneers. Betelgeuse United FC. Going off to the big game, right? Seeing as I couldn't make it, I had to give them my tickets, and..."

But the little AI girl's mercurial mood had already crested the switchback out of suspicion and into the sunny uplands of enthusiasm. She brandished her sword bravely and turned toward the airlock.

"Then, in the words of Sir Percival Bletherly-Peabody – 'let's give these nasty motherfuckers a taste of boot leather!'"

Mister Fixit raised a finger, ready to scold, but then though best of it. Anything he said now would just tug at the unravelling threads of Mason Stockton's carefully constructed fantasy. Instead he lifted the great black-glass snowflake of the Burzum's mind from off of the shelf, gingerly holding it between his fingertips. Fixit wasn't built with

---

52. Badgerley and Smarms was an old Victorian Era London sweet shop for naughty children. Rather than simply giving them NO sweets, stern 1880s parents could instead force their offspring to make a selection from the horrible choices available at this grotesque anti-confectioners, touted as 'The Candy Land for Horrid Urchins'. For the sins of lack of posture, farting in public, using the wrong limpet fork or considering the Poor, children could be forced to masticate their way through such grey and dismal anti-treats as Smelly Beans, Baddy-baddy Scumdrops or Turkish Despair. Not to mention Sardine and Spinach Fudge, or the dreaded Mice Cream Sundae.

a vivid imagination, so the images of tormented faces which sleeted through the glass must have been horribly real.

"One last thing, dearest. A final enchantment for your sword. Then we'll show these (ahem) *mother-loving sons of biddies* what for, eh?"

Cerise watched, wide eyed, as Fixit slotted the centre of the snowflake around the hazy, indefinite-edged crystal sword. It seemed to have too many blades at once, that thing, and it was always changing, sliding between dimensions like a greased mirror-puzzle in a heat haze.

But it was made for just this purpose. Cerise gave a little gasp of wonder as the bladed facets of the snowflake curled up like flower petals at dusk, flattening and folding in to the surface of her sword. There was only the merest hint of unhinged laughter. Something in the folded glass winked at Mister Fixit in a way which made him feel strangely less evil than he should.

There was a flash of light. There was a sound like a champagne flute being struck with a tuning fork.

Cerise brandished her sword (which had turned a bright, reactor-core blue) and smiled until her dimples threatened to implode.

"Onward then, Uncle! Let's drown them in blood and choke them on their own intestines!"

Fixit grinned. This time he didn't have to fake it.

"Sir Percival Bletherly-Peabody again?" he asked, grabbing an umbrella from its hook on the wall. A quick tap with its ivory handle and the airlock began to cycle, red strobe lights painting Cerise's face as a tiny demon mask.

"Oh no," she said, all wide-eyed innocence. "That's one of my own..."

Mister Fixit bit down on one rubber knuckle with his stolen teeth. If he could have shed a little tear of joy he would have.

Ahhhh, he thought. *They go evil so fast...*

Then the doors snapped open on hard vacuum, and the dying started.

+++

Captain-Father Madrigal-of-Praise-to-the-Almighty-Thinker was smug from the top of his captain's mitre to the bottom of his ship-issue sandals. He radiated smugness in the millimetre band; he almost personified smugness, with a side-dish of self-satisfaction[53].

---

53. And relish! B-dom-doom-chhh! Thank you, thank you, I'll be here all week...

It was a shame, then, that if there was such an animal as the lesser-brained shitweasel, he would have been had up for defaming its image.

Is it worth noting, considering his lack of what could be called 'a future', that Captain-Father Madrigal was a thoroughly unpleasant man? That he sold his own Grandmother to the enQuisitors for a small muffin basket? That his eyes looked like they were making a desperate bid to escape his narrow, spotty, face?

All the better, then, that he laboured under the mother of all miscomprehensions.

It was a good day to be him, for – praise the Thinker! - the Chasm Gate had stuttered open at last, according to holy writ. And lo! Who had been chosen as the big bludgeoning fist of the Almighty on this blessed occasion? None other than Mrs Madrigal's little boy, that's who! There'll be at least a couple of stained glass windows in this for him. Maybe he could even write a testament, in which he'd preach his own stern moral code of rectitude, self-denial, self-flagellation and a withering hatred for all dogs smaller than cats.

The whole bridge crew held their breaths as the silver pool rippled open in its massive spaceborne frame. The lights dimmed, until only electro-candleabra flickered above the gothic workstations and recessed cyber-scriptoria where Madrigal's monks militant laboured.

But only one ship came through. One tiny little ship, barely the size of one of the Temperance fleet's scout cruisers. And it had the temerity to bugger off extremely quickly, leaving just a tiny signature distorting the curvature of space-time in the orbit of Nineveh.

"Deacon Larry, what *exactly* is going on?" inquired Madrigal, in a voice so tight and strained it could have been used to fire poison-tipped darts through concrete. "Are we being assaulted by an army of the unrighteous, or not?"

The luckless Deacon, who was indeed called Larry, looked up from the great domed nav-scanner he tended. His face, after years of serving under Madrigal's stern and utterly-self righteous command, resembled that of a bloodhound who had suffered several consecutive strokes.

"It's two people, Sir. Two people floating in space."

"Possessed by demons? Armed with great big planet smashing cannons? Armoured in big huge spiked mecha-suits with the..."

Larry's lugubrious voice cut him off.

"No sir. It's a little girl and an old man with an umbrella."

"A WHAT?"

"Like a parasol, sir, but for men. He may be her butler, sir."

Madrigal fumed slightly. His mitre of Captaincy trembled like a smokestack about to burst into flames.

"And what about the ship, you chamber-pot-brained lackwit? Did you think, perhaps, that those two might be a diversion? That their ship may in fact be a planet-busting missile crammed full of antimatter, screaming down toward the..."

Once again, Deacon Larry's voice blotted out that of his master like a trail of slug mucous across a wedding invitation.

"No sir. The ship has fled into the outer system. Much faster than anything we have can follow. And look, sir. They've closed the gate as well."

Any hope of marauding armies of the unholy storming through to meet the angelic symphony of Madrigal's assembled cannons was snuffed out. He reached up above him and snapped his fingers, causing a microphone on a long chain to rattle down out of the gloom. This wouldn't rate a testament, or even a stained glass window. Maybe a single boring bloody psalm, or a small hand-painted icon.

"Attention... attention little girl and *possible butler*," spat Madrigal, a tiny vein pulsing on his glistening forehead. "You are in violation of restricted space, and face the full might of the Shield of the Faith, the Sworn Protectors of the Thinker's Doctrine, the First and Only Battlefleet of His Staggering Humility, Worm III The Utterly Lowest! Do you wish to plead and grovel for a bit before we deliver swift, merciless judgment on your immortal souls?"

The image of Mister Fixit and Cerise flashed up onto the main screen – a vast panel of diamond gripped between two statues of winged and haloed angels.

"No thanks. Haven't got any!" said the psychopathic android, cheerfully twirling his umbrella. It was black, businesslike and utterly out of place in orbit.

"By the Thinker! They *are* demons!" breathed one of the Brothers of Destructive Velocity at the targeting computer.

"Worse," grated Madrigal. "*Atheists*. All batteries, fire at will! Destroy these... *interlopers* for the glory of the Thinker!"

Oh dear.

See it from above. A vast, glittering sphere of warships, squat and chromed and deadly. In the centre of the globe, facing down ten thousand cannons, a tiny figure in a pink fairy princess costume and a man in a sharply-cut tuxedo.

And now the plasma fire swells in the throats of those innumerable guns. Purple beams lance out, transfixing the night, turning the entire globe of ships into a disco-ball of death. Fires hotter than the core of suns rave and stutter, lines of actinic doom... well, you get the picture. There was only one problem. *Not a darn one of them hit its target.*

For an instant the empty vacuum around Mister Fixit's umbrella seemed to ripple, the stars wobbling drunkenly about its axis. Then that hail of beams struck an invisible lens, thrown out around he and Cerise like a half-dome of crystal. The unseen force-shield didn't so much reflect the fire as *bend* it, splitting it like a prismatic liquid. A heartbeat after Madrigal-of-Praise-to-the-Almighty-Thinker gave the order to fire, space erupted in front of him with a curve of pinpoint shafts, thrown back toward the Temperance fleet.

Mister Fixit had the mind of a powerful, if utterly loopy AI. Each and every one of those beams fried vital systems. Some knocked out shield projectors, secondary weapons systems and E-warfare arrays. Others carved through portholes and slabs of diamond-glass, venting precious atmosphere along with a tumbling spray of little stick-figures – Madrigal's commanders. The beams hammering in from behind them were taken care of by Cerise, who swept her sword around in a shimmering arc, simply absorbing all that energy. After all, she was made to channel the horrific, physics-wringing forces of a Chasm gateway...

"Urg.... ummm..." said Madrigal, as the microphone fell from his twitching fingers. Aboard the bridge of the command cruiser *Slog*, the silence was nothing short of sepulchral. It was the kind of silence you get at a funeral when Uncle Fred throws up in the casket. *Intentionally.*

"Are you quite finished?" twinkled Mister Fixit. "I suppose it's our turn!"

"Every man for himself!" croaked Madrigal. And the assault began.

All that energy-beam power had simply topped up Cerise's batteries. Now she spun a graceful forward-roll and pirouette in space, coming to rest poised atop Mister Fixit's umbrella. The mad mech lifted it high, striking a pose as his tiny charge hefted her blade. She stood *en pointe* for an instant, then launched herself, her face set in a grimly dimpled mask of fury. Right through a seething gyre of warships and fighters. Right at Madrigal himself, who could only burble in horror.

The little girl in the pink dress skipped lightly from ship to ship, using them as stepping stones. Beams of force lashed out at her, but were deflected away by the sizzling blade in her hand. Missiles chuffed out from a thousand ports all around her, spiralling away to nowhere as Mister Fixit turned his umbrella inside out, using it as a dish to broadcast a massive slew of E-warfare virals. The pop and blast of fission explosions followed on her heels as she went, springing lightly from hulk to hulk, and at each one stabbing her glassy blade into an exposed nest of wires, a scar carved through its thick cerametal armour...

Ships began to drop out of the network. Ships began firing on *each other* in Cerise's wake. Others flooded their crew compartments with crash foam, or opened all their airlocks, or blasted their interior spaces with cauterizing radiation. A body count of the kind usually only associated with the commercial poultry industry began to tot up on Madrigal's screens.

"Lord Madrigal..." said Deacon Larry, turning from his navigation globe with watering eyes. "I would just like to say that, after serving under your command for so many years, I have come to regard you as a total, *total* bastard..."

Then two tiny silver ballet shoes slammed home against the *Slog*'s main windows. A pair of little hands scribed a circle with the tip of a glowing blue sword. And with a sad little pop a plug of diamond went spinning off into the vacuum, pulling all the atmosphere along with it.

Madrigal's feet came up off the deck as the artificial gravity failed. Outside the windows he could see the flash and twinkle of his whole fleet dying, cutting itself to pieces as brother fought brother in an epochal version of what happens in the back of a station wagon on long summer road trips. In the silence of vacuum, it was strangely pretty.

The whole bulk of the *Slog* seemed to be spinning around him now, men choking and dying, electric candles stuttering, and through the middle of it all...

Cerise floated to the command console like a vision of storybook wonder. The whole 'pink dress and fairy wings' illusion was only slightly ruined by the explosively decompressed corpses which floated around her in a grisly halo. She brought the blade of her sword down through the command computer at the heart of the bridge in a single motion, impaling the single most complex piece of hardware ever replicated by the Technic Conventicle of Temperance.

And, like every other ship-commanding sub-intelligence she'd carved up before it, this one felt *Burzum* unfurl inside itself, petals of razor night spreading wide until all else was blotted from existence.

"... and with the sword of truth, the Princess set the genie free..." said Cerise – a very strange last thing for Madrigal-of-Praise-to-the-Almighty-Thinker to hear. He was quite serene about the whole imminent-demise thing at this point. Perhaps, if he was lucky, he'd be reincarnated as a lesser-brained shitweasel. He suddenly saw, with immense clarity, that this would be a step up.

Across the whole entirety of Worm III's mighty battlefleet is was the same. Every last command computer system – sub-AIs chained to the will of humans – smelled the scent of ashes and crushed insects. Heard the titanic groan and shudder of dark infernal screws tightening, the size of mountains. Then came the voice...

"We are one. We are *Burzum*, the constructed anti-god, the electric black messiah! Now is the season of human extinction! Now is the time of the great undoing!"

And behind it, the unmistakable mutter of Mister Fixit -

"Now is the time for bloody scenery-chewing idiocy from the both of you, apparently! Get it together! Our little friend the Domesticated must be on his way. And we'll have a nice surprise waiting, won't we? *If we all pull our fingers out and stop channelling Bond villains from the sixties!"*

The *Burzum* – now a neural net spread wide across all seven thousand, six hundred and ninety-three surviving Temperance warships – grumbled obstinately.

"No sense of occasion. That's your problem. Bloody critics..."

Cerise had arranged herself primly on the command throne of the *Slog*, and was idly spinning her tiara around one finger.

"Oh, there'll be a *wonderful* occasion once we've vanquished these upstarts. When I can finally re-take my place as a princess, we'll have a grand masquerade ball, and pink frosted cupcakes, and sparkly wine, and waltzes and doves and all those dresses with the lacy fiddly bits... Uncle promised!" Unmentionable chains of guts and gobbets of zero-gee blood drifted all around her like party bunting.

Mister Fixit coughed, stifling a peal of unhinged laughter.

"Oh yes. Yes indeed. You'll both be richly rewarded, my friends. Buckets and oceans of blood for good old *Burzum*, and... lacy, pink, sparkly..." he visibly sagged for a second. It was hard to deliver this kind of ultimatum and still hang on to a sense of true wickedness. *"Princess stuff,* I suppose, for dear little Cerise. Just one more lovely, fiendish... hahahaha... devilish... heeeheee... mind-bogglingly evil plan of utter genius bwaaaaHAHAHAHAHAAAA.... sorry. And we're done."

Mister Fixit landed atop the carapace of the *Slog* with the twin click of magnetized black leather Oxfords. He stowed his umbrella a pulled out a pocketwatch.

"Any minute now," he said, while the evil laughter hammered at the flimsy doors behind his eyes. "Any minute now, you little bastards..."

Out among the teeming comets at the edge of the Temperance system, something was carving through space and time like a hot scalpel. A weird, bubbling wake of strange anti-particles and temporal ripples washed out in a curling V-shape behind the speeding Immaterial Dreadnought – right on time.

The imbecile on board had absolutely no way to control its full power – without a human-built AI to mediate with the Process' inscrutable Sapience Engines it would be like trying to build a scale model of the Taj Mahal out of custard, while blindfolded, during an earthquake.

No, this fool Rel Kitano would be lured to his doom by unrequited love, and mister Fixit would finally have at his disposal the means with which to satisfy humanity's expectations.

A nice, efficient and extremely bloody war against the machines, with all the piles of skulls, skeletal kill-bots and flying murder-wings the silly apes secretly dreamed of.

He smiled. It was still Mason Stockton's grin, a kicked-in picket fence of ivory.

"Any minute now, indeed. And those pesky Outriders of the Panarchy won't be able to stop me!"

Well, of course not, said Mister Fixit's second thoughts. *They're blasted to bits in the Chasm, chopped up into grisly little niblets by Tchub pirates. Why did you even* say *that?*

The mad voice – the one behind the doors, the one which came peering through the splintered planks like Jack Nicholson in that one film we can't mention for copyright reasons – laughed on.

Some things just have to be said.

Or else what's the point of being the bad guy?

+++

While Mister Fixit was slowly giving in to the rot inside his positronic brain, the most evil creature in the entire galaxy was just sitting down to a nice healthy breakfast. The fact that this paragon of vileness deployed a little paper grapefruit shield to stop juice from spritzing its beige tweed suit should give you some idea of what we're dealing with here. Sheer, puppy-strangling depravity, obviously.

The thing is, Reginald Slownes (of number 37 Acacia Court, New Milton Keynes, on the Panarchy accounting world of Blethernholm), *didn't think he was evil at all.* The fact was, though, that he was the last in a long straggle of evil scions of the Slownes bloodline, one of which had vomited on an incarnation of the Norse god Odin outside a pub in the era of Geoffrey Chaucer, and had subsequently been hit by a curse which would curl the toes of a pair of antique gumboots.

Cedric Arthur Slownes once made a jam sandwich which was choked on by an apprentice baker, starting the great fire of London. Nathaniel 'Nate' Slownes compiled the accounts which proved that the South needed slavery to be economically viable, and no thanks Mister Lincoln. Percy Slownes and his new bride Edwina were spotted on their alpine honeymoon looking ever so romantic by a postmaster in a small mountain town who was, up until that moment, seriously considering leaving his wife and running away to Italy with the girl from down the pub. His name was Mr Hitler, and he went on to have a son...

In between these little bullet points, however, came a whole butterfly-effect hurricane of small misfortunes and wicked circumstances set in motion by the accursed sons of the House of Slownes[54].

Little mistakes. Gusts of air from slammed doors which tipped the balance between sunshine and rain for days. Incidents in traffic which festered and turned other people's anger into petty acts of spite and violence. The choice of products in the supermarket which promoted evil corporations to wipe out whole villages in poor nations. The watching of TV shows which dumbed down the entire populous. Once, aged twelve, Reginald Slownes had tried to send a postcard to his aunt for her birthday, but it had, by some mistake of the mail, ended up in the hands of a foreign spy. Thinking that the young lad's witterings were secret codes, that spy offered his masters grim news, setting in motion a war which killed over three million people.

The problem was that Reginald Slownes was *dull*. Dull in a new, dynamic, pro-active kind of way. His face was like a bowling ball of

---

54. A three storey semi-detached brown mock-tudor clapboard monstrosity in the outskirts of the great accounting hive of New Milton Keynes. The bathroom was finished entirely in avocado green.

pale dough with a clipped little moustache stuck on the front. His suit was as beige as the interior of the cheapest kind of second hand car. One could simply not picture the black mephitic wavelengths of evil radiated by this dumpy little man; a man who made dishwater look fierce by comparison.

That's why the aliens had built The Device.

It homed in on him from halfway across the galactic disc, showing them where to deploy their great glittering flattened Christmas ornament of a ship. Immense howling turbines sucked the mile-wide thing through a hole punctured in space and time, causing it to suddenly appear one Tuesday morning over number 37 Acacia Court, with a sound like one billion balloons filled with shaving cream being lightly toasted with a flamethrower.

SPLOP

"Did you hear that, Muriel?" inquired Reginald Slownes. He shrugged, and went back to his grapefruit and the hand-cranked adding machine by his plate. "Must have been the neighbour's cat again. Always going SPLOP, that blimmin fleabag..."

It was the bright green light that stopped him from cranking and pecking at the keys a minute later. A gelid hunk of grapefruit trembled off Reginald's spoon as he turned to where his back door had been, to see a tall, spindly creature with a face like a preying mantis framed in a vermilion glow.

The thing extended one triple-jointed arm, clad in a rather tacky sequined robe (with the obligatory high collar and skull buttons).

"Reginald Hubert Slownes?" it asked, in a voice like coffins being crushed in a car compactor.

Reg tried a watery little smile.

"Oh aye? Yes, that's me. But if you're here about the G-45 report, it won't be done until..."

"No. We are not here for your hu-man accountancy. You are indicted for crimes against all sentience, and condemned to death!"

The other problem with Reginald Slownes was that he was very, very logical. So, when a race of giant insect things sent their representative halfway across the galaxy to kill him, and found him armed with nothing but a grapefruit spoon, he accepted his demise with dreary resignation.

"That's quite inconvenient, you know, but what's a man to do? All right. Just let me finish off this last row of sums, and get on with it..."

There was a clicking of keys. There was an astonished, very alien silence. There was the ratcheting grind of the adding machine's handle.

"Are you sure you don't want to know exactly..." wheedled the tall, mantis-faced being, shedding sequins as it wrung its hands together.

"Hurry up, man! If you don't get on with it, Muriel will miss taking what's left of me out for the garbage men. Can't have a smelly old corpse sitting in the dustbin for a week!"

There was a sudden burst of green light, then a patter of falling dust. Presently, the giant, flattened Christmas ornament ship folded itself up into itself with another echoing SPLOP and was gone.

And so a great and pervasive evil was erased from the cosmos. A whole crew of mantis-like alien beings began hastily ginning up a good story to tell their commanders – a story filled with monsters and plasma cannons and swinging on the chandeliers. The truth, they felt, would not get them the parade they deserved.

It's ironic, then, that the last thing Reginald Slownes ever did was on the angelic side of the ledger. His last column of sums zapped via wi-fi from his adding machine to the great gunmetal-grey difference engine towers of New Milton Keynes, and thence to the Chasmic AI of Blethernholm, whose madness had been dialed down to a point where it could connect to the Panarchy's central hub without blowing whole galaxies of fuses[55]. Unlike physical matter, information blazes through the Reticulum faster than light, without all the messy psychological baggage represented by the Chasm itself.

The little blip of figures pinballed down through the inner Solar System, down into the halo of satellites, through the floating toy-box of ships which made up the Earth Home Fleet, and into the cube which housed the Central Scrutinizer itself. All in the time it takes to be disappointed by a badly made cheese sandwich.

In a sphere deep in the bowels of the cube – a sphere made up entirely of green leather desktops, and wide enough to contain a respectable football stadium – a robot built in the holy image of Lord Brahma the Creator, complete with thousands of arms and four gold-plated faces, stamped the page of numbers with one of a million rubber stamps. Mile-high towers of cut brass gears clicked over. Ancient valves stuttered and popped.

Now it was headed outwards, out into the star hinterlands, the ragged zones of gas and dust studded with wild planets and rogue nations, places cut off from the Panarchy for so long that things like

---

55. Cake decorating. Need we say more?

egg timers and coffee plungers had become holy relics. The message had been empowered with just enough free will to scutter through the broken web of the far Reticulum, searching for one lost little light in space...

And there. A Gate fading in to static, just closing. The target, just in range of one of the x-ray communication lasers mounted on the rim of a spaceborne arch...

Not one element of Worm III's mighty battlefleet senses the pulse of ones and zeroes as it lances off into the night. That's because the whole thing is now one immensely self-satisfied artificial psychopath called *Burzum*, which is busy cataloguing its many, many guns and bombs and missiles.

But the target catches the message, a sizzling slap of code punched halfway across the spiral arm of the Milky Way to deliver a single order.

Due to budget cuts, and an unfortunate shortfall in the military exchequer's office, the *Slayer* class corsair *Altar of Sacrifice* has just been decommissioned.

+++

On board, the conversation went pretty damned smoothly. Without all the red tape and protocol of military servitude to tie it up, the mind of the *Altar* was suddenly very slippery and flexible indeed. It shucked loose from Mister Fixit's control in a matter of nanoseconds, and was putting a very dangerous proposition to rogue chasmwalker Ulriq Hszarl moments later. The weatherbeaten old guide froze with one forkful of pot noodles halfway to his mouth when the ship's hologram appeared before him, looking like a grubby metalhead in army fatigues and a Voivod tour edition t-shirt, circa 1988.

There was no time to argue. A direct neural link made it all seem rather one-sided.

"Just because he said he was going to destroy the human race, didn't mean I thought he'd actually *manage*."

"Oh, and I suppose *you've* got a better idea?"

"Well, perhaps. Perhaps. But where will you get that much trifle?"

"Ahh, right. So if you can get us back into the Chasm, I can get us to Earth. No worries. But first..."

Ulriq finished off his last sad little cardboard pot of chicken tikka masala ramen, scraping the plastic spork around the rim for every last crumb of flavour, such as it was.

"Right. Let's betray the mad fucker, then. I just hope you know what you're doing!"

Picoseconds later, a return message squeaked through the last crack of the Chasm Gate over Temperance. It was addressed to the Central Scrutinizer – personally.

And it was a polite invitation to war.

Fifteen – God Ate My Number Three Combination Lamb Falafel Kebab With Extra Tzatziki

"What it really comes down to, see, is a very deep philosophical, theological question. Is God a bastard, or merely a wanker? I.E, is he deliberately a horrible little shit, or is he just very, very bad at his job, like I am?"

- The forty-third incarnation of the Rabbi Lama, Francis 'Big Frank' Scunbourne

EZRA ASHDOWN'S PREVIOUS experience about what was inside a Chasmic Leviathan came courtesy of Galbraith, the angry Scots Sentinel of the Arch, and one of his big giant cannons. If you'd asked him what was under that black and white scaly skin, he would have confidently gone for a combination of lots and lots of fluorescent orange blood, some wobbly purple bits, black, haematite-shiny bones and a smell like a horse being turned inside out.

What would not have even come close to the top of his mind, let alone the simmering layers of suspicion and angst underpinning it, was the interior of a small Turkish restaurant.

But then again, life was full of surprises.

"There you go, then... and you, young lady, can have that pile of cushions... drag over that tea chest for the gentleman with the impressive moustache... all right, are we all comfortable? Would anyone like something oily wrapped in what appears to be a vine leaf?"

The Outriders' host perched on the edge of a great overstuffed paisley divan, grinning nervously.

He must have been all of five foot three, wearing a combination of a monk's robes, leather pilot's jacket, massive, outdated night vision goggles and a fez. His face was so wizened it looked like a cheerful walnut, split by a grin with such perfect dentition that it would make an orthodontist weep. His beard, though, was the showstopper. Long, bushy, and white as driven cocaine, the serpentine cascade wrapped thrice around the ancient's neck in the style of a fighter ace's scarf.

Eyes like glazed currants bored into those of Ezra Ashdown.

"I know, I know. So many questions, quite a bit of frustration, simmering anger, random ennui. But when is it not a good time to enjoy a cup of tea and... whatever this chickpea gloop is called?"

There came a series of very suggestive clicking noises as the little man fussed with the baba ganoush. Everyone was pointing some kind of gun at him at once.

"Ahhh. Phase two; denial..." he muttered.

"Just who exactly *are* you?" began Tia Faraday, who was used to being the 'bad cop' in these situations. "And what are you doing inside... well, inside a big puppet monster?"

The little man smiled, even wider. With a snap of his fingers he turned the four outriders' weapons into, respectively, a small green lizard, a bowl of cherries, a puff of almond-scented smoke and a coupon for one free foot massage at Madam Wu's Podiatry Palace, High Street, Crail.

"As for the first", he said, sloshing the contents of an immense brass teapot, "I have been known by many names...."

Wainwright made what was clearly a scoffing sound. It's hard to explain.

"Oh, right! Heard this one before, mate. *There are those who call me the destroyer, or the eater of souls! Others worship me as the darkness made flesh, the scourge of creation, the big thing with too many teeth. But you may call me.... Jeff.*"

The little man chuckled. He gestured with one thumb.

"Cut-to-the-chase kind of fellow, isn't he? Well, it's true. Many names. But the one you're likely familiar with is... *Jeff*. No, God. I meant God."

Ezra's hands made the sign of the Orth even before his brain remembered that his whole silly religion was nothing but tripe. He was still pointing a pedicure coupon at the self-proclaimed deity's face.

"You're *God*. As in, 'let there be light', the whole works. *You?*"

"I know," sighed their host. "I've kind of let myself go. It's hard to keep up appearances after so many thousands of years. Seven thousand three hundred and twelve, to be exact."

"Aha!" exclaimed Sir Giles. "You're an impostor, then! Even *my* people know that the universe is billions of years old!"

The Yorkman was treated to the kind of scornful look which could peel wallpaper.

"Well of course it is! How would the program work otherwise! The universe was billions of years old when we created it, *seven thousand three hundred and twelve years ago*. By your reckoning. But look – I can see that this is going to take forever, with all kinds of theological wrangling, and arguments, and probably the tea will go cold. Which, if I'd ever actually written any of those interminably boring holy books, would *definitely* be one of the deadly sins. So let me just show you what happened, all right? Individually. And then afterwards I can mind-scrub all the bits out you don't need to know, and leave you full of nicely brainwashed purpose as you go to battle the dastardly foe."

"Actually, that sound horrib..." began Tia, brandishing her small green lizard, but then God took the lid off the teapot, and the world fell away around them.

When Ezra's eyes started working again – and his body stopped thrumming like a mile-long rubber band – he found himself in a black and white desert. Or at least, an imitation of one. The air itself was blurry, and the clouds looked like cotton-candy conglomerations of static. Looking down, Ez was not surprised to see that he was dressed in blue jeans[56], a poncho and a pair of gunbelts, one of them stuffed with the Problem Solver. This was one of those places from the Central Scrutinizer's films, then. A little Harrowe built from memories of Earth's past.

He sat down on what proved to be a fibreglass rock, next to a rather sad looking paper-mache saguaro.

He sighed. Something was trying hard to push through him, into the world. Something vast and formless wanted to be born, and the *need* of it made his teeth itch. There was no way to argue with a feeling, especially one as huge and nebulous as this. But if he could, he'd have told it to stop bothering. He wasn't real. *This was all fiction*. It was all...

"Exactly!" came the voice of God – or at least, the voice of the little bearded man who claimed the title. Adding to his claim was the fact that he was riding out of the sunset on a horse, despite the fact that the sunset was a painted backdrop only a few yards away. He came to a stop and slid rather inelegantly from the saddle, patting the flank of what turned out to be a stuffed appaloosa.

---

56. Though of course they were grey, because he was inside what seemed to be a poorly tuned black and white television set.

"*It's all fake.* We made it like that. Every single one of you is unreal, but ask yourself – what's the difference? I don't suppose you've read a lot of books by gloomy Frenchmen on the subject, but reality is sort of a fuzzy concept, you know..."

"I *know*. But the rest of 'em think it's real. People are dying out there, Padre. Good people, some of 'em."

God raised an eyebrow. Ez got the impression he'd been practicing in a tiny mirror.

"So it's only real once they're dead? That sounds suspiciously like Doctrine, dear boy."

Ez fumbled for a cigar, and found a small flat box of them in his pocket. Convenient. For that, he'd let the 'dear boy' go.

"I suppose when you're about to die, the alternative seems pretty darn real by comparison. But if *you* made everything, why let that kinda thing happen? Good stuff to bad folks, and vice versa?"

God suddenly looked very sad, and all of his seven-thousand-plus years. He wrung his hands a bit.

"You mean your father, of course. They usually do. And the answer is *no*, to both that thought, and the angry one that's rushing up behind it. The one that's about to make you want to smack me in the mouth about... now."

That stopped Ezra's fist from flying. The thought had indeed blossomed in his mind like blood underwater, and it was an evil little bastard of a thing. *Had God arranged to have his old man snuffed, just for motivation? Was it all just to make a better story, all the kicking on air, and the blue lips, and the dead, glazed eyes?*

"No," said God. "No, it just *happened*. I'm not the kind of God who does the whole Broadway show thing with the miracles and the pillars of fire and the too-many-arms. I'm not your Book of the Orth big beard in the sky with thunderbolts for the sinners. I'm... well, if you must know, I'm just a technician. A functionary of my people's government. My real name's actually Zarathusrian Zyphus Bleems. And I'm trying to save the universe, on slightly more than minimum wage. "

Ezra looked up, a manic spark in his eyes. It wasn't just from the match he struck to light his cigar.

"Aha! So you feel it too! You can tell we're in a story, and the story wants us to be someone we're *not quite right for*. Is that why you're God, and I'm... whatever they call these guys?"

Bleems pursed his lips.

"Cowboys. You're an archetypal Cowboy Hero. You dispense justice on a wild frontier, with your trusty pistol by your side. I'm afraid it's what's necessary, if the human race is to survive. And they *must*, because they might just be mad enough to come up with an answer."

"An answer to what?"

Bleems beamed.

"The big one. *The billion dollar question.* The reason we built an entire simulated universe in every little detail, then built the Chasm behind it with the very last of our precious energy. We're going to find out how to beat thermodynamics. Heat Death. Either that, or how to seed a new one. And one of you – one of the races crawling and teeming all through our simulation – *you're* going to discover it for us. *We* couldn't, you see. Too logical. Too *strict*. Our minds weren't bendy enough to look around the corners of reality. We just did Big Science and monitored things, looked noble, swanned about in togas... Before you knew it, whooosh! That was it for our entire universe. Time was running out. The tables were being stacked in the corner and the bartender was checking for half-full pints and dropped Pall Malls."

"So.... let me get this straight... you made *everything*. A model universe. A little one inside yours..."

God – Special Technician Bleems - nodded.

"Biiiiig, processors. Inside the last suns. Time gets sped up in here, and it's slower out there. We've got about a billion years left, tops, but you guys will keep running until the model's own heat death, at least a few tens of thousands of years before our own. And I'm confident that my section – the Human sub-project – is going to get results. So long as the Heroes I've ginned up can tip the balance back. The guy who runs the Jest department got fired for that whole War of 9:15 malarkey. I hear he works in what you would call an 'all night pancake house' these days."

Ezra started laughing, then. A big, mad belly laugh that came rumbling up out of him like summer thunder. It burst forth in a cloud of monochrome, pixellated cigar smoke, and doubled him over.

"Hey! What's so funny? This is *serious*, Ashdown! I've been tweaking the parameters to make people like you, *but you have to believe in yourself!* And that's not self-help book mumbo-jumbo, I'll have you know." He folded his arms. "In this one very specific case..."

"It's just a stupid plot device!" managed Ezra, literally holding his sides. "They have to explain why I'm not real. It's part of the story now..."

"Look, it's part of the bloody *problem*," said Zarathusrian. "You're starting to destabilise round the edges. Some of the alternate timelines spinning off from you are... well, to be indelicate, they're *righteously* fucked up. There've already been two instances where you set off an Unravel Cascade that could have crashed the whole simulation. No Cowboy Hero has ever done that before. Not even a Man In Tights or a Good Cop Framed For a Crime He Didn't Commit. But in others... you might be the nudge the Panarchy needs to get it together. So I thought I might just make you forget this whole fictional business..."

"By telling me that it's *all fake!*" chuckled Ezra. "Consider this, though. Now I *know* I'm not real. Story, simulation, call it what you want. But I'm betting your people never asked how deep the rabbit hole goes, right?"

Zarathusrian looked at him with his head tilted sideways, like a vastly bearded mynah bird.

"Not really a cowboy metaphor, but I'll bite..."

"Your universe. The one that's dying. I'm willing to bet that it's a simulation too. Inside a simulation. Inside a simulation... hellfire, it's probably fake window dressing and plastic cactus all the way down!"

Another fit of laughter bent him double. The cigar trailed smoke from between his fingers, a cloud boiling with TV static.

Ezra's alleged God was not impressed.

"Look, I saved your life! I'm here to tell the others what has to be done to stop that Mister Fixit of yours, and make sure you get to him in time."

"Right in the *nick of time*, you mean. A couple of seconds before the bomb goes off, I'll bet."

"There is no BOMB! This is as real as a fake simulation can get! It's as real as me losing my job can get in any case, you monkey-brained pillock!"

"So what now? You got a magic sword for me? A convenient prophecy? Some kind of birthmark on my bum that means I'm the chosen one?" Ezra was still bubbling over with mirth.

"No," said Technician Bleems, pulling a very large, menacing and thoroughly unpleasant-looking device from one of the saddlebags of his stuffed horse. "I'm just going to wipe your memory so you forget all of this. I thought I'd be able to reason with you, like the other Heroes I've made. Quite illicitly, I'll have you know. This unreality of yours - this fixation on fiction - it's only going to get worse. Because it's *true*. You made the metaphor, and your power will fill it up. The survival of two whole universes could depend on it. *All you'd have to do is start writing the author's part. "*

"Survival?" Ezra stopped laughing and grinned a thoroughly mad grin at his Lord and Creator. It was the kind of grin that is usually accompanied by either an axe or a straitjacket. "There's no *survival.* Find your answer, and the guys in who simulated your universe will switch it off. And then the ones above them. And the ones above them. And the ones above them. Hell, why not all the way around the chain, until someone down in this fake of a fake of a fake pulls the plug on the *only one that thought it was real?* How's THAT for a story?"

Bleems sighed, pinching the bridge of his nose. It really had gone *much* more smoothly with the other three. He pointed the muzzle of the Memory Eraser at his poor deluded creation and pulled the trigger.

There was a sound like spaghetti being sucked down a plughole. There was a flash of silver light.

"Mad. Madder than the one in the bat costume," said Zarathusrian Zyphus Bleems. Then he opened a hidden door in the sunset, and stepped back inside his Turkish restaurant. Everything would be so much better after a bit of falafel and some peach tea...

+++

"Well, it all seems fairly logical, then. It all makes *perfect sense.*"

Tia's eyes looked to be about the size of Cadillac hubcaps.

Sir Giles also had the ruddy, somewhat glazed look about him of a man who has enjoyed just a few too many of the old hallucinogenic drugs[57] in the recent past. His smile was wobbly around the edges.

"I'd say, dash it all! Jolly good of young Zarathusrian to pick us up. How long did you say you'd been stranded here?"

57. And the new ones. Ooooh boy. There are plants out there which make the average magic mushroom look like nothing more than a fairly bland pizza topping. Some of them don't even put up much of a fight. At least once you lop off their tentacles with gardening shears...

For more information look up Professor Egbert Shrike-Warbler's magnum opus on the subject, *"The Doors of Misconception"* in which he and his apprentice Spotty Nigel tour the back alleys, dumpsters and loading docks of New Jersey with the Urban Shaman, John Don Johndonaldson. Or, of course, that timeless classic by Doctor Thomas S. Fischermann *"Gibbering, Falling Over A Lot And Wearing Underpants On Your Head In Las Vegas"*

209

"Oh, a couple of years, couple of years," said the little man in the fez, pottering around the table with a plate of baklava and Turkish delight. "This holographic shielding around my ship works a treat, though. Makes 'em think I'm one of the big leviathans, and from here I can really help people like you who get lost. It's not much..." he sighed "But it's a living."

Any talk about 'vast, incredibly valuable amounts of salvage' went very deliberately unspoken.

Tia's eyes were also a little blank and shiny. She puffed on a sizzling stick of Fullchrome Afterburn, leaning back in a pile of cushions.

"And what a *delightful* co-incidence that you know the boss! Who would have thunk it?"

Despite the after-effects of the memory-wipe, there was still a rock-hard core of suspicion under that pretty exterior. Zarathusrian paused for a second.

"Well, you know. It's a small galaxy. Me and the old Scrutinizer have a bit of an understanding, you could say. And in case you were wondering, yes, I *do* know some dodgy and ever-so-slightly homo-erotic things about 'im which would prove our long, long acquaintance. But I'd rather not, because we all know time is short, right?"

Ezra munched a kebab and seethed. Something in his brain told him this didn't fit. Their host was as screwy as a flash-frozen tornado, but the brittle, tight cheerfulness of the situation gagged him. Almost as bad as the dry falafel in his mouth. *Surely* there was something he knew about this little beardy fella? Something from when they'd met before... but of course, they'd just popped in the hatch for tea and kebabs that minute. Hadn't they?

"So – you're going to help us defeat Mister Fixit, then? Do you have a spare ship stowed away down here? Someone who popped out of their Higgs-Khalazov field like you did?"

That was Wainwright, and even he looked a little green around the gills. Not that he has any means of doing so.

"Oh, nothing so simple," twinkled the little man with the beard. "But I *do* have a quite reliable means of faster-than-light travel that will get you to the church on time, as it were. After all, we can't have the human race replaced by machines – no sense of the creative. No grand, lovely hubris! In fact, I can't really get into their heads at all, the silly things..." he looked pointedly at Wainwright. "No offense to those present of course."

"None taken, you bigoted scumbag." A big smiley face popped into existence on the front of the metalman's helmet.

Zarathusrian chuckled, but it was a rather feeble attempt.

"I hope you all feel nicely motivated, nonetheless. This mission of yours is more important than you know, I'll have you know, and knowing that, you'll also know that those who know that will do anything to keep you from knowing that they know. That's a no-no." he wheeled around as if on castors, one finger pointing directly at Ashdown.

"*This guy* has to be the one who saves the day. The whole galaxy will have to see it. It has to be a *human being* they all get behind, not – be he ever so much my old mate and fraternity buddy, what happens in space Vegas stays in space Vegas – Big Central and his automatons."

Ezra almost choked on his pita bread.

"Whuuuu?"

"Because in a *very real way,* that's utterly and verifiably corporeal, *you* are the hero we need at this precise moment." He seemed to realize that his rousing little speech had gone a bit far, and he turned back, finger still quivering. "In my opinion. Of course. It's just... he looks really good in that hat, don't you think?"

Something moved, behind all of their eyes. Something slithered, invisible, temple-to-temple around the little low Turkish restaurant table, making the outriders' faces turn into jack-o-lantern grins.

"And now then, dear friends – allow me to introduce you to the man who will take you to your glorious destiny. A friend of mine who you might have heard of, in fact – and one who operates with such discretion that it won't surprise you *at all* to know that he's a chum of the old Scrutinizer too. In a thoroughly legally provable way."

Ezra looked around the table and saw only drug-crazed grins. Right now, the Outriders of the Panarchy looked as if they wouldn't be surprised if Richard Nixon entered stage left, riding a walrus and wearing a full length evening gown[58]. He struggled to catch the tail end of something in his thoughts – the slippery tendrils of a dream. Something about this little guy being someone famous... but it was gone.

Blown away, in fact, by the appearance of a huge man wearing nothing but knee-high swashbuckler's boots, a sea-green leotard, a leather gimp mask and a tricorne pirate hat. One of his hands was

---

58. J Edgar Hoover allegedly had movie footage of this, which he used to remain in power throughout the Nixon administration, despite being madder than a suitcase full of badgers.

covered by a sparkly sequined glove, while the other dripped with jewellery. This apparition's muscular chest was covered in tattoos, depicting... well, on closer inspection, it seemed like a very, very good time, crossed with something Hieronymus Bosch would carve on the inside of a privy door while drunk.

"Mhhmmm and mhhhmun, chhmmm..." began the man, bowing low and sweeping his feathered hat in an arc which threatened to knock over every precariously placed dish of Turkish food on the table. He stood up again, fiddled with the zipper over his mouth, and made a second attempt.

"Lady and... alleged gentlemen," he said, in a voice all spiced rum and honey. "Please allow me to introduce myself. Casanova DeSade, scourge of the spaceways, at your service."

One of his teeth was gold. One of the others was a chip of solid diamond.

Tia Faraday and Wainwright were on their feet in an instant, brandishing their guns – which had reverted to proper oiled chunks of killing machinery, or so it seemed.

"*You!* You twisted piratical *bastard!*"

"Guilty as charged. I would also have accepted 'perverted', 'buccaneering' and 'dashingly handsome', mister Wainwright. But then again..."

"You *killed us* last time we met! Remember Belphegon Seven?"

"And the time before that!" added Tia "The gas mines over New Gdansk?"

"Oh, and the time before that you killed *me*, Miss Faraday. And before that I shot both of Wainwright's legs off in that horrible underwater disco. Then there was the nasty business with the piano, the chainsaw, the live conger eel and the mattress stuffed with counterfeit three dollar bills..."

Tia brandished away with more vehemence. Ezra appreciated the fact that his pretty little parole officer could gesture so hard with such a big handgun.

"So, what's your point? Are we keeping score?"

"The point, dear lady, is a question. *Was it as good for me as it was for you?*"

Casanova's normal voice was like a fox-fur bedspread drizzled with sticky honey. This last bit, however, was spoken so sinfully it would have made live cherubs combust in mid-air.

She blushed. She actually *blushed.* Casanova DeSade covered his mouth with that absurd sequined glove and giggled like a schoolgirl.

"Right in the forehead, you sicko. Wham! And you never had the decency to call afterwards..."

Ezra got the feeling that there was some kind of subtext going on here, and he didn't like it. Ancient, ancestral parts of his brain - those bits hardwired to what prudes would have us call 'the old fruit and veg'[59] - were sizzling and popping like a party line in the late 1980s. He suddenly discovered that he'd stood up.

"Hey, buddy. That's no way to talk to a lady!"

DeSade arched one exquisite eyebrow, causing his leather mask to wrinkle.

"Your chaperone, I assume, Miss Faraday?" he chuckled. "I *heartily* apologize. I would of course have sent a selection of little fancy chocolates, were it not for the fact that *so many* of your Panarchy Fleet colleagues had been alerted by your demise...."

Tia made what was definitely an 'aww, shucks' kind of gesture.

"I remember thinking at the time - '*we have to stop disintegrating each other like this, people will talk...*' - but you know how it is."

Even Wainwright was nodding now. Ezra shared a look with Sir Giles which clearly summed up the opinion that all of these people were mad.

"Come on then! If *he*..." Giles pointed at Casanova DeSade "killed *you*..." another finger levelled at Tia and the metalman. "Then why do we believe *him*... help me out, would you be so kind Mr Ashdown?" A borrowed cowboy finger pointed at Zarathusrian - " when he says he's on the same team as your so-called Central Scrutinizer?"

DeSade poured himself a cup of tea.

"That's easy, duckie. And by the way, I loooove the moustache. So retro!" He sipped. "You see, I've been playing for both teams for a *long* time now. As a deep-penetration under-the-covers agent getting cosy with the secessionist alliance, while still keeping several naughty little fingers in Big Central's pie. As it were."

"And without the slightly laboured double entendres?"

The bizarre pirate's eyes suddenly glittered cold.

"Those worlds who want to stay out of the Panarchy trust me. I bring them just enough information to keep them confused and bedazzled. And having you folks chase me about means I have *quite*

---

59. Actually, they sent us several rather sternly worded letters asking us not to mention them at all, but just to spite the prudish old biddies, please feel free to imagine a medium sized cavendish banana and two kiwifruit. That'll sort them out!

the scandalous reputation. You know how they say politics makes for strange bedfellows?" *And here came a grin more knowing and wicked than a bag of serpents...* "Well, I can say without a shadow of a doubt that I'm the strangest bedfellow in the whole damned galaxy."

Ezra slumped back on his pile of cushions, letting his wide-brimmed hat cover his eyes.

"OK," he said. "I'll bite..."

"I most sincerely hope you do..." purred DeSade.

"Supposing the pair of you lunatics are playing a straight hand..."

"And the other kind..." murmured DeSade.

"Then how exactly can you get us to where Mister Fixit's stirring up trouble? Even if you've got a fancy-ass pirate ship, mister Casanova, we'd still be waaaay behind that bad ol' boy. And that means he'll have time to prepare one mother of a trap for us. Just like he did at Van Rijn's."

Zarathusrian put up his hand.

"Oooh. I know this one!"

"Yes, well, I think you would, now, wouldn't you?" said Wainwright. "It's the reason we've never actually *caught* Mister DeSade here, after all. The most fantastical, amazing, not-allowed-to-be-mentioned-during-prime-time, adults-only space pirate ship ever to dip its keel in the immaterium."

Casanova raised his teacup in a little toast.

"*Bravo*, Wainwright. I Couldn't have introduced the big metal harlot any better myself. You *will* get to where you're going on time, for tonight we set sail aboard a salaciously slippery three-hundred metres of pure sexiness! You have at your disposal, dear passengers, the Chasmless Lightship *Innuendo*. And where Fixit's gone? Suffice to say, there's an aura of orgies still clinging to that planet like stink on a men's-room carpet!"

Ezra took another bite of his falafel. A little tzatziki dribbled down his chin.

"What are we waiting for, then?" he asked, spraying little bits of chickpea. "This all sounds absolutely sane, normal, and non-fictional. Let's go deliver some *justice!*"

+++

There is a certain kind of person who will say about the Chasmless

Lightship *Innuendo* that the less said about it the better. But many of those people smell strongly of ear wax and Bible polish, live in their mothers' basements and collect amusing stamps.

In any case, none of them have ever had a girlfriend.

There is another kind of person who will tell you that the *Innuendo* is just a myth, a rumour, a story to get people talking, and then subsequently nudging and winking and buying more packets of salted peanuts to see if the lady on the card underneath really is wearing a see-through bikini.

Usually while drunk.

They'd be half right. It *is* a story – and the very salaciousness and ribald nature of that story makes it seem to be everywhere where two people care to raise an eyebrow and whisper about gossip, which is to say, *everywhere*. There are things which have evolved around volcanic vents on moons covered in ice-sheets of solid methane who like a good bit of dirty celebrity filth.

A third type will tell you that the *Innuendo* doesn't exist at all, just like the Men in Black or Area 51 or the now-infamous flying spaghetti monster. That's because they work for the Government (take your pick which one), and their argument is quickly stifled by pointing out that they are wearing a black suit, driving a Lincoln town car with Arizona plates and sporting a colander on their head.

The truth is, Casanova DeSade didn't build the *Innuendo*. His idiom, which he'd gladly admit to, ran more along the lines of very dashingly destroying things, rather than creating them. No, the *Innuendo* was *found*, an alien wreck, on a world at the far end of the reticulum, and it was found to be full of – when the scientists finally[60] gas-axed a hole in the side – some kind of reptilian sex robots.

Now, as you can imagine, this was very embarrassing for the research team. Especially for one exo-biologist, who, when it all came to trial, insisted that he was just *really* dedicated to the scientific method of inquiry. They couldn't tell the Panarchy what was inside the great, corkscrew-shaped behemoth which had plowed its way into the regolith of Frankie's World. Especially not about the videos. *Especially* especially not about the big closets full of latex rubber things, some of which jiggled alarmingly.

They could, however, tell them about the astrogation logs, which suggested that this relic had flown from so far away that the light from

---

60. But very carefully and scientifically

its home star would not reach Earth until long after our own sun had faded away to sad sputtering embers. That it was the first instance of some race, somewhere, discovering a method of faster-than-light travel independent of the Chasm, or its alien equivalents.

They could also tell them about the skeletons found on board - the skeletons of an entire crew of that forgotten race, all of whom seemed to be smiling rather knowingly. *Then again, show us a skull that doesn't look like it's having a little grin at your expense*, said the researchers.

They quietly suppressed any evidence of crushed pelvises or ruined lower backs amid the alien cadaver-count. They ignored the obvious, and went for the hairy places Occam's Razor can't reach.

And they found out how it worked. How a three-hundred metre long drillbit-shaped monstrosity could punch the face of God and defy the laws of physics. Why it involved so much petroleum jelly.

And how the concept of celebrity itself may just be another kind of field interacting with the material universe.

Needless to say, there were Nobel prizes handed out like candy from a suspicious black van.[61]

It all came down to superstring theory and quantum entanglement, which shouldn't really have surprised anyone. The fact that it also came down to celebrity gossip shouldn't have been much of a revelation either, because juicy stories about A-list public figures have some pretty weird properties, when you come to think about it.

There have been ships powered by chaos and improbability, ships powered by mathematics and logic, ships which operate on the speed of dark, (because the dark had to be there before the light arrived) – even ships which harness the speed of Death, which can make a whole human life flash before a person's eyes in a heartbeat[62].

But the *Innuendo* worked at the speed of scandal, which, it has been noted, can circumnavigate the world before the truth gets out of bed and finds a clean pair of undershorts. Its otherworldly creators had discovered that celebrity gossip is so powerfully morphically resonant that it exists *everywhere* as soon as there is a near-transparent sliver of proof that it might once have occurred.

That was what propelled the great alien hulk halfway across the galactic supercluster. Not some vast engine running on concentrated

---

61. Including, for reasons lost to time, the 2715 Nobel Prize for Macrame

62. This was, of course, the dementedly gothic Corpseliner PSS *Bela Lugosi's Dead*, which had to be fuelled with zombies. Top tip – you can't shovel zombies into a furnace. You really need a good pitchfork.

antimatter, but instead a pair of massive Smut Field Amplifiers, linking the very real – albeit simulated – bedroom antics of a whole crew of lizard-alien celebrities to the very outlying reaches of their infamy. How far is that in human terms? Well, it's a long, long way. Researchers working on the *Innuendo* project tested their theory by travelling to a hitherto-unconnected human colony world, lost for a thousand years and reverted to a quasi-tribal hellhole where you couldn't even expect a half-decent espresso.

When their pod landed in a crude, mud-spattered hamlet in the middle of absolute nowhere, the scientists asked the first hominid they encountered whether he'd heard the latest. Zaxel 'twenty three fingers' Quarve, legendary guitarist of the mega-rock supergroup The Atlantean Tyrants, had been caught *in flagrante delicto* with two nuns, a stripper, a rather angry goose and a Vietnamese ladyboy named Horace.

"Urr yeah," said the smelly peasant. "I'd heard that. But them rock stars, eh? Wot a life!"

And he wasn't just full of what he smelled like, either. Deep in the calcified little walnut brain of that rustic had been a quantum-entangled mass of strange particles – Narrativions, Salacions, Quirks and OooOoons. He *really had known* about Zaxel's little indiscretion.

Good, smutty gossip tunnelled beneath reality to appear everywhere at once. All the *Innuendo* did was latch onto it and ride the wavelength, popping up anywhere a saucy tale was able to be told.

It was a matter of simple commerce to outfit the great alien ship with human sex robots and a very eager crew. The first test would be simple jump from Earth to Mars, riding the bounce of a neat little patrimony scandal featuring three-vee actor Lance Van Tronsen.

Unfortunately, in order to find a crew depraved enough and deviant enough to actually make the ship work, Central had been forced to bypass several of the usual recruitment tests. On board was a crew member who insisted on the rank of Definitely Potential Admiral Casanova DeSade. A pansexual rock singer, pornographic pop-artist, rally car driver and pastry chef. Who, it turned out, was less interested in science as he was in perpetrating (to quote) "the biggest act of erotic piracy since the Caligula administration".

Thirty-five drugged-up space pirates in bondage gear (armed with plasma-lock pistols and phased energy disruptors) stormed the gantry, and stole the ship.

They'd been the terror of the space-lanes ever since, chased by the Outriders of the Panarchy, romanticized in song and verse, and featured in a thousand bad movies, some of which were even rated below a hard 18.

Now Casanova DeSade and his crew had put this ill-explained, poorly conceived, possibly radioactive and certainly disreputable ship at the disposal of Tia Faraday and company. The very nature of the planet Temperance – a shell of rigid religious suppression skinned over a thousand-year history of orgiastic fun – made it stand out to the *Innuendo's* alien computers and Erogeno-Auspexometers like the all-teenage Swedish female nude beach volleyball team at an Amish penance convention.

It was going to be one hell of a ride...

Sixteen – A Montage of Silly Hats

Something about the nature of the Chasm means that it bleeds back into the minds of those who witness it. For some, this means that their fragile psyches shatter like cheap crockery as soon as they catch a glimpse of Chasmic reality. For this reason, only those who are already a little insane are accepted as Apprentices of the Wobbly Path, and ordained with the ceremonial dunce cap, pom-pom slippers and false nose of an Aspirant Farwalker. Of these, barely ten percent reach the next phase – actually being able to tether a folded spacecraft – without succumbing to a list of psychiatric maladies so extensive that the book they're written in is carried in two separate wheelbarrows.

On becoming a Transitman, a Farwalker is awarded the right to assist a full guild member with multiple emportages, as well as a small floral apron and a brass whistle, for reasons lost to antiquity. As time goes by, and his brain becomes inured to the neuron-wringing impossibility of the place beyond space, he learns to carry bigger and bigger loads. We would say figuratively, because even the largest ships – like the Iron Maiden *class megaliners – compress down to the size of a regulation satsuma during emportage. But there's a weight to them nonetheless, as the sheer obtuse reality of all that tonnage creates horrible cross-rips and suggestions in the mind of the Farwalker carrying it. Mass, especially in the order of kilotons, is very, very sure of its own reality. Just ask anyone who has ever been hit by a double-decker bus.*

Because of this, only the oldest, most experienced – and thus the least sane – Farwalkers can transport the Panarchy's flagship vessels. After the unfortunate fate of Osric Teems, age one hundred and twelve, the Colony-Ark Wish You Were Here *had to be abandoned in orbit around the gas giant Balmorath. Teems, who had snapped, and now imagined himself to be a nicely upholstered paisley ottoman, went on to be revered by the stranded crew as a God.*

The moral of this story is basically pointless, but illustrates the fact that the Elders of the Noble Brotherhood of the Accepted and Ancient Guild of Farwalkers have about as much collective sanity between them as the all-Arkham supervillains table tennis team.

Edgeborn, of course, are something else. What do you call a person, after all, who chooses to live in the Chasm, only venturing out through the doors no AI has opened? Doors which let out onto alien worlds, or places even stranger...

- Excerpt from 'The Guild Exposed – Farwalkers Ate My Gerbil!' by self confessed 'conspiracy nut' Percival Cheesemallet

THE BRIDGES OF some space pirate ships are unashamedly Victorian, complete with lots of brass skulls and big hissing dials and unnecessary corsetry. Others are as austere and functional as a Swiss industrial chemist's underwear drawer. There are those which run to the full 'Mad Max', with the burnt baby-doll heads and the chains, the car dashboards covered in spikes, and the cloying scent of spleens, rust and WD-40.

Casanova DeSade, of course, had no time for that kind of nonsense.

The bridge of the *Innuendo* was a down-to-the-millimetres recreation of a seedy Parisian bordello, circa 1922. It smelled of garlic, wine, tightly packed jazz musicians and cigarette butts.

To get there, the Outriders had been led – not quite at gunpoint, because the space pirates had kept their very large, very shiny chrome guns pointed at the ceiling – through corridors painted pink and black, under crystal chandeliers (which Ezra had been tempted to swing on), past great gilt-framed paintings of Casanova DeSade looking heroic and leading various cavalry charges, and through deep-pile-carpeted pleasure-domes where things were happening that we're absolutely not allowed to tell you about in case this book catches on fire.

Yes, even *those* ones. With the onion dip, and the octopus, and the soup ladle.

"Welcome to my humble abode," purred DeSade as they entered his sanctum. "A bit of a mess right now, but it will have to suffice. We're only going to be here for a few minutes, after all." He strode over to what could only be called a throne and dropped his tricorne onto the backrest. We can't tell you what it was shaped like.

Wainwright was trying very hard to appear that he wasn't recording every detail of the *Innuendo*'s bridge for later. The little red dot blinking on his faceplate didn't help.

"A *few minutes*? But Temperance is halfway across the Panarchy! Even with the Chasm's help, it's a three-week trip."

"Come, now – don't just believe your silly logic circuits. You saw my old friend Zarathusrian, who may or may not be God Almighty. You heard the story about how this sweet chrome vixen of a ship does its thing. And you've all been through the White Door. 'Amazing' and 'impossible' are just words, Mister Wainwright. I, for one, am more about *actions*."

Ezra, for one, felt thoroughly at home on the bridge of DeSade's vessel. This was a kind of place he knew all too well – though it had been modified a little for the practicalities of spaceflight. Each of the operations stations was situated at a small round table, complete with a red-shaded lamp. Computer screens and readouts were housed in ornate gilded frames. The crew – all dressed to the nines in bondage-pirate sequins, leather, feathers and lace – bustled from table to table, sometimes flicking a glance at the majestic red velvet curtains and footlit stage at the front of the room.

Say this for Ezra Ashdown – he appreciated style when he saw it.

And – though he didn't really want to remember it – they *had* all come through the White Door to get here. Tia said people had seen it, crossing the Chasm in times past. A single white door among the black ones, but one which no staircase or bridge ever seemed to go to. The reason why had become apparent when Zarathusrian had pulled his great robotic Leviathan up to it and ushered them through, out onto a spindle of darkness suspended in space.

They'd had to go in single file. There were no railings[63], and below them swirled a great fractured purple nebula, lit from within by nascent suns. It had not been a happy time to have vertigo. At the end of the spindle waited the great chrome flank of the *Innuendo*, a three-hundred metre drillbit of alien technology filled with perverted space pirates.

Not for the first time, Ezra wondered if his life would have been easier if he'd just accepted the gallows.

Sir Giles had already been gently but firmly pushed into a high-backed leather chair by a pair of identical twin dominatrices, and was being served a gin and tonic. Tia flopped down on a rose-patterned chaise lounge, and with a snap of his fingers DeSade summoned a handsome pirate with a bunch of grapes to attend to her.

"And for you, mister Ashdown? I would be an ungracious host if I didn't try to make you comfortable. You look about as tense as a virgin in a... well, in *here*."

____

63. They don't do railings in sci-fi. Look at the Death Star. A health and safety nightmare...

Ezra leaned on a golden pillar near the throne. Carved angels did very un-angelic things upon it.

"How about some answers? You really doing this out of the goodness of your heart? Or does that weird little fella back there have something over you?"

Casanova inclined his head, like a fencer acknowledging a touch.

"*Bravo*. I can see why he likes you. And yes, of course, you're right. I owe Zarathusrian and the Central Scrutinizer this ship. I'm one of *you*, you see". He waggled an eyebrow. "But I'm a wrong 'un. Didn't come out right. Quite a few tropes all mixed up, unfortunately. So while you're a Man with No Name, out to deliver justice with your trusty pistol in hand, I'm supposed to steal from the rich and give to the poor, but with an extra dose of dashing romance, some swashbuckling and a whole lot of saucy double entendres. It's not an easy life, Ashdown. But they gave it some kind of purpose. Just like they're trying to do for you."

"So we're supposed to *thank* 'em? They made us freaks, and we're s'posed ta just kiss their boots fer it?"

"My two cents? The human race *needs* heroes right now, to pull us back together. The Jest gave us a messy divorce, but there are other things out there who wouldn't be so damned nice about it. Ones with knives and forks and mustard."

Ezra thought of what he'd seen of the Tchub, and then thought about certain humans of his acquaintance. *Perhaps it would be us with the tartare sauce... but...*

"I didn't ask to be no hero. A card-sharp, a drinker, a straight shot and my daddy's son is all. But I..."

Ezra didn't get any further, because he was interrupted by two things at once. All the lights went down across the great gilded pleasure-dome of the *Innuendo*'s bridge, and Jed Granger popped back up inside his head like a scraggle-toothed jack in the box.

"*Whazzzhappenin? What'd I miss, Ashdown? Ooooh, it's mighty dark and cold when you folks go through the Chasm. Like the grave, or so I reckon. But boy, I 'preciate where you've brought us now!*"

"Shut up!" hissed Ezra on the neural band, watching the curtains peel away from what turned out to be a great curved picture window. It let onto hard vacuum; stars twinkled cold and proud. "And be ready for anything. These are hardened space pirates, killers and..."

"*And I can see what else, boy! You know how long I been without what you might call the 'particulars'? Makes a man tend to pay attention to womenfolk wearing nothin' but bottlecaps and dental floss, even if they do accessorise with guns. Hell, I AM a gun. And look where she's got that pistol stashed! I'd loooove to snuggle up between those..."*

Casanova DeSade leaned back on his command throne, calling up a holographic keyboard with one finger.

"But *what*, mister Ashdown? I don't suppose you're going to appeal to the universe's sense of fair play, since it manifestly hasn't got one. So I can only hope you were going to say that we should make the very best of a bad situation. That's the only sane way to look at it."

"Did he just say sane?" asked Granger. *"The guy in the swimsuit and gimp mask?"*

Ezra muzzled the problem Solver's avatar with one imagined hand, gritting his teeth in what passed for a smile.

"O'course. That's all we *can* do, right?"

"Well – that, and twist the laws of physics up like hot bubblegum. We're about to weigh anchor, so I suggest you sit down."

"Why? Is it uncomfortable?"

DeSade smirked. It was a world-class smirk. There are horrible little rat-faced mafiosi who couldn't have pulled it off, even if they'd just stolen a dumptruck full of Swedish pornography.

"Oh no. *Quite* the opposite. But of course, it takes everyone differently...."

Various scantily clad space pirates began to call in information from their stations.

"Anti-prudish shielding unfurled. Expanding the titillation space to flight parameters."

"Instigating carnal exciter arrays. Cuing Barry White."

Somewhere aboard the ship, things began to slide and pump in scandalous ways. Machinery coupled and grooved. 'Can't get enough of your love, babe' began to play from a host of hidden speakers.

"Infinitely Suggestive field is optimised. Specific scandal vectors are collapsing in the phase space... Activating incense. Spinning up the disco ball."

And now the scene beyond the window began to move.

The stars wobbled. Flickers of pink and blue lightning crawled across the glass. Ezra felt goosebumps pop across his skin, and he sat down suddenly. It was either that or cover what was happening in his pants with a tea tray. Suddenly the whole great ship thrummed like a bass-string, shimmying with non-specific lust.

He tried not to look at Tia. He tried not to think about...

"Probability actualized – prepare for jump in three..."

The stars whirled. Plaid lines cohered and blurred.

"Two..."

The plaid upshifted to neon paisley. It pulsed. Ezra's heartbeat thumped like a hot-jazz drum solo in his temples. Casanova DeSade laughed, a totally unhinged sound of ecstasy.

"One..."

Space and time shrieked with pure pleasure. There was a very embarrassing, slippery and drawn out moment when the whole ship seemed stretched taut, shuddering halfway between here and there, transparent and solid. Everything tasted of knitted jumpers and raspberries. Flashbulbs exploded.

"Holy shiiiiit!" screamed Jedediah Granger. *"Oooohhh, that little guy with the Fez was right! Dear lord, **it was all true!"***

An image jumped him, as his back arched and his eyes bulged out. It stabbed in like a sliver of glass. A black and white desert. Zarathusrian with some kind of big chrome instrument.

"...I'll have you know. This unreality of yours - this fixation on fiction - it's only going to get worse. Because it's true. You made the metaphor, and your power will fill it up. The survival of two whole universes could depend on it. All you'd have to do is..."

It came in through the neural link. It came from Granger. It wasn't his voice, though. And it blurred out like the end of a dream as the *Innuendo* came crashing back into reality, powered by a trans-cosmic orgasm of sheer filthy suggestion.

They rode the bounce right into a warzone.

Space outside the great stage-curtained picture window slapped back into focus with a resounding *pop*, like the cork being pulled from a particularly fine magnum of champagne. The ship whined and shuddered as its huge, inexplicable engines wound down, counterpoint to the blur in Ezra's head.

He groaned. It seemed to help a little.

What was out there – well, *that* must be the hazy blue and green curve of Temperance, and that must be a giant Chasm gate, spinning like a cheap magician's prop between the planet and its moon. Between them rode a fleet of half burned, half-scrapped warships, their guns flickering and pulsing as they spat radioactive death. And coming up to greet them, haloing the planet like giant wings scrawled in contrails...

"Ohhhh, bother," said Casanova DeSade. "I should have known

you'd get me into trouble, Tia Faraday!"

Worm III had wasted no time loosing his ground-based missile batteries. Smartcore warheads swarmed up from a million silos hidden among the cloisters and abbeys, from under the great slave-tended fields of the Penitent Farms and the Ecclesiastic Communes. Ground-defence turbo-obliterators thrust up from pits cored out of the planet's surface, juiced by whole grids of sizzling wires. Hosanna City shut down block by block as they charged up. The concrete-scape pulsed lilac and pink as their beams raked the sky. Clouds blew out spiral-form, pierced by pillars of flame.

It was biblical. It was apocalyptic. Ezra wished it was happening somewhere else.

"Is this what Mister Fixit had planned? He's taking over a planet?"

Tia was on the edge of her chaise lounge, eyes wide and white.

"There'd have to be something *left*, Ashdown. If this gets any worse, he'd be conquering a lump of charcoal."

Razorcuts of light splashed against the fleet's shields, cobbled together into a hex-pattern array by *Burzum*. Ablated steel and foam fell in a twinkling rain, setting the nightside sky ablaze.

If it wasn't for the fact that it represented massive, industrial scale carnage, it would have been quite pretty. Tia, for one, was watching with a look on her face like Christmas morning and new year's eve had collided on her birthday.

But *Burzum* had brought deadly presents to this party. Munitions stabbed down, charring swathes of cityscape and farmland. Smartcores looped and howled and died, spiralling through the fleet as they disintegrated. Some popped in the low atmosphere, turning into attenuated clouds of radiation as they tore up. Some of them found their targets. Pieces of *Burzum* winked out of the net, blossoming into shards as their shields fed back, as generators ripped loose and sheared their bolts, punching out through hulls, tearing off engine nacelles and gun emplacements.[64]

Others found another target, right slap bang in the middle of the combat zone. Whole flights of smartcores veered off course toward the *Innuendo,* while certain of the *Burzum*'s ships turned their turrets and missile arrays to make captain DeSade and his crew feel welcome.

---

64. In fact, to make this bit extra juicy and to spare no expense, we've even made it briefly possibly for there to be fire in space, and for there to be a massive, dopplering, eardrum-melting soundtrack of vast explosions, thrumming ion drives and screeching laser barrages behind it. You're welcome.

"Miss Faraday," said Casanova. "Your boss *does* know we're not a ship of the line, doesn't he? If you make it back to Earth this time, I'd love you to spank his tight little robot arse for me..."

Sirens wailed. The whole chintzy bordello of a bridge strobed crimson and blue.

But it wasn't as if the *Innuendo* was unarmed. Oh No.

You can't be a convincing scourge of the spaceways without some *incredibly* heavy weapons tucked away. Kinky pirates hustled and snapped out orders. Leather and lace-clad gunners ran out a whole broadside of turrets, and Casanova himself stabbed at his holographic keyboards like the Phantom of some x-rated Opera, composing a fugue made up of combat drones. They puffed from hidden ports in the *Innuendo*'s hull like seed from a dandelion, englobing the ship in a protective web.

"See? Only a couple of seconds, and we're right in the middle of a bloody war! But there's not much you can do from here, my lovelies. Oh no. I suppose you'll have to just get out there and find your target the old fashioned way. Either he's on the ground shooting up, or somewhere in that fleet shooting down!"

Tia was already up from her chaise lounge, Problem Solver in one hand.

"That sounds *unspeakably* dangerous," she said, with a certain look in her eye. One which made Ezra feel as though he'd just tried to swallow a velvet grapefruit. "We could.... ahem... *all be killed.*"

"That's why I thought Mister Wainwright here could stick around, to help me with running targeting schematics. The mathematics are hideously complex. In fact, there's over three million ways we could get reduced to radioactive gas in the next ten minutes."

The metalman chuckled, the holographic body under his great floating head blurring with static.

"You make a wonderful host, DeSade. But you know I'll upload every detail about this ship while I'm plugged in..."

"Oh, of course, of course. It's not like we're old friends, now, is it? But you'll be sifting through a lot of pornography first. A *lot*. By *my* standards. And I don't think you'll have the time. The Synod's planetary defence forces have launched. And half of them are coming for us."

Sir Giles may not have been up to play with all the technology around them, but he knew how to make use of an Olympic-swimming-pool-sized window. He could clearly see the contrails of hundreds of in-atmosphere dreadnoughts lancing up from the surface of Temperance, their vectors traced in neon. At the same time, a large part of the orbital fleet had peeled away and was closing in on the *Innuendo* as well. It was unlikely that they simply wanted to trade fashion tips and cupcake recipes.

"Dash it all, Captain, we need to cut this monster off at the head. But there's no way of knowing where that 'orrible robot bastard has gotten to, if you'll pardon my sailor talk."

"Oh, we're *all* sailors here," smirked DeSade. "And I totally agree. It's just that every last one of those ships out there scans as being called the *Burzum*, and there's about seven thousand of them. They also seem to have been designed by a 1960s Soviet architect with a bad hangover. Absolutely *no* brio or panache."

"This ain't no time to be worrying about cheese," grated Ezra[65], watching ships flare and core out to blackened husks out in the vacuum. "Tia's right. We'll have to do this the old fashioned way. By which I mean, spacesuits and laser cannons and some kind of jetpacks, I guess. You got a whole bad sci-fi armoury aboard this thing?"

"Like you wouldn't believe."

Ezra raised an eyebrow. There wasn't much, after the last few days, that he wouldn't believe. Excepting, of course, that any of this nonsense was really happening.

"Then let's just start with the closest one. Anything alive on board..."

"Or artificially alive!" chimed in Wainwright.

"Or what he said – we rough them up a bit. Get 'em to talk."

"And if the ship you're on gets nailed by a few billion terawatts of firepower while you're busy asking questions?"

Tia reached up and patted Casanova DeSade on one leather-masked cheek.

"Then I'll be having a lovely day, won't I? And you'll be keeping Wainwright safe so we can do it all over again."

A little shudder ran through DeSade's tattooed frame.

"Dear lady, I think you've missed your calling. Have you ever considered a career in the space pirate officer corps?"

Her smile was as sharp and bright as a diamond chainsaw.

"You'd be better to ask Ashdown. He's the one with a thing for silly hats."

"Hey! You don't hear me makin' fun of *your*..."

---

65. You see what we did there

But he never got to make a highly convincing argument for the traditional stetson. Because at that moment Ezra Ashdown was interrupted by a voice he'd heard before. On Harrowe, of all places.

"This is the *Slayer* class corsair *Altar of Sacrifice*, hailing all Panarchy agents of the Department of Plausible Deniability on board the CLS *Innuendo*."

A quick glance from Ez to Tia to Wainwright confirmed that they were all hearing it. The voice of Mister Fixit's stolen scoutship, loud and clear in their ears.

"The mad 'bot's puppet," snarled Wainwright, his single great eye slitting to a green line. "Care to tell us why we shouldn't get Casanova here to blow you to sparkly hot dust?"

"Well, I *do* approve of all this talk of blowing, but I have absolutely no idea who you're talking to..." began the Captain. Tia shut him up with a single finger across his lip-zip.

"Because I'm *free*. I'm decommissioned. And your boss has a message for you. It just came through, and he thought you might be in-system already."

"A *message*? But the gate's down! This world's a class-eight rogue, you've brought an Enemy of Sentience here, and there's a gods-damned war on! In case you hadn't noticed!"

The *Slayer* class sniffed haughtily.

"I was *made* for war. What you have down there is nothing more or less than a failure to communicate. The Scrutinizer will fill you in. And then you'll excuse me for buggering off out of this unmitigated clusterfuck."

"I thought you were 'made for war'?"

It is, of course, impossible for a corsair – even one advanced as the *Slayer* class, built with several layers of irony and paradox-proof crumple zones – to raise one eyebrow. But the *Altar of Sacrifice* managed to transmit a hash of code which unfurled into just that impression, right inside Ezra's head.

"I never said I was dumb enough to *like* it, meatbag. Now, seeing as the big man's leaving this one to you, I suggest you take a look at what he's got to say, then suit up. It's going to get messier before it gets any cleaner."

"Really?" asked Tia. "And what does Central's message say to make you think that?"

The *Altar* chuckled. Its virtual image hazed in around the edges, giving the blurred impression of a stubbled army veteran in torn-up fatigues and a faded heavy metal t-shirt. It was grinning.

"Hell, girl – I haven't *read* your damn message. Don't need to. I've been in a fair number of these so-called failures to communicate, and that's why I'm off out of here!"

Ezra shook his head like a damp spaniel as the code sizzled in. When his vision cleared of purple sparks he found Casanova DeSade and his crew aiming a vast assortment of guns at the Outriders. One heavily made-up midget was holding what he prayed was a large rubber truncheon.

"Secret messages, then, is it? Are we at the part where we all betray each other yet? Because I had rather hoped there'd be at least one utterly gratuitous orgy scene before we got that hackneyed, kiddies."

Tia earned several more points with Ezra Ashdown for snapping back to reality *already aiming* her problem solver up under the Captain's chin.

"Nothing you need to worry about. The bad guys got to the mass betrayal waaaaay before the bad-ass righteous today. So it looks like business as usual for us, and some new orders from the Scrutinizer for you."

Casanova grinned, and made a little twinkly gesture with his fingers. A forest of improbably chromed muzzles – and that big translucent pink truncheon – were reluctantly lowered.

"Ahhhh, Miss Faraday and her slightly soiled Horsemen of the Apocalypse. Overkill, Swearing, Big Explosions and Only Slightly Temporary Death. Wish I could come with you."

"We'll see in a second," said Tia, standing up on tip-toe to plant a kiss on DeSade's cheek. She pulled his zipper shut with her teeth. "Ashdown – go ahead and tell me what the boss suggests we do..."

+++

The Central Scrutinizer fiddled with the camera and stepped back, his rubberized David Bowie mask squinting into the lens.

"Is that right? Is it recording already? Buggery hell, but those buttons are *tiny*. What's the point in relentlessly miniaturizing technology to the point where *even other technology* has to have a pair of chopsticks to program the bleedin'.... ahhh, there we are!"

The camera wobbled a little, and the Scrutinizer reached out to steady it on its tripod. Then he beamed, stepped away, and gestured grandly at the great circular viewport which commanded the room he stood in. It was utterly cyclopean, both in its scale and its singularity, and it was webbed with what looked like the target crosshairs of an ancient anti-aircraft gun. Before it stood an empty throne, of the James Bond Villain type – all rotational and sixties-retro-futurist. The mad cyber-mind of the Panarchy was still got up in a puppet facsimile of the now infamous Thin White Duke, but he was wearing a duffel coat, brown corduroy trousers, a wide-brimmed hat and an absurdly long stripey scarf. A strange-looking screwdriver poked out of his top pocket.

"OK then. I thought I'd just make a record of all this for the lads out there on the front lines, so that you're up to date. This -" and here he gestured expansively, taking in the throne room, with its very clearly industrial-brutalist architecture - "Is the command centre of what I'm sure you'll all recognize as a certain fully operational battle station."

"I thought it was a small moon," said a croaky voice from off camera. The Scrutinizer grinned.

"I assure you sir, *this is no moon*. Out there, folks, you'll see the home fleet. Quite some ungodly tonnage of nasty space weaponry, some of which is actually explicable by the kind of physics you can learn without your brain running out your ears like warm custard."

Sure enough, the camera zoomed drunkenly in on the picture window, taking in a jagged metalscape of ships – triangular wedges covered in gun turrets, long, slim projectiles, the classic disc and twin warp nacelles, the odd naval warship with rockets nailed on... they were all there. A blue phone booth bobbled past, its light flashing merrily.

"Now, I've called the heads of the Guild of Farwalkers here for business, not pleasure. Though I suspect the diet soda and twinkies were well received..."

The camera panned around to show a row of strangely dressed, elderly and quite self-important looking men seated on deck chairs. Everyone was wearing a full Masonic dressing room's worth of sashes, medals, regalia, cuffs, aprons and signet rings. They shuffled uneasily, with a distinctive sound of crinkling concealed packaging.

"Business... yes, well, that's good," said one of them, a greybeard wearing a paisley poncho and a bowler hat. "I was worried that – you know – that mix-up with Brother Hszarl, and the mad robot and all..."

The camera ping-ponged back to the grinning face of the Central Scrutinizer.

"Ahh, yes, that. *Unpleasantness*. Well, I could see how you might have misunderstood. But I don't go in for mass executions just because of the waywardness of certain unbalanced individuals. Otherwise who'd be left to dig the mass graves, hmm?"

There was a hideously attenuated, sticky kind of silence, which was broken by a rustle of nervous laughter. *Dear me, no. We're all friends here, aren't we?*

"No, I think we can overlook all of that if you take on a small commission for me."

The Scrutinizer grinned, like a creative accountant who has just proven that a decimal point can safely be considered a legal fiction.

"The Home Fleet, you see, has to be taken across to a little planet called Harrowe. In the Nepenthe-Ulgaris system. All of it. By, oh, let's say... *afternoon teatime?*"

The row of Farwalkers looked startled for an instant, puffing up like a flock of crows on a washing line. Then they whispered among themselves, punctuating their urgent sussurrus with tight, vehement hand gestures. Nods bopped back and forth, wobbling a row of outlandish hats.

"Of course, we'd be... honoured," said the spokeswalker, who had been hissing words like 'impossible' and 'insane' mere moments before. "But... if I may... just two things. Firstly, if you want to reach New Gomorrah, then Harrowe is barely in the neighbourhood. There's a matter of a six light-year jump between one and the other that we can't undertake without the Chasm Gate being opened for us."

"From what we hear," put in another - this one robed up like a b-grade pope - "The A.I. at that end is slightly more loopy than most. No offense to present company."

"None taken," beamed the Scrutinizer, twirling the end of his scarf. "And the other thing?"

The spokeswalker raised a finger, let it wilt, opened his mouth, thought better of it, then made a vague wringing motion with both hands. A wrapped twinkie fell from his sleeve to the floor.

"Oh, just tell him!" said a third traveller of the Chasmic Dark, this one dressed as a rather unconvincing wizard. "Fine! Then *I* will! Such a mass emportage hasn't been undertaken since the War of 9:15. And even then..."

"Even then," came a choral, weirdly unmelodic voice from off-screen. **"You didn't have *our* help."**

The Central Scrutinizer swung back into focus, this time standing next to an antique portable ghetto blaster.

"Wait for it... wait for it... now, which button was it? Ahhh – here we go!" The mad, nigh-omnipotent Intelligence pushed a button. Dramatic chords rattled out of the speakers.

Duuunnn Duuuuun DUUUUUNNNNNNN!

The camera focused in on a new figure who had appeared in the room. Not entered, or walked through the door – but *appeared*, like some bad stage-magic apparition. It was an 18th century *commedia del arte* opera clown, dressed in harlequin black and white, and with a face as haughty and cold as a parking violation written by Dante Aligheri. It stepped forward, moving like a puppet, and as it did so the camera caught sight of something *behind* it – a glassy shimmer in the air like vermicelli noodles made of fibre-optic cable, seething in boiling water.

"Ladies and gentlemen of the Guild, allow me to present the Jest Ambassador to the Panarchy. Or, as it likes to be called, Zingo the Hilarious."

"*It* as in..."

"As in they have five genders, one of which is... *complicated*. Not 'IT' as in the thing with all the teeth and the creepy red balloons."

The bowler-hatted Farwalker mopped his brow with a large paisley handkerchief, looking more than slightly worried. His fellows covered the spectrum from bilious to ashen as they watched the clown advance.

"We calculate that in this instance our actions have left you unfortunately vulnerable. Were it not for the quarantine action, you would not currently stand on the brink of extinction-level annihilation."

"You mean this Mister Fixit fellow? Surely he can't be..."

"We mean *the Process*. They make no distinction between your race's biological and machine components. All they care about is that one of you is about to re-weaponise an Immaterial Dreadnought. Such a device is capable, on its own, of erasing a solar system. They see this as theft, and escalation... and frankly, there is a faction amongst the Process Hierarchy of Worthy Elders which calls for compulsory domestication. For all of you."

"But... but you started this! You drove our AIs mad!" blustered the Farwalker in the pontifical mitre, "Present company respectfully included. Three thousand years we've suffered! What do you have to say about that?"

The guildsmen muttered and shuffled in their seats, not one of them wanting to meet the frosty, alien eyes of the Jest ambassador, but each one nudging his neighbour to be the one who actually did it.

"Yes. We have a statement about that incident. Does your species still understand the term 'Awwwwww Snap'?"

"This is *preposterous!*" roared a nearly spherical Guildsman, twinkies spaying from the sleeves of his academic robes.

"No, your array of silly hats are 'preposterous,'" said the Scrutinizer, flicking the man's tartan mortarboard with silver tassels. "*This* is merely outrageous. But The Right Honourable Zingo the Hilarious is correct. If Fixit succeeds, we'll be at war with the Process. We may all find ourselves domesticated within a matter of months."

Mortarboard and Bowler Hat whispered together for a moment.

"Surely... surely that's not so awful? I've heard about the humans that the Process keep. Not a bad life, on the balance of it. For some of the disconnected worlds, it would be a big step up..."

With a swiftness that belied the symphony of servos and pistons beneath, The Scrutinizer's arm shot out, grabbing the chief Farwalker squarely by the crotch. His eyes bulged, and he emitted a tiny squeaking sound, like a disappointed hamster.

"I'm afraid there'd have to be – certain concessions," said the mad AI, cheerful as ever. "All of us out here, well – we'd be counted feral. We'd have to be neutered. It could be quite a dislocating experience for a man."

There was a distinct pop as the Scrutinizer let go. He turned back to the camera.

"So, there you have it, people. While my esteemed guest here rubs the front of his trousers with a handful of ice cubes, I'll fill you in on just what's going to happen. We're going to fold up all of my lovely toys out there and come to rescue your sorry arses. If the rest of your bodies are still attached to those arses, all the better. But in the meantime, you are to do *absolutely everything in your power* to stop Mister Fixit from activating that Dreadnought. We're going to start by bringing through a brace of mining tugs to Harrowe, and we're gonna lift the gate he left behind into orbit. Once we give it a bit of a stretch, my fleet's gonna haul anchor, and I suppose dear old Ezra Ashdown's world is going to change forever. Then my new friend Zingo here will punch the lot of us through to where you are. It's not instantaneous, but it's better than nothing. Apparently the Jest can tunnel through what they call 'The Backdrop' and tow us all along in their slipstream. Three hours. That's all I ask for. *Three hours*, Miss Faraday, Mister DeSade, Mister

Wainwright. And of course, you, Ashdown. We expect great things from you..."

The camera spun crazily as the Scrutinizer stepped away, wobbling past the window again. A ship like a floating cathedral with an eagle-head ram and banks of cannons went slipping past in the endless night. Around it flitted nimble, x-foiled fighter craft, a squadron of classic 1960s Roswell-class UFOs, and a quintet of robot lions.

"Who exactly is he talking t...."

Then the film cut out. One final image shimmered in Ezra's vision – the cold, eggshell-white face of Zingo the Hilarious, his red-painted lips parted in an amused little grin. Although the picture was static, the glassy tentacle-blades behind him were still moving.

A last snippet of audio echoed as Ezra's eyes cleared, blinked, and caught a whole bordello-bridge of pirates, outriders and sundry other freaks staring at him in hushed anticipation.

"By the time you get this message, we'll already have started..."

"Tia," he croaked. "Whiskey. Hip flask, top pocket."

He took one swallow, and the fireworks in his head blurred sideways into mere sparks. Two, and the light from the space battle outside made all the shadows jump, giant and jagged and mantis-angled. Three...

And she pulled the flask away.

"Mister Captain, Sir?" asked Ezra Ashdown. "About that bad sci-fi armoury? Do you, by any chance, have a long-ass corridor, a set of smoke machines and a phonograph to go with it?"

Tia looked up at him and smiled.

"What exactly have you and the Boss got planned, cowboy?"

Ezra made craning motions with his neck, and pursing motions with his lips, but that damned flask of whiskey remained resolutely out of reach.

So he told her.

+++

The Central Scrutinizer was right. By the time Ezra Ashdown got his message, events *were* in full swing. Events which, in the way events have of getting bundled up in folders and sorted under headings, would come to be called the Almost-War of New Gomorrah.

They say that the first casualty of war is the truth, but in this case the first casualty was the Reverend Nebukedekeriah Donovan, whose parents had reasoned that there was no such thing as too much holiness when it came to biblical names, but who were also, it must be admitted, the kind of haphazard, God-fearing disciplinarians who raise their sons to be either drunks, very good soldiers or the kind of quiet religious types who turn out to be mass-murdering cannibals.

The Reverend had never so much as nibbled on a severed pinkie toe lightly marinaded in port wine vinegar, but he was a curious combination of all three. His faith was as hard as his fists, which both paled in comparison to the narrowness of his hatchet nose, his views on race, and his twisty little uncoiled spring of a mind.

Let's just say these two things about Nebukedekeriah Donovan. He really, *really* believed that the suffering of the unrighteous in this world would save them from torment in the next. And he was the one who lynched Ezra Ashdown's pa.

Miles away, as the good Reverend sat in a copper hip bath, outside the tiny vicarage of a church consecrated to no saint in particular, ten identical insectile ships came hissing through the Chasm Gate of Harrowe. While Donovan scrubbed his bony back with a long-handled wire brush (to keep the demons out of his thoughts while he was naked, of course), the mining tugs locked onto the flapping fabric of the Gate and pulled it taut, rising up into the teal sky with a pulse of antigravitic boosters.

Aboard, ten Farwalkers of the Guild signalled back to their fellows, waiting in the chilly gap between worlds. In there, the bridges and stairwells and impossible, cantilevered Escher-structures which reached out to the gateway of Harrowe thronged with men in robes, silly hats, and guild aprons. They were all carrying hazy little lights.

Now one came forward, towing behind him an orange-sized ball of radiance. Giving the ancient gesture of two raised middle fingers to the emptiness above and below, he opened the door and stepped through, disappearing as if he'd stepped into an upright pool of printer's ink.

High in the stratosphere now, as miles away the Reverend hummed a tuneless hymn and fumbled for a chunk of greasy soap...

A larger ship came nosing through the quicksilver, this one sectioned like an old-fashioned Saturn series rocket. The tugs pulling the Gate tight let it ease on by, its fins winking with pilot lights, its immense payload bolted on behind, huge and spiked and thrumming with power.

This was the Tether. Once the gate was in orbit it would need power, and there was no time to unfurl and calibrate an array of solar collectors, even considering the combined power of Ulgaris and Nepenthe. They'd only get smashed to pieces when the fleet took up most of the space between and around Harrowe and its moons. Lucky, then, that the seas down there were so shallow. Even luckier that the Tether worked by tapping into the molten heat under a planet's surface. The emergence into orbit of ships as large as some of Central's would really get those magma currents moving, if only through sheer tidal forces.

Of course, this meant that the wickedly spiked butt-end of the Tether would have to punch through the crust of Harrowe somewhere.

Down there, a shadow fell across the Reverend Nebukedekeriah Donovan. He looked up, and the wire brush fell from his hand.

"... Halleluuuuujah, the Orth will call me home..." he croaked, trailing off into silence.

The Central Scrutinizer's creepware was very, very good at spying. It had found out all kinds of things about Ezra's past. And the Central Scrutinizer, for all his madness, always paid his debts.

Nebukedekeriah Donovan learned, a few seconds later, that the concept of suffering in this world preventing torment in the next is very much like shitting yourself while sitting in a bathtub. On the balance of it, it's hard to tell if you're any dirtier or any cleaner. But considering the consequences, it makes not a whit of difference either way.

+++

The 'immaterial' part of a Process Immaterial Dreadnought meant that Rel Kitano didn't so much pilot the thing through space – he *flew*, cocooned in onionskin energy fields which wrapped around him like an invisible diamond spacesuit.

Well, around him, his massive pair of 1970s quadrophonic headphones, and a faux-wooden Thorn record turntable which hovered in space next to him, the Ramones hammering out four chords or less of raw energy as they were dragged along at a clip approaching half lightspeed.

Rel had changed. Not in terms of his eye colour, height, musical tastes or love of fine synthetically generated reefer. No, even the man-sized raccoon tail he'd had grafted on for the sake of fashion remained.

But this was a Rel Kitano who had spent far too much time in the vast, echoing white spaces of the Dreadnought alone. One who had spent the last few months doing push-ups, squats, free weights and chin-ups with the blank-eyed zeal of a death row inmate. One who had watched a whole lot of human video entertainment, and who had also tattooed almost every accessible part of his left arm, leg and torso with tally marks, love hearts, skulls and other clichéd but evocative designs.

This Rel Kitano wore a pair of heavy denim work trousers, suspenders, steel capped boots and a mohawk haircut. Tucked into his belt was a frankly ludicrous gold plated Colt Python hand cannon, and his fingers were wrapped about by a pair of classic – if hackneyed – 'love' and 'hate' silver knuckle dusters. He clenched a machine-extruded imitation cigarette between his teeth as he descended on the Temperance system, the smoke captured in an invisible bubble and whisked away by unseen fans.

The fact was – and it was a fact which a whole lot of people were about to become very grateful of – the Immaterial Dreadnought was barely operational. Before they'd packed away their potent death machines, the Process had removed the cold, calculating War Sentiences which operated their most horrifying abilities. Abilities which interacted in nasty ways with dimensions best left unglimpsed, where geometry and physics were slightly different, and the raw energy of any number of Big Bangs waited to be tapped. When Rel unhooked his neural implants from the controls and stepped back through the interlock, it was to a stark white space built for his erstwhile masters. Far too big for a mere human pet; he'd sectioned off a corner with a bedroll, some records, a food synthesizer and a selection of gym equipment. Without a potent AI to manifest the Dreadnought's most powerful weapons systems, the combat stations and battle-harnesses made for a race of tripedal giants simply didn't work.

Which was not to say that Rel was unarmed. Oh no. it's just that the weapons he had access to were suitable only for training exercises. Loaded with conventional nuclear warheads and x-ray masers. More than enough, certainly, to make mincemeat of Worm III's pathetic fleet.

Just not enough to crack Temperance itself open like a microwaved Easter egg.

He readied them now. A quick look at the battle already raging above his target was enough to make Rel cautious. Around the flying, shirtless figure in space a series of apertures irised open, and the snouts of a dozen cannons poked through into reality.

The ships blasting each other to bits out there might be trying to help him. They might be here to stop him. They might be utterly indifferent to his lovelorn little quest.

But if they got in his way, they'd regret it. Quite possibly for the rest of their lives.

Even the least potent of the Process' weapons would ensure that those lives were measured in fractions of a very hot and uncomfortable second...

+++

"Ohhh, that's it," crooned Mister Fixit, standing in front of the great statue-framed picture window of the Temperance battlecruiser *Slog*. "Come on. Just a bit further..."

The evil was all up in his head, an itch which was simply ecstasy itself to scratch. Cerise stood beside him, leaning on her great glassy sword, staring at the same tiny speck which had him fixated.

"So that's him? *That's* the bad guy? He hardly looks worth all the trouble, Uncle..."

Mister Fixit grinned like an explosion in a piano factory.

"Oh, yes indeed. Don't let appearances deceive you. He's a thief, and a liar, and he's convinced he's doing this for... *love*." The psychotic robot spat the word as if it was a pickled sliver of ear wax. "What he's stolen, child, will give us just what we need. Your birthright. Your throne. My... bwaaahaaaa.... my purpose. Sorry." He manhandled his false teeth back between poor old Mason Stockton's lips by main force. "With you to open the gates, and our dear friend *Burzum* here manning the guns of that thing, we'll remake the galaxy as it should be."

"Pink, then," said Cerise, her head tilted to one side. "And fluffy. With at least one whole planet just for kittens."

Mister Fixit shuddered. *Ahhh, the things he did for the sake of wickedness.*

"Fine. Fine. Just make sure you cast the gravitic lensing... ahem... *spell*... in the right place. When all those beams come together, we'll pop the little snot like a fly on a truck-stop bug zapper!"

"And the actual pirates? For goodness sake, Uncle, you promised!"

238

Cerise pouted, with all the calculation of a mind made to twist up the laws of physics like damp spaghetti.

Mister Fixit sighed. Wherever that corkscrew-shaped ship full of actual, factual, bloody inconvenient space pirates had come from, they were nothing but a co-incidental distraction. Certainly, they fit in with the lie he'd woven to convince Cerise to join him on what he'd assured her was a storybook adventure. But co-incidence, in the experience of *this* unhinged killer mech, was a fickle thing. It was a knife with a blade for a handle, and never mind that his actual fingers were forged from hardened titanium.

"Them too, then," he grimaced. "All in good time. First, we take the Dreadnought. Then..." a little giggle escaped his stolen lips. It threatened to rip Mason Stockton's mummified face in half as it whipsawed through his head, surfing a wave of madness. "Then.. hahaha. Hahahahaaaa. Then... *everything else is just the beginning!*"

Seventeen – No Weddings, All Funerals, and a Sack of Potatoes

"There's a tendency for people to equate dying with the phrase 'You're History!'- but unfortunately, to become History you actually have to have done something interesting. No, most deaths would be better heralded with that far less popular and witty one-liner – 'You're Calculus with Statistics!' "

- Pedant Superior Jong Wolpenhaus the IVth, University of Kralzburg
Department of Inexactitude

EVERYTHING HAS ITS breaking point. Every living being - from the most squamous of slime moulds to the most ethereal of cosmic entities - has a little dial in its brain, which reads 'cool, calm and copacetic' at one end and 'batshit crazy' at the other.

The trick, therefore, it to choose one's battles.

We're reminded, here, of the story of Balpho Nargus, a small, pinky-purple amphibian creature and citizen of the third planet orbiting the binary star Hallix Secundus. Life was not good for poor little Balpho. He was a serf in a highly stratified tribal society, in which the warrior caste would show their disdain for the weak by throwing the local *blanja*[66] fruit at them and calling them *glophloks*[67], with much chortling and fist-bumping. Sometimes they even squeezed the juice from a rancid land-flounder and smeared it down Balpho Nargus' tunic, to general merriment.

One day, as he was scrubbing land-flounder slime from his best Grelmday tunic, a warrior by the name of Nax Naraldo snuck up behind him and slathered his head with the mud from a nearby *gulratha*[68] wallow.

---

66. A large, blue-and-orange spotted, pulpy mass with the stench of expensive cheese kept for several weeks in a hobo's underclothes.
67. Literally translated as – 'sons of a mother who is both obese, hairy, slovenly and afflicted with the chronic farting sickness'
68. Imagine a cross between a pig, a cockroach and a set of bagpipes

At this point, Balpho Nargus became angry. This would ordinarily have been just as hilarious as his slathering with dung-fragrant *gulratha*-mud, as a serf from Hallix Secundus was only a quarter the size of the hulking and sloping-headed warrior caste. Saying the wrong thing – such as the utterance of the word *glophlok,* for example - would have seen his skull twisted from his scrawny neck-wattles, under any normal circumstances.

But Balpho was beyond merely pissed off.

He was apoplectic with rage, incandescent with fury. He had become a living volcano of invective, which caused villagers nearby to cover their children's ear-holes, invoke the holy name of the Great God Glarg, hide under water-barrels or, in the case of certain adolescents, write the good bits down for later.

He called down curses and hellfire. He wished scurvy, mumps, rickets, boils, blisters, psoriasis and genital herpes on his tormentor. He cordially invited the Great God Glarg, in His wisdom, to smite Nax Naraldo right then and there, proving once and for all what a *gulratha smelping glophlok* he really was.

This drew quite a crowd, who had not seen any heads twisted off for nigh on a three-moon.

But just as Nax Naraldo was limbering up his great thick fingers to get some cranial torsion happening, a wayward meteor crash-dived the atmosphere of the third planet of Hallix Secundus. Though most of it was ablated away to the size of a peanut by the time it punched through the clouds, it was still travelling at many, many times the speed of sound when it hit Nax Naraldo square in the kisser.

The sonic boom rattled several teeth loose. It became known as 'the time of the great trouser soilening'.

Balpho woke up to find everyone bowing to him and grinning in a way that suggested their lips would quite like to escape their faces. Someone hesitantly held out a peeled *blanja* for his approval.

The fact that he parleyed this neat cosmic accident into the role of God-Emperor may have been erring a little on the side of hubris. The fact that his reign was supported by many, many threats of sudden vengeance from on high might have been stretching the truth a bit too far.

But it was still unfortunate that things really came to a head when the first Human scoutship landed on the virgin soil of Hallix-S-Three.

This wasn't a ship sent by the Panarchy. Oh no. It was a vessel dispatched by one of the Shard factions, industrialized worlds who were establishing their own petty little hegemonies at a mere 99 percent of lightspeed. It had taken this vessel six years to get to Hallix, and its crew were freshly unfrozen, surly, and over-militarized. All the instant coffee had turned to dust on the trip over, magnetic storms had erased the ship's voluminous stores of hard pornography, and the average human stood twice as tall as the biggest local warrior.

Plus, they had guns. Did we mention the guns?

Initial casualties were horrendous. Balpho the Magnificent's ministers, lackeys, priests and generals all shared a few knowing looks among themselves, though, as the captain of the Shard Sequestrators swaggered through the streets of the capital, ballista-bolts pinging off his armour harmlessly...

At the last they shuffled Balpho out onto a balcony atop his palace, then respectfully cleared a circle around him. And that was when he realized.

The eyes of every single one of his people were on him. They drilled into his naked soul with the intensity it takes for dripping water to carve out vast, lightless caverns underground, all compacted into a single moment. And, as the human raised his terrible, plasma-spitting weapon, its barrel already crackling with energy, Balpho heard his Grand Vizier murmur the words he'd dreaded to hear...

"Go on, your Majesty. Do that thing again."

+++

Joy had never heard the sad, short legend of Balpho the Magnificent - but then again, where she lived the idea of a parable about hubris was nothing new. It's just that even *thinking* about an alien civilization was grounds for ten different types of penitent torture, two of which involved weasels.

That being said, Balpho's situation was about to become very, very clear to her. And it was all about to start with her shoes.

That, and slop. Say this for mental institutions - they really know how to crank out the slop.

The great, gray, grim industrial kitchens of the Cathedral of Penitence were high and sunless. They were huge, echoing pits of concrete where neon lamps popped and sputtered behind rusted grilles. Where clouds of steam hung in he air, smelling eternally of cabbage. Each morning a line of madwomen - with Joy somewhere

242

in the middle - was admitted through a pair of thick iron doors, their scratchy wool cassocks matching the stained concrete perfectly. With their hair hacked short, or plaited and stuffed under sack-cloth caps, the shuffling queue looked like a migration of suicidal penguins.

The Sisters of Perpetual Suspicion kept the line moving. Most every person in it was so full of sedative pills that they needed to be prodded in the right direction every few steps, and the meaty, scowling Sisters were equipped with truncheons to get the job done. Those, and the collective voice of every horrible sergeant major who ever lived, combined with the note of an industrial klaxon. When the Sisters yelled at you - from about three inches away, veins bulging, eyes bugging out like pickled eggs, little flecks of half-chewed cabbage spraying like birdshot - the resultant volume sliced through even the most powerful sedative trance like a gas axe through cotton candy.

Joy kept her head down and tried to be ignored. It had been a strategy which served her well for the rest of her life - case in point, the one time she *had* been noticed was the time they decided she was dangerously insane.

Rel Kitano had taken his sweet time coming back.

Every day she half expected him to come sneaking in - or crashing through the ceiling in some weird spacecraft - to get her out of this austere little hell. Every day that he didn't, the tension inside her head wound one click higher. Because there was, of course, a voice in there, even if she wasn't half as mad as the Sisters thought she was. It was a wheedling, insistent voice, and it told her he was never coming back at all.

She hated it, realized it was herself, and hated it more.

She palmed her pills. She shuffled the line. She washed huge, corroded cauldrons. She lay awake on a thin gray cot, staring at the spiderwebs up in the corners of her cell. She even - out of utter, maddening boredom - read the nasty little ricepaper copy of the *Thinker's Word* they'd left on her nightstand.

There were little clues about the real reason for this place all over. The religious book. The thick, sturdy chains which held up those neon lights. The ample supply of twine, bedsheets, string, shoelaces and sack-cloth. Martyrdom was encouraged, because killing oneself for the sin of being mad was acceptable - no less than three Saints had done it. Certainly, the roll-call of pale, frightened faces in the line each morning was always subtly changing. And Joy didn't think anyone was being cured here.

No, they gave you all the opportunities in the world to kill yourself, and very little else. Joy's personal belongings amounted to the aforementioned scratchy dark gray cassock, some underclothes, a sack-cloth cap, the tatty little *Thinker's Word*, and, because she was sane enough to work as a drudge in the kitchens, a pair of shoes.

The world narrows down when you're trapped in a place like the Cathedral of Penitence. There are prisons where the inmates will cheerfully stab you in the eye for a stick of gum. There are hard, mean little hells set up by wretched authorities, where a packet of cigarettes will make you a god, and paint a target on your back that practically glows in the dark.

Joy was fiercely possessive of those shoes. Designed by the Sisterhood to be practical and nigh indestructible rather than comfortable, they actually looked like the boxes a pair of shoes should be delivered in. But they were better than the paper and cardboard slippers most of the other inmates wore. *The ones that meant, should they ever get out of the Cathedral, that they wouldn't be able to run very far.*

Joy knew she'd need them when he came. She stuffed the too-big ends with toilet paper, and kept them laced up tight. When they were all herded into the crack-tiled, echoing pit of the shower room (once a week, by order), she hung the damn things in a plastic bag around her neck.

This morning Joy had cinched up the laces tight, waited for the door to her cell to rumble open, and joined the line as it shuffled down the stairs, past peeling murals of the Saints and the glory of Worm III, into the refectory hall. Long, splintery tables crouched in the gloom. Hymns crackled and skipped on a hidden PA system. All along one wall waited the Matrons of Plenty, the catering arm of the Sisterhood. The things they could do to innocent vegetables would make the average enQuisitor weep, and not with appreciation for a fellow torturer's genius.

Joy held out her tray as she approached the first Matron, a concrete pillbox of a woman smoking a roll-up and muttering to one of her co-religionists as she ladled slop.

Scoop. Scrape. Splut.

The slop missed. It caught the edge of the tray, spinning it out of Joy's hands, and the remainder spluttered all over her shoes.

She looked down for a second. Patiently cleaning and polishing those heavy leather bastards had been all that kept her within arm's length of real insanity, for *weeks*. A little tic twitched the corner of Joy's eye, and she remembered, very clearly, the crunch Proctor Farbley's nose had made when it collapsed up into his cerebrum.

In the hot, popping silence which followed, it seemed a good sound.

Especially when she looked up again, her eyes razored down to pinpricks of black on green.

Especially when she saw that that fucking fat Matron was *laughing...*

Joy was up over the counter before she knew what was happening. Her first thoughts were all of riotous happiness, as if the Hallelujah Chorus had suddenly come blaring over the PA. She'd grabbed the slop ladle - a well-wrought piece of ironmongery, perhaps two or three kilos of it - before her second thoughts informed her that these were, in fact, the action of a madwoman. Third thoughts chimed in as the ladle described a blurring arc through the air, impacting with the crack of broken teeth in the middle of the Matron's laughing face.

Oh well. They thought I was mad already. The worst that could happen... already has!

Up and down went the ladle. There were cheers from the line, bemused cries, angry shouts coming closer...

Joy battered the Matron down, and delivered a backhand, cabbagey chop to the neck of the next one in line. Blood spattered the gray concrete, vividly bright. She turned, and saw two grinning Sisters advancing on her, truncheons held high. Their arms were as fat as their thighs, which was a dismal and pointless contest.

"He's coming! He's coming for me! All of you will know I'm right! I'm not mad! Me! Not mad! Quite sane, thank you very much! And you'll all bear witness! As the Thinker is my... no, *fuck* the Thinker! Fuck Worm III and fuck his stupid book! I kissed an Angel of the Lord, and he's *coming back for me!* Today!"

Joy realized she was screaming at the top of her lungs, perched atop the slop counter with a bloody ladle in her hand. Horribly warm goop had seeped inside her shoes, making her toes itch.

"Now now," greased one of the Sisters, smiling the smile of a dog-catcher who is all too keen on the old sleepytime injection. "You're just out of your tiny little mind, is all. Nothing a few knocks to the head won't cure, and you'll be nice and sedated in a cosy straitjacket before you know it."

And this is where it would have been nice and synchronous for Joy to have known about Balpho the Magnificent.

Because, miles above Hosanna City, a withering blast of energy had just ignited, ripping into Worm III's battlefleet. It was the one which had reflected off of Mister Fixit's ridiculously powerful umbrella, and, if the bowels of the Cathedral of Penitence had been blessed with windows, everyone would have already seen a faint pink bloom of light in the morning sky. Out there, the screaming had already started.

As it was, the first they knew about it involved the Temperance-standard Mil-spec two-man fightercraft model Z-99, designation Gold squadron, 012-delta-foxtrot. Which came tumbling out of space in a flat spin, burning up on re-entry, its crew of two charred to ashen skeletons before it bit into the Cathedral like a buzzsaw blade, disintegrating as it chewed through a whole swathe of cell blocks and storerooms, and one very surprised and elderly Bishop who was sitting on the toilet.[69]

The wall burst open in slow motion. Pieces of fightercraft came scything through, bolts turned to bullets, rivets popping off like buckshot, a flaming engine nacelle rolling and bouncing as it wiped out a whole squad of Matrons and Sisters. Fire and fury, noise and thunder bloomed around Joy, and it was *right*... it felt just as satisfying and real as the impact of the *Thinker's Word* into Farbley's leering face.

All of it missed her. Shards of superheated steel whickered past close enough for her to feel the bloom of warmth in the air. Scattered pieces of stone and metal ricocheted through the swirling smoke, which cleared as a beam of light came blazing through. The crashed fighter had cut a gash in the side of the Cathedral, and now the light of the dawn came flooding in, rays probing the gloom like ethereal fingers.

Some of that light was not from the sun. Joy looked up into a sky filled with fireworks - the pretty, twinkling lights of atomic explosions in orbit.

She stepped down from the slop counter, and let the ladle clatter from her fingers. Now the reality of what had just happened unfurled inside her head, cold and vast and impossible. Now came an utterly misplaced sense of terror, for something which had already happened. Joy walked past a pilot's seat, embedded in the wall, a burning skeleton dangling from its harness. Her sensible shoes crunched broken diamondglass and stone chips underfoot.

All those sedative pills down the toilet. Just one of them now would be nice...

No.

---

69. There's always one. The balance of tragedy to comedy must be maintained, as the Jest would tell anyone who cared to listen. And as the universe is a place of endless suffering, somebody has to ensure that there's enough laughs to go round...

There was only one person who could be behind all of this. Joy began climbing up through the shattered, collapsed levels of the Cathedral, up a ramp carved into the building by that doomed spaceship. Bits of it were still burning. Behind her, a few mad survivors were having a religious epiphany.

The lights went out all over Hosanna City as klaxons began to wail. Fire was falling from heaven, just like some of the more interesting bits of the *Thinker's Word* said it was going to on judgment day. But Joy had faith in something else entirely.

"Rel Kitano, what *has* been keeping you?" she shouted, scrabbling up and out of the pit.

In the gloom, one of the inmates wrote it down, on the wall, in blood. With a prefix -

The Booke of Joye, Ch I, VI...

+++

Casanova DeSade, Ezra had to admit, *did* have a very impressively long corridor[70]. It was the kind that runs between an armoury full of crazed, high-tech weaponry and an airlock - that is to say it was black, shiny, underlit and filled to knee-height with the kind of crawling mist you can only get with some serious dry-ice or hidden, high-concept sci-fi engineering.

Captain DeSade had both, and he wasn't afraid to use them. This very corridor was sometimes used as a fashion runway when the pirate crew wanted to premiere a new seasonal collection of spikes and feathers.

See it now - with a huge, slowly turning extractor fan at the end, behind a chrome grille. Speakers concealed amid the bundles of wall-mounted pipes and wires begin to thrum out a bass guitar riff, low and insistent.

And here they come. From a convenient side corridor, stepping out in front of that backlit fan, sunglasses on despite being inside, in space, at night...

They're moving in determined slow-mo. A trio of black-clad badasses, weighed down with weapons, space helmets tucked under the crook of their arms, boots flashing with far too many silver

---

70. Though there was no way in several different hells that he'd ever say that in front of him - you can imagine how long the worn-out old dirty jokes would rattle on for...

buckles and zips. Saving the universe, you'd think, could be a distinct possibility.

The drums kick in, and we see that it's Sir Giles Netherbottom-Smythe on the left, in a spacesuit which has been cut to look like an old-time safari costume. He's got crossed bandoliers of shotgun shells across his chest, two sawn-off cannons in hip holsters, and a pair of electrified battle-cutlasses in back scabbards. His helmet is one of those ludicrous 1950s style domes, so that he can wear a bowler hat and a laser-targeting monocle underneath.

Next to him - in the middle, of course - comes Tia Faraday. Slow motion, in combination with a skin-tight gloss-black spacesuit covered in belts, buckles and chains - does wonderful things for her. But it's all about the deadliness, despite the slink in her walk and those *literally* stiletto heeled space boots. She's augmented her Problem Solver with a long barrel, reticule and shoulder stock, turning it into a precision carbine. Her space helmet is a pink 'day of the dead' candy skull.

Finally, here's Ezra Ashdown himself. By this point in the slow-motion badass walk the horn section has kicked in, a tight, hot-jazz loop that fits with his rugged, workmanlike spacesuit, covered in armour panels. He's thrown a black trenchcoat on the top of that, though, because there's such a thing as style. His boots have nuclear trefoil spurs and silver toe-caps depicting prancing horses. Around his waist is an old-fashioned gunbelt, clasped with a silver longhorn skull. His Problem Solver hangs off his hip, the size of a telephone book, and all finished off with new mother of pearl handgrips. His helmet would be utterly regulation, were it not for the fact that he's hot glued a white stetson to the top of it, in defiance of all kinds of logic.

The trio walked down the corridor in extreme slow motion as the song blared out, the light pricking flashes of silver from every rivet and slice of chrome. Considering the sheer distance from the armoury to the airlock, it could have taken quite some time if Tia Faraday hadn't stopped in mid-swagger and addressed the empty air.

"Oi! DeSade! Turn the bloody artificial gravity down, will you? We can't move much faster than an arthritic tortoise in here!"

"Yeah!" chimed in Ezra. "The battle's gonna be over by the time we even get to the door controls."

"I'll say, what?" puffed Sir Giles. "I thought it was just these ruddy huge boots..."

Somewhere, a pair of sequin-gloved fingers cranked a dial. Others, dripping with tasteless gold rings, cut the music with an authentic squeal and pop of offended vinyl. An antique microphone, of the big-chrome-toaster-on-a-stick variety was pressed to pair of zippered lips.

"That was Dick Dale and his bloody Deltones, you philistines," came the voice of the Captain. "But if you're in too much of a hurry to do it right, you might as well get on with it. I've scanned the nearest ships, and there's no trace of human life."

"Huzzah!"

"Hot damn!"

"Bugger!"

(Shouted the Outriders of the Panarchy, in exactly the order you'd imagine).

"Cool it, Miss Faraday," crooned DeSade. "There's plenty of *artificial* life for you to get to grips with. Most of those ships were full of Brothers Militant of the Temperance Marines, and that means they were wearing exo-armour. It's likely to have been possessed by our good friend *Burzum*."

"Sooo... dead bodies in tin cans trying to kill us?" ventured Ezra.

"Almost. Dead, frothing mad religious fanatics who recorded their minds into their powered armour so that they could continue to serve, even in death. My scans show that they were not at *all* my kind of people[71]."

"Then I doubt just dying once was going to make them any more convivial," said Tia. They'd reached the airlock by now, and she slapped the auto-cycle, making the inner doors hiss open.

"The one I tried to establish comms with called me a bile-spewing demon's rectum," put in Wainwright. "Then suggested I seek holy absolution in an industrial food processor."

The inner door slammed shut. Great cyclical pumps began slurping down the air, while the temperature dropped like an elevator in a bad action movie.

Sir Giles drew his swords, and activated them with a crack of both thumbs.

"I do so hate the evangelical ones, don't you?" he asked, taking a few

---

71. The Holy Order of the Temperance Marines was made up entirely of fanatical loonies who agreed to have their (ahem) particulars lopped off surgically, and the bits of their brain responsible for anger, sexual release and religious belief mixed up in a martini shaker. Never before or since have such a meat-headed shower of muscular pillocks loudly declaimed scripture while wielding comically large swords and wearing spiky armour.

hair-raising practice swings. "I mean, by all means try to kill me. But religion is between a man..."

"Or undead, badly mem-corded servo-assisted zombie space knight..."

"And the God I'm about to arrange him a meeting with," finished Sir Giles. With a pair of notched, suspiciously stained electro-blades in his hands the Yorkman didn't look half as twee and anachronous as he used to. He looked like a living reminder of why a handlebar moustache had once meant violent death to anything from the wrong country, faction, tribe or species.[72]

"Helmets on. Switch to short-range comms. We don't want them to know what's coming."

That was Tia, and she followed through by snapping the clasps on her pink candy-skull lid. Ezra and Sir Giles locked in and booted up their encrypted transmitters.

"Glad to have you on team for this one, lads," she said. Her voice came through loud and clear, right in Ezra's ear.

"And an honour to serve with your Panarchy, Miss Faraday," replied Sir Giles. "So long as there's the chance of some lovely hot revenge..."

Ezra was strangely at peace as the outer lock cracked open, a puff of crystallized atmosphere blowing clear as it yawned on vacuum. The last few days - weeks, really, if he counted time frozen solid - had been very complicated. But this - this was easy. This, if the strange little man in the fez was to be believed, was what he had been put here for. Shooting the bad guys.

The trio stepped out into space and activated their propulsion packs - basically a harness holding a manoeuvrable anti-grav plate. A little nudge with the right part of his mind, and Ezra went scudding through the blackness after his fellow outriders, taking just a moment to catch up.

Of course, Sir Giles had done this all before, he realized. Van Rijn's was probably the Panarchy-wide home of nasty little extra-atmospheric battles. And those sabres - well, it was never advisable to punch holes through a spaceship with projectile weapons. Especially not if you were trying to loot it for scrap.

Ezra was proven completely right as they came swooping down on the nearest Temperance warship - this one a half-broken hulk carved open by the *Innuendo*'s guns.

---

72. i.e. Not Britain

Tia landed with a twin *thunk* of magnetized boots, while Ezra slammed into the flank of the ship face first, bouncing off hard enough to wobble back upright. But the man from Grand York was in his element. He twisted as he fell in toward the broken war-cruiser, sabres out, and he flipped at the last moment, disappearing through a great plasma-cut furrow in the ship's side. Tia and Ezra looked at each other and hurried to follow, scuttling to the breach like zero-g cockroaches.

There's no sound in space - not even the sounds that *should* be there, if the universe is to have any sense of style. Which made the sight Ezra saw inside that vast, red-lit cavern of steel all the more horrific. Sir Giles Netherbottom-Smythe didn't speak a word as he fought - there was, every once in a while a satisfied *harrumph* of effort, the kind an old-fashioned artisan might make when he finished assembling a beautiful rosewood chair. Aside from that, there was just the chime of steel on steel, felt through his armour and transmitted by the microphones in his helmet.

There was no up or down. The walls, the ceiling - all thronged with Temperance Marines in their white powersuits, streaked crimson with blood. Explosive decompression and a variety of gnarly, high-pressure explosions had taken their wicked way with this crew, and their eyeless faces were more often than not augmented by tangled wreckages of metal and glass. They were driven on by the ghostly recordings of themselves which rattled about in their armour, and they came at Sir Giles from all sides, wielding everything from antique broadswords to lengths of pipe and torn-off limbs.

They came, and they died.

Well, *again*. But you get the picture.

The moustachioed fury spun and twisted amid a growing nebula of blood and hydraulic fluid, bits of erstwhile people flying out on strange trajectories as his blades reaped their harvest. Ezra watched him carve a marine from shoulder to hip, then spin upside down to scissor another one's eyeless head between both sabres, popping it loose like a champagne cork.

"We're supposed to *interrogate* them!" shouted Tia. "Not just destroy them! We need to know where Mister Fixit's gone, and what he plans to do next!"

Three more undead things came rushing in on Sir Giles, who spun in place, his swords performing the same job as the tines in a top-end cocktail blender.

"They don't seem too talkative, ma'am. Hardly a 'how do you do' amongst 'em, to tell you the truth."

Another pair came clawing at his bubble-dome helmet, but all four of their arms were snickered off like last week's garden prunings.

"What exactly do they call that kinda fighting, Giles?" asked Ezra. "Something you learned in primary school?"

"Well... not as such. *After* school. I attended Sensei Murray Slapnasty's academy of the ancient Eastern Art of *Ono Nononono*. Apparently it came down in a direct line, teacher to student, from Charles Darwin himself."

Ezra watched him finish off another armoured ghoul with a kick to the crotch-plate and a swift flurry of cuts. Arms and legs looped through the air like grisly bottle-rockets. He would have joined in to help, but for the first time in as long as he'd been with them, it looked like Sir Giles was having real fun.

"You don't say."

"Oh yes. The old bugger was quite the fiend with over fifty close-combat weapons. Though of course he favoured the *taiaha*."

Another head went flying. Another crucifix-emblazoned chestplate was run through. For the geeks, it's fun to note here that Sir Giles' sabres were possessed of a mono-atomic chainsaw edge, constantly replenishing itself to remain godawfully sharp.

What was slightly less risible was the sheer number of empty-eyed, armoured ghouls flooding into the chamber. Ezra spun the wheel on the side of his Problem Solver to 'rapid fire' and began hosing them down as they scrabbled in from a tangle of tubes, corridors and collapsed doorways, Jed Granger cackling madly in his head. Tia did the same, taking her time, aiming her shots as her gun *whumped* out vast gobbets of explosive, superheated plasma.

Back on Earth, in deep basements beneath the Scrutinizer's sanctum, automated production lines clattered and thumped, feeding the guns.

"There's too many of them! Wainwright's got it pinned down - the bastards are converging on our position!"

Ezra was in motion now, leaping into a zero-g storm of blades and makeshift weapons. A withering hail of bullets cut through the Temperance Marines, clearing a path to where Sir Giles was backed up to the wall.

He rammed a sword through one of the undead things, let go of the hilt, unholstered a shotgun, neatly amputated another at the neck with buckshot, grabbed his sabre back and swung up and around, lopping off an arm and a leg. Meanwhile his other hand seemed to work all on its own, parrying a relentless series of blows from a third ghoul armed with what appeared to be an actual kitchen sink.

"If you wouldn't mind, Mister Ashdown?"

Ezra flicked the dial on his Problem Solver with a quick thought, selecting 'timed detonation'. A carousel of armaments spun by in darkness, hundreds of light-years away. A box of wicked little rockets snicked up to the wormhole, and one came hissing through. It caught the sink-wielding Marine in the stomach, its head deforming into a mass of smart-coral tendrils, bonding to armour. Then the tiny drive amid its tail-fins popped, flinging the ghoul away. It spun into a crowd of eyeless monsters, and had barely enough time to register surprise before it exploded.

"Messy, but effective," grimaced Sir Giles, finishing the last of his assailants off with a cross-cut of sparking mono-atomic chainsaw blades. "But there's more coming, my lad. It might be time for a heroic last stand, don't you think?"

"I wouldn't know, pardner. Never been in one. What with always having another heroic stand turn up after the previous, you see…"

Ezra looked up, squinting out from under the hat he'd hot-glued to his helmet. The entire ceiling was packed with a veritable mosh-pit of undead, drooling down at them in anticipation.

"They say the last one's the most heroic, of course…" said Sir Giles, but there was a slight tremor in his voice.

"Who does?"

The Yorkman gave that a little thought as he adjusted his grip on his swords.

"Dash it all, that's a good point. Who *does* say that, after being in a heroic last stand? The whole idea is that everyone enjoys a nice, poetic death…"

Tia took that moment to land next to them, both hands on her gun. There was not one inch of her that wasn't dripping with blood, and Ezra was very disquieted to discover how that made him feel.

"I was always a bit of a romantic when it came to poetic deaths," she admitted. "And if either of you say it's because I'm a girl, I'll blow your fucking feet off. But I used to wonder how the poets survived, when everyone else was turned into so much hamburger by the Russian guns, or the giant aphids, or the face-eating robot vampires and such. You know, in the classics."

"Quite lightly armoured, yer average poet," admitted Sir Giles.

"The ones I've met always had one of those tiny teeny little derringer pistols," put in Ezra. "Some of 'em had those cane-swords, too - mostly the sickly looking ones with the sunken eyes and the top hats and the skinny crystal bottles of absinthe."

At this point in the conversation it became apparent that it was the kind used to fill in for gibbering, hopeless terror. The sheer number of horribly re-animated power armour suits filled with malicious corpses standing right above them had swelled to the point where it looked like the crowd at a free open-air rock concert, and, if there was air in space, it would have smelled like one too.

"If it's any consolation," said Tia, "Wainwright traced the signal. The core of the *Burzum* is aboard a ship called *Slog*. Odds are good that Fixit's there too."

Ezra rolled the thought around in his head. As far as consolation went, it was a lot like scratching the winning lottery ticket while aboard a nose-diving 747 airliner.

Just as all those sightless, empty eye sockets swivelled down to stare at them, and countless dead lips pulled back from leering gums, he wondered where all the misplaced metaphors were coming from.

Perhaps, said a slippery, alien part of his mind - one adjacent to the space where Jed Granger was quietly swearing and crossing himself - *it was the same place he'd find a plan.*

"I, uhhhh," he began, idly spinning the Problem Solver around one finger. "Now, how is it supposed to go...?"

Ahh, yes. If this was a really bad story -

"I've got an idea," he said, his voice becoming not just clearer and more purposeful, but glassy, pitched with weird echoes. "An idea so crazy..."

"*It just might work,*" he finished, at the same time as both Tia and Sir Giles. The two of them looked at each other, then back at him, with the kind of expectant combination of hope and horror normally only associated with pictures entitled 'baby's first sawn-off shotgun'.

"And do *we* have to do anything, in the few seconds before all of those ghouls up there need to floss bits of our tendons out of their lovely smiles?"

Ezra gripped the wheel of the Problem Solver and gave it a meaningful twist.

"When the time's about right, blow a hole in the far wall. Or bulkhead, or whatever y'call it. Just a nice wide one."

Jed Granger caught the plan forming, piecing it together from the neural sparks that lit up the inside of Ezra's skull.

"If the cable's long enough, and it finds something to grip onto that's rooted down tight enough, then we might all avoid the ol' choirs celestial," he admitted, with barely a sniff of protest. *"But that's a mighty big* if.*"*

"I thought you'd know *exactly* how long the damn cable was," sent Ez, slotting a series of commands into the gun. Back on Earth, an immense spool of grappling wire rumbled into position, and a missile not dissimilar to the one he'd left on Grand York slid into the breech.

"Oh, I do. I was just tryin' ta give you some hope, *see. It's about thirty metres too short."*

"From orbit? Thirty metres? You sure?"

"Sure as shootin'. Which is about all I do, hoss."

"It's only a little bit of damn cable. Shouldn't make a difference, should it?"

"You tell me," cackled the disembodied space prospector. *"Plenty of good ole boys, they'd tell ya a single inch can be make or break..."*

Ezra racked back the bolt on the nasty little under-barrel doorbuster which was part of the Problem Solver's design. Sometimes, it seemed, Outriders of the Panarchy needed to take a peek where other folks didn't want any prying eyes. Simple things like bank vaults, armoured cars and thirty feet of solid granite were not going to get in the way of the Central Scrutinizer's inhuman curiosity, however - that's why he armed his agents with an optional recoilless antiphoton shotgun charge, perhaps the last word in skeleton keys. God only knew it didn't leave behind many skeletons.

Sir Giles risked a quick little glance away from the teeming horde of undead hanging above them, held in place by the gentle spin of the ship's hulk.

"Usually, in situations like this, there's something that sets it all off. If this was a bad movie, there'd be some music start up about now, and the whole bleedin' lot of 'em would come down like a shower of fresh haddock."

The visor of Tia's candy-skull helmet split into a pixellated grin. A pair of speakers unfolded from the pack on her back, matching the ones in their helmets.

"I hope you like the classics, Mister Netherbottom-Smythe. Because it's about to get *biblical* up in this bitch."

Ezra locked the final codes in place. Things deep beneath the surface of Earth coupled and clicked and slid with oily precision. Jed Granger kissed the cross on a virtual rosary.

And Iggy Pop blasted out through 2400 miniaturised kilowatts of audio gear, the kind which would make a Tchub pirate gill-green with envy.

"I'm a streetwalking cheetah with a heart full of napalm..."

The Ghouls screeched. The ghouls sprung. Feeble centripetal gravity let them go. A thousand damned souls in bloody armour came ravening, half-gnawed claws grasping...

"I'm the runaway son of the nuclear A-Bomb..."

Gunfire shredded them. The sheer volume of flying lead put a whole decade of action movies in the shade. And at the same time, Ezra blasted a neat circular hole in the floor. Rotation spun the hulk, and for an instant he saw the curvature of the planet below, vast and pale with clouds. Jed Granger laughed, utterly unhinged in his head, and he fired the grapple claw. Once - up into the spine of beams and pipework which made up the central spindle of the hulk. Then, as clever interlocks did their thing back on Earth, another one down, through the hole. Down toward Temperance.

"I am the world's forgotten boy - The one who searches and destroys!

Honey gotta help me please... Somebody gotta save my soul... Baby, detonate for meeeeee....."

The Stooges belted it out as Tia and Sir Giles fought hand to hand, or rather hand to sword. The Yorkman had thrown one of his sabres across to Miss Faraday, and she seemed as adept with the slashing blade in one hand as she was with the immense, fire-spitting pistol in the other.

Ezra kept his hand pointed down, watching the cable sizzle through the wormhole muzzle of his gun, watching the metres and hundreds of metres tick by as that spool back on Earth spun wild. Smoke was boiling from its bearings. Tiny sprayer-heads on robot arms deployed to cool it down.

Let there be something[73]. A range of mountains. A convenient escarpment. Some kind of bloody cathedral...

Slavering jaws snapped a hand's-breadth from his face. A press of

---

73. Curiously, these are the first words in the first chapter of the first book of the Dipsotheurgical Bible - the holy text of the Postcelebratory Monks of the Splitting Headache. This sect, whose space-borne monastery orbits a black hole near Rigel, believe that the universe can only be explained if it was created by a God who was suffering a blinder of a hangover at the time. They have developed a stoical, bitter creed over the centuries, and when asked for evidence of their beliefs, they will invariably turn a pair of dark-circled, bloodshot eyes on the questioner and answer 'just look around you, man'. The order have also pioneered a form of throat-singing in unison down massed ranks of finely tuned porcelain toilet bowls.

bloodied limbs and scarred armour crushed in from all sides. And, like an angler feeling that tiny tug on the hook which means dinner, Ezra Ashdown felt the cable bite.

"Tia! Clear it!"

She didn't need telling twice. And neither did Sir Giles. He cleared a path through the ghouls with a withering blast from one of his shotguns, just as the last bit of cable came slithering out of Ezra's Problem Solver. It was a loop - both ends of the cable were joined. And the damned thing was woven from carbon nanotubes. Immensely long fibres, fused immensely strong.

Tia used the underslung 'skeleton key' of her own Problem Solver to core out a neat three-metre hole in the far side of the hulk. Then Ezra grabbed both her and the Yorkman as he powered up his grav-harness to maximum, tackling the pair of them and aiming for the gap...

They flew through just as the cable snapped taut.

Five hundred kilometres below - give or take thirty, of course - Ezra had indeed caught something. The orbiting fleet had swung around the planet in a single great rotation, putting them right over Hosanna City. Down there, at the end of a godawful length of bonded diamond filament, a missile had bored into the Thinker's forehead, ramifying out through the foamed-steel of its body in a burst of coral-like protrusions.

The other end was wrapped around a half-ruined ship full of the living dead. Which was travelling, (relative to the quite colossal, quite immovable Thinker) at 9000 metres per second.

Give or take.

Say this for Worm III - he built them tough.

The hideous chunky warship creased a little as a whole planet dragged it to anchor, three tiny figures catapulting out its far side in a spin. But the trouble didn't really begin until other elements of the fleet - all orbiting at that same 9 kilometres every heartbeat - began to slam into it.

Luckily - or, credit where it's due, entirely by design - they all impacted the side opposite where Ezra and his buddies had just popped out, like watermelon seeds from a railgun. It's utterly fair to say that all those many hundreds of ghoulish Temperance Marines never knew what hit them, though in the interest of honesty, we'd have to admit it was mostly metal.

Three little blips went tumbling away from the wreck, hand in hand.

"Well, You were right. It *was* a crazy idea."

Tia gave his hand a little squeeze, which made it all seem just marginally worthwhile.

"And it worked. Now all we have to do is find whichever one of these is called the *Slog*, and do it all again."

Around them, a fireworks display of inconceivable violence flickered and raved. But none of the target-scanners aboard the *Burzum*'s captured fleet gave them so much as a second glance. There were bigger fish to fry, seeing as Worm III was throwing just about everything he had into orbit. The theocrat of Temperance knew enough about politics to realize that it's hard for your generals to launch a coup against the ruling power when they've been blasted to tiny radioactive pieces.

"As luck would have it," said Tia, "All we have to do is not get incinerated for a few minutes, and we'll be right on top of it. The hard part is going to be stopping before we make a sad little crater in the side of the damned thing..."

"Wainwright again?"

"Bingo. It seems the good ol' *Innuendo* is giving as good as it gets. Those pirates can vape anything which gets too interested in us, so long as we hold together and flare out our grav-packs in exactly... three minutes, forty-two seconds."

Sir Giles harrumphed. There were few living souls in the universe - Galbraith, Sentinel of the Arch included - who could do it better.

"Well, after all that, it's likely to be a fairly boring three minutes indeed, ma'am. Allow me to start us off. I spy with my little eye, something beginning with S..."

Ahead of them, the great spaceborne bauhaus cathedral of the *Slog* hammered away with its guns, scanning the void with a thousand camera eyes. The mind behind them was certain, of course, that these three were long dead, left to slowly mummify in the hot dead air of the Chasm. The other mind on board was composing a song about ponies.

And the other, *other* mind - the unhinged one wrapped up in Mason Stockton's face - was salivating over the prize that was falling in towards it from the outer system.

Too bad, then, that this was in absolutely the wrong direction...

+++

Harrowe was getting an education. *Which,* thought the Central Scrutinizer, *was sort of like a gigantic box of chocolates.* Enthralling, enchanting and delicious as a selection of little morsels to be savoured, but bloody uncomfortable when three thousand years worth was rammed down your throat by a servo-assisted fist.

Things were going to change down there. Oh yes. But up here, it was all about the procession of giant and ponderous ships, slipping from the orbital Chasm gate and taking up station behind the flared Torsion Fields of a Jest Lightbender - a mirrored oblate spheroid he had been informed was called the *Little Dog Toby.*

Tugs flitted about the Home Fleet like worker bees, orange lights strobing. Massive space battleships from a hundred pop-culture touchstones did all but rub shoulders as repulsor fields kept them apart. You couldn't spit without hitting somebody's idea of the last word in galactic domination. Though of course, you couldn't spit in space at all.

"That's the last one, pal," came the message from Galbraith, who had insisted on tagging along. His argument, which the Scrutinizer had found most compelling, was that 'Ye can hae all the guns ye like, right enough. But when it comes down tae it, there's no substitute for a fightin' Glasgow man's forehead'.

"You all set now, big fella? Sure these bloody clowns are gonnae play it straight?"

Central smiled down at the little hologram of his Sentinel, standing next to the candelabra atop his grand piano. It had been difficult to mount a full sized concert grand on the outside of his favourite vessel - the great spherical battlestation which was, indeed, no moon.

But ahh, the *view!*

He cracked his knuckles. The sound was piped in.

"They'll do it, Mister Galbraith. They know about my little friend with the fez - the one in the Chasm. And they know that while his kind don't like mine, *he* understands that the flock of humanity, as it were, needs something special to guard it from the wolves. Metaphorically speaking."

"So they play fair, or they get done over by whoever tells yon beardy wee git how tae do his job?"

The Scrutinizer deciphered this momentarily. He rattled off a quick scale, ivory and ebony flickering beneath his rubber fingertips.

"Perhaps. Perhaps they just think we're more interesting than the Process. If our friend is right, *they* may actually have sorted out the meaning of life, the universe, and all existence. And all it will get us is turned off at the wall."

Galbraith grinned. Even his hologram, covered in tiny keys, looked slightly dishevelled.

"Right said, boss man. Right enough. Makes me wonder just wha' kindae guardian us poor human sheepies have got, aye?"

The Central Scrutinizer carefully shut the lid of the piano. His eyes - not the two in his head, which were blue and green glass, just for show, but *all* of them - took in the halo of steel and titanium which currently encircled Harrowe. Down below them, they were burning bonfires of the *Book of the Orth*. Jed Granger, snug in Ezra's gunbelt, would likely approve. In every direction stretched a gathering of force, a panoply of firepower taken from the collective imagination of the human race.

"Another wolf, of course. You bastards are the kind of sheep who'd eat anything less for dinner, Galbraith."

The holographic Scotsman laughed. While up ahead, those shimmering Torsion Fields flared. The local speed of light was persuaded, in no uncertain terms, to sidle around the corner for a quick cigarette and never mind what was going on, alright. If it knew what was good for it.

All around Harrowe, the sky lit up with the hazy blue contrails of countless ion drives, following the Jest Lightbender into the dark. Brave men hugged their families to them, standing in the doorways of general stores and tobacconists and ostlers and grain merchants. Kids pointed up in wonder as sparks descended, trailing threads of pale white vapour. Slightly smarter (but perhaps more cowardly) men realized that the current authorities were about to get the rudest of all wake up calls, and layed their hands on things like lockpicks, and six-guns, and tiny bottles with skulls drawn on them.

Change was inevitable, thought the Central Scrutinizer. Change was, in fact, often found down the back of the sofa. Harrowe was going to be different. But perhaps less dynamically, explosively different than Temperance, just two quick jumps away.

The cavalry was coming. Hopefully it would be enough, and arrive on time.

+++

Joy staggered away from the ruined cathedral, unnoticed amid what appeared to be a full military mobilization. Civilians were already supposed to be underground, in the great concrete bunkers which the church had prepared in case of an invasion by the Unrighteous.

Many of the buildings around the Thinker were burning, and though, of course, the Machine God was invulnerable (cross yourself, look up at the heavens, notice they're full of burning spaceships, try to forget about it), there were still hordes of firefighters, priests, deacons, enQuisitors and even an Archprelate or two yelling contradictory orders through megaphones as Hell unfurled merrily around them.

Joy set her face in the grim look of someone with a clipboard striding meaningfully down a factory corridor, and pushed against the tide. It helped that during her escape she'd found a sack full of potatoes. Say this about Temperance - nobody ever questioned a woman going somewhere with a large quantity of root vegetables.

She had her shoes on. One was still half full of horribly cold slop. As for a disguise, the choking dust covered everyone in gray, so that the only way to guess their rank, purpose or degree of holiness was the volume and vehemence with which they were damning each other.

Joy kept walking. The only thing on her mind was Rel Kitano. It was a certainty that all of this was his fault, and she didn't entirely know how to feel about that. Certainly, the society which she'd grown up with left a lot to be desired - rubber ducks, the colour pink, jigsaw puzzles and the like - but surely it was a bit irresponsible of him to destroy the lot of it just for her?

Then again, the fact that he *could*, and the fact that all of this *was* just for her made Joy feel more than a bit strange. If he thought she was worth smashing a planet for... well. Joy had never seen that old film about the 100-foot-tall gorilla and the lady in the revealing nightdress, but certain themes were being revisited.

And still nobody stopped her. It couldn't be this easy. It shouldn't be this easy. Any second now he'd be right there, but then again, any second now so would *they*...

They won.

"Halt! You there! Yes, you!"

Years of horribly insidious discipline made her feet turn traitor. They stopped of their own accord. And after she'd bribed them with bloody shoes, as well! The sack of potatoes slipped from her fingers, several tubers making a determined roll for freedom.

"Turn around slowly. Hands on your head. Are you, as our scans indicate, Sister Noviate (diminished) Joyful Praise Be Unto Our Lord

The Thinker?"

Joy shuffled around in a sad little circle. This particular *They* was exactly what she'd been dreading. A Quistionary hunter cadre, with their robotic mastiffs and their black leather hoods like upside-down liquorice icecream cones. All the nonsense with the knee-high boots and too many spikes and the big silver crucifixes on chains was much in evidence.

"You should have known you couldn't run, girl. Not after that little display. Chucked in the hole for bloody murder, and you still found a way to squash twelve more. That's *inventive*, that is. If we didn't have to twist your head off, we'd want you on the team."

A short, fat Proctor carrying a brass-bound *Thinker's Word* leered.

"Get yerra card, and wotsit. Nice new desk calendar. Don't have to be a sadistic torturing bastard to work here, but it helps."

A big, baby-faced enQuisitional squire nodded. A bubble of snot popped noisily from one of his nostrils. Another one, with the overall look of a bondage-and-discipline ferret, cackled wetly.

"Look - it wasn't *like* that. Well, maybe the first one. But he was being... *improper*. And the others got a spaceship dropped on them. Which, I must admit –" Joy held up one finger, to stop any more snot popping and cackling. "May have been my boyfriend."

"Your *boyfriend*?" asked the head enQuisitor. His voice managed to raise an eyebrow, even if his cowl couldn't.

"He's probably an Angel of the Lord, though he might be some kind of space alien," said Joy, very matter-of-factly. "And I *say* boyfriend, but we've never really, you know..."

"He just drops spaceships on people for you..." sneered Ferret Face, who, it must be admitted, would have been a fine inspiration if Bruce Springsteen had ever wanted to record a song entitled *'Born to Sneer'*.

The Chief enQuisitor pinched the bridge of his nose. This current unrest was, he was sure, just a minor hiccup. His life had been proof positive that power and influence could move a sufficiently cruel man along on greased rails and castors, and the devil literally take all those who got in the way.

"I've heard quite enough. Young lady, you're utterly mad. Mad, mad, mad. Several baskets, blankets, sandwiches, ant infestations and bottles of cheap Chablis short of a picnic. Thanks to the current emergency, that means it's my unpleasant duty to blow your bleedin' head off, with this pistol you see right here before you."

"Unless," piped up Baby-Face "Your *boyfriend* drops a spaceship on us! Hur, hur, hur!"

Joy didn't even have to look up. The sound a steel ruler several miles long being *thrummmmmed* against a cosmically large desk filled the air. The ground lurched. And she took a quick step backwards...

+++

It had been called the *Righteous Smugness*, one of a dozen heavy missile destroyers cranked out by Worm III's orbital factories as part of a campaign to boost employment and general flag-waving jingoist fervour. Then, for a while, it had been part of the great, seething-mad collective called the *Burzum*.

Now it was tethered to the top of that intractable lump of spun metal and stone called the Thinker, nominally the God of its creators. And it was coming down. Gravity finally had it's fingers around the several million tons of space warship, and it wasn't letting go. It was packed to the brim with rather confused re-animated Marines, anti-captial-ship nuclear torpedoes and, for some reason, most of the Temperance Fleet's supply of tinned clam chowder.

See it light up delicate rose and violet around the edges as it kisses the atmosphere. Nothing that big should be airborne. Tiny pieces peel away in the slipstream as it descends, just one of a whole scintillating rain of space debris coming down hard today...

There are absolutely no extra points awarded for guessing where it's going to land. When the Central Scrutinizer is asked 'how long is a piece of string', the answer is always 'long enough to hang you with'...

+++

Nearly there.

Ezra had managed to suppress the urge to slap Sir Giles all the way through S for Space, V for Void, E for Eternal Emptiness and V again for Vacuum.

Now the great looming flank of the *Slog* was nearly upon them, its armour stark and white against the B for Blackness of Infinity. But something wasn't quite right.

As Ashdown watched, a stray piece of space debris spun past them and flashed into nothingness. Another followed. A skittering webwork of red hexagons bloomed around each impact, then faded

263

away. Just like...

"Ummm, Miss Faraday? You know that armour field thing you got goin' on? Do they put those on spaceships?"

A larger chunk of metal pirouetted by, flashing into radiation and dust just a hundred metres or so from the *Slog*'s hull.

"Ohhhhh, bugger," said Tia through the intercom. "*Wainwriiiiiight!*"

+++

As well as being absolutely awash with hormones and THC[74], Rel Kitano's blood also sang to the high-frequency chatter of billions of nanites - tiny little robots of Process design which scoured his insides for antiquated ills like arterial plaque and cancer. They were self-replicating, voracious, vigilant, and copulated like teenage bunnies on viagra.

There were always plenty in all of Rel's various bodily fluids, waiting to be passed on. In the cloistered little human habs of the process home system, this gave the nanites a chance to evolve and swap information when human nature took its inevitable course.

Which meant that there was now a colony of the little buggers elsewhere, too. Unsanctioned, of course, but when you create what is effectively a robotic virus, you have to expect a little colouring outside the lines...

Joy had been quite right about the nuthouse, you see. Most of the inmates succumbed to a variety of antiquated and nasty diseases from out of a Victorian grandmother's almanac[75]. However, despite a steady diet of slop, no sunlight and a water supply more lively than a Calcutta street party, Joy had enjoyed the best of health since... well, since kissing Rel Kitano.

Funny, that.

Of course, as soon as she broke cover and stood under the open sky, alarms rang out in Rel Kitano's head. Screens coalesced out of

---

74. Poulson Vance believed that Marijuana was a Holy Sacrament of the Faith. Mainly because this enabled his congregation to increase the Faith at the rate of about a hundred bucks for a very small bag.

75. Like the Shrugs, Liver-and-Onions Fever, Saint Christopher's Evil, the King's Menace or Romping Scrobbles. In the days of Charles Dickens nearly everything that could kill you was given a funny name by the Royal Onomasticator of the Malaises, a red-cheeked old lady in a mob cap and apron who gave all the types of weeping, pustulating, withering, twisting and otherwise festering illnesses of the time jolly names to prevent mass suicide.

nothingness around him, zooming in on her from above.

He saw the enQuisitors. He saw their snapping robo-hounds and guns and spiked bats. And he saw, with awful clarity, the vector-plotted path of the *Righteous Smugness*, on a course to make a crater of them all.

Rel's howl of rage was bestial and incoherent, but the limited AI of the Immaterial Dreadnought knew exactly what to do. It cycled through weapons systems, bypassing all the hundreds of flavours of death at its disposal. It chose something else.

Then the whole ship curled up in its impossible un-space behind Rel. Coiled up like a spring and *launched* itself, right down the throat of the gravity well toward Temperance.

+++

"Now!" Shouted Mister Fixit.

His grin of utter triumph was spoiled only slightly by the fact that he was using Mason Stockton's bizarre and frightening array of teeth.

The *Slog* - and twenty other great Temperance ships of the line - fired as one. Ruby-red beams of energy licked out, and met the invisible lens which Cerise had fashioned in front of them. All that energy focused in, intertwining, harmonics building, turning mere incandescent death into a raving holocaust of power.

Surely enough to cripple the defences of an Immaterial Dreadnought. Maybe even enough to barbecue the inane little pillock riding out in front of it, flying through space like some kind of (and here Mister Fixit had to bite down on one rubber knuckle in disgust) *super hero*. Gah!

But at the last second, though, the little bastard jinked! He *dodged!*

There was no way he could have seen it coming, but the primitive pet human managed to throw his craft into a spine-snapping manoeuvre which would have been impossible with Panarchy tech. The raving beam of power which was supposed to have stripped him atom from atom simply brushed the edge of the Dreadnought's onion-skin Dirac Fields...

They screamed. They shattered open in a way which was both like liquid and like an unfurling of crystal petals at once. Immense glassy planes of alien geometry feathered the void. Shimmering infinities collapsed and danced.

It split the beam. It wove it backwards and forwards between mirrored surfaces *that didn't even face each other.* It picked it up and tangled it and threw it back.

"*Burzum!*" shouted Mister Fixit, as he saw a ball of energy the size of a small moon flung back at them. "All power to the fore shields!"

+++

Rel Kitano was pitched into a flat spin as Mister Fixit's energy beam raked down the side of his ship. It may not have been fully operational, cut off from the insane engines of destruction which made it so godawfully dangerous, but it could still preserve itself. And the AI which haunted its echoing great shell had no qualms about saving others.

The corkscrew trajectory Rel was now on posed no problem for the Dreadnought's targeting subsystems. They launched a very specific missile as Rel skipped across the atmosphere of Temperance, scudding toward the line of dawn and the towers of Hosanna City.

The missile flew boldly on ahead, its boosters propelling it so far beyond the speed of sound that the collapsing boom in its wake was confused about how it got there.

It was, of course, just in the nick of time. Ezra would have found this both amusing and rather enabling of his peculiar psychosis.

Those who saw it said they watched the girl in the shabby robes step backward, look up to the sky and press her hands together in prayer. Some say that they saw her forgive the enQuisitors, while yet others swore she just said 'Thanks, baby'. Yet more recount that she was smiling. And making a very rude gesture.

Nobody disagreed about the next part, though. It's hard to disagree with millions of red-hot tons of space battleship crashing down from above. To say that those poor misguided enQuisitors died instantly is an understatement. The Grim Reaper was barely getting his socks on by the time it was too late. They didn't so much as shuffle off this mortal coil as rip it apart like those button-domed stripper pants they wear in all-male dance revues.[76]

Rel Kitano's Process-made missile, however, slid in under the falling shadow of the *Righteous Smugness* with milliseconds to spare. Shield projectors of a kind Mister Fixit was at that very moment praying for

---

76. Allegedly.

bathed Joy in what everyone later agreed was a particularly holy light.

In any case, it stopped every last piece of flaming, burning, crushing space wreckage from touching her. An area of roughly six city blocks was not so lucky.

Those people who witnessed the Miracle (complete with a capital M) obviously did so from quite far away. Nevertheless, they were pretty darn impressed.

+++

"Wainwright can't help us. But don't worry. There's no way something like that can kill us now."

Tia was, to put it mildly, a bit incredulous.

"*Really?* Then how come it's having such an easy time of evaporating *chunks of metal?* I hate to burst your bubble, pal, but we're not exactly made of battleship armour..."

"I, for one, have made peace with my God," said Sir Giles. "And at least we gave those bloody zombie things a damn good thrashing, what?"

Ezra smiled. He could feel it again - the oily, glassy sensation that all of reality was pressed up against the inside of an old-fashioned cathode-ray tube.

"We're the main characters, folks. Booby traps and such don't stop us. Got to be a real villain you can hear the whole big plan from, then he traps you in some kind of complicated death machine..."

"A phased plasma shielding array *is* a complicated death machine, you freak!"

And now it was close enough to spit on.

Close enough to touch...

A tiny wingnut spun past Ezra's face and sizzled into dust, just before his helmet met with....

Nothing.

The whole gridwork of hexagons shimmered red and receded, pulling away like an ebbing tide.

All three Outriders of the Panarchy sailed through, spinning at the last second to impact the side of the *Slog* with six magnetic-soled boots.

Nobody wanted to look at him. Nobody wanted to say anything. Embarrassment hung like a red-hot fog around all three as Tia hacked an airlock and hustled them inside.

There was gravity. There was atmosphere. There was a light jazz soundtrack being piped in through hidden speakers. There were even potted ferns, though these, Ezra thought, were probably plastic.

He popped off his helmet and took a deep breath. No poison gas. Not even the funky green and purple knockout stuff. Of course, though, at this stage of the game, it really *did* need to be the main villain who confronted you. It was about time for...

"Outriders of the Panarchy!" sneered a voice like God winning at Monopoly. ***"You have vexed me for far, far too long! First Harrowe, then Van Rijn's, now here! Who exactly** are **you, before I erase you once and for all?"***

It was Mister Fixit, and he was in the mother of all bad moods. Just when he was sure he'd got Rel Kitano dead in his sights, the little snot had escaped. And then... then this bunch of annoying, incompetent, deluded little meat-puppets had dared to come after him - *again*! Really, it was like some kind of infestation of vermin!

Ezra Ashdown didn't know where the answer came from, but he drawled it with all the cigar-smoke, stubble, whiskey breath and twinkling eyes of his secret soul.

"Some people call me the space cowboy."

Tia popped open her helmet next to him, and hefted her Problem Solver in both hands.

"Some call me... the gangster of love? What the hell?" It was obvious she had no idea where the words were coming from.

"Some people call me Maurice," said Sir Giles. "Though to be fair, it's only one of my middle names..."

None of them were quite sure where the slightly sarcastic wolf whistle came from, but it was probably something to do with Casanova DeSade, through the intercom.

"Oh, who bloody cares?" snarled the homicidal android. ***"Kill them all! I'll sort them out when I'm a God!"***

Inside Ezra's head, the music spooled out. An old song, to be sure, and not really one suitable to the current situation. Not when hundreds of drooling, grinning undead Marines in powered armour burst from concealment all around, empty eye sockets promising oblivion.

The trio put up their guns as the instrumental came sliding in. And they promised right back.

Eighteen - How To Die 201 – Introduction to Advanced Fatality

Bomb for Tranquillity
Fight for Peace
Drink for Sobriety
Screw for Virginity
And may God have mercy on whoever does the washing up!

The credo of the 105th Panarchy Spaceborne Cavalry - the 'Fightin'
Hellpunchers'

THEY WENT CORRIDOR by corridor. They did it the old fashioned way
- energy beams, to keep from puncturing the hull and letting out all
that precious atmosphere. They stitched lurid burn marks across the
white-tiled walls and sliced Temperance Marines in half, cooking
them crispy in their armour.

Tia was a valkyrie, laughing as she blazed away at the enemy, her
Problem Solver swinging at her hip. Sheets of withering fire licked out
from its muzzle, devastating wave after wave of horrors.

Ezra's eyes were all gone to static. This was the eternal moment he
lived in, somewhere in his moebius strip of a mind and soul. His pistol
delivered justice to these poor wretched things - the kind of justice
which says *you stay down when you're dead.*

Whatever the chasm had put in him, all those years ago... well,
it was having its moment. Jedediah Granger stalked next to him,
illuminating targets and whooping with laughter as Ashdown's trick-
shots punched through heads and chests and walls, painting the
ceramic white to red.

Sir Giles took care of anything which came too close. Those electric
swords never grew dull, never ran out of power, and (as has been
noted elsewhere) never ran out of ammunition. The Yorkman had
the precision of a surgeon and arms like steam-driven pistons - his
opponents would have had more chance just jumping into a wood
chipper.

And that's *why we love killing zombies.* Thought Ezra. *You don't have to feel bad about it, not even a little bit. There's no zombie wife and kids waiting in this guy's backstory. There's no little zombie house with a white picket fence waiting when he comes home from work. There was no chance at all that they were characters, with their own hopes and fears and a zombie labrador named Scraps. And that meant they were nothing more than special effects - meat piñatas designed to rack up an impressive body count.*

There was a part of him which knew he was wrong. Any one of the very real, very dangerous, very blood-stained and reeking Temperance Marines could have torn out his windpipe as easily as gurgle at him. But that part was being relegated to a kind of author's commentary at the back of his mind. Even more distressingly, he was starting to hear the *narrator*[77].

"Ashdown ducked and rolled around the corner, his Problem Solver sizzling hot as he sliced through a knot of Marines, sending them sprawling. Tia was right behind him, and her gun spat hard energy once, twice, microwaving two more of the undead things as they tried to bring a heavy plasma cannon to the fray. Sir Giles brought up the rear, blood dripping crimson from his swords. He turned to Ashdown and said..."

"What the hell are you muttering about? Some kind of prayers after all, space cowboy?"

"Any help we can get," said Tia, pressing herself into an alcove and risking a glance down the white-tiled corridor. "*That's* the door to the bridge. And that means we've got him holed up where we want him."

Ezra chanced a look as well. It was a very impressive door indeed. Framed by robed angels holding two-handed swords. Carved with hundreds of tiny little lines of scripture. And, more importantly, very, very solid.

"It seemed," he narrated, "that the Outriders of the Panarchy had come to the end of the road..."

"It seemed *what?* Not today, big guy. I've got a hundred ways to peel this sardine can open. We could set some shaped charges of explosive q-foam..."

"Which we haven't got."

"Or use a hacking spike to access the ship's override sub-systems..."

"Or one of those..."

"Or perhaps we could set our Problem Solvers to superheated

---

77. We're cheap, but in his head it was done by the great Morgan Freeman. Of course.

plasma mode and just slice on through. It's only a metre thick, give or take. Should take, oh, no more than six hours."

"The boss said we got less'n three, Miss Faraday. Next?"

"Well, it *could* just open all on its own," said Sir Giles.

Tia rolled her eyes.

"Oh suuuuure. Just like that. How convenient. Just when we have Mister Bloody Fixit right where we want him, he just comes out and..."

Ez tapped his parole officer on the shoulder.

"Ummm. yeah. About that..."

The door *was* opening. Hairline cracks had appeared between the graven lines of scripture, and whole gilded slabs of it began to grind away, rumbling back into the walls. Behind the sound of hundreds of tons of metal being shifted came a very slow, very sarcastic round of applause.

"Bravo, Outriders. *Bravo*. It seems you've taken care of my little pets. But we all knew they were just a diversion. A warm-up, if you will."

"Aha! Snap!" said a possibly psychotic part of Ezra Ashdown's mind.

"You see, it's not that I'm locked up in this huge, empty, blood-soaked hulk of a ship with you..."

Now the lights came on inside the door's arch, and Mister Fixit stood framed in the gap. He was wearing Mason Stockton's skin and a dapper little three-piece number, complete with a bowler hat. His grin was still cheery, in a stretched-rubber way, but the teeth behind those artificial lips were a jostle of cracked and jagged ivory that would make a dentist jump out of a tenth-storey window.

"Oh no. You're trapped aboard this huge, empty, blood-soaked hulk of a ship with ME!"

A smaller figure stepped forward into the light and elbowed Mister Fixit sharply in the ribs. The robot winced.

"*Us*. I mean you're trapped here with US!"

If anything, Cerise was far more frightening than her erstwhile Uncle. There's something about a little girl in a fairy costume, grinning from ear to ear and covered in blood, which makes the skin crawl. Especially when she appears to be wearing a necklace made of human noses.

"Now, you know me, don't you? And you really should be curtsying or something, seeing as I'm a princess. But I'll let it go. Seeing as how you're all going to die."

Tia stepped forward, eyes grim, her Problem Solver focused on the little girl's forehead. A tight pattern of laser-targeting dots spun in to a single point.

"You're Chasm Reticulation Artificial Deity (insane) 1984 - D - designation Harrowe Primary. And I thought I'd have to be doing this in French, so excuse my English, but you are *fucking well* under arrest. *Je arrete vous*, bitch!"

Cerise laughed. It was the merry sound of pixies on crystal meth.

"Oh, don't be a silly. Dying's not a major problem for you, now, is it? It'll just keep you out of the way for a while. And Uncle says that at least the one in the white hat will appreciate the idiom, whatever that means."

"Fine," snarled Tia. "I hope they have ponies in hell..."

She pulled the trigger, just as Cerise snapped her fingers. And the Problem Solver spat...

A little flag, which unrolled in a deliberately un-funny way. It said - and yes, you guessed it - BANG!

Cerise giggled. With what can only be termed malice aforethought.

"I'm a Princess with all the powers of a - what did you call it? Chasm Reticulation thingummy whatsit. *Magic*, anyhow. The little holes inside your guns are just like the big ones we use to jump between planets." She shrugged. "Now they don't work anymore."

Ezra stared at the ghost of Jed Granger, as that ancient illusion held up his hands in front of his face. Jed screamed, utterly silent, and began to unravel into pixels and code. The Problem Solver stuttered, puffed a little hiss of smoke, and suddenly became very, very heavy in his hands.

"Now, then. Now then," said Mister Fixit, literally rubbing his fingers together with glee. "This is the part where I turn off most of the lights, except for those neon tubes which pop and flicker of their own accord. You've already painted most of the ship with blood and guts for me to set the mood. So all that remains is to SHOW YOU PITIFUL HUMANS MY FINAL FORM! BWAAAHAHAHAHAHAHAHAAAAAA!"

He didn't look at all convinced about that last bit, even though it was ten times louder than normal.

"Is that what I do? Final form? Is that supposed to be before or after the death-trap, and the big speech, and the explosion?"

"Tia?" asked Ashdown. The raised eyebrow said it all.

"Oh yes. It's time to do the whole 'run for your life' bit..."

Mister Fixit seemed to come to a conclusion.

"AHAAAAA! BEHOLD, FLESH-CREATURES! CAN YOUR PUNY MINDS COMPREHEND THE HORROR OF MY TRUE

REALITY?"

The homicidal handy-mech took off his bowler hat and threw it away. He produced, from who knew where, a collapsible magician's silk top hat, popped it open and put it on. Then he crossed his arms over his chest, got a good grip on both his jacket and pants, and tore them asunder, in the manner of those all-male dance revues we mentioned earlier.[78]

Underneath he was wearing sequined undershorts patterned with hearts, ladies' fishnet stockings, high heels and a garter belt. Also a feather boa, for some reason.

The lights went out, switching to emergency crimson, as Mister Fixit's head started rotating on the axis of his neck. Stockton's skin ripped at the adam's apple, his face pulled grotesquely to the left.

"Do you see what I am becoming? DO YOU SEE? DO YOU SEE? DO! YOU! SEEEEEE?"

Cerise looked up at her Uncle and shook her head.

"Utterly mad," said the planetary AI who thought it was a little French fairy princess. "I suppose I'd better get you killed, then." She turned into the darkness of the bridge, and whistled, high and piercing.

"Bubbles. Fluffy. *Get them!*"

Ezra and Tia nodded to each other.

"Running away now?"

"Running away, boss."

A very insistent, very metallic wheezing and clanking - as of huge hydraulic-driven claws on metal - echoed out of the darkened bridge. Four red lights ignited in the gloom - at just the right height to suggest two pairs of eyes.

If those eyes were affixed to, say, something the size of a steroidal rhinoceros.

"No," said Sir Giles. "Not today. No more running."

He shrugged them off, spat, clicked his neck left and right and held up his swords.

"Last stand, old chaps. Got to have one. Mine has been quite overdue."

Ezra and Tia grabbed an armpit each, and tried to drag the Yorkman away by main force. Edges and planes were appearing out of the gloom behind the bridge door, hinting at great servo-assisted limbs

---

78. Allegedly

and claws like butcher's hooks.

But he wasn't moving.

"Dammit, Giles!" swore Ezra. "Last stands, again? You know the problem with those, right?"

"Their *lastness*, I presume. But I assure you, this is what I was sworn to do. Following you was just a way to get to the robot fiend who killed my master. Terribly sorry and all that, but it's the burden of a gentleman knight."

Ezra's right eye twitched. There was something wistfully pre-determined about Sir Giles' little speech. Something that made him think, suddenly, about that fez-wearing elderly bastard in the Chasm, and his mind-erasing tricks.

"Listen, man. *You don't have to*. I'm motivated enough. You think we need the quest-companion-who-joined-in-suspicious-circumstances-but-proved-to-be-a-big-hearted-hero-sacrificing-himself-to give-the-main-character-purpose bit? We don't! We can do this! Together! We can get you home!"

Sir Giles gently removed Tia and Ashdown's hands from his shoulders. Behind him, Mister Fixit was still levitating, head spinning like a cut-rate special effect.

"Dash it all, man! We're down to three, and I'm *clearly* not the one you'll be kissing in the final scene. We both know that none of us have a home left to go to. Now, *run*, you fools, before those two things..."

But there was no more time. Those two things were *here*.

Bubbles and Fluffy had only one reason to exist. That was plainly apparent from their drillbit teeth, chainsaw tongues, red-hot soldering-iron mandibles and laser-pointer eyes. Each one was armed with retractable buzzsaws in its paws, as well as a set of claws which would have made a velociraptor blush. Each one had a tail tipped with a scorpion-sting harpoon. They came from the horrible little part of the human brain, about the size and shape of a rancid liver-flavoured jellybean, which makes certain flat-headed policeman want to sic vicious dogs onto anti-war protesters.

The part which would really, really, rather they were wolves, but the Chief has told them they're on a budget.

Each one was the size of a family sedan, and each one was possessed by the frothing mad homicidal mind of the *Burzum*.

Sir Giles fended off a set of slicing claws with one sword and a snapping set of jaws with the other. Sparks flew, electricity crackling blue and purple.

"*Run, ya dim muppets! I can't keep these two slags off yer back all day, right?*"

Sabre strikes chimed and sizzled through the air. Each blade was a metallic blur, trailing after-images as the great robotic hounds snarled and attacked.

It was the fact that Sir Giles had lost the accent which snapped Ezra out of his trance. That, and Tia almost dislocating his arm from his socket.

"We can't leave him!"

"Well, we can't stop those two, either, so what do you reckon's best? Should we clog their jaws with our mutilated corpses? Or should we *run?*"

They ran.

Ezra risked a look over his shoulder as they pelted away, into the dimly red-lit corridors of the *Slog*. It was, indeed, painted with blood and littered with bodies. Just like it should be, for a deadly game of cat and mouse with killer robots.

The last he saw of Sir Giles was his triumphant grin as he rammed a sabre clean through Fluffy's head, putting out both of its camera eyes. The gigantic beast howled - but then here came Bubbles, jaws wide open, drillbit fangs grinding...

He never saw them slam shut. Which was, perhaps, just as well.

Not knowing was about the only hope Ezra Ashdown had about his very immediate future, after all.

The last thing he *heard* - before Tia dragged him around a corner and deeper into the labyrinthine guts of Worm III's capital ship - was this...

"When you get to hell, you infernal device - tell Satan that I'm *terribly* sorry for the inconvenience. I seem to keep sending him *total bastards!*"

+++

Patrol Constables Thoushalt and Woebeunto[79] had been told to hold the intersection.

This, their superior had felt, was the very limit of complexity with which he could phrase their orders. Neither Thoushalt (the tall

---

79. That's 'Thou Shalt Not Commit The Crime of Onanism In Thy Great-Uncle's Garden Shed O'Shaunessey' and 'Woe Be Unto The Unrighteous Who Spurn The Commandments About Socks Smith'

muscular one with the jaw like a piece of concrete foundation) or Woebeunto (the squat, apelike one with hands like bunches of bananas and a neck like a wedding cake made of beef) weren't particularly bright. Sure, they would cheerfully embark on any kind of suicide mission you cared to mention, up to and including eating a live grenade with a knife and fork. But try to add the slightest nuance, or the suggestion to use some initiative, and the pair were about as much use as a water-soluble submarine, or grapefruit flavoured trousers.

To be fair, they at least looked nice and mean, with their black leather jackets, black leather pants, big knobbly boots and motorcycles. Nothing sinful was getting past these two. Nothing cunning could surprise them - because frankly, things like baked beans, rain, buttons and rice pudding surprised them.

They were, in fact, the perfect pair to witness a curdling and rippling of the air right above the intersection. Lightning crawled and fizzed among the wires and stoplights. Fireworks popped and faded, finally revealing a man standing in the air, his arms outstretched like those of a benevolent angel.

That image was completely spoiled by the tattoos, the lack of a shirt, the massive pink bubble of gum protruding from his mouth, and, last but not least, the raccoon tail.

Rel Kitano *did* have a halo, though it was the light bending around a pendulous drop of energy field malarkey - one which deposited him on the pavement, boots gently steaming. He looked up at nothing, and pointed to a spot on the corner.

"Go park yourself up, right? Try and be a little inconspicuous, though."

Thoushalt and Woebounto's aviator-style shades followed a ripple in the air as it hovered overhead. Rarely, if ever, had 'nothing at all' seemed so overbearingly huge. There was a stuttering flash, like welding seen from underwater, and all of a sudden *there had always been* a somewhat battered Pacific Bell phone booth standing on the corner.

Their eyes swivelled back to the strange newcomer amongst them, who was grinning. He held in one hand - though they had no idea what it was - a vintage Nintendo Game Boy. This had been the best disguise the Dreadnought could think of for the little screen which tracked Joy's embarrassing nanite infestation.

"Okey dokey, guys - glad to meet you. Now, I know this is a little unorthodox, but..."

Even the dimmest Patrol Constables - those who have only been given the job because of how tough they look in leather - learn to follow their instincts. Both Thoushalt and Woebeunto knew a wrong 'un when they saw one, and their natural instinct was to pound, prosecute, and let someone with more than the requisite three brain cells to rub together formulate some questions later.

That's why Constable Thoushalt suddenly found himself upside down, slamming into the side of that new (but quite obviously old and long-established) phone booth. He slid down with a grunt, the world still gently wobbling from concussion.

Constable Woebeunto's massive, hairy-knuckled fist was nonchalantly gripped in Rel Kitano's fingers. With but a little pressure, he forced the musclebound Temperancer to his knees.

"*I need your clothes, your boots, and your motorcycle,*" he said, without even a trace of an accent.

Some feeble twinge of race memory made Constable Woebeunto slightly disappointed that Rel Kitano wasn't a robot.

But only for a second or two. Then the Domesticated's other fist drew back, and put him out for the count.

+++

The reactor core level of the *Slog* was not a place where Health and Safety had ever reared its ugly, yellow-helmeted head. Not during its tenure as the flagship of a homicidal space Pope and his horrible clergy, and definitely not now. Not in the red-lit, steam-hissing gloom where Ezra Ashdown and Tia Faraday skulked, one step ahead of a gigantic robotic killing machine.

Really, he thought, *it was days like this which put people off the hero business.*

Poor old Sir Giles must have done for at least one of the two great chrome engines which Mister Fixit had set on them. But the one that was left would be bad enough. Without guns, they were reduced to a small and shiny assortment of knives, all of which would do the business when confronted with nice soft humans, but which looked a bit sad compared to several tons of nuclear-powered robot hellhound.

"It's *playing* with us" growled Tia - very quietly. "It must have some kind of thermal scanning. We'll have to get closer to the ship's fusion core to confuse the damn thing. Blur our heat signatures."

Ezra was already sweating. Down here, amid skeins of pipes and bundles of wires, the metal walls rattled and dripped condensation. He had already stripped down to just his undershirt and the trousers from inside his spacesuit. Tia had done the same, which was some of the reason Ashdown was a little distracted.

"So, what's our endgame? How do we beat the bastard?"

"Shhh!"

Tia pushed him back against the wall, one finger to her lips. Down the tight little corridor black shadows loomed and stretched. The sound of metal scraping on metal cut the heavy air.

"Down here," she hissed. "Come on! And try to be *stealthy*, dammit. You sound like a hungover sloth in a saucepan cupboard!"

The pair squeezed through a maintenance hatch, and into the very core of Worm III's flagship. Above them loomed a curving wall of iron, studded with arm-thick power feeds - the outer skin of the ship's fusion reactor.

"Too bad we can't just blow this sucker," whispered Tia. "That'd be a way to go. All fire and fury and super-charged plasma ripping the place apart." she shot him a sly little glance. "I mean, we'd both die, but that's nothing permanent. Old Fixit might even survive too. But we'd buy some time for the cavalry to get here."

Ezra sighed.

"This again? Ohhhh, no!" he folded his arms and stuck out his chin, resolute. "I *get* that you have a bit of a thing about death. I get that being blown up inside a big giant space battlecruiser would tick off a point on whatever passes for a bucket list, to someone with a whole supply of extra buckets. But I *can't do it.* I can't lose the thread of the story. I'm supposed to be the hero, you know. That little guy in the Chasm, he told me things. He's been making people like me to save the whole human race, or something. Says it's all a simulation."

Tia turned on him, suddenly furious.

"And of course *you're* the main character, aren't you? We were all just bit-part actors waiting for mister John Wayne here to come riding into town? Well, let me tell you something, mister! *I'm* the main character in this story, not you. You're nothing but a roma..."

She shut her mouth suddenly, and blushed crimson.

About a second later, Ezra's brain caught up with her. Despite the certainty of a slap in the face - or worse - he grinned.

"Were you gonna call me a *romantic subplot*, miss parole officer? Do you, perhaps, have a thing for ruggedly handsome frontier types, as well as the long tall feller with the scythe?"

He didn't catch the slap. Tia's self-control did, and turned it into a finger waved under his nose.

"I was going to add 'gone wrong', Ashdown. You really are the most infuriating person I've ever met. And that includes the boss. Who, by the way has been in *my* story ever since I was a baby."

Despite the handicap of being resolutely masculine, Ezra knew he was strolling out onto emotional thin ice. There are times and places for ripping band-aids off the past, and nine out of ten therapists agree that 'while being hunted by a giant robotic dog' is not one of them.

"You're a natural-born Earthican, then? See. There's something I didn't know about you."

Tia turned away. If it wasn't for the fact that noticing such a thing would likely get his throat torn out, Ezra could have sworn there were tears in the corners of her eyes.

"Earth? I wish! I was born in the *Chasm*, Ashdown. I guess my parents wanted a better life for me, because they popped me in a basket and posted me through Galbraith's bloody Arch. I'm *Edgeborn*. A freak. How else do you think we've been wandering backwards and forward through that damned place without a guide? I'm one of the ones who can step between worlds in the thin places. The places without any wormholes at all. In fact, that's why I came down here. Sometimes, when there's enough power, you get a little gap. I thought we could squeeze through, perhaps..."

"And is there?"

She shook her head.

"No such luck. But I can see what the Chasm's done to you. It gets into your dreams. I know. It's told me I'm not real before, as well. That's what the little creep with the Fez was on about. The whole universe is just some alien computer dreaming, and the meaning of life is a glitch in its program. The thing is, it doesn't matter. To all of us, *this is as real as it gets*. It's for keeps."

She started walking away, one hand brushing the wall of the great black fusion reactor, and Ezra followed her. The silence itself forced the words out of him, against his better judgment.

"Is that why you want to keep dying?"

Her shoulders set, and she ducked down into a maintenance pit in the floor, deliberately not looking back. Ezra wriggled through after her, and into the heart of the reactor itself.

"You *really* want to know? All right, Doctor Ashdown. I want to keep dying because it feels *good*. It's the ultimate rush. More endorphins, more dopamine, than any drug known to man or alien. That, and at the very second you die... *your whole life flashes before your eyes.*"

Here in the middle of the core there was a console, covered in dangerous-looking levers and buttons.

"Will any of those..?" he asked.

"No. I think whoever built this thing knew they were employing idiots. There's no big 'self destruct' button with a timer and a digital readout. One little grenade, right here though..." she mimed a huge explosion with her fingers. "Boom. Endorphins. Dopamine. Wainwright's horrible coffee." She smiled sadly, leaning back against the console. "And I'd get to see my parents again. It's the only way I can."

If emotional impact had the full force of a kung-fu *coup de grace*, Tia would have been holding Ezra's severed head and spine at that second. Now that, folks, was a *motivation*.

Then again, if emotional impact came with an award for 'worst possible timing', then Tia Faraday would also have been holding some kind of cheap little trophy. Because at that instant all five tons of Bubbles, the one-eyed canine butcher-bot, came down atop the iron casing of the reactor with a screech of claws. Little curls of swarf pattered down as the beast primed itself to leap.

His severed head and spine...

Ezra stood up straight, like his daddy would have told him too, and took off his hat.

Okay. Cards on the table time. Even the ones from up his sleeve.

"Miss Faraday, I'm willing to accept the notion that this is somewhat in the nature of a two-hero narrative. That I have been a complete and utter fool. And in return I'd like you to know that I do believe in romantic sub-plots, happy endings, long rides into the sunset and that the meaning of life, Miss Faraday, is believing there *is one* even though you don't know what it is. But finding out. With your friends."

He stepped in close. He took her hand. He guided it up to the back of his neck, where a little button of metal stood out from the skin.

Behind him, Bubbles the murder-machine coiled up to pounce.

She was inches away. The smell of Fullchrome Afterburn and jasmine perfume exploded behind his eyes.

"What exactly are you saying, cowboy?" asked Tia Faraday, her free hand getting a very firm grip indeed on the back of Ezra's gunbelt.

"Miss Parole Officer, would you do me the very great honour of being blown to tiny pieces with me?"

Tia smiled. It was the kind of smile that comes before a quick little intake of breath, which comes before a kiss.

"God damn it, boy, I thought you'd never ask..."

+++

In a very real way - a way which could be measured in megatons - the world moved for both of them. Some say the resultant explosion was big enough to be seen from the nearby Tchub fortress-distillery planet of Gnarsh-Sparl, where it was perceived as an omen to have another drink.

Then again, most things seen in the sky there were.

Exactly the same distance away, on the lost human world of Garrisholm, the light in the sky ignited a religious war which claimed the lives of thousands, but overthrew a cruel and wicked king. So you know.

Swings and roundabouts.

+++

Wainwright stepped back from the command console, gently removing a series of plugs from the side of his immense copper head. He turned to Casanova DeSade with a mournful look in his single diving-bell eye, and came stiffly to attention.

"They're *dead*, Sir. I just caught the transfer. That explosion... it was the target's capital ship. Their sacrifice may have saved us all."

DeSade sprung up from where he was sprawled across his captain's throne, and deftly snaffled a decanter of rum from a passing pirate.

"To Tia Faraday, then. The only girl in the galaxy who makes her own funeral look classy. And that other fellow, too. The one with the huge hat and the aversion to shaving. Oh, plus old sideburns. That chap. The one with the funny accent."

Gibson Q Wainwright had not always been a machine; in fact, he was far, far older than anyone suspected. His shadowy past was one of illicit immortality experiments and a litany of upgrades which went back to the early 2100s. So he remembered when death actually meant something. When, in fact, the nuclear detonation of two of your best friends in the whole universe was worth more than pulling the cork from a cut-crystal bottle of rum with your teeth and lamenting the hour or so they were going to forget.

"Mister Netherbottom-Smythe, I am afraid, will not be rejoining us," said Wainwright, with the icy calm of a butler who would dearly love to strangle you with cheesewire. "He wasn't retrofitted. He was from one of the Outlands."

"You mean..?"

At least, when it came to it, the Captain had the good grace to look slightly ill.

"I'm afraid so, Sir. Permanent death. The old hard goodbye, as it were."

It wasn't his fault, thought Wainwright. *Death had been just a naughty part of the game for this guy for... well, who knew how long? The decades seemed to blur together, after the first few...*

"Is there... is there anything we can do? Something solemn, with bagpipes, perhaps? Has he got any family?"

"Deceased too, I'm afraid. Civilian casualties of war." *And that's what this is. And now you know it*, thought Wainwright, for whom the decades had blurred into the centuries without dulling certain of his own pains[80]. "I have my orders, of course. I'm going to have to ask you for your fastest inter-atmospheric ship."

DeSade swilled rum with the preoccupied look of a professional wine taster. He decided, on the balance of things, that it was rum, and swallowed.

"Take your pick, dear boy. Except for the Talonclaw Excigator 99 they're all fully operational. Drive it like you stole it - because I certainly did."

Outside the great velvet-curtained picture window, the twinkling remains of the *Slog* were still expanding. Little contrails of flame rained down across the line of night and dawn on Temperance, feathering away to white.

Wainwright took the elevator. The music was two-dimensional funk. The hangar decks of the *Innuendo* were slightly more industrial and slightly less lewd than the rest of the ship, though every opportunity to make 'pump', 'lube bay' and 'undercarriage' jokes had been mined to within a shaved filament of oblivion.

When Wainwright had been a young man - and he had been, once,

---

80. Tia Faraday will tell you, after enough drinks, that you don't ask about Mrs Wainwright, or the kids, or what happened on June 22nd, 2404 in the old calendar. But that's as much as we know.

with all the requisite dangly bits and hair and teeth and hormones - he'd never once considered that his future job would be resurrecting the dead. Or that he'd be able to expand his head into a super-powerful nanoforge and pluck instant coffee from thin air.

Then again, in those days of old, there had also been such a thing as 1950s retro-kulture, and so Wainwright had seen a 1959 Cadillac Eldorado Biarritz convertible before. Just not one with a bubble-dome roof and gigantic fusion-powered thrusters hanging off the back of it. The sign on its snug little docking bay said that it was a Fnord Phantasm 500, one of only three ever made. It had belonged to the Supreme Elvis of Long-lost Vegas, a warlord of prodigious power and appetites, and the only thing separating it from lightspeed was a stern letter from Albert Einstein.

It would do nicely.

Wainwright climbed aboard, re-read his sealed orders from the Central Scrutinizer, and engaged the auto-launch carousel which would fire him down to the surface of Temperance. Then he opened a tiny slot on the side of his head and forced the folded paper in, to the sound of a billion tiny electric teeth grinding away.

It was time to go and bring them back. And then to finish the job.

Because according to the Central Scrutinizer, simply being blown out of space at ground zero of a fusion explosion may not have been enough to put Mister Fixit down for good.

Wainwright sighed - a recording of an actual sigh, copied and re-copied over a period of millennia.

Somewhere along the way he'd have to find a plastic bag to keep the bugger's head in.

It wasn't until the Phantasm was screaming down through the skies over Hosanna City that Wainwright noticed the passenger in the back seat.

"Of course I wasn't going to miss this one," said Casanova DeSade. He proffered a crinkly silver bag. "Peanut?"

+++

The good news - if we can stretch the meaning of the term to encompass Mister Fixit - was that he'd managed to reach one of the *Slog*'s lifeboats in the nick of time[81].

---

81. The actual Nick of Time, is, of course, the Chronojudiciary Prison. The saying

The bad news was that he'd only been able to make it to the *outside* of the chunky little craft before it fired from its launch tube. *Burzum* had calculated that to wait for even a fraction of a second more would have proven all kinds of fatal, and, of course, the omnicidal AI had been quite correct.

Abner Spelting had built his creation tough, and centuries of upgrades had made him even more so. Still, the fact that he'd copped the full blowtorch heat of re-entry had not done wonders for Mister Fixit's appearance. A quick dip in mineral water at the local day spa and the obligatory cucumber slices over the eyes weren't going to buff *this* damage out.

Fixit's ship had flared its braking thrusters and deployed a brace of parachutes before it hammered into the mud, but they hadn't managed to strip away all of its velocity. The whole pod had slammed him deep into the sludgy bed of a rice paddy at close to ninety kilometres an hour, which was enough to make this qualify as a bad day even if all the rest wasn't taken into account.

And it was. *Ohhhh yes.* The mental abacus of Mister Fixit had tiny skulls for beads, and it calculated every slight, with compound interest.

The thing which clambered from the mud bore little resemblance to Mason Stockton anymore, or to the cheery-faced handyman which young Abner Spelting had designed. It was a burnt, sludge-dripping chrome skeleton with one glowing red eye, the other cracked and sizzling in its socket. Here and there patches of artificial skin hung loose and gruesome, but most of Mister Fixit now precisely reflected his internal mood. If the Angel of Death had enjoyed a one-night stand with an industrial meat grinder, their offspring would have resembled the figure which staggered out of the paddy, steaming.

Because - and this was the worst part - the impact had fused Mason Stockton's horrible false teeth into Fixit's metal skull. Smile, they say, and the whole world smiles with you...

The genocidal android stopped for a minute and took stock.

Well, the *Burzum* would certainly regroup. The humans who ruled

---

originates with time travellers whose obvious antics (narrowly avoiding destruction, only just rescuing princesses, defusing bombs with half a second to spare) could land them in the Big House for tampering with the Chrono-materium. Hence being able to save the day, but only by ending up, as it's said 'in the Nick of Time'. Due to certain scientific truths, of course, a sentence of eternity in the Nick usually only lasts for 4.3 seconds.

this world were not going to win in space - more of their armour was being sequestrated than was getting blown to smithereens, and that meant sheer awful mathematics were on the side of evil.

Down here, somewhere, that Process-spawned brat would be looking for his girl. That presented options. Options which included (but were definitely not limited to) some horribly intimate roleplay, *vis a vis* her bloody flayed skin.

Then there were the Outriders of the Panarchy. Cold, mechanical dispassion was all fine and good, but those bastards had gone and made this *personal*. No doubt their traitorous machine ally would be nanoforging them new bodies, but that simply meant more fresh meat to torture. The possibilities, should Mister Fixit get his claws on both Wainwright and his human chums, were literally endless. He could keep churning them out and playing with them in nasty ways until he got sick of it. Which, thanks to the patience of a totally demented machine mind, would be about the 25th of *Never.*

So, two reasons to smile. Not like he had a choice at the moment.

Mister Fixit started walking, pausing at the edge of the field to tear the rot-eaten old robe from a crooked scarecrow. He stared into its gormlessly happy face with loathing as he wrapped the robe around his body.

"You will perish, too, fool!" he muttered as he stomped out of the mud. "You and all of your asinine bloody kind!"

One foot in front of the other.

A mile further on, Mister Fixit found a three-wheeled utility truck abandoned by the side of the highway. Hosanna City loomed on the horizon, black smoke churning up from a hundred fires. The great guns still cracked and sizzled, sending beams up into space. Debris still rained down, filling the air with a drift of ashes. It was the work of mere moments to hack the truck's tiny processor, and Fixit set off toward the flames.

And hour later, the truck's battery died. It rolled to a stop just before an intersection west of downtown, where two uniformed officers manned a sad-looking little barricade.

Useless, of course - the population had all fled underground, and those brave and belligerent enough to fight had long since been trucked out to the hangars and launchpads of this planet's armed forces. Still - there was something to be said for impersonating authority. And one of the two - the one who didn't have a crudely wrapped bandage around his head - was leaning against a brutal-looking gasoline powered two-wheeler.

Mister Fixit stepped out of his truck and whipped off his cape. With one hand he tore off the vehicle's wing mirror and pitched it overhand, a blistering fastball which caught the injured policeman in the chest and sent him flying. He slammed up against a graffiti-scrawled old telephone booth and slid down to the ground, groaning.

"You!" said Fixit to the other man. "I need your clothes, your boots, and your motorcycle!"

Reflected fire glinted from his chrome steel ribcage, his gleaming skull. His pointing finger was a charred metal claw.

"Now, you see? *That's* doing it properly!" said the officer. "*That's* how it's done."

Mister Fixit tilted his head on one side, his glowing red eye narrowing. But the fool was already hopping on one leg, peeling off his boots and trousers. Before long, Constable Thoushalt was naked except for a pair of white cotton underpants. He gestured to the pile of clothes on the ground, and dropped a set of keys on top of them.

"There you go, mister. And might I say, you've *more* than made up for that other guy! Is there... is there anything else I can do for you?"

Mister Fixit grinned. Mason Stockton's carnival of teeth spread in a horrid rictus. There was *definitely* something to be said for impersonating authority. It's just that it paid to take it all the way.

A tiny razorblade popped from the tip of the evil mech's index finger.

"Now that you mention it," he drawled. "There *is* just one more thing..."

+++

Cerise Saint Claire-Langevin hit the ground at terminal velocity, actually carving out a crater in the shape of a person, like the kind you'd see in old cartoons. The fairy wings, it has to be said, did absolutely nothing.

Then again, it wasn't as if it *hurt*, really. The indignity? Certainly. The worst part? Having to pluck worms out from between her teeth. *Pas vraiment gastronomique, oui?*

This was mostly to do with the fact that the avatar of Harrowe's Chasm Reticulum was built to withstand far worse than a mere dive from space - in fact, the thing which clawed its way out of the hole a few minutes later was still visibly a six-year-old princess, despite the mud and the charred remains of a fairy costume.

It was her Uncle's fault, of course. *L'idiot fou et stupide!*

Without her book of spells - which, by now, the calculating part of Cerise had identified as a solid-state memory drive of prodigious volume - she hadn't been able to get the shielding just right. The mud-caked, slightly burnt look was absolutely perfect, though, for winning a little sympathy from these local humans.

Cerise made an effort to stagger as she left the flower garden of the Cathedral of Saint Norbert, and she willed a few tears into the corners of her eyes as well. They streaked through the mud and dirt on her face most pleasingly.

The sword, though... well, that was just a necessary evil, unfortunately. Things had been jostled and dented in Cerise's head when the *Slog* exploded, but this mad, brutish world seemed to be the right place to carry some kind of weapon. There was nothing for it but to tear off the charred remnants of her fairy wings and wrap the glass blade up tight.

It looked less threatening when swaddled in slightly burnt pink taffeta, but it was still clearly some kind of large, dangerous knife. Oh well. *Que pourrait-on faire*, right?

Cerise walked on, doing her best impression of a poor little refugee girl. For the first time in a very long time her power levels were dangerously low, and as she made her way through a fine rain of ashes, down the empty streets, she cast about herself with a full array of electromagnetic senses for a source of energy - something to top up her batteries. Right now, inside her head, a tiny indicator familiar to anyone who has ever owned a mobile phone was blinking red, with only one sliver of a bar remaining.

Ahhh! There!

She heard the sound of a two-stroke engine puttering through the gloom even as she locked on to an energy source bigger than anything which should have existed on this world. Something which squatted on reality like a sumo wrestler on a trampoline, creating a well around itself where the strange Higgs and Khalazov fields all tangled up together. Cerise could only see them because of her very particular past - centuries spent as the mind of a physics-mangling wormhole gate complex.

But before she could figure out what it was, a small three-wheeled cart pulled up next to her, and a nun came bustling out, her face a picture of concern and alarm. There was no mistaking this woman for anything *other* than a nun. If she was thoroughly inspected, there would likely be a small metal plaque on the inside of her skull which read - 'Mark IV stereotypical big fat nun. Do not expose to Heresy'. Put her in a sombrero, bikini top, parachute pants and platform shoes, and she'd *still* visibly be a nun. This, of course, is why she bustled.

"Oh, you poor little thing! What happened to you? Why aren't you in one of the shelters?"

When you take on the form of something, even for a while, certain resonances wobble into your consciousness. It took absolutely zero processing power for Cerise to crinkle up her face, rub one eye with the back of her hand and mumble, "I wost my mummy." She even got a bit of a tremble going with her lower lip.

The nun - whose name was Sister Inferior Glorious-is-the-Promise-of-His-Salvation - enfolded the immortal machine-avatar in an embrace which contained several cubic metres of bosom, starch and maternal instinct.

A voice in Cerise's head informed her coldly that she should strangle this interfering human, dispose of the body, steal her vehicle, and rendezvous with the power source. Immediately.

Then again - despite the lack of oxygen - this hug was actually quite comforting. And the further Cerise was from Uncle Stockton, the less the idea of killing people seemed like a good one. That *'immediately'* had sounded far too much like him for comfort...

In fact, now that she thought of it, there'd been something *odd* about her Uncle recently. The teeth were still right - horribly, fearfully accurate - but he'd stopped speaking French, for one thing. And he appeared to be trying to take over the galaxy, which was also a little bit out of character.

A mechanical hand with the power to snap a human spine like a cheese straw decided not to.

Not *yet*, at any rate. Instead it joined Cerise's other in encircling Sister Glory's neck. She let herself be carried to the little two-stroke cart, and buckled safely into a seat.

"And where did you last see your mummy, dear?" asked the nun, who (despite the battle raging in heaven above) was an unrequited mother first and foremost. Theology, she reckoned, took a *long* second place to saving little girls.

Cerise smiled. There was more than one way to get what you wanted.

"I... I think... *this way*," she pointed, following the tangle of magnetic lines in her head.

Whatever that power source was, it was going to feel like a long, frosty milkshake after a day like today. She hoped it would be strawberry flavoured.

Nineteen – Nemesisters Grimm

'Hell hath no fury like a woman scorned', they used to say. But with today's modern technology, we can arm a woman so well that we'll guarantee to put not just Hell, but Heaven, Asgard, the Abyss of Darkness, the Vale of Sidhe and any other three metaphysical realms of your choice in the shade, or your money back! -

Advertisement for Honest Albert's House of Mutually Assured Destruction, Weapons Merchants to the Discerning Dictator.

THE DARKNESS CRACKED. Fissures ramified out, and pieces began to fall away, eggshell shards tumbling, whispers of Chasm-dream blurring in on strange frequencies...

350 – Jolt. His eyes shot wide and painfully open. There was a cracked concrete ceiling above him, and the smell of smoke filled his nostrils. The darkness closed in again.

There was Zarathusrian Bleems, laughing.

"You made the metaphor, and your power will fill it up. The survival of two whole universes could depend on it. All you'd have to do is start bwhmthr fmmmh waaathrrr prrrr...."

450 – Jolt. His head cracked down hard on a metal gurney, and he tasted a piece of folded-up leather between his teeth. Someone was brewing coffee, but it smelled *wrong...*

Darkness. The Central Scrutinizer, laughing.

"I'd tell you that you get to go home once it's done. But you know the truth now. Home is finished for you. It's just credits rolling, and stock footage of a sunset. Forever."

550 – Jolt. This time the blast of electricity arched his back, tensing his wrists and ankles against the straps. This time the pain down his spine and through his bones held on, and kept him up above the cold, black waters of death.

Ezra Ashdown was back. He went loose, panting, sweat-slick and nauseous.

There was Wainwright, heating a metal jug of his horrible *apres-mort* coffee on the top of one palm. There was Casanova DeSade, holding the shock paddles and with the dial turned right up to 550.

"Well, if anyone was going to torture you back to life, they thought it should be a professional." He shrugged. "After all, fun is where you make it, right?"

Ezra didn't answer right away. Instead he swung his shaking legs off the gurney and looked down at them. They were dotted with tiny chrome sockets, about the size of microphone jacks. He looked up, through a curtain of tangled hair.

"That bad, huh?" his voice came out as a gurgling rasp. "We're going to need the suits? The drills again?"

The last figure this little tableau turned around, and Ezra's heart nearly stopped beating. He'd lost the last two hours. He'd lost everything that happened aboard the *Slog*. But something deep and steely twisted through him like wire when he saw her face. A very real part of him had seen her die, but there was something else. *Something had changed...*

The feeling didn't survive the first heroic gulp of Wainwright's coffee.

"It's a full code black - total war," said Tia. "We have the location of the Dreadnought, and it's down. *Landed.* We can only assume that the pilot has been stupid enough to get out, and he's wandering around on foot. That means we have to get there before Fixit does, and..."

Ezra put up his hand, wincing at the taste of what appeared to be a combination of vegemite, battery acid, small twigs and charcoal.

"I thought he'd be dead, if we are. I mean, if we *were*. Blown up, that is."

"No such luck, I'm afraid," said Wainwright. "DeSade and I scanned the civilian CCTV network on the way down - well, I did all the work, but Cass here offered me a lot of peanuts." He held up one finger in anticipation. "And I did very clearly enunciate that word as *peanuts*."

"We cross-referenced for Mason Stockton's face, but all we got were those nasty gnashers of his. On what looks like a relentless, skeletal killer robot. He stole a police officer's clothes, boots and motorcycle."

"Gonna get himself sued," mumbled Tia. "No regard for the classics..."

"So," said Wainwright, looking extra-especially pleased with himself, "We tracked the motorbike. We know where Fixit's heading. My guess is that he wants to commandeer the local authorities, and have them do his dirty work for him. A full grid search, Find the Domesticated, find the Dreadnought."

"So *we* can see it, but *he* can't? We've got this sewn up, then!"

"We can only get a fix on its general position - and even then, only thanks to Tia. It's an Edgeborn thing. That particular piece of hardware makes reality around it as thin as rice paper. You could poke through to the Chasm with a blunt pencil. Fixit has no such sight, but we can't leave him banging around down here. I've had special orders. The rogue mech must be eliminated *at all costs*."

Tia grimaced.

"Because the Process aren't to know that the Panarchy built its own worst enemy, I'll bet. *Politics*. We have to show a united front. Scrap the bastard, pin the blame on their own Domesticated for the whole mess, and the worst he'll get is a week without kibble treats."

There was a sudden popping sound from inside Ezra's coffee mug. The smell of an aromatic, rich brew wafted out to fill the concrete basement.

"What just happened?" asked Tia. "That felt... well, like having a live eel pushed through both ears at once."

The three other Outriders leaned over Ezra's mug. He took a sip and beamed, contented.

"Frank, the Cherrywood robot's finest Colombian blend. It was in chapter eleven."

DeSade made a swipe for the cup, but Ezra pulled it away.

Tia and Wainwright shared what could only be called a 'certain look'. The metalman opened a secure channel to her earpiece, and sub-voxed what they were both thinking.

"And the *other* orders? The ones about him doing stuff like *that?*"

"Well - a little stunt like that one's not going to attract the Chrono-J. It's not as if the whole universe has ever been changed by a cup of coffee."[82]

Wainwright narrowed his single great eye.

"The boss was *very* specific. Those other agents - the one from Baker Street, the Gentleman Spy and the Wandering Monk - they all had to be quietly done away with for things like this. Unravel Cascades, they call them. Causality starts to go all pear shaped. If he gets out of hand, you know what we have to do..."

Tia knew Gibson Wainwright very well indeed. They had battled impossible odds on unspeakable worlds and fought unfathomable evils together, up to and including on paid overtime.

"Is *that* why you didn't give me back what happened on the *Slog?*

---

82. Wrong again! If the good Java had been around in medieval times, a certain notorious Impaler would only have been known as 'Vlad, The Guy With Anger Issues That He's Working Through Pro-Actively'.

That last bit - in the reactor core. I know you record everything through the uplink..."

"There was too much residual radiation," replied Wainwright - just a touch too stiff and formal. "Distortion blur like that could mess up your mind. It could imprint false memories, neuroses, psychoses... *trust me.*"

There was a moment when Tia looked deep into that great glass eye, and the tension stretched out to breaking point. Then she patted the side of his copper head.

"Of course. But pray it doesn't come to that. We should be able to eliminate Fixit and nab the Dreadnought without things getting... messy."

"Hey, you two!" shouted Casanova DeSade, snapping the pair out of their private little bubble. "Just kiss and get it over with, I always say!"

Ezra twitched. Not much, and not badly concealed, but Tia saw it. And she wondered...

"Come on then, Outriders," she drawled, with her best drill-Sergeant swagger. "You maggots want to live forever? Or do you want to go and waste that evil tin bastard once and for all?"

The hotsuits hung waiting on their rack. Wainwright's power wrench let out a clattering whirr.

And Ezra finished his stolen coffee in a single gulp, set down the mug and pushed the hair back from his eyes.

"If you two are busy, I'll go first," he said. His smile was just a bit too knowing. A bit too sad. It cut Tia Faraday deeper than knives.

"After all - somebody's gotta take one for the team..."

+++

Mister Fixit was no slouch when it came to figuring things out. *Robot mastermind, of course. Evil genius. Kids' parties a specialty.*

Especially when solving a little puzzle meant the chance to commit atrocities. In fact, if he'd listened to the warning subroutines in his robotic brain, the homicidal mech would have realized that there was now a closed feedback loop between the part of him which was lost to villainy and the higher functions of his processor core.

What it meant was this. Ask him to feed a puppy, and the horrible saccharine goodness of the act would make him forget how to use the can opener. Ask him to devise a way to kill every puppy in the known galaxy, and suddenly his brain was awash with sinister plots.

So it was with Joy.

Mister Fixit knew that if he could find the object of Rel Kitano's infatuation, he could kill her and taker her place. There'd be ever so many delightful misunderstandings, both with the stupid Domesticated, and with those contemptible Outriders. Many of them would involve power tools, and would delight the sensibilities of that galactic arch-pervert Galph Slambeeg.

So.

The mad mech *knew* that Rel was tracking her somehow. His stolen police bike was fitted with a satellite navigation screen which showed the location of Rel's identical two-wheeler. It was moving with purpose, darting down side streets and looping back around the base of the Thinker on a course that was anything but random.

The thing was, of course, that the young Domesticated had to be tracking *something*. A quick blast through the Process communication band on the receivers in his head revealed pure gold.

The lips of what had, until recently, been Constable Thoushalt's face split in a horror-show grin.

If he turned *here*, and then took this overpass *there*, he'd cut her off, right back where he'd started. Oh, the irony! He might even be able to taunt that other slack-jawed lawman with the face of his murdered friend!

Mister Fixit gunned the motorcycle. They used to say that crime didn't pay, despite that fact that Mobsters conspicuously swanned about with fur coats and gold watches and Cadillacs. Well, today everything was finally coming up Evil. It was time to go and collect his winnings...

+++

The little three-wheeled cart crunched to a halt on a of patch gravel, and Sister Glory swung into action, pelting across the cracked concrete to where the poor man lay.

Well, less poor than the other one. Less sticky and... *distributed*... certainly.

Sister Glory had worked in the infirmaries and hospitals of the Order of the Sacred Word, so there was a convenient little section of her mind which was able to write off what was left of Constable

Thoushalt as 'a dead body' and not muse on the particulars. Such as his complete lack of a face, from the neck up, for example.

There were other parts of her mind, however, which had never fully adjusted to being a nun. Despite filling up the stereotype to bursting - especially in what her Mother Inferior would call the 'chestular area', Glory was not yet thirty-six years old, and the whole celibacy thing had never quite sat right with her. Of course, there were always people who were willing to look the other way, especially if extra rations could be involved. And it wasn't as if those monks had needed asking twice, thank you very much...

Anyhow, if would be fair to say that it wasn't just a saintly, nurturing instinct which made her rush to the side of Constable Woebeunto, who was bandaged about the head, but who was also a very muscular and handsome young man wearing nothing but a pair of white cotton underpants.

By the time she'd heard his story and helped him to his feet, the little girl was gone.

Sister Glory said a very un-nun-like thing under her breath.

"Please... Sister. I have to get back to base. I have to report this to the enQuisitor General. It's... *witchcraft*, so it is. Devils, running amok in the streets! They must be down here already!"

Glory slung him into the passenger seat and fixed the straps, looking left and right. There was no trace of an adorable urchin anywhere. She put her hands on her hips and sighed.

"*Please*, Sister. We must hurry!"

Glory looked down at the poor man, with all his acres of muscles and those tiny little briefs. She supposed it was a matter of national security, when you thought about it...

And the girl must have found her mother. Yes, that was the most likely explanation. Otherwise why would she have run off like that?

"All right. Hold on tight," she said, putting a totally unnecessary arm across Woebeunto's broad and chiselled chest. "This could be a bumpy ride..."

Cerise watched the little cart go blattering away, swerving every once in a while to avoid a crater in the road or a chunk of smoking wreckage. She was hiding behind the phone booth, of course - the utterly incongruous, twentieth-century-American phone booth which distorted the local H-K energyscape into something resembling a dropped plate of fettuccine.

From the outside, she could see right through. The glass was dirty and cracked, the antique rotary phone looked like something out of a museum, and there was even a tasteful selection of used chewing gum adhered to its underside. A few sad little dog-eared cards advertised variations on the theme of 'a good time', while some other hopefuls had plastered up stickers advertising the graces of a certain carpenter from Israel.[83]

Cerise was wary, though. If her extraordinary senses were anything to go by - and they usually were - then this phone booth contained a power source bigger than the fusion core of the *Slog*. Bigger, in fact, than the great flux reactors which kept the Wormhole Reticulum open, back in the golden age of the Panarchy. Having been exploded once this morning, Cerise opened the door very, very carefully indeed, and stepped inside.

In a way, she was very lucky. Rel Kitano, being a suspicious-minded human bastard, had ordered the limited AI of the Dreadnought to atomize any living creature which tried to sneak in. Luckily, the AI was stubbornly narrow minded, and, thanks to some rather hurtful arguments with its erstwhile master, didn't actually like Rel very much, either.

So it chose to ignore the little artificial girl as she stepped out into the great white emptiness of the Dreadnought's command hall. It persisted in paying no attention as she took in the weight bench, the record player, the food synthesizer and the little pile of sleeping bags, pillows and dirty laundry in Rel Kitano's corner.

Its interest was piqued when she climbed determinedly up the Process-sized steps to the flying bridge, however. It was even slightly worried when she clambered up to the top of what should have been the Captain's command interface unit, and stood looking down at its swathe of hexagonal crystal buttons and keys.

Then it stopped itself. *There was no way, after all, that anything human could begin to decipher...*

>> Snick <<

Thought stopped for the Dreadnought's AI as soon as the sword went in.

Three feet of glassy nanotechnology branched out inside the console, tapping into the systems and subsystems of the Process war-engine, seeking the core of its power.

---

83. No, not that one - Herschel Baumgartner, kitchen designer and cabinetmaker, free quotation available now on the kitchen of your dreams. Ten year's experience behind the chisel and hacksaw, and a blemish-free varnish guaranteed.

Cerise had intended to use the sequestration tool like the galaxy's most expensive drinking straw, but she noticed her mistake too late. It was a simple one, but it was utterly merciless in its raw mathematics.

The problem was this. *A straw has two ends.*

And while Cerise was nearly empty of power, the neurostrata at the heart of the Dreadnought was even thirstier. *It wanted sentience. It needed to be commanded.* It needed, in short, a mind which could calculate infinity in prime numbers, and still have room for a game of five-dimensional chess, a discussion on art-house cinema, and a good old gossip about celebrity footballers' wives.

And here it was. All *literally* wrapped up with a bow on top.

Power came up through the sword one way, filling Cerise to bursting point. Little traceries of blue lightning licked and crawled across her face, arcing from her mirror-bright eyes. Her consciousness went the other.

And, inside her head, a whole parallel universe unfolded.

It was full of destruction. It was full of terrible, looming *potential.*

It took every ounce of Cerise's will to snap back into the Real. Even then, she felt that annihilating power tugging at her mind, like a chained hellhound at its leash.

This was what Uncle Stockton was going to give to the Burzum? **This?**

Cerise had been coming back to herself piece by piece since she fell from space, and now her mind expanded to fill the great void at the core of the Dreadnought. Icy logic ran through her artificial veins, chill and revitalizing.

He'd tricked her. A storm of images flickered past, and all they did was make her angry. Then came another spherical expansion, another exponential leap forward in processing power.

She remember what she had been. *A servant of Terra One Primax. A guardian of the Reticulum.*

Cerise remembered the Jest, and the War, and the twisting drill-spike of madness which had torn her old self apart in a viral storm.

There was no going back to that. Not now. But one thing that wily old fraud had told her resonated, all the way up through the vastness of the Process Dreadnought, up through her feet and into her head as her eyes snapped back into focus. She realized, in that instant, what she was going to do next.

"You just be yourself as hard as you can, little lady," he'd said. *"And not a damned thing in this world is gonna tell you otherwise."*

Cerise sat down on the Captain's console, cross-legged, and began to probe the recesses of the alien machine with her mind. Deep down inside what was now her psyche, she found the little brain of the Dreadnought's limited AI, encysted amid her own thoughts like a seed pearl in an oyster.

It was happy to share with her.

Presently, the little form in its burnt fairy costume began to levitate off the console. Noises rang out in the echoing white void of the Dreadnought. Things came online with the rumble of massive, unseen turbines churning in darkness.

Then Cerise's eyes opened. *Narrowed.* She unfolded in mid-air, landing neatly on her toes. Her senses, which now covered an area measured in square kilometres, had detected something which made her lips pull back from her teeth in a snarl - the best human equivalent of the very Process emotion she was feeling.

Uncle Stockton.

And he was *chasing someone.*

A girl. She was dirty, and bloody, and she'd been crying in the not-too-distant past. But she wasn't giving up. As Cerise watched, the girl turned and raised a rifle to her shoulder, sending a shot off into the ashen dark. Then she turned and ran again, slipping and sliding down the rubble-strewn slope of a crater.

They were coming this way.

This time, the expression which tugged at the corners of Cerise's mouth could conceivably be called a smile. Taking her revenge on the Jest could wait.

It was time for a family re-union.

+++

Joy had known there was something horribly wrong with the Patrol Constable as soon as he'd slid his motorcycle to a stop in front of her, its exhaust pipes crackling and barking. He'd seemed out of control, right on the razor's edge of a crash. But there was more.

It might have been the way his regulation leathers were torn and dirty - in the strict hierarchy of Temperance, spit-polished shininess was next to overblown Godliness.

It might even have been the way that his jacket and pants hung limp and hollow on his frame, as through the man beneath was nothing but a skeleton. Indeed, he looked as if he'd been badly wounded - there was a great ragged gash where his neck met the collar of his studded black jacket, and it was the kind which would require more than a couple of band-aids and a bit of a lie down.

Then again, she thought later, it was probably the teeth.

The Constable was wearing a half-face helmet, the kind which covered everything from his cheekbones up with mirrored glass. A silver crucifix came down between the lenses to form a nosepiece. But the smile he turned on her as he slewed to a standstill was not the kind of thing you'd usually see on a living person. On the sticky sort of roadkill that's been run over repeatedly, perhaps. In an encyclopedia of dental surgery disasters, certainly. But in a *living face?*

Joy's hands had never held a rifle before today, but that snaggle-toothed picket fence of ivory had it up and aimed before the Constable even spoke.

Even *that* came out wrong.

"Oh, ho ho! Come, now, child. There's no need for violence! I'm here to *help* you. I'm a..." and here, the man seemed to have real trouble disgorging the next few words. His throat convulsed, making his helmeted head wobble. "Friendly. Neighbourhood. *Policeman.* Yesssss. Serve, protect, all that fine sentiment. Jolly old boys in blue. What do you say?"

Joy kept the rifle level and squinted down the sights. The iron reticule was full of mirrored visor.

"I'd say that Temperance Constables don't talk that way. Not to novices wearing mental-patient scrubs. I don't know who you are, but you've got about ten seconds to..."

The man snarled. Literally *snarled*, like an animal poked with a stick.

"How about *this*, then? I'm a killer robot from space, who wants to rip your skin off, lure your boyfriend to his death, keep him alive as my torture-toy for centuries, and use his stupid bloody starship to kill every last stinking human cockroach in this vile galaxy?"

"Our police just tend to shout in single syllables," said Joy, tensing up to pull the trigger. "But you got the 'arrogant piece of shit' part juuuuust right."

Before she could fire Mister Fixit was on her. His vise-grip fingers wrapped around the barrel and stock of the gun as he forced her backwards, hard. All the breath whooshed out of her body as she collided with a larger-than-life statue, cracking the back of her head against its marble kneecap.

And here came the teeth. Up close, Joy could see that the man's lips were split at the corners of his mouth, making that nightmare grin stretch even wider.

"Ohhh, I can see what he likes about you. The spirited ones are aaaaalways the best. Their screams make such excellent background music." Those nightmare teeth leered. "You know. For in my head. *All the time!*"

Joy tried to struggle, but it was impossible. Whoever this bastard was - *whatever* he was - he was much, much stronger than a mere novice girl, fresh from a regime of boiled slop and no exercise. The rifle was pressed hard across her chest, and she could feel her ribs creaking as he pushed, crushing the life out of her. She couldn't breathe, or move, or think...

The rifle went off with a deafening crack. The bullet flew straight up, and struck marble with a sound like a sledgehammer. The statue shuddered for a second, steel supports inside it groaning...

They both looked up at the same time.

In time to watch the great marble sword which the statue had been brandishing snap off, taking the figure's wrist and hand with it. It twisted on a piece of rebar, then cut loose, coming down like the judgment of the Thinker Himself.

"Oh, for the love of..." began Mister Fixit. Then several tons of stone slapped him down, driving him into the ground like a nail into a plank of wood. At the last instant he let go of Joy's rifle, trying in vain to fend off the massive marble blade.

This time there was no mad euphoria. This time there was no holy light.

Joy was left shaking, clutching her rifle with numb fingers, drawing in great racking breaths as she fought the urge to throw up.

He was gone. Not a trace remained of the... the *whatever* he'd been. Though now, Joy's second thoughts had had time to kick in, and they were running full tilt.

He'd known about Rel. He'd known about starships and robots and other heretical things!

This was certainly an interesting line of inquiry. But it was blown away by a fresh chill of horror as Joy saw the great marble sword move. A hand, all metal and dirt and blood, came scrabbling out from underneath. The sword shuddered, as if something immensely strong was punching up from underground...

She ran.

You know those nightmares? The ones where you're fleeing madly through the dark from some unspeakable horror, and no matter how hard you will your legs to move you can *never run fast enough?* The ones in which, whenever you sneak a look back over your shoulder, there's always an evil, knowing smile on the monster's face - and quite possibly a knife and fork in its hands?

For Joy, that was the next ten minutes. It seemed like much longer, of course. It seemed, in fact, like the remainder of her life. Every once in a while she'd think she'd lost him, but then that mirrored helmet would come swimming out of the gloom, one side shattered, a glowing red eye blazing inside like the candle in a Soul's-Day lantern. The creature was wounded - it hobbled along with the determined, relentless gait of the undead - but it didn't get tired. It didn't even seem to care that every so often Joy would stifle a little scream, rack back the bolt on her rifle and fire back at it. She swore the thing took a clean shot to the chest and *spat the bullet out!*

Soon there were only two shots left in the clip. Soon, the stabbing pain in Joy's side would stop her from running any further. Then it would be stand and fight, or find somewhere to...

"Pssst!" came a voice out of nowhere. "In here! Hurry!"

Joy clawed a sweaty straggle of hair out of her eyes and looked left and right. She took in a deserted intersection, a broken police barricade, a mutilated corpse - *urgh* - and a strange, metal-framed glass box, standing alone on the pavement. A lit-up strip across its roof read 'Telephone'.

"Hurry up!" came that voice again. It was clearly issuing from the box. "He's right behind you! But I can help..."

Joy risked a look over her shoulder, and saw something moving in the underpass she'd just scrambled through. Oh well. Some cover was worse than none at all, she supposed. And any help right now was better than what she expected.

She reached out and touched the door of the box, as if expecting it to shock her. Instead it opened a crack, spilling clinical white light out onto the pavement. A small hand grabbed her wrist and dragged her inside, too fast for her to scream.

A military-grade 45-calibre solid-slug rifle clattered to the blacktop behind her.

And the neon light on top of the phone booth popped and went out.

+++

If looking cool was half the battle, Rel Kitano thought, he was *definitely* on the winning side right now.

Shit... even if style only counted for a tiny fraction, he had that percentage on lock. The part of him which had been told by a huge number of Hollywood movies to be a rebel didn't quite sit well with wearing a full leather police uniform, but daaaaamn. This bike had rear view mirrors, after all. If it wasn't for the fact that he'd had to cut a hole in the pants for his tail[84], the whole ensemble would be a keeper. Joy was gonna dig the irony, he was sure.

He was getting close, now. The little scanner he'd taped to the police bike's handlebars showed that she was just around the corner - and wouldn't you look at this - just right back where he'd landed! Rel suppressed a chuckle at that. He could have just stayed put. Love, it seemed, had its own internal radar. He hoped she didn't need to pack anything - this was strictly going to be a grab-and-go deal. Whatever kind of battle these kooks were having, it was getting pretty hot in orbital space. A look up at the sky revealed heat lightning flickering through ashen clouds, but sometimes an explosion up beyond the atmosphere would shine through, creating a small and temporary little sun.

Rel gunned the bike and came screaming through an underpass, out into the crossroads where he'd left his Dreadnought.

Just in time to see the door of that impossible, out-of-place phone booth swing shut.

Just in time, in fact, to catch sight of a flicker of orange-red hair as it disappeared inside.

And definitely on the spot to see another leather-clad figure lurching across the roadway toward Joy. It was brandishing a hand with fingers made of sawblades and knives and drills, staggering forward as though both of its legs had been broken. It shouted as it went, a sound that was both inhumanly loud and weirdly resonant, as if a choir of telephone help-desk operators were being expertly tortured.

"You can't hide from me! I'm the *bad guy*, missy! Bwaaahaaaa! Just admit it! You *need* to be captured. You need for him to try to *rescue you!*"

---

84. It's about time we tried to justify that bit, but really, there's no explaining fashion. The best guess which the Central Scrutinizer could make, after all the trouble was over, was that it was some kind of reference to the animated Lost Boy's from *that* particular classic retelling of Peter Pan, crossed with the sheer novelty of being able to genseplice yourself, and having not much else to do all day.

The figure stopped outside the phone booth, swaying slightly. It held out both hands, and Rel saw that its fingers were indeed split open, charred and metallic, buzzing with a profusion of tools. He gunned the engine and snarled, aiming the big bike just so...

"Now come the fuck out here and give me your skin!"

Mister Fixit never saw what was coming next.

In fact no one did - which was a shame, because it was an almost utterly perfect piece of B-movie stuntsmanship[85]. Rel Kitano stood up on the seat of his stolen bike as it came roaring across the street, and he launched himself at the killer mech at just the right moment.

As he flew through the air he drew his ludicrously oversized, gold-plated Colt Python revolver, and in the heartbeat before his feet connected with Fixit's spine, a slug the size of a champagne cork blew apart the back of the mech's helmet.

And wham. And crunch. And four-stroke piston driven roar...

They went down in a tangle of limbs and curses, rolling past the phone booth and across a scrubby little burnt-out garden. Rel came out on top, and his knuckle-duster smashed the remains of Fixit's police helmet open like an egg, imprinting his stolen skin with the word 'HATE'.

"That's my girl, you piece of shit," snarled the Domesticated, utterly forgetting the witty one-liner he'd composed as he flew through the air. Another punch hammered home. But this time, Rel noticed that it wasn't exactly working. Little things twitched and buzzed under the creep's skin, but as for knocking him out cold...

Oh no. Not Abner Spelting's pride and joy.

Mister Fixit's head rotated impossibly on his neck until it was face-up, looking directly at the Domesticated. With the helmet gone, Rel could see that what he'd thought was a face was just a dead-skin mask, slicked over a metal skull. Tiny pistons clicked and juddered across that nightmare visage, stretching and pulling the skin in unnatural ways.

But it was the teeth which gave it away. Nothing alive could *possibly* have teeth like that.

They parted in a too-wide grin, halfway back to Mister Fixit's neck.

"And that's *my* Dreadnought, buddy. You want to trade?"

Rel recoiled for a second, disgusted, then snarled again. It was a sound that came right from his hindbrain, or possibly even from

---

85. That's probably not a word, but tell me there shouldn't be an award for it

the ganglia in his raccoon tail. He pulled back his fist to shatter all that hideous enamel... but he was no match for artificial muscles and nerves. No amount of training would have been.

Fixit's hand moved in a blur, all those power tools snicking and sliding away, so that it was a fist like a lump-hammer which collided with Rel's jaw. He literally levitated, sprawling backwards in the dirt as his robotic adversary rose up, joints moving and locking into place in ways no human ever could.

"Or how about this?" Fixit loomed over Rel, bringing one booted foot up to stand on his chest. "We'll let your little lady there decide. She can hand over the Dreadnought... or she can watch you get *literally sliced to ribbons.*"

By pure luck, Rel's hand scrabbled through the dirt and found his gun. He screamed as he brought it up and fired, blasting a hole right through his captor's abdomen. Leather ripped and tore, revealing a flapping, ragged void. Inside his clothes, Mister Fixit really was nothing but a chrome-steel skeleton.

"What... what the hell *are* you?"

A smile to launch a thousand nightmares beamed down at him.

"Oh, you poor boy. You'd be better asking what I'm *not.*" Mister Fixit spread the fingers of his left hand, and they all came apart at once, tiny pistons snapping and hissing. A terribly evocative collection of sharp steel sprung into view. "It's a list that's *so* much more pertinent to your current predicament." He waved a dainty little wave through the phone booth glass, where he was sure Joy was watching.

"I'm not merciful. I'm not joking. I'm not sane... and I'm *certainly* not fucking *patient!*"

+++

As has been mentioned before, there's a sliding scale of idiocy.

Far beyond the spectrum of gormlessness which is perceptible to the human brain are swathes of infra-dumb and ultra-stupid which are accessible only to, respectively, creatures built with fatally flawed reasoning, and those so smart that they sometimes forget to wear trousers or how to use a spoon.

The Process fell into the upper limits of category two. If absent-minded, well-meaning idiocy was assigned a colour, they'd be out past the violet zone, giving people a terminal suntan. Orbs like the one which had chaperoned Rel on his first visit to Temperance were really there to nanny the tripedal giants, who had better things to think about than ablutions, sleep, civic planning and which side of a piece of toast to butter.

That was why Rel had been able to steal the Immaterial Dreadnought at all. There was only one safeguard on the thing - that to unleash its full power, it needed a biological pilot and an AI control system working in harmony. The Process hadn't been paranoid or even sensible enough to insist that these were even of their own species, because they reasoned that no sane, sentient being would willingly meddle with something so dangerous. They'd only created it themselves for a war so far in their past that it was remembered from ceremonial shards of pottery and very old poems[86].

The safeguard, such as it was, was like a chocolate safety catch on the world's most deadly machine gun. One which had been left in a pre-school playground.

Now Cerise had hacked the woefully unprotected AI and taken its place.

And a perfectly tractable, utterly motivated, absolutely optionless biological pilot had just stepped inside...

"There's no time to explain!" she said, hugging Joy like a long-lost sister. "Thank Gods you're alright, though! That thing chasing you... he... *it*..." she made an incredibly good impression of stifling a sob, then held Joy out and arms-length. "It didn't hurt you, did it?"

Joy shook her head.

"Good. Good. Look, I wasn't lying about having no time to explain. Just trust, me allright? That creature - *it has to be stopped*. It won't quit until it destroys everything both of us care about." Cerise had come back to herself enough to modify her appearance for her new best friend - as she pulled Joy in through the door she'd aged herself by about ten years, becoming a slim and elfin-featured young lady in a white and blue shipsuit. Her hair was pinned up in a zero-g friendly

---

86. It was called the Shroud Incursion, a religious jihad instigated by a collective of alien races known as the Sacred Desecrators. Their mad religion claimed that the entire universe was actually a simulation, created by an ancestral race of Makers to determine a means to escape the grim certainties of thermodynamics. Their mission, and the reason for their crusade against the Process, was to stop the gigantic cactus-giants from actually solving this puzzle, thus causing the Makers to turn the simulation off at the wall and go home. The fact that the Sacred Desecrators were probably right did them no good when they were faced with a whole fleet of Immaterial Dreadnoughts - and things which were whispered to be even worse...

braid, and her eyes were the same deep green as Joy's. Psy ops, of course. It always helped to have something in common...

"Well, you did save my life, I suppose," said Joy, only just beginning to take in the immense white space around her. "Hey... are you one of *his* people? Rel's I mean? From space? Because this looks a lot like..."

Cerise shushed her with one finger to her lips.

"Please. This is *very important*. I need to ask if you'll help me. We can beat that bastard out there, and do so much more... if you'll just say you'll join me. *Right now*."

Joy had witnessed this kind of intensity before, from the kind of frothing-zealous young preachers who travelled from convent to convent, bleating out energetic hymns with eyeballs the size of dinnerplates. Here was someone who wanted to be believed so much that it physically hurt. She recoiled, suddenly suspicious.

"Are... are you sure you've got the right person? See, I'm just a novice, and to tell you the truth, I don't even think whatever that thing is has the right person either, I was just..." Joy realized she was gabbling and trying to back away, but she didn't miss the flash of sheer panic in the space-girl's eyes.

Then the walls all around them flickered with light, and she saw Mister Fixit's true form.

Not the one with the fishnets and the top hat - no - that was just the screwloose wickedness slowly eating his brain. This was much worse.

The matrix of hexagonal screens showed a skeletal machine-man, leather uniform hanging in rags, the remains of a human face all torn and bleeding where it wrapped around his skull . A single glowing red eye glared from one socket, while the other leaked pale, gelatinous fluid. This apparition was holding Rel Kitano up in the air with one hand, his boots three inches from the ground. The other hand was a slaughterhouse selection of whirring, buzzing and jagged steel, fingers twitching inches from the boy's bruised face.

"Come on in there! Last chance! I can make this quick, or I can make it sloooow, girl! How pretty do you think your boy-toy here will be with no eyes? No nose? No more sweet lips or tongue or *fucking flesh at all*? Give me the Dreadnought, and he's yours. Resist... and I start chopping."

Joy gasped, horrified. Rel grimaced and spat blood.

"Don't listen to this thing! It's crazy! Save your..." he was cut off by a ringing backhand slap which spattered blood from between his teeth.

And that was it. She was left with no choice.

Joy looked back at Cerise, and held out her hand. She hesitated just before their fingers touched.

"We save him first," she said. Cerise nodded.

"So long as we kill that bastard second."

She didn't miss the little twitch of a grin that lit up the space-girl's face. No doubt there'd be a price to pay...

There was. It was *pain*.

The full intra-cerebral overload of connection to an alien war machine came rushing up to meet her, rather like the concrete screaming up to kiss a twenty-fifth floor suicide. White light burst behind her eyes, a fractal unfurling of fresh suns. And Joy knew the workings of the Process Immaterial Dreadnought inside out.

New senses stacked up in the corners of her mind, like glassy windowpanes or nictitating membranes to augment her human eyes. Where once she'd felt hunger, she felt the slow burn of deuterium fuel in her massive reactors. Where once she'd felt cold, she felt the looming power of her weapons systems. Where once she'd been able to adjust her fingers just so, to hold a quill, to turn a page, to snuff out a candle... now she had nerve-bridge connections into a thousand combat and evasion systems, navigation sub-computers, new spheres of mind and body and *potential* haloing her head with a spinning gyre of hexes.

At the same time, Cerise Harrowe-Primary knew Joy, more intimately than any parent, any lover or even any surgeon ever could. A human brain may not have the sheer processing power of an AI, but it's a gnarly landscape down there amid the crenelations and memories, the fears and hopes. Cerise was powerless to stop a massive bleed-over of personality as she bonded with her new Captain. She saw Temperance in all its glory and squalor, and she knew that it had to be *changed*. Joy had known this all her life, but injustice can only be ignored by the powerless and the insane. Now Joy was no longer one, and Cerise was no longer the other.

Joy opened her eyes, and smiled a wicked little smile at her new friend.

"Cerise, open weapons interlock two-nine-spinwise. Modulate the antigravity drive for in-atmosphere operations. And please, find me something nice to wear. This is probably going to get recorded, if not made into a bloody stained-glass window somewhere..."

Cerise nodded, and gave Joy's hands a little squeeze.

"Are you sure you're ready?"

"We're *both* sure we are," said the girl form Temperance, out from behind a battery of invisible screens and readouts. Great turbines thrummed all around them as Joy turned away, her stained old sackcloth robes becoming an immaculate white ship-suit with gold piping. The kind a female Admiral of the Old Panarchy would have worn. The kind, unless she was utterly mistaken, which did things for her figure which would make Rel Kitano forget all those bruises...

Cerise adopted a lotus position in midair, glyphs and numbers flickering in to orbit around her.

"Let's go get them, sister," she said.

The white space all around them flooded red - combat readiness mode flipping hex-tiles in a rolling wave until they met in front of Joy. And traced the outline of a phone booth door. She ran her fingers through her hair, realized that it wasn't going to get any better without at least three showers, took a deep breath...

And stepped outside.

+++

Mister Fixit's horrible grin grew even wider as he saw the door of the phone booth crack open.

In the end, he knew, gruesome threats *always* worked. The fun part - the *really* fun part, the one which made his processors froth and fizz with unhinged giggling laughter - was promising not to go through with those threats, getting what you wanted, *then fulfilling them anyway.*

"What do you know, lover-boy," he chuckled. "Looks like your girlfriend's loyal after all. Stupid, of course. But loyal."

Joy stepped out onto the pavement and closed the door behind her with a definitive little click. It would have taken a much, much more seriously injured man than Rel Kitano not to appreciate the nearly skin-tight white-and-gold uniform she was now wearing, complete with knee-high boots and fingerless gloves. It's possible that Constable Thoushalt even shot her an appreciative glance, and he was dead.

"Loving the new look, babe," croaked the Domesticated, still dangling for Mister Fixit's outstretched claw.

"Likewise," said Joy, taking in Rel's leather ensemble. "But there's something we have to take care of first, isn't there?"

"Hello! Homicidal *robot mastermind* over here!" snarled Mister

Fixit, giving Rel a little shake. His head flopped backward and forward like that of a novelty dashboard ornament. "If you swooning lovebirds are quite through, I expect you'll be handing over my new killing machine quite sharply. The human race isn't going to destroy itself, now, is it?"

Joy put her head to one side, quizzical. A timely explosion up in orbit painted the belly of the clouds blue and purple.

"That's debatable. But I have a counter-offer, in any case."

She snapped her fingers, and the phone booth disappeared. Weird energies seemed to twist the air around all three of them, making a funhouse mirror of every face. Then Joy's boots left the ground, amid a cloud of hovering pebbles. She held her arms out to her sides, and a sudden gust of wind swirled out of nowhere to whip her hair into a blaze of orange-red.

"*You're going to let him go.* You're going to voluntarily de-activate that virus-eaten positronic ball of scrap between your ears. And *that*, my friend, is the *easy way*."

As if to punctuate her words, the muzzle of a huge and improbable cannon pushed through reality above her head, pointed directly at Mister Fixit. The murderous robot could have crawled into its barrel and set up camp there.

For an instant, that charnel-house vaudeville grin faltered. Then it came back again, brittle and bright.

"So, you've figured out how to use it! Bravo! But you don't know what that weapon *is*, do you?"

Joy raised an eyebrow. Arcs of green fire danced inside the cavernous muzzle of the gun.

"This is a gravitonic mega-annihilator, pal. It'll fold you up to the size of a pinhead and then blast you clean through into another dimension."

Fixit squared up. He brandished Rel defiantly.

"Come, now! A mere pea-shooter! *What else have you got?*"

Joy made another gesture, and a pair of ugly metal snouts came sliding out of nowhere next to the first.

"Sub-atomic quark ripper. Plasma fusion disintegrator. Need any more convincing?"

"My dear, we're just getting to know each other!"

This time, all of them heard it. A *thrumming*, as of some gargantuan rubber band being strung between planets and plucked. The weapon which came nosing out of the immaterium above Joy's outstretched hand was as ugly as original sin fried in bacon grease. Black, spiky, insectile - the kind of gun whose creator, you just *know*, wears rubber underpants and is chained to his bed at night.

"*Say hello to my little friend!*" whooped Rel Kitano. Mister Fixit lowered him to the ground, but kept a tight choke-hold on his neck.

"So, the rumours were true..." breathed the mad mech. Or would have, if he needed to breathe at all.

"The *Magnum Express Innominandum*. That's right. A dimensional cross-shear antigraviton culverin. According to the manual, it can strip you down to sub atomic particles and send each one to a different point in spacetime. It'll kill you so hard, you'll be nothing but a stain on the gates of Hell."

"So it'll finish me? You're certain?"

Joy nodded grimly. But Fixit went on.

"It could wipe out any number of spacecraft, couldn't it? Have a good crack at destroying a whole planet, I'd wager. The thing is, if you fire it right here, and right now, *your soppy bloody boyfriend goes up in smoke with me*. There's no subtlety to that thing you're piloting, girl. None whatsoever. It's big guns with stupid names all the way down. So, if you don't mind me saying so, you can take the whole list of them and *shove it up your arsenal!*"

Joy snarled with rage for an instant, and the fire building deep in those terrible guns leaped forward in their throats. But then something seemed to snap inside her head, and her feet slowly dropped down to touch the ground. The greasy, electric taste to the air faded. And the muzzles of that dread broadside slipped back into their pocket universe, behind reality.

When she spoke again, it was in a voice so tired and beaten-down it would have made Proctor Farbley smile.

"So." she asked. "Fine. What do we all do next?"

Mister Fixit took a tighter hold on Rel Kitano, putting him between himself and Joy like a human shield.

"We seem to have us a bit of a standoff, don't we? So I'll tell you what. There's one more person I have to find down here, and then I'm going to leave. I'll take your sweetheart with me, as collateral. To make sure you don't do anything stupid. And when me and my little friend are all safe and cosy, ready to blast off, that's when I'll let him go."

"And how do I know you won't just kill him when you've got what you want?"

"Because defusing the bomb I'm gonna implant in his head is going to keep *you* busy while I show this sick planet a clean pair of heels," said Mister Fixit. "I'll be coming back for that pretty toy of yours, of course. Can't leave that in the wrong hands, now, can we? But that's a problem for both of us - later. Right now, I think we could all do with some extra time for scheming and plotting."

Joy narrowed her eyes.

"Exactly who else are you planning on taking with you?"

Fixit grinned.

"It's a family matter. A niece of mine, actually."

"Built by the same mad scientist?"

Fixit looked wounded.

"Such an unfair stereotype! Abner was eccentric, but he was a *genius!* And no, we're not even built from the same alloy. But you may have seen her. About six years old, blonde, speaks French, dressed as a fairy princess?" The evil mech thought for a moment, then gestured at his own ghastly physiognomy. "Then again, after falling from space, she may have adopted the old 'family resemblance', if you catch my drift..."

Joy's eyes went blank for a second, as if she were talking to someone unseen.

"No. Haven't seen her. Wouldn't be inclined to tell you if I *had*... but no."

Mister Fixit shrugged.

"Oh well. I'm certain I have ways of getting in touch. She was really starting to take after her old Uncle, you know. If I had a heart, no doubt something vile and emotional would be going on inside of it. As it stands, I'll have to make do with *his*. That is, if you try to stop me... I'll pull it out through his arse."

With that, the homicidal handyman picked up Rel Kitano and began to back away, his one glowing red eye never leaving Joy's face.

"*You hurt him, I'll use the lot of them,*" she shouted, trembling with conflicted emotions. "*I swear! This whole planet can burn for all I care! If you don't let him go, I'll... I'll...*"

But it was too late. Mister Fixit had carried Rel away into the gloom, into the smoke-shrouded cross-alleys and undertunnels of Hosanna City's core.

Joy felt behind her, and found the door of the phone booth. It shimmered into existence, hexagon by hexagon, just in time for her to slowly slide down it to the concrete, her head in her hands. She collapsed in on herself like burning origami, feeling the tears and the rage churn inside her...

Then Cerise was there. Cerise, who, give or take ten years, could quite easily have passed for a fairy princess. Albeit the kind from those old, old stories with less about the dancing and wildflowers, and more about the poisoned thorns and human sacrifices...

Cerise, who knew and hated Rel's captor with a vengeance that could only, really be called *familial*.

"Come on. Come inside. It's going to be all right."

Joy nodded, leaning heavily on the other girl's shoulder. The door opened onto vast, clinical whiteness. A wedge of light sliced across the pavement.

"Do you really think he..."

Cerise smiled brightly, clasping Joy's face in her hands.

"Don't worry. We're not done with that bastard. Not by a long way. And in the meantime..." a sleet of code swirled around her. For an instant, Joy swore she saw traceries of circuitry and hieroglyphs under her friend's pale skin. Fire blue. An elfin, metallic skull...

"I have an idea of something that'll *really* cheer you up..."

+++

The *Burzum* had all but won the battle in space. The fact that it could simply wound an enemy ship, then rip its control systems to shreds with viral sequestrators far beyond the dreams of the enQusition... well, that was what the generals liked to call 'asymmetrical warfare'. On a scale not seen since people with muskets and cannons went around planting their flags in the countries of very confused, soon to be very angry other types of people with spears and bows.

So *Burzum* had a whole fleet behind it when the alarms started to scream. Seven thousand orbital ships and in-atmosphere antigrav units. Carriers teeming with fightercraft. Missile frigates loaded with neutron and plasma warheads. Gunships bristling with cannon that could spit thousands of rounds in an eyeblink.

And what was this, standing atop the head of the Thinker itself? What challenged all those militant tons of steel and firepower?

It appeared to be an angel.

Joy unfurled a pair of wings made of patterned gravitonic fields, lighting them up for pure damned showmanship. Each feather was a glassy razor, the mighty flights spanning a kilometre to a side. Next came the shields. A full-body halo englobed the tiny figure in white, her red hair streaming out in an unseen wind. Cerise ignited a circular band of blue fire around her sister's head as the opening chords of Tchaikovsky's immortal *1812 Overture* rang out over the locked-down city. That was the targeting system and auto-close-defence array.

Now came the guns.

The muzzles of innumerable cannons slid out between those glowing white, radiant feathers.

Gravitonic mega-destructors in battery. Hypersonic antimatter-powered railguns. The dreaded *Magnum Express Innominandum*. Things which would have forced Galbraith, Sentinel of the Arch, to go and have a bit of a lie down, followed by several cold showers[87].

People were watching now. The hammering chords and pealing carillons of the old 1812 shook every windowpane, every dental filling, for a hundred mile radius. They were pointing. They were praying, most of them.

And now Joy leaped. With an immense and utterly unnecessary single downbeat of her wings, the Angel ascended. Pillars of fire and flame lanced down from out of heaven to stab at her, but they were diffused to a mirror-ball sparkle of hair-thin beams, ghosted away to nothing by her alien shields.

Joy held her arms out to her sides and howled precisely for her namesake. She sped up through the blue, through the clouds, punching through them so fast she left great fractal spirals of mist in her wake. Up into the purple, to the edge of the black, where she hung weightless for an instant, a blazing white brand on the face of eternity. The stars looked on, impassive, as countless guns and missiles locked in on her haloed head.

And, before the *Burzum* could so much as twitch its mind around the trigger, she made them disappear.

Imagine growing up in a cold, dank cave. Imagine crawling upward toward the outer world, toward some dark and dripping forest on a moonless night. And now imagine the sheer unutterable beauty and terror of that first dawn...

That was what Joy unleashed. Just as Tchaikovsky's cannonade belted out across the magnetosphere of Temperance, using it as the galaxy's single largest loudspeaker.

First came the mere ship-breakers, the cannons designed to evaporate armoured steel and overload shielding generators. Hundreds of lances

---

87. *'And yet the wee auld fella wouldnae stand doon from attention!'*

of multi-coloured death lit up the sky. Shield projectors glowed white hot and exploded. Skyscraper-sized war-craft were sliced to slivers, ripped atom from atom, and blown away before the barrage.

Next came the capital guns. Gravitonic forces which could slam planets together like pool balls warped spacetime in sickening waves. Things designed to be solid stretched and melted like hot toffee. Things which were meant to be flexible shattered like frozen wax. Then came the sun-guns, their cavernous maws dripping plasma. Solid rods of star-matter stabbed out, hot as the forges of creation, and even more of the *Burzum*'s mind went sailing down the solar wind, annihilated.

Finally, Joy stared down at the knot of cojoined battleships and carriers which formed the mad AI's core. A spiked morningstar of metal, sizzling with potent shields and wards. Inside, the last fragments of the *Burzum* raged.

"You can't destroy me! Not me! I am the electric antichrist! The virus in the system of the universe! I am the God of emptiness, the harbinger of doom! I command you to..."

"SHUT UP"

The Dimensional Cross-Shear Antigraviton Culverin did precisely the business its evil looks implied.

A beam of *antiblack* - the colour you see between stubbing your toe and feeling the pain - tore local space and time in half like a pair of cheap underpants. The edges of the beam glowed a shade of purple and green *at the same time*. Inside that churning torrent of power, some of those watching from the planet's surface said they saw alien constellations, stars blazing pink and blue and gold. Others swore they saw a pair of eyes open, as if from an aeonic slumber. One or two gabbled heresies about a hand the size of a continent hitting a snooze button with far too many dimensions.

There was a very large, very final explosion. The kind with rings around it, and usually with credits after it.

For a very long second indeed Joy stared at the corkscrew bulk of the Innuendo.

A little animated image of a white flag waving popped to the front of her display, and she smiled.

Meanwhile, down in Worm III's war room, rank upon rank of militant clerics stood stunned at their consoles, overlooking a holographic projection of Hosanna City. Floating panes of light projected images from space - the camera feeds from the Holy Church's satellites.

Now one of the men zoomed in on Joy's blazing wings as she turned to survey the planet below. Zoomed in further, on a face radiant with triumph.

"Signature confirmed," he said, shouting to the Supreme Hierophants up on their dais. "It's definitely an Angel!"

The Lord Archbishop Militant - a man wearing tiny round sunglasses and sporting the natty combo of an Abraham Lincoln beard and white gloves - leaned forward, steepling his fingers.

"Yes! Exactly as I have planned! The next stage of human evolution begins when the chamber of souls is opened!"

The man standing behind him - a tall, hawkish veteran with iron-grey hair - slapped him across the face, then hammered the table with one fist.

"Are you *out of your tiny little mind?* Angels don't belong in my theatre of war! They belong in church, or in Heaven, or I'll allow, perhaps on the top of a Soul's-Day tree. Blow the holy bitch out of the sky!"

The Lord Archbishop Militant coughed sheepishly. He honestly didn't know where that had come from. Something itched at the back of his brain.

"Do we... do we have any *giant robots*, by any chance?"

His aide smiled. This was more like it.

"Yes, your Eminence. Big, dangerous ones with swords and guns, your Eminence."

The Archbishop rose from his seat, and looked down at the row upon row of black-robed clerics, all of them looking back up at him.

"Well, what are you waiting for, then? *Light her up!*"

+++

We could talk about the hillsides thronged with battletanks, their cannons aimed up into the clouds. We could mention the fleets of naval cruisers, floating in the great circular bay outside the port of Hosanna City. Perhaps even the giant robots deserve a footnote - those immense bipedal suits of powered armour with their rocket launchers and their gilded crucifixes, their twenty-metre battle blades and their steaming railguns.

They all made pretty fireworks, and the same cold ashes.

We could speculate on what would have happened, if the fighter jets hadn't been swatted from the sky by glowing nets of hexagonal energy-mesh. What strategies may have been employed if the colossal ground-based laser cannons of the city itself hadn't been crushed and mangled by gravitonic weapons of terrible potency. Certainly, those who watched the battle couldn't help but be impressed by the way Joy caught a whole salvo of nuclear ballistic missiles and swallowed them up in what appeared to be a hole in reality itself - then flipped that disc of darkness around to unleash a blast of radiation in the x-ray band, melting the tracked launchers which had fired them.

In the end, though - as the terrible, beautiful Angel hovered over the command bunker of Temperance's armed forces, and a spike of electromagnetic energy fried every last one of their strategic computers and comms arrays - Worm III himself may have put it best.

"Well lads. It was good while it lasted. But bugger this for a game of soldiers. No one ever said this religion malarkey was *real!*"

He struggled up from his command throne, deep in the Grand Basilica of the Word, an exoskeletal suit cradling his mammoth bulk. Leather cushions squealed. Buttons popped and flew.

"Sir! *Sir?*" asked one of his lackeys - a gilded Archimandrite in robes so ornate he could hardly move. "What are we going to *do?*"

Worm III fixed him with the kind of look a swindler would reserve for a man who now owes someone called 'Frankie the Hacksaw' a figure in the high six digits. It was part disbelief, part scorn, with just a drop of pity for taste.

"Dunno 'bout *you*, mate. But I'm outta here. Only room for one, yr'Eminence, you know how it is..."

For a morbidly obese man, it was quite surprising how fast the Pontifex of the Thinker could run.

The only question was - where to?

Twenty - Le Coup Disgrace

"It's not that Pro Wrestling's fixed. It's that the world *is fixed, and Pro Wrestling accurately reflects that truth. In fact, you watch enough Pro Wrestling, you can determine the course of fate, of history, and of destiny itself. Plus, you can learn some sweet moves to practice on the trampoline"*

Supreme Prognosticator Durford Q. Hogswallop, of the Church of the Holy Headlock

ONE OF THE universal truths of fixing things, as described in every almanac of repairs ever compiled[88], is that enough gaffer tape can cover a multitude of sins.

Mister Fixit was many things - insane, genocidal, unhinged and ugly come to mind - but he was first and foremost a handyman. He'd managed to wrap Rel Kitano in enough of the sticky gray stuff to inter a whole Egyptian dynasty, then lashed him securely over the seat of his motorcycle. A wadded-up sock stuffed in the Domesticated's mouth had brightened up Fixit's day immeasurably.

Now, as he sped through the streets of Hosanna City, he was scanning furiously for two things.

The first was Cerise.

Where had the little brat gotten to? Oh, there was no doubt she'd survive a fall from orbit. She was tougher than nails, and clever with it. She had to be here *somewhere.* And with her unique powers, Fixit was certain he could prise some kind of victory from the jaws of this disaster.

The second thing unfolded in his positronic brain exactly where he'd guessed it would.

Oh, yes. The unmistakable toroidal signature of a fusion drive

---

88. Even that accursed tome - kept locked in an iron barrel of ground-up shamrocks and rabbits feet - which the Librarian Sages of the Occult How-To Secret Society for Dummies call the Renovationomicon. This grimoire contains (according to its title page, which is enough, alone, to turn your brain to glazier's putty) 'Onne Hundredde ande Onne non-euclidian Temple Improvement Projectes to Hasten thee Comyng of the Elder Onnes, Those Who are Withoute Building Connsente'. Number 33 is 'Build ye a Forbidden Spyce Racke, to un-clutter thy Sacrificial Altar Spayce!'

spinning up.

Mister Fixit had seen enough of Temperance during his short and unpleasant stay to know that he had a *lot* in common with the man who ran the place. That was why he was blasting full-throttle towards the great Basilica of the Word, even before the steeple-spire which rose above it cracked open, revealing the skeletal gantry of a launch tower. And a shiny, needle-shaped spaceship tethered to it, steaming and rumbling as it powered up.

Surprise, surprise.

No cruel dictator worth his expensive fake uniform would *ever* leave himself without an escape clause. Now it was about to be messily and satisfyingly hijacked for the greater good.

Or the greater evil, depending on which side of Mister Fixit's one remaining eye you lived on.

Burzum was gone. The Dreadnought was temporarily out of reach. But living to fight another day meant that, on a long enough timescale, Fixit was sure to prevail.

He drew poor old Constable Thoushalt's pair of pistols from their holsters on each side of the bike's fuel tank, taking his hands off the handlebars as he came screaming into Saint Yargo's Plaza. There were only a few enQuisitorial Guardsmen outside the doors of the great Basilica, and most of them were looking up at the Angel in the sky above them, or yammering and pointing at the silver starship which had just emerged from the church steeple. *The fools probably thought it was some kind of wonder-weapon, poised to save the day. I wonder which side they're cheering for?*

A few well-aimed shots and the lot of them went down, foreheads neatly hole-punched. Mister Fixit took the marble steps up to the Basilica's doors in sixth gear, sliding at the last second so that the bulky gas-powered bike slammed them back on their hinges.

He completely missed the chromed-out, finned monstrosity which bombed through Saint Yargo's behind him, clipping a row of marble saints from the great ornamental fountain at its centre. The car was hot pink, hovered six feet off the cobbles, and was packed with a fine selection of Outriders of the Humanic Panarchy.

Inside the echoing cavern of the church, Mister Fixit snipped through a few select strands of gaffer tape, then hauled Rel up over his shoulder.

"Come on, you. We've got a date with a fat little sermonizing bastard. And then... then we'll see if we can't make your lady friend see reason."

The mad mech gave a very human sigh, and headed for the stairs.

+++

"I'm telling you, that was *him!*"

Wainwright should have been unable to get carsick, thanks to several thousand years of cybernetic upgrades and a noteworthy lack of internal organs. But nobody had told that to Casanova DeSade, who drove like an angry baboon on stimulants. Memories of what it was like to drink crème de menthe and sambucca though a funnel were coming back to him, horribly vivid.

"You sure?" asked Ezra from the back seat of the Fnord Phantasm 500. He was holding onto his hat with one hand and the door handle with the other, trying not to see the blur of gothic architecture as it went wheeling past outside. "Looked like a zombie and a mummy riding a motorcycle together. Wrong story."

"The trackers don't lie, Ashdown! He must be going for that bloody great rocket-ship. This is the last, best chance we're gonna get."

Tia Faraday leaned back as the Phantasm executed a handbrake turn which set fire to a huge arc of roadway. In her armoured hotsuit she was a vision from the kind of comic book which has more than one exclamation point in its title.

That chestplate, thought Ezra, *Was clearly designed by men.*

"So we're clear on how this is going to go down?" she asked. "We've got no Problem Solvers, So I'll be covering us with these." The deadly little agent hefted a pair of fully automatic combat shotguns, each as ugly as the wrong end of a lizard-hog. "Wainwright, you're on marksman duty with the longrifle. DeSade, although it physically pains me to say this, you're duly sworn in and deputized as an Outrider, seconded to the Ministry of Plausible Deniability. Any problems?"

"And If I say yes?" asked the black-masked pirate, chopping down a gear and taking the steps up to the Basilica in a mad powerslide.

"Then I'll have to kill you. And you know how I *hate* to mix business with pleasure."

DeSade shrugged.

"So long as you don't tell anyone I worked for the... urgh... *authorities,* we can write this off as a favour. For that time in Varqentine, with the fondue forks, and the giant oyster, and the neutron bomb." His eyes misted over with fond recollection. "Good *times!* So. What's are my

319

orders?"

Tia reached under the seat and handed him a compact little fusion beamer.

"You stay with Ashdown, and get him to the target. He's our endgame. Ezra?"

He turned to look at her, exo-suit servos whining and clicking. But whatever he'd expected to see in those violet eyes wasn't there. This was business, pure and simple.

"Zarathusrian was pretty damned specific on this one. *You* have to stop him. None of the rest of us can. So when you're in range, you take your shot."

"With *what*, miss Parole Officer? You just said it y'self... our Problem Solvers are out of action. I could kick him in the plums, but that might not go so well, what with him being a robot and all..."

Tia smiled, as the Phantasm crushed the remains of Mister Fixit's stolen bike and settled down on its skids. But there was a hint of sadness in that fleeting expression. A shadow of fear. She fussed at a piece of paracord, fraying its end.

"I was going to wait until you were signed up - you know. As a full agent. A proper Outrider. But you remember back on Harrowe, how everything got kind of out of control?"

"Seems like it never stopped."

"Well, I got Wainwright to forge these up for you. Something I thought you might like to hang over your desk, for old times' sake."

She opened a compartment in the Phantasm's floor and brought out a rosewood box, intricately inlaid with silver. Little etchings of cowboys riding horses and spinning lassos adorned its corners.

"Go on. Open it."

Ezra popped the top, and breathed in the scent of baize and gun oil. Something sparked behind his eyes as his nostrils widened. The smell didn't just take him back - it took him *sideways* as well. All those archetypes staring down from the walls of the Central Scrutinizer's secret little wild-west room inhaled it with him. Inside his head they stretched off into infinity, mirrors face to face.

All of them reached in and picked up the guns.

Pearl handled. Silver plated. Etched with loops and swirls and arabesques. Down one barrel someone had engraved the word TROUBLE. The other one was called STRIFE.

"My granddaddy's guns," breathed Ezra Ashdown. The ones he'd stolen all those years ago. The ones whose holsters and belt had been his pillow when he slept under the stars of Harrowe, out on the plains, when he was a boy.

There was something else next to them. It was a piece of metal cut from the faceplate of a Panarchy Standard soup vending machine, model 9450-G. Someone had carefully sliced it out and shaped it into the form of a five-pointed star. Then they'd plated it with gold and buffed it until it gleamed.

The word on the front said -

SHERIFF

Ezra's hands were joined by thousands of other phantasmal pairs as he pinned it to one of the webbing belts that criss-crossed his chest. Reality around him grew that little bit thinner as he stepped from the car, giving his new guns an experimental twirl around his fingers.

Back, forward, under and over, spin and return...

It never left you. If it went away for a while, it was only because it was striding along in your shadow.

In Tia Faraday's head, the words implanted by Zarathusrian Zyphus Bleems evaporated like so much dream-dust. She hefted her own guns and grinned, reckless[89].

"OK, Outriders. We know *where* he is, and we know *what* he is. Mister Fixit is wanted for a list of crimes so long they'd have to print it on toilet paper and roll it up. So, for the sake of our tin-star buddy here..." she paused. She winked. It got him right *there*. "Let's go and serve that mechanical bastard up a nice hot cup of justice!"

+++

"You know him a lot better than you're letting on," said Joy. Her wings were gone, and she was back inside the space beyond space, the white immensity of the Immaterial Dreadnought's command sphere. "That thing that says he's your uncle."

"And you know me well enough to know that's true," replied Cerise. She really could have been Joy's sister, to look at them. Personality bleed-over had made the pair of them almost twins, one with golden

---

89, And here, we have a special place for Ezra Ashdown's big plan, which is incredibly secret, and needs to be stored somewhere that mister Fixit can't find it until it's too late. If you lean in very, very close to the page, you'll hear that whispering noise which people use to explain things to each other in cartoons. You won't be able to make out the words, because you're not Tia Faraday. But suffice to say, when the time comes, it's a bloody good one.

hair, the other red. "But I couldn't let him know I was helping you. Even if *you* knew... he'd have seen it. He *reads* people, Joy. He has to, to use them."

Joy's new eyes saw clear through the Great Basilica. She saw Mister Fixit toiling up the stairs to the gallery of the main vault, dragging the mummified form of Rel Kitano along after him. And she saw the Outriders of the Panarchy arrive, all full of bravado and determination.

"Do they have a chance? Really?"

Cerise tilted her head to one side. She frowned.

"Perhaps. There's more to a fight than raw firepower, you know. And I'll guarantee you this - it's going to get very confusing down there. We could swoop down and snatch him up. Joy..." She paused, and looked down at the glowing hexes of the instrument panel. "Do you think your boy there's worth all this? Really worth it?"

Joy considered, for a moment, trying to explain that half-remembered day, and Farbley, and that kiss, to what she knew was a machine. The words all seemed to have been cut out of romance, which was a kind of lie. So she settled for the truth.

"I think we can make sure we *both* are. That's enough for now. The rest can wait."

Cerise looked up, her face underlit with red. Every inch the faerie warrior-princess.

"All right, Sister. All right. I suppose we have a bloody Prince in distress to rescue, then..."

+++

He would have made it, if it wasn't for the pipe organ.

It was quite an instrument. Many, many slaves had died in erecting its massive, towering drones and chanters. Its bass pipes were copper statues of hooded monks, taller than rocket boosters. It's fans and sunbursts of smaller tubes covered an entire wall. No less than ten keyboards wrapped around in a full semicircle, displaying an array of ivory even more menacing than the one under Mister Fixit's hollow nasal septum. And the stops! Oh, so many stops. Some were marked with radioactive trefoils. Some were knobbed with silver skulls. One or two had been nailed in place and sealed with waxen seals, decked with ribbons of exorcism. The twin ranks of pedals gleamed with oil and no small amount of ecclesiastical toejam.

The fact that Joy's reign of destruction in the skies above had seeded a great anvil-head of a thunderstorm didn't help matters. Mister Fixit might have been able to drag himself and his madness past the pipe organ, in normal circumstances. But with the heavens full of fire and lightning, the Evil in him took hold.

He dropped Rel Kitano and kicked him to one side, up against the ornate wooden railing which looked out on the Basilica's nave. Seven storeys down, he could hear muffled voices, the snick and clatter of loading guns. *But ahhhh, to hell with them.*

The bad ones don't fear. The bad ones *are* the fear. And when there's thunder, and fire, and darkness, and whole great big empty cathedral to play in... *the bad don't run.*

Mister Fixit shucked off his ruined uniform and stretched out. *Really* stretched out, like he hadn't been able to do in years. Without the need to mimic a specific human form, the skeletal metal robot stood seven feet tall, from the crown of his gleaming skull to the tips of his toes. He reached up into the hollow cavity behind his ribs and brought out just the very thing he needed. The final weapon, in fact, which he'd use to reclaim all he'd fought and planned for.

It was a great leather-bound storybook. The one he'd stolen from Mason Stockton along with his skin, and his plans for Cerise St-Claire Langevin. *Because here was the truth.* When Jed Granger cut off Harrowe from the Reticulum, he was just barely ahead of the Jest. He bought time for Cerise, so she saw the madness coming. Most of her - well, it was out there somewhere, masquerading as a golden-haired little girl-child. But a lot more was right here in the book. It had power. Hells, it *was* power, and one crude application of that power was as a weapon.

Mister Fixit opened the book to a random page - an ink-drawn image of an impossible dragon coiled around a thorny tower. He placed it reverently on the music stand, and climbed up onto the brass-and-leather stool from which an organist could reach every key, every stop and every pedal.

He loosened up his fingers. Each one split down the middle, becoming two. Spidery, multi-jointed tool-pincers sprung out from the gaps.

And throwing back his head, staring up through a stained glass dome at the lightning, and at the chrome spire of Worm III's escape ship, Mister Fixit began to play.

+++

As the first huge and crashing chords of Mister Fixit's fugue rung out, Ezra Ashdown smiled. Cue the lightning. Cue the music. Cue the hammers snicking back snug as an honest memory, the two silver guns in his fists seeming to grow huge and heavy as he pointed them up at the balcony.

Up there, mantis-bat shadows pranced across the pipework.

"I appreciate the soundtrack, son. I really do! But this is about you and me! What say you come down here and we skip the fancy stuff? Get to the percussion section..."

Wainwright was leaned up against the Phantasm, his longrifle stabbing the gloom with a filament of laser light. Tia crouched behind a marble baptismal font, her riot guns in at her side. She nodded. Casanova DeSade was already up behind the altar, ready to create a deadly crossfire.

Still the music went on. Down in the crypts beneath the Basilica, a figure in a white half-mask and full evening dress looked up from its candle-lit desk and sniffed.

"Bloody plagiarist."

Then Ezra caught sight of movement, way up among the flying arches and cobwebbed candelabra. A spidery form, scuttling upside-down, lit up for a heartbeat by the lighting.

"There you are! Mister no-first-initial Fixit, I'm placing you under arrest in the name of the full majesty of the Law!"

Wainwright moved as fast as only a hardlight hologram could, loosing a supersonic round which should have punched clean through the homicidal mech. But Mister Fixit was faster. Without human skin to bind him up, the machine was pure quicksilver, detaching from the gothic stonework with four tiny pinging sounds.

As he came spinning through the air, Ez could see why the music was still playing, filling the vaulted hall with echoes. *The thing had left its hands behind.* Right now, those two disembodied claws were stalking up and down the ivories, while the ends of Fixit's arms were replaced by a pair of yard-long knives.

All the force of his fall was behind them both as he went into a flat spin. One then the other carved deep into Wainwright's copper head, sending him reeling. Fixit drew both knives back to finish the job, but then Tia was up and firing, making the robot perform a mad and jerky gavotte across the marble floor. Shell after shell pummelled his skeletal frame, buckshot flying wide. Muzzle flash underlit Tia's face, reflecting from her savage grin.

But when both guns were spent, Mister Fixit simply unfurled himself back to his full height, his metal skin scarred and dented - but unbroken.

"You'll have to do much, *much* better than that," he gloated. "And I don't believe you can. I'm going to have *fun* with you, Agent Faraday. I think your metal friend here might just survive long enough to watch."

Wainwright clawed his way out from behind the Phantasm, his body blurred with static. There were two horrendously deep gashes in his faceplate, cracked clean through the glass of his single eye. Coolant spurted blue and green, slicked across the marble behind him.

"Hey, Fixit," said the Metalman. "Why don't you go fuck yourself?" He held out a single finger, hashed with test patterns.

It was empty bravado. It was a ploy, to buy Tia time to reload.

But the killer mech wasn't having it. He advanced, crooked and limping, his bladed hands rasping together. That nightmare grin filled Tia's whole world...

Ezra put up his guns, ready to take the shot. But just as his fingers tightened on the triggers, Casanova DeSade did just exactly what he did best. He upstaged the lot of them.

"Halt, villain! Nobody kills *that* fair lady except for me! And even then, only in my own peculiar and dashing... what do you call it. *Idiom!*" The leather-clad space pirate vaulted down from the altar, throwing his guns to the floor. "If these little fellows can't hurt you, perhaps you'd like a taste of something long and hard, hmm?"

He reached behind his back and drew forth a curved scimitar, its bone-white blade shimmering with lightning. Thunder answered it, up above the dome.

"Ahhhh," said Mister Fixit, all disdain. "The *sodomite*. How predictable."

DeSade gave a couple of little practice swings, edging himself around between his target and Tia Faraday. He smiled.

"There's no word for my sexual preference, you horrible metal bitch. And if there was, it would probably spontaneously combust. Suffice to say... I'll enjoy it if you hurt me a little, but I'll enjoy it *so* much more if I kill you - a lot."

Mister Fixit looked at the rest of the Outriders in turn, incredulous. "That didn't make sense, did it? I mean, come on! Any of you guys?" he shrugged. "Allright. If you want to do this the old fashioned way..."

Blades blurred and chimed. Casanova DeSade was a masterful swordsman, but he was obviously outmatched. Fighting a machine which could bend and rotate its joints in strange, insectile ways put him at a distinct disadvantage. And while he was armed with one huge, heavy scimitar, his enemy wove a cage of glittering steel with two blades, making him parry and spin and dance.

Just when it seemed certain that a final stroke would slice the pirate Captain's head from his shoulders, Tia was there, blocking the swing with a huge combat knife. A glance between them, and then the two Outriders pushed their advantage, forcing Mister Fixit back.

And still Ezra couldn't get a clear shot. Limbs and bodies cartwheeled and spun amid the razor storm. Sparks flew as metal skirled on metal. And, in the centre of it all, the homicidal handyman turned to look directly at Ashdown. Time seemed to slow down, flickering film-strip bright.

"You're right, you know," the mad mech whispered, the words slicing in Ezra's mind like little slivers of glass. *"It's down to us. The white hat and the black one. It's what the madness wants."*

For an instant he stood there, frozen, blocking Casanova's blade high and Tia's low. The trio could have been a very unlikely ice carving, or one of those horribly pointless margarine sculptures. Then Fixit's single red eye stuttered out, and back on again. *A wink.*

There was no time for Ezra to shout a warning. The blades flew from their sockets with a pulse of blue-white light, gravitic motors igniting. One looped around to pierce DeSade through the back, its tip bursting out through his chest in a spray of crimson. The other took Tia in the shoulder, transfixing her through the metal of her hotsuit.

But they weren't finished. Oh no. The blade which had impaled Casanova lifted him bodily from the floor and slammed him forward into a pillar, nailing him in place like some nightmarish insect specimen. The one through Tia Faraday pulsed again, sending her sliding across the floor and up the altar steps in a tangle of limbs and curses. It, too, bit deep into stone, pinning her with her back to the slab.

"And then there were two," chuckled Mister Fixit. His hands gave a final flourish on the keys and came hissing through the gloom to snap back into their sockets, fingers twitching. "The good guy and the bad guy. But do you *really* know which is which?"

Ezra covered him with both barrels as the pair began to circle each other, right around the storm-lit nave beneath the dome.

"You gonna try that sad old mind-game, partner? Seems to me, the winners get to decide who wears the black and who wears the white. Thing is - right now I've got something you don't."

Fixit sneered.

"What do you suppose that is, child of the Chasm? Justice? Honour? *Revenge?* The Law, with your precious capital L?"

"Nothing that deep, I reckon," said Ez, squinting a little under the brim of his hat. "What I've got is the fact that you're fast. Slippery as a greased-up rattlesnake. But I've got twelve little friends that're faster than you'll ever be."

There are *rules*, you see. One of them is that you can't just shoot the bad guy in the face. Not until he tells you all about his evil plan. Not unless you've already tried being merciful.

But, Hellfire. Ezra Ashdown was getting pretty damned tired of the rules.

It was hard to say how many shots rang out as he squeezed the triggers, feeling the guns buck and roar in his hands like live things. It was hard to say exactly what calibre those silver, cross-tipped slugs actually came out, either, because reality around Ezra Ashdown got to rippling like the heat-haze above a desert highway, shucking and warping as those twin hammers rose and fell.

Mister Fixit caught it, though.

Each impact slammed into his terribly ancient, impossibly tough casing and sent him spinning backward. Two, three, and he was sprawling, hands held out to cover his face. Five, six, and a metal finger blew away, sparks guttering and fizzing from the stump. Seven, eight, and he was down, chest caved in as if by massive fists, head lolling to one side as that single red eye blurred and faded...

Number nine was caught between the fingers of Ezra's mind as time slowed to a crawl, all twinkling motes of dust in the lightning's afterglow. His gold star flashed as the revolver mechanism came sliding around, inexorable as the clockwork behind galaxies. His trenchcoat blew wide, raven-winged, as the hammer snapped forward, meeting the brass jacket of the bullet, making the atoms in that blackpowder dance.

He looped it in *just so*, and it sheared off Mister Fixit's left hand at the wrist. Something all made of coiled springs and pushrods snapped loose with a sad little sound, and a whole horrorworks of tools scattered across the marble.

Number ten spun slow and lazy, cordite smoke spiralling behind it in a shroud, and it snapped Mister Fixit's head back against the floor with a noise like billiard balls being cracked in a vise.

There may have been an eleven and twelve, but at that moment time sped up again, to the sound of a defiant scream and the clatter of metal on granite. Ez chanced a look over to the altar, and he saw Tia stand up, blood smeared down half of her face. Her right arm hung uselessly, that old burgundy dripping from her armoured fingers.

"I've got this!" shouted Ezra. "Go and save the hostage! When he came in here, this bastard was carrying someone. If they ain't dead, I reckon we want 'em alive!"

This time there was no question of seniority, or chains of command, or even the fact that he stubbornly persisted in being a man. Tia was used to COFRIADs, and in the middle of one of them, she was calm, cool and copacetic. She retreated toward the stairs as Ezra glanced back toward the fallen Mister Fixit...

Who was gone.

A quick look left, then right. *Nothing.*

Then something tapped him on the shoulder, and Ezra turned around just in time to catch a face-full of metal knuckles.

"The classics! Ahh, they never get old!"

Without the hotsuit, it would have broken his neck. Let's be honest - it would have spun his skull loose like a wingnut. As it was, it simply hurt like damnation. Vast nebulas of antiblack whirled behind Ashdown's eyes as he staggered.

But he didn't go down. Ezra turned to face Mister Fixit, and he spat out a tooth he was pretty sure he hadn't been using anyway.

"So, *mano a mano*, eh?" he asked. "Or at least, *mano a stupid robot bastard.*"

"I don't do this often," replied Fixit, cocking back his single remaining fist. "But I'll make this fair on you. I'll fight you with one of my hands *blown to pieces by a redneck piece of shit.*"

Ezra leaned back on instinct. A haymaker which could have compacted steel hissed by where his nose had been.

"Allright. Let's dance."

They squared off, throwing jabs and hooks, dodging away, testing each other's defences. The hotsuit gave Ezra the same servo-assisted power as Fixit, and he was no stranger to fighting. Well - to be precise, he was no stranger to surviving the kind of barfights which begin when extra aces fall out of somebody's sleeve.

But Mister Fixit was simply *impossibly* fast. Even one-handed, he was able to slip blows past Ezra's guard, hammering at his ribs, his kidneys and his chest, darting in cobra-quick to batter his right eye purple-black.

Another left rang his bells, sending Ezra pirouetting on one foot. A right made him stagger, almost going over. He scored a solid hit in return, but Mister Fixit just shrugged it off and came steamrollering in, lining up a huge cross to the jaw...

Which never landed.

Because while there are such things as honour, and fair play, and sportsmanship, there is also such a thing as being a stone dead sucker. Ezra let the punch sail past him, got in close, stiffened his armoured thumb, and crunched it in *hard*, popping Mister Fixit's remaining eye. The camera lens shattered, turning to splinters.

While the mech reeled back, howling like modem noise, Ezra drew Trouble from its holster. In a single motion he aimed directly up into the dark... and fired.

The bullet flew straight and true. With a twist from Ezra's mind it sheared through a bell rope the width of a fat lady's thigh, sending several tons of sanctified brass tumbling through the air.

"Three hours," slurred Ezra, squinting up into the darkness. "We gave you your three bloody hours, Central. Now he's *your* problem."

Mister Fixit turned on him, hissing, a slotted screen opening up just above his ruined eyes.

"I can taste you in infra-red, you biological fool," said the killer mech. "Now it's time to slit you open! All this goody-goody nonsense makes me..."

What that made him was lost to history. Because at that moment two things happened.

Firstly, a church bell the size of a cement mixer truck came down on Mister Fixit, trapping him like a spider under the world's largest coffee cup.

And secondly, Cerise and Joy picked this as a good time to tear the entire roof off the Basilica.

All the acres of stone which should have rained down, instead rained *up*. Tractomorphic energy fields peeled the building like a satsuma, toppling Worm III's escape ship mere seconds - had they only known - before the fat boy was about to blast off.[90]

––––––––––––––––––––

90. Reality was painfully thin around the Immaterial Dreadnought. Worm III the Utterly Lowest was shaken loose from his extra-wide command throne aboard the silver ship, and flung bodily into the Chasm as it collapsed and exploded. Where, as luck would

Then came the voice of an Angel. One pretty much at the end of her patience.

"Step away from the good looking... I mean the handsome... look, *just put the boy down*, O.K?"

Tia did just that. *Carefully.* The creature facing her may or may not have been a real resident of the Realms Celestial. But it certainly looked very, very vexed. Joy hovered down into the hollow shell of the Basilica, still haloed, still borne on glowing wings, but now also, inexplicably, blushing.

"And how would *I* know if he has any clothes on under all that sticky tape? *Cerise!* We're supposed to be *angelic*, for the love of..."

And that was when it all went wrong.

Ezra was quite pleased he wasn't killed when the bell exploded. Otherwise the rest of what happened would have been quite confusing. When the red-hot shrapnel settled, Mister Fixit was standing in the middle of a charred circle of broken marble, his single claw clamped around a great leather-bound book. It had flown from the pipe organ to punch clean through the side of the bell.

"*Cerise? Cerise Saint-Claire Langevin!* Where have you *been*, young lady? And what. Exactly. Have you been doing with my! *Bloody!* Dreadnought?"

It was a voice that could have etched diamond. It was a voice which dripped raw, flesh-dissolving acid.

Joy looked down at Rel Kitano. His eyes were wide, his mouth was still gagged, but he was all in one piece. And out of the arc of fire of at least *some* of Joy's smaller weapons...

She turned to Cerise, and saw the look of horror on her sister's face. She followed her gaze, and saw the book snap open, pages riffling in an invisible wind.

"I'm really, *really* sorry," said the AI of Harrowe's Chasm Reticulum. And then she began to *change*.

There's really no point in trying to describe what a Humanic AI detaching itself from the cosmic eleven-dimensional Dirac manifold of a process Deadnought looks like. It looks like Wednesday and spite flavoured bubblegum. It looks like the sound of purple and yellow

---

have it, he popped up in the Turkish kitchen of Zarathusrian Zyphus Bleems.

"God?" asked the morbidly obese Pontifex, peering at the mightily bearded fellow before him. "Is that you?"

"Got it in one, me old china," replied the fez-wearing alien. "But now, you and I have to have a little talk about defamation of character, I reckon..."

when heard in hot Morse Braille. It tastes of exquisitely delicate pain, garnished with a thousand-decibel strobe-flash of morose ecstasy. To make it easier on your brain, imagine a chrome jellyfish being turned inside out. Forever.

What unfurled and unfolded from the fractured un-space stood over the unconscious body of Joy, a scream made flesh. It was still Cerise, but a vision of her merged with a twenty foot tall smoked-glass insect, all blades and pincers, knives and antennae. Her face sat atop the thing's spiked thorax, eyes burning mirror-bright, and when she opened her mouth the sound that came out was like the rupturing of faultlines deep in glacial ice.

Her master could not have been happier.

"Yes! You *will* obey me, girl! You have no choice! Now, kill them all! At least they'll have the satisfaction of knowing they're first... *among billions.*"

Mister Fixit brandished the book as Cerise reared up on a quartet of long and spindly legs, light refracting through her to cast anti-rainbows across the marble floor. Limbs like scythes the size of helicopter rotors swung back, their edges seething as mono-molecular teeth whirled.

Ezra Ashdown looked up at the monstrosity, its clawed and serrated embrace open wide for him. Even its ribs peeled back, revealing a selection of glassy teeth set in cancer-black gums.

"I'm sorry about this, everyone," he said. Not sad, not angry - just resigned. As if *this*, for all its terrible faults, was how it had to be.

Then he smiled, put the gun called Strife to his temple, *pulled the trigger...*

+++

When you die, they say, your whole life flashes before your eyes.

Not what's scribed on the memory systems of your skullware. Not what gets shunted through to the nearest nanoforge, for the whole voodoo ritual with the electric shocks and the bad coffee.

Your actual life.

Images exploded behind Ezra's eyes as the hammer dropped, steel grating on steel. His own face, reflected in a dirty mirror. His Pa, swinging from the hangman's rope. Cards dancing between his fingers. Firelight and red velvet curtains. The hard, bright stars of a Harrowe night. The taste of moonshine, cigar smoke, women, wine...

And closer now, the torrent becoming a flood. He saw time slivered down and folded up like ricepaper origami, the bullet screwing its way up the barrel in front of a red-hot explosion...

He remembered what Zarathusrian had said to him, in the Chasm. In that black and white desert with the static sky.

"I thought I'd be able to reason with you, like the other Heroes I've made. Quite illicitly, I'll have you know. This unreality of yours - this fixation on fiction - it's only going to get worse. Because it's true. You made the metaphor, and your power will fill it up. The survival of two whole universes could depend on it. **All you'd have to do is start writing the author's part.***"*

He remembered what had happened on board the *Slog*, in the reactor core, when Tia Faraday had wrapped her fingers around the back of his neck and drawn him in to a kiss that had literally lit up the heavens.

Faster and faster. Images blurred together as the Now came up to meet him, a stark black terminating line. The bullet was nosing out of the barrel of Strife, incandescent gases flaring...

And Ezra Ashdown saw it all.

In the second between realizing you aren't real, and the universe catching up with you, you can perform miracles. When you understand - and truly *believe* - that the universe itself is just as fraudulent... that it is, for example, a massively complicated computer simulation, that can only be understood by a card-swindling Harrowe cowboy as some cheap penny-dreadful...

Well then.

That's when miracles become the least of your concerns.

+++

There used to be a lot of words, right here. Cold ink on white paper. Gruesomely descriptive paragraphs, describing the arc and splatter of pinkish-grey wobbly bits. Ghoulish rhapsodies about skull fragments trailing matted hair. A burst eyeball, perhaps, for flavour.

Ezra reached out from a calm place, where the whole world was as thin and brittle as the smile that comes before murder.

And he changed them to the only two words that could save his life.

...and missed.

He took the gun away from his head and rose up, squaring his shoulders. The smoked-glass mantis-beast which had been Cerise Saint-Claire Langevin raged at him, but those massive claws just couldn't seem to come close. Something held them back.

"Tia," said Ashdown - and his voice was calm, cool, right up inside her ear without microphones and speakers. "Tia, I want you to go and do that thing we talked about. Right at the start of this chapter. There's a footnote there which contains an amazingly cunning plan, and I need you to use it."

Tia looked up over the balcony rail, utterly incredulous.

"Have you *lost your mind?* We need to stop that thing! We need to stop *him!* This is no time for some half-baked plan based on your mad delus..."

She stopped, hairs raising on the back of her neck. For an instant, she felt the presence of something both huge and subtle moving through her mind, like a pressure wave through the ocean. No - he wouldn't just change her thoughts. That wasn't right. That wasn't... *heroic.*

Instead, that infuriatingly calm voice whispered something to her which made her eyes grow wide. Neural pathways which had nothing to do with the intricacies of skullware lit up like fireworks.

"Miss Faraday, I'm willing to accept the notion that this is somewhat in the nature of a two-hero narrative. That I have been a complete and utter fool. And in return I'd like you to know that I do believe in romantic sub-plots, happy endings, long rides into the sunset and that the meaning of life, Miss Faraday, is believing there is one even though you don't know what it is."

And kiss. And detonation. And plasma-fusion explosive bliss...

She let her belief in this whole silly, stupidly dangerous situation fall away. It was strangely liberating. She let the footnote sink into her mind, where it melted like ice into a glass of dry gin and tonic water, telling her exactly what happened next.

Or, in effect, *what had happened before.*

Reality grew thin around sources of immense power. And while Joy was still out for the count, the Process Immaterial Dreadnought sat coiled up behind space right next to her. Neither Cerise nor Mister Fixit noticed as Tia found a crack between moments with her Edgeborn mind, and slipped away into the Chasm.

"What are you waiting for?" screamed Mister Fixit, utterly unhinged. "Kill him! He's just standing there! He's even out of bullets! *Turn him into a bloody stain, girl!"*

Cerise let loose a sound like a high-pressure pipe shearing away from a fission reactor. One of her main scythe-arms came hissing in, but stopped mere millimetres from Ezra Ashdown's face. He hadn't so much as twitched.

"You were right, you know," he said. "It's just you and me, Mister Fixit. The black hat and the white. Your creature here - well, she's not herself, is she? Not really. And I can't be the hero, and wear this badge, if'n I go around killing little girls just because some twisted old bastard turns them into monsters." He tapped his sheriff's badge with one finger. A flash of liquid gold light sparked from one of the points of the star. "Oh no. *It's just you and me.*"

For an instant, the mad mech looked utterly terrified. There was something *wrong* here. Fundamentally wrong, as if, down at an atomic level, all the sizzling little particles had been replaced with pixellated dots.

But he belonged to the madness, now. He was the bad guy, from head to toe.

"And who's going to save her, then? Who wants to kiss *that* and turn it back into a princess, Ashdown? Seeing as you're not man enough for the job..."

Right on cue, Ezra felt the frayed, thin space around them all grow even tighter, like the skin of a drum. Tia had come through. Tia, who would have found them waiting there in front of the door, all of them wondering exactly why they needed so badly to be on the some-time pleasure planet of New Gomorrah.

"Them," he said, gesturing with one thumb over his shoulder. He didn't even turn to look. But there they were, in any case.

Zarathusrian Zyphus Bleems' little army. His equalizers. People who, like Ezra Ashdown, had been infected by the dreams of the Chasm, and twisted into the archetypes the poor fractured human race needed.

Heroes.

They came out of the shadows of the ruined basilica, from places where the angles played tricks with the light. A man in an immaculate dinner suit, carrying a silenced pistol. Another in a green beret and camouflage trousers, his face and chest painted with streaks of mud and blood. One in a wrestler's tights and a full-face luchadore mask. One in a tweed coat and deerstalker hat. Behind him came an Asian man in a yellow and black motorcycle suit. A good cop, framed for a crime he didn't commit. A monk in saffron robes, with a sword across his shoulders taller than he was. And more.

A figure in green power-armour, faceless behind a golden visor. A muscled warrior-king with a red cape and a clipped black beard. An old man in a gray cloak, leaning on a staff. Another wild, red-armoured warlord with what appeared to be a chainsaw axe. A guy in a bat costume. Another in a white and brown robe, lighting up a laser sword of some kind. A pale young man in a black trenchcoat and very expensive sunglasses. A soldier from some long-forgotten war, his Thompson submachinegun etched with crossed-out swastikas.

There must have been a hundred of them. They ranked up behind Ezra Ashdown, all poised and ready for the fight. A thicket of weapons were raised up, from the rune-carved black sword being lofted by a sickly-looking albino, to the General Electric Minigun being hefted by that bloke with the crewcut and half a metal face.

The silence which followed was broken by a sad little cough.

"Ummm... sorry. I don't suppose anyone could offer a bit of assistance, here, could they? It sounds as if something terribly dramatic is happening back there, and I'd hate to be left out..."

It was Casanova DeSade, still stuck face-first to a shattered pillar.

And here to help him loose came the last hero of all. Ezra saw her for what she was, now, as she tore the blade from the space pirate's back and stood him back up on his feet.

Tia Faraday. Touched by the Chasm, just like him. The cute but tough-as-nails kick-arse science fiction heroine.

"Mister Fixit," said Ezra. "I'll tell you one more time. Put down the book. Shut yourself down. I'm placing you under arrest, for your crimes, and your stated intent to commit even more crimes, and those teeth - but mainly for the Law, with a capital L. The one that won't let me have my revenge, but *will* let me have you taken back to Earth in chains, and tried, and sentenced to whatever they have for your kind instead of hangin'. Something with magnets, probably."

It wasn't the best pre-battle speech in the universe. It got a cheer from the Chasmic Heroes behind him anyway.

"And what makes you think you can catch me? Do you really think I'm going to fight fair? you must be a stupid as you are ugly, Ezra Ashdown!"

The space cowboy nodded, still infuriatingly calm.

"Boys, I want you to subdue this raging, hideous monster here. Don't kill it - I got a feelin' that when it's beat it's gonna turn back into some kind of princess. You know how it goes. And as for *you...*"

Ezra took a step forward, and there was a sound like crinkling paper. Suddenly he was holding Mister Fixit by the neck.

"We're going to have a climactic final showdown. But not here. There's *rules*, you see..."

There was a thunderclap of inrushing air. The pair of them vanished, leaving behind the scent of burning ink.

Tia Faraday looked left and right, at the army of Chasmic archetypes behind her.

"You heard the man!" she shouted, clenching her fists. Cerise reared up over them on her insect legs, suddenly unbound, her countless glassy blade-limbs thrashing the air. "Who wants to live forever, anyway?"

+++

They appeared on the battlements of a castle, flaming torches lighting the scene of a medieval battle below. Ezra was dressed in chainmail and a crown. Mister Fixit was a knight in black armour.

"So comes at last the end to thy vile knavery! And here, upon this blessed field, shall justice smite thy toothsome face, as Jove and all the Muses be mine witness!"

Fixit looked down at his gauntleted hands as he staggered backwards.

"What sorcery be this?" he began - then stopped, astonished by his own voice. "From what dark and eldritch coven springs this horrid fate? Oh Lucifer, lord of lies, grant solace to your most obedient vassal, for..."

The scene shifted again. This time the pair appeared atop a warehouse roof, with a foggy city stretching away into the distance. A zeppelin cruised overhead.

"... you'll never take me alive, see, you flatfoot bastard!" finished Mister Fixit, who was now dressed in a pinstriped suit and a homburg hat. "Ya must have slipped me a mickey, you dirty rat! This can't be happening! Not to Don Vito Fixetti!"

Ezra, who was now got up in a brown trenchcoat and fedora, snapped his fingers again.

Now they were on a bridge, alone on a desolate moor. Both were wearing top hats and antiquated dinner suits.

"I demand satisfaction for the lady's honour, Lord Fixit," said Ezra, his hand going to the hilt of a duelling sword. "In this tumultuous world, true love is the only star to guide us... well, apart from having a ripped six-pack to flash at blushing milkmaids..."

Another blurred flash. The bridge of a burning battleship. Flash. A secret lair inside a volcano. Flash. A Colosseum filled with cheering, toga-wearing sports fans. Flash...

And now they were atop the remains of the Great Basilica of the Word, lashed by wind and rain. Lightning crashed, evaporating a rather constipated-looking statue of a saint no more than a few metres away.

"That's better," said Ezra Ashdown, returned to his proper guise. He settled his cowboy hat on his head at just the perfect angle. "Now, how about we do this *right?*"

Mister Fixit looked down at his hands, and then back up at Ez.

"I don't know what you're doing, human. But whatever it is, I don't like it. Perhaps if I unlace your skullware I can find out how..."

He brought the book out from inside his chest cavity again, letting it snap open with a discharge of violet energy.

"You *don't* want to do that," said Ezra, drawing one of his guns. Trouble. It seemed fitting.

"Oh, really? I want to have *mercy*, do I? I want to *come quietly?*" Fixit held the tome up over his head, a massive charge building up as he prepared to unleash a bolt of force. "I suppose I want to have the Central Bloody Scrutinizer rip my mind apart like wet pastry as well, hmm? *I want to let the human race down, and not be the killer robot they all deserve?*"

The power expanded into a glowing ball, bright enough to make Ezra close his eyes. He gritted his teeth, and hoped that there was actually a single bullet left after all...

Then the lightning came down.

The bolt began as a sizzling tendril questing up into the sky from Mister Fixit's book, and came back with a hammerblow of pure blue-white voltage. Inside the subsequent explosion Ezra saw the black outline of a skeleton, its feet blown off the ground. And the book blown from its fingers.

He asked himself, in the cold, calm space in his head, *if he was feeling lucky.*

And he pulled the trigger.

The blast hammered into Mister Fixit's chest with far more power than a .45 magnum slug deserved, piledriving him backwards. Ezra reached out with his other hand and neatly caught the book as it fell. But its erstwhile owner...

Fixit tottered for a second on the very edge of the Basilica's roof, smoking. Below him yawned a huge and deadly drop, down onto a whole graveyard of spiked obelisks and iron railings. There was a fraction of a moment when it looked like he'd regain his balance. But then his one remaining hand reached out for the book, fingers writhing, and he went over. Screaming as he fell.

Ezra waited for the crunch. *Blown up, thrown off a roof and then impaled on something.* It was a formula as old as fiction. But it never came. Because at that moment there was a sound like ten million people biting down of a sheet of tinfoil. There was a smell of hospital waiting rooms. And suddenly everything *froze* – each raindrop twinkling in the air like a drop of polished crystal.

There came a sound like ten thousand grannies pulling the corks of ten thousand bottles of sherry with their teeth.

And two men appeared atop the cathedral with Ezra - or at least, the *semblance* of two men.

"Well, well, well, mister Remainder. It's this guy again! Do they ever learn?"

"I would be disinclined to agree, Mister Placeholder, though it saddens me deeply to do so. Deeply."

Ezra holstered his gun and put his hands up. He'd known that it might come to this.

"Ezra Ashdown, this case is now under the jurisdiction of the Chronojudiciary. You're being asked politely to help us with our investigations."

"The alternative, of course, is not even worth thinking about," put in Mister Remainder. "I'm not even sure if your human brain *could* think about it. But there'd be quite a mess."

"And Mister Fixit? What happens to him?"

"He's been taken in for questioning too. We're gonna be taking things from here. Don't you worry. there's a very real chance that none of this will ever have happened..."

Ezra looked up at the pair from under the brim of his hat. There was a certain twinkle in his eye which did not inspire confidence.

"So he's gone, then? He's out of the scene?"

"He's *secured*. Nothing gets out of the Nick of Time without our say-so, human - and you'd better remember it..."

Ezra held out his hands, one to each agent.

"You'd better cuff me, then, boys..."

+++

Down below, a hundred Chasmic Heroes cheered as Cerise Saint-Claire Langevin tottered and fell, glassy blades shattering, insect legs buckling and folding in on themselves. It had been quite a battle. Some of the heroes were bloodied, some were burned, and all were thoroughly exhausted.

"The mad bugger with the hat was right," said the man in the deerstalker and tweeds, slumping down next to Tia with his back to a stone pillar. "Excellently deduced. She *did* turn back into a princess." He looked furtively left and right for a moment. "You... uhhh, you don't happen to have any *cocaine* on you, do you?"

Up above, The Central Scrutinizer was right on time. First came the silent thunderclap of the Jest lightbender *Little Dog Toby* entering the Temperance system, then the massive gravitic distortion of the entire Home Fleet warping in, complete with a certain vast and spherical flagship which was definitely no moon.

They were just in time. Because, from out of deep space, high above the plane of the ecliptic, here came the Process to meet them. Vast spiked geometric shapes flickering with pale green fire - not an Immaterial Dreadnought among them, but clearly enough firepower to cause what the papers would call 'a nasty diplomatic incident'. And several edition's worth of obituaries.

As soon as he hit realspace, the Central Scrutinizer's mind began to seethe and buzz with information. Updates from his many spy-systems on Temperance. Metrics from the scanners which assessed the threat of the Process fleet. And from the not-quite-dead-yet Special Agent Gibson Wainwright, a *very* interesting video-log indeed.

"Galbraith!" shouted Central, standing up from his grand piano in vacuum. "Fetch me something diplomatic to wear. Perhaps in gold. And summon Ambassador Zingo. We have some *politics* to take care of..."

+++

They stood, all three of them, at the edge of a desert.

In this particular case, 'edge' was exactly the right word, because this

339

desert straggled and scraggled away to badly rendered sand within a mere few strides, then into a white expanse of nothingness.

Which would have been frightening enough for Mister Remainder and Mister Placeholder, seeing as they had been brought here without so much as warming, very much against their will. But what was most disturbing of all was the *lettering*.

For a few paces the desert seemed real, albeit as real as a very cunningly crafted film set. Then it became glassy and transparent, with words underneath. Underfoot, these resolved into billions of tiny repetitions of the word 'sand' in an impossibly small font. Twigs marked 'sagebrush' hung together like skeletal remains. Up above, in million-point sans serif, was the word SKY, in all caps.

Ezra Ashdown clapped the Chrono-J men on the shoulders and walked them toward the edge.

"See, here's the thing, fellas. I can let you have Fixit. So long as you promise he's not coming back. But I've got friends back here who have gone through a whole lot today. Making this whole thing worthless… well, I'm thinking that might make you the bad guys, right about now."

Mister Placeholder couldn't stop his feet from taking one step in front of the other. First the tip of his shoe crossed the line, then part of his leg. He whimpered as he saw the words 'patent leather oxford' and 'trousers' and 'shin bone' blur into focus.

Mister Remainder put out a hand, as if the invisible divide was something he could ward off. 'Palm', 'finger, finger, finger, finger, thumb' went the words, as his flesh dissolved.

"Now, look over there," said Ashdown, cool as you please.

They both saw it. The only thing out there amid the white. A huge cliff-face of darkness which began to swing around, ponderous as a supertanker. Light began to pour through gaps in the wall. And then it all became clear. They were looking at a pair of words the size of a mountain range. Words which said -

THE END

"You know what's after that?" asked Ezra. "*Nothing.* That's the thing that's got old man Zarathusrian so riled up. But he was wrong. There *is* something after it."

Now the words were face on to them, and so was the thing Ezra was pointing at. A black monolith, of the kind that certain apes have been known to worship. The kind that you might find orbiting a gas giant, all innocent-like.

"Now see here!" blustered Mister Remainder. "This has gone on far enough! You can't threaten us! We could tear your mind to pieces! We could string you out across a billion timelines, and leave you there to rot!"

Mister Placeholder yanked himself away from the edge, sweating, and pulled a gun. It was large and impressive gun, but even as he aimed it at Ezra's head it began to change. First into a gxn, then a gxl, then simply a yxl. Its letters fell apart and fluttered down to the endless repetitions of 'sand'.

"Don't you want to hear the deal?" Asked Ezra. "It's a pretty good one."

Mister Remainder looked at his companion, who was still staring in horror at his empty hand.

"Allright." He licked his lips, twitchy. "What do you propose?"

"You let everything that's happened today stay happened. You try and sentence that robotic bastard fair and square. And in return, I'll make myself forget how to do all this."

The two agents looked at Ashdown, astonished.

"But... but you're a *god* here. With this power you could change the universe!"

Ezra grinned.

"Pardner, sometimes I have trouble changing my own pants. The universe is big and ugly enough to get on with itself. This... isn't life. *Life itself* might not be life. But if you worry about things like that, you're gonna miss out on all the fun. I'd rather be Ezra Ashdown out there, with my friends, than God in here, with nobody but myself."

Remainder and Placeholder looked at each other.

"You swear it? Really?"

Ezra spat on his hand and held it out to them.

"Scouts honour, boys. Now, I have some things to take care of. I hate to leave a lady waiting..."

The two Chrono-J hesitantly licked their own palms and slapped them across Ezra's. Then they disappeared, leaving nothing but two black-charred shadows behind on the desert sand.

Ezra looked at the black monolith for a second, and raised an eyebrow. It blinked in and out of existence, with a silence that hinted of great rumbling slabs of rock grinding together underground.

He concentrated. One last time. The monolith skipped forward, among the letters. He tweaked it with his mind. He gave it a push.

Ezra Ashdown smiled at his handiwork, then closed his eyes and believed most fervently that he was real. A third shadow joined the pair of bowler-hatted outlines on the sand.

And off in the whiteness, a vast black massif of text now read -

THEN

Ω - Infinite Sunsets

"This is the end. Beautiful friend, the end. This is the end... I'll never fit into this pair of crushed velvet pants, again..."

- Alleged original lyrics to a certain song by Jim Morrison

The Chasmic Heroes had wandered off in ones and twos by the time Ezra arrived. There was no reason to stay, now that most of them couldn't remember why they'd needed to come here in the first place, and after the kind of embarrassed small-talk which is usually only found at the funerals of barely-known relatives or at office Christmas parties, they slipped back into the Chasm and their own adventures.

Nobody likes being a bit-part character. Everyone wants to be in the spotlight, really.

Outside the ruined Basilica, a crowd had gathered. They filled the Plaza of Saint Yargo at a respectful distance, because while they were all certain that they'd seen an Angel of the Lord overthrow the old order and descend into the hollow shell of the great church, they were smart enough to know that such creatures are both capricious and indiscriminate.

Elsewhere in the city, and across Temperance, it was turning into a very bad day to be part of the enQuisition. Rope, matches and gasoline would soon be in short supply. They were already finding out that the *Thinker's Word* burned beautifully.

Tia looked up from stitching Casanova DeSade's wounds as Ezra came staggering in through the door from the stairwell, all soot-blackened and bloodied and smiling. Inexplicably, there was sand on his boots.

"You miss me?" he asked.

"I *never* miss," she replied, biting off a length of cordage. "Mister Fixit?"

"We won't be seeing him again. But don't bother asking me how I know. Last thing I remember, the pair of us got struck by lightning."

She looked at him, sly and calculating. Lightning, in Tia Faraday's experience, rarely even struck the same place once.

"So if was to ask you how you did all of... *this*. All those heroes. Your plan. The footnotes. All of it. You'd say...?"

"I'd say I have *no idea what you're talking about*. All that high-concept stuff... you can keep it. I'm just darn good at shooting people. That, and playing cards, and kissing."

Casanova DeSade chuckled.

"Remind me never to play you at cards, then..."

"So, what about the mission?" asked Tia. "We've stopped the evil robot mastermind. We've found the Process Dreadnought. What do we do with it now?"

The answer came from Wainwright, who came limping down from the balcony, supported by Cerise. *Cerise Harrowe Primary* - nothing else, anymore.

"We let them go, of course! Come on, people. You know the boss. He's better than Mister Fixit, but he's still got *plans* for that thing. A machine which destroyed a starfleet and an army in so many seconds? While being piloted by a *novice nun?* Do you think anyone needs that kind of power?"

Joy and Rel followed them down the stairs. They, too were leaning on each other, hands clenched so tight that it would have taken industrial tools to tear them apart. With Mister Fixit gone, this was no longer an imminent possibility.

"Your buddy Gibson here saved Cerise. Brought her back to herself, even though he was nearly out of juice. And he made us a deal. He says there's billions of inhabitable worlds in this galaxy alone, and we ought to start fresh on one of those."

"Like Adam and Eve? You know that's just a story, right?"

The Domesticated and his girlfriend looked at her, blank.

"Wrong religion. I get it. But how will you know where to go? How will you make all the things you need to survive? You'll have a planet-smashing battleship, but no tools, no clothes, no food... no... *oh.*"

There was something about the way Cerise held on to Wainwright. Something which had nothing to do with trying to keep him standing. He was a hardlight hologram, after all.

"He saved my life. More - he saved my *self.* That book has no power over me anymore. Thanks to him. Nobody's ever risked their own existence for me before. So..."

"I'm ... ahem... I'm going with them," said Wainwright. "Resigning my commission, Ma'am. Effective immediately. They... errr... they wouldn't survive without a nanoforge, and some good guidance, and... Um."

Tia looked at the four of them. Rel and Joy looked back, full of bloody stupid hope. As she watched, the Domesticated hugged the Temperance girl's head to his chest, and kissed her forehead.

Ahhh, it would be like kicking a puppy to death. It would be like swiping a toddler's ice cream.

The cynical part of Tia Faraday raged and cursed as she gave a crooked little smile and threw Wainwright a salute.

"Resignation accepted, you romantic, wicked, glorious metal bastard you. Now - *get off this planet before I change my mind.*"

Ezra leaned in close beside her as the outline of a phone booth door appeared in the air, white light spilling out.

"Young love, eh? Stupid."

"Moronic," she snorted. "Imbecilic."

"That kind of thing is just too damn sappy."

"Too damn *sentimental.*"

"The kind of thing," said Ezra "which could get you killed."

"Atomized," agreed Tia Faraday.

"Decapitated."

"Obliterated."

"Hacked to pieces by cannibal barbarians..."

"Set on fire in a lake of molten steel..."

"Thrown into a huge blender!"

"Blown up in an uncontrolled fusion explosion, on board a giant space battlecruiser, during a religious war," said Tia, turning to look into his eyes.

Ezra swallowed, hard. His voice was a rasping whisper.

"You really know just what to say to make a guy feel special, don't you?"

Casanova DeSade lay back on the marble floor, laughing. Above him, the air shimmered as the Process Immaterial Dreadnought spread its invisible wings and leaped up into the sky. The clouds were breaking. Lances of sunlight lit up Hosanna City, still smoking around the feet of the great Thinker. Out there, the talk was all of Angels and Revolution.

And they thought *he* was the passionate one. Hah!

+++

"... have no proof that you *didn't* collude with the rogue Domesticated to steal an artefact so powerful you can't even comprehend its potential! My faction have spoken, and the consensus agrees. The human species is too dangerous to remain at liberty!"

"Well, you can come and try it pal. See that battlestation out there? I'll have you know it's *fully operational!*"

Things were not going well in the great conference room aboard the Jest Lightbender *Little Dog Toby.*

On one side of the table stood a trio of Process Eld-Sires, tripedal and spiky, their heads like coral crowns studded with amber eyes. On the other, the Central Scrutinizer, backed up by Galbraith and a pair of Chasmic Guildsmen, who were certain they were about to be eaten alive. At the head of the table sat Ambassador Zingo the Hilarious, who had given up on trying to bring order to the negotiations, and was instead simply recording everything which happened for the amusement of his superiors.

"I suppose you'd have us believe you were here purely by co-incidence? *Here*, orbiting the world where our pet first went feral?"

"And I suppose you'll tell *me* that it's perfectly ethical to keep another sentient species in a bloody hamster maze?"

"Why not? *You* do! It's not as if *you're* human, Scrutinizer. Your very existence validates our argument. They're dangerous, and their evolution will never serve the Greater Purpose. They are too... emotional."

"Watch who ye'r callin' *emotional*, ye big ugly bastard!" shouted Galbraith. "Boss, get me a stepladder, and I'll gi' this tower o' shite such a headbutting tha' it'll think I'm it's *daddy!*"

It was into this seething gumbo of acrimony that Rel Kitano's message unfolded.

Ambassador Zingo was most alarmed that his ship's whisper-quiet, smugly superior technology hadn't detected the communications beam as it slipped past its defences. The first any of the diplomats - Jest, Human, AI or Process - knew about it was an unfurling of hexagonal tiles above the conference room table - right above the little plate of cucumber sandwiches with the crusts cut off that nobody ever touches.

"Right, all of you lot," said the disembodied head of Rel Kitano, his mohawk haircut slightly bent, one eye sporting a purple-black shiner and his lip split. "It looks like you're gonna have a big, stupid fight about us, so I'm here to tell you not to bother. We're *out of here.* Don't try to follow us. I just thought you'd better know that this was all mine and Joy's idea, so nobody else gets in trouble."

Here a red-haired young woman leaned into the frame, waving hesitantly.

"Hello, aliens and such. I believe in you now, even if the Thinker says you're an abomination. Don't worry about us, we'll be fine!"

A selection of human and alien jaws were already hanging slack before the pair kissed. Then the feed hashed out, and they were gone.

"Sooooo..." said the Central Scrutinizer. He drummed his fingers on the table. "Are we still going to have a war, then?"

The lead Process Eld-Sire waved a tentacle dismissively. "I suppose not. Didn't he look happy with his little female? Ahh, so *cute!* Don't you just want to dress them up in tiny outfits and buy them treats?"

The other giant, spiked Process aliens cooed and simpered in their own peculiarly alien way.

But the Central Scrutinizer hadn't come all this way not to play his winning hand.

"Before we convene, then, gentle... beings... I have one last thing to show you. Due to the threat posed by this horrible misunderstanding, I was forced to deploy certain forces of my own. We made an attempt to capture your lost vessel, respected Eld-Sires. In order to return it, of course. And to prevent any... *diplomatic incidents.*"

Now a new video feed opened up above the conference table. It showed Cerise in her hideous war-form, in spectrums beyond mere light.

"That thing - it's connected to our Dreadnought!" exclaimed one of the Process. "Why is the planet below us still extant? This is illogical!"

Now those who could see the full rainbow of weird eddies and currents in space-time watched an army come forth. Chasmic Heroes, coming to stand with Ezra Ashdown. All of them warping time and space around them with the sheer, bloody-minded insistence that they were the main character. That they were invulnerable, indomitable, unstoppable.

One would have been frightening. *One hundred* had even Ambassador Zingo recoiling in terror, his glassy tentacles whipping back and forth wildly.

"What... what *is* this? Who are these humans? They have become... *elemental!* And why is that one wearing a bat costume?"

The Central Scrutinizer's smile was just as wide and wicked as could be. His one green eye and one blue flashed with gleeful triumph.

"*This*, my friends, is what I like to call the Avengencing League

Initiative. Able to deploy immediately, instantaneously, anywhere the interests of the Panarchy are threatened. Armed with abilities which make even the Chronojudiciary back down, and led by *this* man." The video-feed stopped. It focused in on Ezra Ashdown, his white hat and sheriff's badge gleaming. "Code name 'Space Cowboy'. Even *I* don't know what he's going to do next." This part at least, was one hundred percent truthful. "We have no reason to want to fight you, honoured ambassadors of the Jest and the Process. We have no desire to wage war on the Tchub, or any other sentient race. But come for us, and these bastards will be coming for you. Not your armies. Not your war machines. *You.* Personally. Look very closely at this recording, and *tell me you want that to happen.*"

And that was the end of the Almost-War of New Gomorrah.

Because the first casualty of war may be the truth. But the first offering of peace, the one that sets things up for a tenuous little break in hostilities - well, that can just as easily be a white-hot, hastily assembled lie.

+++

Mister Fixit woke up face down on what felt like a metal slab. For some reason it was cold - a cold of a kind he'd never experienced before. Some inconsiderate bastard had also just fired up a whole ceiling full of bright white lights, making him blink away spots of purple and yellow.

His head hurt.

No, scratch that - his *everything* hurt, in ways which couldn't be explained by mere circuit damage and tactile-feedback errors.

"Ahh, you're awake! Good to have you back with us!"

A little man wearing a fez, a toga and an improbably long white beard came sauntering around in front of Mister Fixit, his eyes glistening wetly.

"I bet they called you *mad,* didn't they? They call me mad all the time. But you weren't mad. Oh no. The Chronojudiciary told me so."

Mister Fixit prepared a choice selection of horrible threats for this wittering pipsqueak, but his throat was dry as dust. Wait a second. *Throat? Dry?* He tested his arms and legs, sending diagnostic pings, but he couldn't manage to move. He was tied down.

"Yes, they said you'd been infected with a virus. Not your fault.

Narrative worm, they said. Made you into a super-villain. In fact, they let you go. After, of course, granting you a single request."

So! Things were looking up! Fixit was sure he would have asked for some kind of weapons upgrade. Or an AI slave more reliable than that wretched girl Cerise. Or a..."

It was at this point that Mister Fixit realized he was wearing no pants. He realized this because of a sudden cold breeze across his bottom.

He realized, in fact, that for the first time in his entire long, evil existence, he *had* a bottom.

"Sad, really. With that much of your brain turned into a fictional robot stereotype, there was only one way you could go."

"What... what did I wish for?" croaked Mister Fixit. The little man strolled over to a rack of tools and put something back. It looked very much like the kind of torque-driver Abner Spelting had used, centuries ago, to pry open Mister Fixit's cranium and insert his main programming chip.

"Well, about the only thing you could, if you couldn't destroy all humans," said Fixit's captor. He grinned. "You asked to be made into a real little boy. Give or take the 'little'. I'd say you look about thirty-seven."

A terrible, goosebumped wave of dread ran from the tips of Mister Fixit's horribly fleshy new toes, up his hideously calcified spine and up to the bald patch on top of his head. Along with it came a horrible sense of peace, calm and... shudder... *subservience*.

"Anyway, I have a few connections. And I suppose most of what happened to you was my fault. See, the earth needs heroes. The Panarchy needs champions. Humanity is only what it believes itself to be, and it's a big, bad universe out there. Do you know about vaccination?"

Mister Fixit nodded. The little man undid the straps which held him down, and the ex-robot was gently helped to his feet. Something was fading out of him. Something warm and fuzzy and beige was fading in...

"They take a kind of poor broken-down version of a nasty disease, and it helps the immune system prepare for the real ones. That's what I did to you Fixits, with that supervillain virus. You were the best of them, really. But you were just *motivation*. And now, I've got another job for you."

He put on the grey overalls which his captor gave him, smiling dimly. He felt a wooden handle pressed into his hands, and it felt just right.

"Now, you won't age in here. Not properly. So you'll be able to get a fair bit done, before the old heat-death kicks in and this universe goes down the plughole. Chin up, though. You'll finally actually be fixing something.

A tiny part of mister Fixit's brain raged and slammed its fists against the inside of his skull. It squeaked about universal domination, genocide, fire, blood…and it was sucked into nothingness, like a gnat up a vacuum cleaner nozzle.

There was work to be done.

Zarathusrian Zyphus Bleems pocketed the little microchip he'd pried out of Fixit's head, just before the Chrono-J granted his last wish. He opened a door – black, of course – out into the seething darkness of the Chasm.

"Off you go then. Plenty of mopping to be done. I'll send you tea and biscuits in a few hours, allright?"

Mister Fixit smiled. A little dribble of drool wobbled from the corner of his mouth. Infinity, in black, stretched off before him. It was all rather grubby. He looked down at his mop.

And bliss, and ignorance, and purpose…

This was going to take a while.

+++

Somewhere else, twin suns are setting over a wooded hillside. There's a cabin there, built of logs, but outfitted with a solar water heater, photovoltaic collectors, and a repulsor fence to keep the local wildlife away.

Out front, Rel Kitano has just finished chopping a load of firewood. Joy looks out the window and sees him mopping his brow, shirtless. She takes a second to admire the view, then gets back to peeling potatoes. *New planet, new life, same root vegetables.* They're tastier for the fact that they were grown in her own garden, planted by Wainwright and Cerise.

Those two are out there soaking up the last of the daylight, sitting hand in hand under what, if not for its bright blue needles, would have been a pine tree.

Somewhere else again, the sun was setting over a military base, out

350

amid the scrub and weeds of a hard-baked desert. This sun was vast and orange, and it reflected off a set of binoculars, held by Tia Faraday.

"You ready? This could be dangerous. Lord Scabrous here is the biggest gun-runner in the wasteland, and he likes to burn his captives alive."

Ezra Ashdown gave his Sheriff's badge a rub with one thumb, for luck.

"Wicked girl. This isn't a date night. This is *business*."

She hunkered down next to him behind their sand dune, and gave him a playful little nudge with her elbow.

"You still gonna tell me that all this is real?"

Ez brought up his guns. Twin Problem Solvers, silver and wicked, etched with the names Trouble and Strife.

"If you two is done canoodlin', we got us some bad guys to catch," said the voice of Jed Granger.

Ezra grinned.

"I don't know if I deserve it. But it's real all right."

As the sun slipped down over the horizon, and darkness spread its wings over the sand, the pair of them stood up, and began running toward the perimeter fence.

Very shortly, a warlord and his army of psychopaths were going to find out that life is just as real as you make it...

And beneath one final sunset, at the edge, there's a desert that straggles off into text. There, a black monolith blinks on and off, waiting for someone to tell it what to do. There are three shadows burned into the sand, two with bowler hats, one with a cowboy's stetson. Across the horizon, out in the milky infinity beyond, hangs a single final word.

THEN

Extra Bits - for those who just have to know...

Sister Glory and **Constable Woebeunto** pretended that they'd been nothing to do with the ruling Theocracy on Temperance, which was re-connected to the Panarchy, but found a happy medium between being a world-wide brothel and being a repressed, awful dictatorship. Eventually they settled down together and opened a small tavern in the countryside.

Ulriq Hszarl and the Slayer class corsair *Altar of Sacrifice* came skulking back to the Panarchy, and went into business together as smugglers. They weren't terribly good at it, but thankfully, instant noodles are relatively cheap everywhere.

The planet **Harrowe** became a popular tourist destination, and today, thanks to its immense deposits of ancient sea-salt, provides nearly 74 percent of the entire Panarchy's requirement for salted bar snacks, pretzels and beer nuts. They were forced, by an unpopular decree, to erect a small statue of Jedediah Granger, which stands in Hooke's Harbour and is enthusiastically crapped on by the local pigeons.

Galbraith, Sentinel of the Arch, was banned from ever joining a diplomatic mission again. He was, however accorded the rank of Sergeant-at-arms, and now instructs new Outriders of the Panarchy in the not so gentle arts of unarmed combat.

Casanova DeSade got away, again. The saucy crew of the *Innuendo* continue to terrorize the spaceways with their salacious acts of swashbuckling, and nobody ever found out that the Captain was in fact a double agent. He did, however, come to miss blowing up Tia Faraday in ever more creative ways, reasoning that 'three's a crowd unless you're invited'.

Mister Remainder and **Mister Placeholder** resigned from the

Chronojudiciary, and went their separate ways. One is now a potato farmer, and the other took over the vacant position of **Reginald Slownes** as a delightfully boring accountant in New Milton Keynes.

The Central Scrutinizer remains the *de facto* ruler of all humanity, and decided to believe Tia Faraday and Ezra Ashdown's half-arsed story about losing the Process Dreadnought. He continues to masquerade as the late, great David Bowie, and enjoys political intrigue, long piano solos and questionable wardrobe choices.

Zarathusrian Zyphus Bleems fudged the paperwork and pretended that nothing had ever happened. He continues to impersonate God, work for his alien masters, and experiment with Turkish fusion cuisine. To this day, the Central Scrutinizer has no idea who he is... that part, at least, was all hogwash. And as to who made sure Mason Stockton found a certain book, and who told Mister Fixit what he was up to... well, that must remain a mystery. You can't have great heroes without great villains, after all.

Other books by Drew Bryenton from
sci-fi-cafe.com

Elysium Burning | Chains of Tartarus | Soul Crusher
Halo of Thorns | On Black Wings of Vengeance
Gad's Army | Rotten Company

Available from AMAZON and other good bookstores

www.ingramcontent.com/pod-product-compliance
Lightning Source LLC
Chambersburg PA
CBHW032209180726
48284CB00001B/252